From The Women's Press Ltd
34 Great Sutton Street, London EC1V 0DX

Caeia March

Caeia March was born in 1946 of white working-class parents on the Isle of Man. She grew up in industrial South Yorkshire, graduated from London University in 1968, was married the same summer and became a social studies teacher.

She has lived alone as a lesbian since October 1980, some five miles from her sons in S E London. Her part-time work as a clerk for the local council pays the rent. She pays the other bills by working two evenings a week: tutoring a discussion, support and study group for women in the Albany community centre in Deptford; and teaching creative writing in an adult education class in Brixton.

She has had several stories published, in *Everyday Matters* Vol. I (Sheba Feminist Publishers), *The Reach* (Onlywomen Press) and *Girls Next Door* (The Women's Press, 1985); as well as pieces in *Spare Rib* ('Diary of a Feminist Teacher', under the name of Kate Elliott, 1978) and *In Our Own Words* ('Writing as lesbian mother', Hutchinson, forthcoming). She is working on another novel.

CAEIA MARCH

Three Ply Yarn

The Women's Press

First published by The Women's Press Ltd 1986
A member of the Namara Group
34 Great Sutton Street, London EC1V 0DX

01992680

British Library Cataloguing in Publication Data
March, Caeia
   Three ply yarn.
   I. Title
   823'.914[F]   PR6063.A6/
   ISBN 0-7043-5003-3
   ISBN 0-7043-4007-0 Pbk

Typeset by AKM Associates (UK) Ltd
Ajmal House, Hayes Road, Southall, London
Printed and bound in Great Britain

Available on cassette from Feminist Audio Books
for blind and partially sighted women.

Acknowledgments

This manuscript could not have become a published book without the encouragement, support and constructive criticism of my women friends. I would especially like to thank Jan Bradshaw, Nancy Diuguid, Bernardine Evaristo, Pat Hextall, Patricia Hilaire, Penny Holland, Gillian Spraggs, Rosalind Weekes and Kerilyn Wood for giving generously of their time and creative energy.

The manuscript was typed by Sandra den Hertog and Pat Angove, and was copy-edited by Janet Tyrrell.

Earlier writings (1980–84) were encouraged by Zoë Fairbairns (tutor for a feminist writing class 1980), Penny Henrion, Alison Light, Sandra McAdam-Clark and Fiona Thompson, who read and commented on them for me, giving me the confidence to write this novel.

I'd like to thank my mother and my sister for being family, and them both and my late father for believing that I could do things. That which began in my working-class childhood lingers on, on the good days.

Recently, the women involved in *Shooting Our Mouths Off* and *The Common Thread* have included my work in public readings, and their efforts are tireless in giving working-class women the confidence to write and publish. Their existence is an inspiration to me.

To Sue Sanders, with whom I have shared the past six years as lover, friend, and co-worker, my deep thanks for her vital contribution to the making of *Three Ply Yarn* through hours of talking, arguing, editing and laughing.

Three Ply Yarn is fiction. I hope that its publication will encourage many other working-class women and lesbians to create our literature from our lives.

Caeia March 1986.

Deanne

Childhood

I wasn't going to let them take me away from Dora. Back to London and put me in a home. Her back in Birmingham, in a different home. Not bloody likely. So we needed a plan, us two. We sat in Mereford Woods in Dorset, near the wild violets.

'I don't want to leave Nell though. Nell's like a sister.'

'They'll sure as hell split us up, Dee. We'll never see each other again.'

'I know. I shan't let 'em. But it still hurts, leaving her.'

'She'll be all right, Dee. She's still got a mum, hasn't she?'

Mereford Village was our home as evacuees, in the second world war. It was twelve cottages and Penny Acre Farm, along a thin lane. Like square stone beads on a string. Ours was the farm.

The ford was a short walk from the last house. A brown gold river ran across the road. We used to play there, the three of us, plopping pebbles. While voles played in the bank, under the pussy willow. Brown voles. Brown like the river. Whiskers just above the water.

We used to say the river was a mirror.

Dora's mum used to be a munitions worker. Before that she was working in a box factory. Her dad was disabled so he wasn't called up. Both of them were killed in 1943. Direct hit. Mine went later in the year. It was a terrible year, that.

The blitz on the London docks got my mum. My dad died in Burma. That's when Dora and me first took to cuddling. Behind the hay barn, while Nellie collected eggs.

Dora said, 'If I start crying, I shan't ever stop. I'll go dry like sand. I will so.' So she didn't cry at all. I didn't either, till the day we decided to run away.

Nell used to cry gallons. We'd lived next door, back in Rotherhithe. Her mum worked with mine in the biscuit factory.

Nell and me was luckier than some 'cos we was sent away, together.

1

Mrs Gilbert came to the church hall, in Mereford Aubrey, to choose us. She saw me and Nell sitting there frightened out of our wits we'd be parted, and she must've took pity, and took us both.

Lots of the others got split up, even brothers and sisters. Nell said, 'They shouldn't do that, should they, Dee?' but they did, so we counted our blessings. And we met Dora, sent away from Birmingham. She was glad. She'd been there all alone till we came.

Then, after my mum died, Nell said, 'Magic three. It always comes in threes. So my mum's next.'

She cried and cried and started her white nightmares after that. White plaster falling from white ceilings; white dust in her eyes; her mum gone white like a ghost; sort of dry white, buried alive in white.

Then Nellie started to wake with her single bed soaked. Mrs G didn't let us call it pee. We had to say 'number one'. We all used to giggle behind our hands.

We daren't wake Mrs G because she was tired and too busy.

When she took us in, she was kind and I think she wanted to be a mum to us. But us three girls was too much for her, what with the dairy to run, and all the other work on the farm. She got just too tired out to be soft to us. We thought she was very very old. Forty or even more. Anyways, she was worn down with Nell's wet sheets. And after her 'duty' wore off, she started to shout if we broke her nights.

So Nell'd shiver in the dark while me and Dora took off her wet nightie. Then she'd climb in the double bed with us. We'd all hold tight till morning.

We grew up, eleven, twelve, thirteen.

Nell slept through by then, so it was just me and Dora cuddling. Touching ever so softly where our breasts were growing, and our hairs were starting. I liked her tongue. It was warm and soft down the side of my neck.

We called those nights our foreveralways nights. We wanted the comfort to go on and on.

We daren't let on to Nell, though p'raps she guessed. She might have let it slip to Mrs G. I knew *she'd* not approve. I could just see her face set hard, down in her shoulders of her huge print apron.

But loving Dora made me feel all right.

The urge went deep in me. For the comfort and the kisses, foreveralways.

So I wrote a note to Nellie and left it on her pillow.

Dear Nellie,

I'm not coming back. Me and Dora are gone to make our fortunes. 'Cos if we don't they'll put us both in homes. We'll be all right I just know it. And I will always be your friend. Dora says you can write. You put the address something called Post Restante. (Funny spelling.) Dora says her brother told her about it, the one that died in Italy. Then you put Central Post Office, Southampton. We'll go and collect it. Please, please write to me. I want to be your friend.

Lots of love Deanne.

Dora and me lied about our ages. We was thirteen but we looked bigger and said we was fifteen. It was easy. We found work as chambermaids. It was the Bronnester Hotel, Coombebury, by the sea.

We were the morning-after-cleaners for the filth of other folks' passion. There was slops in the chamber pots and semen on the sheets. (I found out that was the right word for it later. Me and Dora called it fuckmess.) Hairs everywhere. Long ones on the pillow, curled ones in the beds, shaved ones in the basins, tangled ones in forgotten hairbrushes flung to the back of bedside cabinets.

I suppose they took us on because we was cheap and useful. They just didn't care. They was only interested in where they'd fix us up with a bed, 'cos their attic was bomb damaged. Coombebury hadn't hardly been bombed, but there'd been this one plane that had been offloading before going back over the English Channel, so Corrine, the singer in the hotel there, said. She said that's how one or two of the hotels copped it when the town hadn't hardly at all. Not like Southampton. But then Coombebury didn't have docks or the military there. Only in billets in some of the hotels.

Me and Dora was very lucky. They'd made a thin room over the garage and one next to it. They put us in the thin room. There was only room for one bed for the two of us. And four next door. We was quite ready to say 'we didn't mind sharin' ' but we didn't have to. They never even asked us. That was how much they cared. But the walls were thin as paper, so we hid our grins and kept our kissing very quiet.

There was blood as well. We were teenagers now and we bled too. So we knew now that sometimes it'd start at night. Wives and mistresses mightn't know till they woke shamed next morning. We weren't shamed with each other. But then it was different for us. Besides the two of us usually came on together, being so close, in every way.

So, seeing blood on sheets wasn't too bad. But I never did get used to

3

bloody pillows. I could hardly imagine what they did, to get the pillows bloody.

'Somebody's cut round the face again, Dora. Cut round the face again.' Then I vomited into the chamber pot. It mixed with the slops.

After about a year of that they told us to wait at tables instead. There was quite a to-do about that with one of the other chambermaids. But me and Dora just kept ourselves to ourselves till it blew over. It was more money, though not to write home about. We didn't have homes to write to. But letters from Nell came every so often, and I wrote back.

I liked waitressing compared to chambermaiding. At least at table they didn't bleed on the tablecloths. They hid their passions under their clothes instead.

I learned to balance an *entrecôte* steak on a serving fork and spoon. One-handed. They called us deft then. Deft, not daft.

I learned to put the sugar in real coffee to make it thick then the cream would float. I learned to float the cream from the jug down the handle of a spoon.

I learned to be quick, and to do that without appearing to. No one likes to see a waitress appearing to rush around; but they don't want cold food either, faddy lot. So they've got you no which way.

Dora and me had to be ready for the snap of their eyelids. They snapped for attention, and if we minded them too much, then, while we were listening to them, changing their orders and such like, they'd snap their fingers too, on our behinds. They only got me once or twice. After that I kept my rear end well out of their way though I'd got each ear trained to their every whim.

It was interesting though, listening. They talked with long words and long rambling ways. Took ten minutes to say nothin'. But I was learnin'. I slowly began to want to talk different. I wanted more words. I never did go *much* on words though. From the time I could use a pencil, I liked to draw instead. Cartoons. Doodles. This and that. Dora used to say I could get a whole story in a few strokes. I liked her putting it that way.

I often thought of Nellie back home in Rotherhithe, on ration cards.

'I bet she never has steak,' I whispered to Dora when she sweet-talked cook into a special dinner.

'Eat up and shut up,' she hissed back, but grinning too, 'we'll not get this more'n once in a blue moon.'

We didn't talk about our own mums and dads. Or about death or grieving. We understood it and lived it. We didn't need to ask each other questions. Not about that. We were so close I could finish off her sentences. She could answer me when I hadn't even asked her something, just been thinking about it, instead.

Every night when I curled up with Dora (with nighties right by the bed in case of a fire alarm – you never knew what might happen at the Bronnester), every night I'd send up a message to my favourite star, the one at the end of the Great Bear. I'd ask for Nell to be happy like I was happy.

I didn't pray. Nell and I knew that didn't work. But I hoped she'd know and get some comfort from it.

The hotel had not closed in wartime. It hadn't been a billet either. It had kept going, as a hotel. That astonished me, and didn't at the same time. It puzzled me because of all the people working and dying while some still had holidays.

So trade at the Bronnester Hotel was good all through the war. After the war, when we started there, it was very good. The visitors weren't all tourists. Some were officers on leave with mistresses with real leather shoes. Some were local businessmen. Some came from Southampton too. They had well-groomed wives. Some even had real mink coats.

When we started waitressing we had about five hours sleep. We were never in bed before midnight with the work. We were up again by six-fifteen, laying breakfast trays and tables. I didn't like work. Nobody I knew liked work.

Dora and me worked to put a roof over our heads, to get a bed with sheets on, to put food in our bellies and to stay together.

The Bronnester was the best we could think of for doing all that.

Nell's letters came sometimes. With gaps sometimes. But they did come and I wrote back. Soon she started to mention her new boyfriend, Fred, who was from the local Grammar. She wrote that her mother was ill, worn down with work and the damp; and how they were on the waiting list, but no one ever seemed to move off it; and how she hated school and simply could not wait for the leaving day to come.

I knew that one day I'd meet Nell again, and I wrote her that. But I daren't risk anyone finding me or Dora. So I kept up the lie about where we were for several years.

It hurt, lying to Nell.

On our days off, Dora and I would sometimes go to a matinée. We'd hold hands there in the dark. Romances we saw lots of. And war films. We joked about having a film about us. Girls like us. But our film wouldn't have girl meets a man and lives happy ever after. Ours would tell how the war took away our childhood but gave us each other.

5

'D'yer think men and women love like we do?' she asked.

'Ugh, no,' I said, thinking of the messy beds and horrid pillows. 'S'not the same for them at all.'

'Humph,' she sort of grunted. 'Be nice if we could go to the fleapit and see films about girls loving girls, eh Dee?'

'Nice if the moon were made of green cheese and all. Do you want to come for a walk on the beach then?'

In the thin room, with the thin walls, late into the night, she kissed every inch of my skin. It was good for me.

Loving Dora was like finding a rainbow on a wet Saturday in town. I'd want to shout and tell everyone. And there wasn't anyone to tell.

Except Corrine who knew without words.

She'd been a street walker by the docks of Southampton, when she was fifteen. That was 1934. She didn't make much money, but she didn't get VD. It was her Maggie that got it. Syphilis.

Maggie was to Corrine what Dora was to me. Then Maggie died slowly. Corrine watched her and couldn't prevent it. They couldn't make love like they used to either. Maggie was afraid she'd pass on the symptoms.

So Corrine knew like we did about death and grieving. But she learned to hide it. Very carefully. She went to the Bronnester as a waitress, just before the war started. She told us later that she watched the wives hiding their bruises under their expensive make-up, and she hid her emptiness just as carefully. She wore make-up too, not expensive, and she put on a smile and a song.

One of her regulars for evening dinner was a businessman called 'Dove'. He had money, and a wife with a string of real pearls.

'He had an air about him,' said Corrine, 'and so the proprietor of the Bronnester simply couldn't afford to ignore Dove.'

He heard her singing. He asked her to sing for him. She blushed at his request. He insisted. He called the manager. Corrine sang.

That's how Corrine became the resident singer at the Bronnester.

It amused me, in a sour way, that he had a gentle name. I never liked or trusted him from the start. Ralph Edmund Dove. With men you do it for money; with women for love. That was what Corrine always said.

I don't believe Corrine ever did it with him for love, though by the time we came there, when we were thirteen, she was twenty-six and had been his mistress for four years.

In a small town like Coombebury it should have been a scandal. But in the Bronnester Hotel there was a price tag on everything. A cheap chambermaid; a candlelit dinner for two; a sweet song from a radiant woman; it wasn't a scandal *there*.

We used to go out, the three of us, sometimes on a day off. Of course it was ages before Dora and me found out about Maggie. Corrine had to know us before she'd dare let us into that. She had to be sure we wouldn't let on.

So, I remember one of those days particularly. We sat there in the New Forest. Me and Dora were quiet. We could almost hear her thinking. She told us about Maggie. She said she realised from when we first arrived that we must be like her and Maggie. We were shaky when she said that. We were scared others could tell and we'd lose our jobs.

But she said that we shouldn't worry. It didn't show except to her, because of her loving Maggie like she had. Then we realised why she'd always kept an eye out for us. Helping us from when we first turned up.

So we sat quiet while she talked. I remember the sunshine. It was making the leaves very light green. Like dappled horses on the farm, only green not grey. I did a picture of it later.

'She liked secret places,' said Corrine. 'She said she was drawn to them. You'd have liked her. Everyone did. She could tell tales like no one I've ever met.'

We were quiet for a while, thinking. I was thinking that there'd been her and Maggie. So there must've been others. Others like me and Dora. I think it was fixed in me that it was a happy moment, suddenly thinking that. Loving Dora and knowing that about Corrine made me feel I could face anything. I remember then the wind came up, just a thin wind. Not cold. Then the trees shook, and it was the dappled horses running. But when I thought of Corrine with Dove, I thought of the horses being stabled. It grieved me. But I didn't say it.

We were secret people. Our loving had to be secret. Three of us. We started to talk then about secret places. Or at least, Dora did. She was the words one. Really. I'd be thinking it and she'd say it.

'Have you got a secret place, Corrine?' asked Dora.

I was a bit embarrassed, so I interrupted: 'It's a secret,' I giggled. They both laughed, then Corrine answered: 'I don't know where exactly. A place with music. A lot of singing. Maybe near some stones. Somewhere like Maggie found. Her special place was a stone circle she found. She used to touch the stones. She said she always felt them warm under her hands.' She paused, thinking, then, 'Maybe we could go there together. Maybe I could talk Dove into lending me one of his cars.'

7

'You mean he's got more'n one?'

'Course he has, Dillydim,' laughed Dora at me. 'He's got four.'

'Four?'

They both laughed at me.

On other days off I'd walk by the sea with Dora. I'd imagine then a place with no horizon. The sea and sky would meet and go on forever. I'd imagine four of us, including Nell. We'd have a house with a garden, a dream garden. I'd grow things like I'd seen growing on Penny Acre Farm. There'd be time to watch the sea and sky change.

Time to listen to the sea birds wheeling. Answering and calling, Why? Why? Why?

No one would have to spend a lifetime washing up other people's greasy plates. No one would have to empty other people's chamber pots. No one would catch a disease from a man's thing.

Or we'd go back to the New Forest. Me and Dora, if Corrine couldn't come. We'd get ourselves there all right, on the bus.

Then I'd imagine woods that stretched from there all the way to my dream garden. To the sea in a special place. There'd be insects scurrying there under low bushes. Busy and quiet like me and Dora in bed. Loving in the thin room.

If we went to the New Forest in the autumn, we'd see berries. Orange and scarlet. And rose hips on wild roses.

'Season of mists and mellow fruitfulness. Close bosom-friend of the maturing sun,' quoted Dora. (We were taught that in Mereford school.)

Several times we went with Corrine to the open-air service at Barrow Hill. There was a natural amphitheatre on the hillside. The ministers stood on a portable pulpit. They promised us happiness if we worked hard and prayed often.

I was already working harder than I'd thought possible. I was already happy. I decided praying wouldn't change much.

I'd much rather lie in the dark cuddling with Dora, and put my hands on her, than put my hands together and pray to Jesus.

We giggled. 'Jesus bids us shine like a pure clear light. But he doesn't want us to be cuddling in the night.'

So, after the sermons, I'd pick a bunch of pink campions and ladies' lace for Corrine, and another for Dora.

I knew if I had those two in my life, I was definitely doing all right.

We'd known Corrine maybe three years when she took us down to The Feathers.

There's one in every town. Ask any taxi driver there.

In the summer time in Coombebury the taxi drivers brought in the gay visitors, in ones and twos. There were more gay men than women. We had the back corner. We'd been posing as fifteen from the time we first ran away from Mereford. This was three years on. So it stood to reason we were seen as eighteen, the legal age for buying drinks. Mine was always half a bitter. Dora's was dry cider. She could down it by the barrel.

Corrine knew everyone and made it easy for us.

First we met Irma and Frank who ran The Feathers. To everybody outside of the pub they were man and wife. They'd been married since before the war. She was a huge woman. The same height as him. They never did it with each other, not since their first year married. They tried it but didn't like it, so Corrine said.

Then Irma took up with Erica, this upper-crust woman from London. Wow, was she loaded. She used to buy Irma gold earrings, real gold, with diamonds set in. Irma wore them always in The Feathers, along with her high-heeled pink bedroom slippers and a ring on every finger of her hand. I couldn't take my eyes off her. She was like a walking bank raid.

'Dora,' I whispered, 'why don't she sell that lot and live happy ever after? I would.'

'She likes us lot too much. Likes the limelight. Look at her sparkling there behind the bar. You can tell she used to be an actress before she married Frank.'

Many's the night me and Dora went to sleep muttering about Irma down The Feathers. She had a scrapbook of cuttings of Tallulah Bankhead. From before the war. Girls flocked to Tallulah's shows in hundreds; mobbed her at the stage door; screamed and fainted for love of her. She called them all 'dahrlings' and said she invented camp. She did.

Irma revelled in tales about herself. Like her idol, Tallulah, the more the better. It brought custom, after all. She claimed she kissed Tallulah Bankhead. I wanted to believe her.

Frank was the exact opposite. Quiet, plain, grey haired, and always wearing a tie. He had a gold ring, too. Just one. I didn't know if Irma sold one of hers to buy him that one, or if his boyfriend, Clive, gave it to him. Clive lived in the town and came into The Feathers sometimes for a beer, after work. He was a postman.

Our first friends there were Micky and Charlie. It was them that taught us to play snooker. Micky was patient while we learned. She

9

didn't make us feel stupid. She came there to The Feathers night after night, so no wonder she had so much practice. Dora and me only went one night a week or so. The gay boys usually crowded us out.

Micky had a jacket with five pockets and sometimes I wondered if she kept a knife in one of them. No one crowded out Micky. At least, not in The Feathers. She was the champ. Could beat any man into the ground, playing snooker, that is. I only once saw her in a real fight. Some visitor tried to pick her up. Now everyone in The Feathers, all the regulars, like us, knew Micky only went with women. This straight guy from out of town offered her money. That was after seven double whiskies. She poured her pint over his head.

Then it started. He landed out. She cracked him one back. He fell against the bar and broke his nose.

I have never seen Irma and Frank act so quick. Three men appeared from out the back and this visitor was bundled up and out and we never saw him again. Word has it that they put him on the London train and when he woke up he was in Charing Cross Hospital. I don't know if that's true.

Charlie had tattoos up her arms and short hair shaved up the back of her head. I gulped when I first saw her. She had the flattest chest of any women I'd ever seen. She could have passed for a man anywhere. In the summer Charlie was never without a girl. They fell for her one after the other in droves. It was pick and choose for Charlie in the tourist season. In the winter she was lonely. Slouched there on the edge of the bar in The Feathers without a Dora to go home with. I half envied Micky because she was so tough but I never envied Charlie. Micky had other things going for her, her job – she was a window cleaner, self-employed – lots of friends, women and men. All gays. But Charlie was a loner. I could see terror in that.

Charlie was a gardener on Lady Claymer's estate. It was the edge of the New Forest. She went out there every morning on the bus. I'd always wanted a garden but I wouldn't want to be out of doors in bitter cold winters like Charlie. I'd have hated to travel so far to and from work, and often Charlie would be on her own for hours. Gardening didn't appeal to me at all as a job, only as a hobby. I went with Dora twice to see the grounds, when her Ladyship was jaunting in Europe. Lord Claymer died in glory (who cares!) in 1943. The same year that my mum and dad were killed.

One night, two new women came to The Feathers. They called themselves Mol and Pol. I knew they'd made that up. It suited them. They were mother and daughter, both gays. Mol had the loudest laugh

I've heard before or after. Pol had the prettiest face. How they arrived in Coombebury no one knew or asked. Some things you don't ask.

They came in wearing dresses that matched. They talked our heads off.

Mol ran a clinic, as she called it. She was once a nurse, she said. She knew what was what, so to speak. Pol said she'd never let a man near her, having seen the state that girls arrived in at Mol's clinic. Mol did not advertise. It was word of mouth only. No girl ever suffered or died from anything Mol did to help her.

Mol used to go to the gay pub in Southampton, till she had a row with the man that ran it. Then she came to The Feathers. We always thanked our lucky stars for Mol. She'd had Pol in 1923. Mol said it was worth it, to do it just once, with a soldier, to get Pol. That's all men were good for.

Mol listened to blues. She was white, we all were, but blues was Mol's favourite music.

In years to come it was Mol and Pol who joined up with Corrine in the singing group. Amateur. Singing for the joy of it, they said.

When Pol met Micky they matched like fish and chips. Their laughter was as sharp as vinegar.

Mol herself had a thing on and off for years with Corrine.

'I wonder if they sing in bed', said Dora, laughing.

In 1947, Dora and I had moved out together from the thin room and rented the upstairs of a house, near to the railway. Our landlady was an elderly widow who lived downstairs. There were other pairs of girls in that area, sharing like us. I wondered if they were gay like us, but I never saw any of them down The Feathers, though. We liked our landlady, who didn't interfere, and we kept ourselves to ourselves.

We'd been there two years when Dora started feeling restless. That'd be '49, and we were both seventeen though we looked nineteen. We'd been together for nine years by then.

I still went regularly to The Feathers. Dora didn't always go. We made a raucous crowd. Jostling to get the words in sideways. Playing snooker (it wasn't pool till years later), elbowing for enough space for ourselves in the pub full of gay boys. We had to grow extra skins to cope outside where we were not seen, and to cope in the pub where we *were* seen. I knew some of those gay boys, liked some, but they wanted it all for themselves. We had a time of it keeping our corner. If we let ourselves miss a night or two, then, like Mol said: 'Sure as hell fire they'd grab it.'

I missed Dora when she didn't go, but I was safe there with the other regulars, especially Micky and Charlie, Mol and Pol. And Corrine on the nights she wasn't working.

Three or four times a year someone would have a party. Twelve to twenty of us, all women, dancing, joking, arguing and laughing. Getting each other through the Good Old Bad Old Days.

Esther

February 1983

My secret room. So late that the red London buses have stopped trundling past. Warm red woolly dressing gown. Deep soft red shadows in the corners of this place. Must write, before it all fades.

Another amazing dream.

Densley again, childhood. The night before my eleven-plus results. Me in bed telling tales to my sister, Lotte, while she lay in the dark, in the single bed next to mine. I told stories to keep her safe and my mind off my results. Lotte was giggling. I was telling her about the fat blue dragon, the one who lived under the privet hedge in the back yard at number five, our street. The white flowers on the privet weren't really flowers at all. They were the dragon's beard. It wasn't dangerous, except to Jimmy King and his gang who used to lie in wait for Lotte and pull her plaits on the way home from school.

The dream changed to the back yard. We discovered there that the dragon had eaten the saddle bag of Lotte's second-hand bicycle, her birthday present for which Mum had saved so hard.

The dream jumped. Into the school kitchen in Densley High, after I'd passed. It was full of silent silver custard cauldrons, their lids open, gleaming, as if waiting to gobble up me and the other first year girls. Then in swept Miss Richards, my favourite teacher who taught history, and put down all the lids, so I was safe. That's when, in the dream, I fell in love with Miss Richards. She had red leather boots, knee high.

In the school kitchen, chlorine hung in the air. White tiles gleamed above deep white sinks. Dishcloths hung on racks, bleached. Tea towels dried on high airers, whose ropes were taught, twisted around double silver hooks on the walls. Nooses dangled. Above the serving hatches, which were open, there gleamed rows of stainless steel knives, sharp, poised, waiting. I felt very apprehensive.

The other side of the hatch, my great grandmother, known as Lavender Lil, called to me: 'Come buy my lavender, sweet smelling

13

lavender. Buy some for luck, Essie.' I couldn't reach her, nor properly see her. Miss Richards came and stood beside me.

'I can't see you properly,' I shouted to Lavender Lil.

'Ask your Grandma Clegg,' she called back.

'What?'

'To buy some of my lavender.'

'I will. I will.'

I turned around, and behind me right there, in the school kitchen, was my grandmother, making a banana cake. There, in my dream, in Densley High.

'Why're you making that, in here?'

'Your mum's on shifts. You like banana cake, don't you?'

'Yes, but . . .'

'Soon be ready. Your mum'll be home soon. Give us a hand, Essie, there's a good girl, this cauldron's heavy.'

'Why're you cooking that little cake in that custard cauldron, anyway?'

'Oh, Essie, you always were such a one with your questions. Oh, give it here, love, I'll do it myself. Get on with your book, girl.'

'I thought you wanted me to help with the cakes?'

'Don't answer me back, our Ess. Just get your homework done if there's that much of it, love.' Pause. 'Heavens above, what's that noise. It sounds just like your mum's bus.'

It was. Coming through the school corridor. It entered the foyer, and mum was hanging off the back, holding on to the silver pole, wearing her own bus conductress's uniform. By the serving hatch there was Lavender Lil with her arm out, hailing the bus. It stopped, just in time. I didn't know where I was or what was happening but Miss Richards said: 'Come on quick, Esther, or we'll miss it. But don't call me Miss from now on, because I never missed a thing. Come on, run.'

Mum dinged the bell and we just made it, with Lavender Lil, as the bus moved off. It swayed crazily through the school hall, but we didn't break a single window leaving the building, because there was nothing but air where the walls and windows should have been. We were travelling faster and faster and I said: 'Come on Great Grandma!' to Lavender Lil, whose face I still couldn't see too clearly, and I climbed up the stairs while the bus was in full motion, followed by Lavender Lil and Ms Richards who was now starting to quote Lenin saying: 'To the Finland Station. To the Finland Station.' I began singing and also started unravelling the woven seats on the top deck. Then I started threading the strands of upholstery, with my right hand, through the thin filament windows, whose little silver turning handles I was opening with my left hand.

I was still singing loudly. All this time, Lavender Lil was calling out the windows to passers-by to buy her lavender, sweet smelling lavender. Ms Richards was by now quoting long passages from *The Theses on Feuerbach*, such as: 'The purpose of philosophy is not to understand the world but to change it.'

Downstairs mum was dinging her ticket machine, handing out tickets. I don't know who was driving, but the bus was gathering speed until we were well over the speed limit. I was singing lustily, trying to make up tunes for Ms Richards' speeches. We turned a corner, swerved until we were all flung to the front in a laughing heap, and the jolt woke me up.

This room where I'm writing *is* my secret room. A place to hide away, to think, to learn to write. That's what this den means to me. It's a garage, really, running front to back alongside the bed-sit which I rent here in South East London. I learned to drive ages ago, but I don't have a car, and I didn't need a garage. But as soon as the landlord showed it to me, I said I'd take the place. From the outside it looks as it did before. But here inside I've hidden the entire door with a collection of bookcases, all leaning against each other, piled high and painted dark matt red, to match the ceiling. The other end has a window on to the garden, which I share with the other tenants. In front of the window is a desk with an upright chair, and a table lamp. The walls are white and covered with posters, pictures and photos. I've added a small cupboard, also dark matt red, with a kettle on top of it and two pots for tea bags and coffee. I have mum's old rocking chair, and when I'm thinking I sit and rock, as I did when I was a child.

My den has a past, present, and future quality about it. It is softly lit, with small lamps on the crazy bookcases. My rugs are multicoloured and Grandma Clegg pegged them, inch by inch, from pieces of rag. She called them proggy rugs and they still wash well. I miss her. I shared half my life with her, as I was born in 1946 and she died when I was eighteen. There's a photo of her with mum, who is wearing her busconductress's uniform. There is no photo of my great grandmother, who *did* sell lavender on Densley market.

Outside the window is a spreading wisteria. Its trunk is thick and gnarled.

Lavender Lil wore grey-brown skirts of wool, the colour of wisteria stems, to protect her from the winter frosts on market days. Her arms were tough and sinewy, like the stems are, and they have wrists and elbows too, like she did.

In May and June, the flounces and frills of blossom peg themselves out along these stems, as delicate as the lavender muslin gowns that Lavender Lil might have chosen, if she'd been one of her own wealthy customers.

Deanne

In the spring of '53 I arranged to meet Nell for the first time since we'd parted. I was twenty-one and she was nineteen and every part of me was hurting.

I arrived in Downingham on the bus at eleven. I'd rather have been alone in a quiet place, getting myself ready to meet her after such a long time. Instead I had to walk to the coach station through the market, feeling nervous and excited. Around me people bustled. I was carrying a suitcase. It jostled against women's legs and their shopping bags. My case was almost as cumbersome as their pushchairs balanced with parcels, and just as heavy as it had no wheels.

Above me the sky was the colour of cheap blue china on market stalls. In the market all the colours were brittle and the sounds too sharp. People's laughter was harsh, and babies seemed to shriek, not just to cry.

On some days the old town, high on the downs, miles from the sea, might have been soft and welcoming. Weathered bricks and worn grey stones. But on that day it was disturbing. I left the market and made my way to the end of the High Street. The edges of the buildings were all hard, the red too brash and the grey unfriendly. It was all down to the angle of the sun and to my strange uncomfortable mood.

The High Street had traditional shops, with the original wood panelling around the small windows and the oak doors. I passed the saddlery and the boot shop. The chemist had old blue bottles on display, and they made me shiver, not knowing what was in them.

Up ahead the street narrowed and then widened suddenly and parted around a war memorial from the first world war. It was an unusual four-cornered building rising to a clock with a dome. I had been watching the clock face from some distance away. It had been playing sour games with me. As I walked nearer, for what felt like one minute, the minute hand seemed to speed up and cover what must have been two minutes. It increased my worry about being late for Nell and my obsession about timing. I can't quite explain that. I mean about finding the right words to show Nell what had happened in the past months to me and Dora.

Even the sunshine didn't help me. It seemed to be mocking that day. As if to say that I might be on leave from work, but not to ask any more favours. Enough for it to be shining. What more did I want? I stepped into the street just then to avoid two mothers with prams. They were outside the wool and baby shop.

The rest of the High Street was long and rose from the clock tower to a flat open square so high that I could see almost a full circle all over the downs. They rolled away in all directions.

The coach station wasn't only in the most inconvenient part of the town; it was wrongly named as well. I'm sure it was really a gatehouse to a manor or a huge country estate. It was a one-storey grey stone building with red brickwork around the door. It had a clock on it. I was beginning to think that Downingham was the town of a thousand clocks. This one didn't tally with the clock tower. P'raps I was late. Panic started.

'Oh don't you fret my dear,' said the woman inside, kindly. 'Your friend's more than likely on the one that's been delayed an hour and a half. Late leaving London, my dear. Not expected here until one o'clock now.'

The thought of sitting in a converted gatehouse didn't thrill me.

'Could I leave this here, please?' I asked and pointed to my case, 'and is there anywhere I could walk to in, say, only fifteen minutes, and maybe buy something to eat?'

We put my case in the left luggage and I took the green ticket. Then the woman came outside with me, and started talking with her hands and waving her arms, in the direction of the open countryside, when she realised I didn't want to go back and sit in a crowded café in the town. I said I'd be back for sure in an hour and a quarter, in good time for Nell's coach. She laughed then and told me it wouldn't be early, possibly even later.

I realised then that I didn't have my sturdy shoes on. But then I'd hardly expected to spend half that day waiting and walking. So I had to get my case out again, change my shoes, and put my case back.

I started along the west road out of Downingham and tried to swing into my usual steady rhythm. I had my watch on and I was half glad that Nell was delayed. Leaving the town was a relief. I was aware of birds singing for the first time since hurrying with the suitcase. I missed the gulls of Coombebury, though. And the smell of the sea. The sky was not only china blue; it was also the blue of robins' eggs. I didn't know if Nell would remember those. Eggs were about waiting. And springtime. It would soon be summer. I didn't know how summer could help, that year.

There were no trees along my route, because it was high downland. The hedge bottoms were a treasure though. Some of the boundaries had been hedged and bodged recently. By experts. The raw open cuts were already healing. A hare sprang away and raced over the fields.

In another twelve minutes, I arrived at Mrs Mull's tea garden, just as the coach woman had said. It was an outbuilding, not big enough to have been a barn. There were tables and chairs under the apple blossom in the orchard. Mrs Mull was like someone out of *The Archers*. I had to stop myself from staring at her.

No wonder this place was well known. I was content that everyone was in the damned market town. I needed this orchard to myself.

I ordered a double hot chocolate and three toasted teacakes. There were bluebells in the grass, and wallflowers in tubs by the teahouse. I could hear cows being taken into a field the other side of the main farm; and in front of me the sparrows were being bullied by some starlings. Greedy birds. I tried to feed only the sparrows with the teacakes.

I thought briefly of other people who might meet there; or wait like I was waiting. The old stones were not so frozen as in the town. They had seen comings and goings too but seemed quieter, contained. It made me wonder again about the life I'd built with Dora and the foundations too.

The clock on the teahouse was set into the stones, like a sundial. Now that I had time to sit and think of what to say to Nell, the minute hand seemed to travel patiently across the face. I was grateful for that old-fashioned slow place.

'Don't be old-fashioned, Dee,' Dora had said, not long after we moved into the rented rooms. 'It's not Mereford now. We've got to move with the times now. Get a more modern outlook. Be modern.'

'I am modern, sweetheart. I love the new clothes and all that.'

I didn't understand that, for her, modern meant going with a man. I became afraid after it happened the first time, that some new man would appear and offer the world and so-called normal family life, bliss as it was meant to be.

At first we kept on arguing. I went on about trust and how could I learn to believe in myself, and in a woman's love for me. I said that surely we had something precious that men would only spoil? Hadn't she started out feeling that way too? So why had she done that if I didn't need to? What was wrong with her, or what was wrong with me?

'I wanted a fling, that's all, Dee. Don't hurt me like this by keeping on raking it up. I haven't been with one since.'

'Then why won't you . .? I mean why don't we . .?'

'We don't have to . . . well all the time.'

'It's been ages since we . . .'

'Well all right then.'

'Oh no, Dora. Not when it's like this. I want you to want it too. Like we both used to. Doing it just for me isn't what I want.'

During the two years that followed, we started to make love again, mutually. Sometimes it was very good for us. My trust began to grow again. In her, and in myself. Time helped me. I knew I loved her. I wanted to trust her, again.

Loving Dora could make the backs of my knees go loose, ready . . . I never was one for talking about the physical side. I wasn't used to having people to talk to about it. Oh there were plenty of jokes down The Feathers, but as for exactly what we did, I only talked to Corrine: and that was spoiled for me if I gave half a thought to Corrine in bed with Dove-baby.

I ordered another hot chocolate and a teacake to feed to the sparrows.

Dora's second affair began in early '52. It was April that year when I found the photo. I couldn't imagine she'd left it lying around by mistake. She meant me to find it. There was my Dora with her arm around a black man.

I didn't recognise the place they were, but it was likely some part of Southampton. I looked at his hands, his face, his eyes, his lips. I put my fingers to my face, tracing round my mouth. I was staring into our bedroom mirror then at the eyes in my own reflection.

I hadn't known I could hate so much since the war bombers killed my mother.

Dora's picture was of a woman who had just had pleasure. That glow. A wonder the camera hadn't melted with the aura. That used to be for me. I knew that magic on her, in her. I used to turn her whole body into that. I hated him for being a man and was appalled at him for being black. I loathed him right through her pregnancy.

'I don't know how you could. A man. You wanted another man and not only that, you chose a black man.'

'There's nothing wrong with that, you narrow-minded bitch. I don't care if he is sky blue pink with yellow dots on, I like him. And you're a prejudiced bitch as well as a possessive one. You don't own me and you never have. It's my body and I'll put it where I damn well please.'

'You are having a mixed-up baby. It won't be one thing or the other. Half and half – have you thought of that, my love?'

'Don't you call me your love in that tone of voice. That's half the trouble with us. I haven't stopped loving you, Dee. We had some good times together. Till you tried caging me in. I do love you, I actually love you a lot, Dee. But I want to be free. I will love who I want to, when I want to. Without being possessive. I'm mine. Mine. I insist on being free to love. Free love. That's what I hold with.'

'There's no such thing as free love for women. You won't face it. You're already pregnant and you still won't face it. You haven't even thought about the brat. You're having a bastard. This is Coombebury, not London. You're living in cloud cuckoo land.'

'If anybody's doing that it's you, Dee. How the hell did you think we were going to carry on here, like this? At least I'm normal.'

'Oh you are, are you? Well let me tell you this. Nobody else is going to see you as normal. But you won't talk to me about that. Just go around the edges all the time. I'd be okay if I could just walk out on you, but I still can't. I'm going up the wall, Dora. Waiting and being messed about. I never felt that way for a man. Any man. I never wanted a child. I can't understand you. I can't understand. I can't. I can't.'

'You aren't damn well trying. That's what.'

'Don't you tell me what I'm trying. I'm trying to work out what the hell is going on in your head. Why didn't you get rid of it? You won't admit it's happened this time will you? You must think that if you ignore it it'll go away. Well it won't. This time it'll come out brown. And you know as well as I do there aren't any others like it here in this place. You . . . you . . . you leave me speechless.'

'It'd be a relief if you damn well were. Know-all. Bloody know-all. P'raps I don't care if it's brown. I'm not a prejudiced cunt like you. Besides . . .' She stopped. Was she deciding whether to tell me? 'He wants to marry me. He wants me to go to Trinidad with him.'

'Oh my sweet mother. I swear on the life of my dear dead mother that I wasn't meant to hate *you*, Dora. I hate him and I don't want to hate you too.'

We still lived in the rented rooms down by the railway. Unable to move apart. Clinging but repelling. Like two south poles trapped in the same wretched magnet.

The tearoom clock showed half past twelve. I paid my bill and started back to the coach station.

As I walked towards Downingham, I saw that some clouds had moved in low over the town. They lay there uncomfortably on the house tops, on the churches and chapels, pierced by the many clock towers. I thought of the clouds there, and then of me and Dora in bed, and they seemed like feather mattresses on a bed of nails.

Esther

February 1983

I dreamed about my sister Lotte who was roller-skating up and down the sloping roof of our house, in Densley.

I was calling out of the window to her, 'Come down, Lotte. Tea's ready. Grandma Clegg's made potato cakes. Come on, she says you're not to roller-skate on our roof. It's going to crack the roofing slates. Come on down.'

Next, she was paddling in our back yard in a woven boat, like a Welsh coracle, and the water was lapping gently along the back door step.

Lotte floated out of the back yard in the coracle, towards a wide open area of very beautiful marshland. There were reeds and bulrushes, birds soaring, using the air currents with magnificent wings.

A mist came down, until I couldn't see my sister. I called to her over and over. 'Lotte, Lotte.' She didn't answer but when the sunshine evaporated the mists I could see that she was no longer paddling, with the oar, but was drifting happily, knitting. Like Grandma Clegg. It wasn't with wool but instead it was with bus tickets, from one of Mum's buses after they changed from little thick cardborad tickets to long thin paper rolls, which were produced in a continuous flow, printed in pale purple ink.

'Lotte, when did you start knitting?' I called to her.

'Who you talking to?'

'You, Lots, what'you knitting?'

She laughed then, in my dream, and didn't answer me.

'I love you, Lotte.'

But she didn't hear me, though I called four more times and my voice was becoming fainter and fainter and the mist came down again, over the marshes. When it brightened, I was by a waterfall. I was spinning, with apple peelings. I spun and spun, and the peelings were fine and thin and started to pour through my fingers like liquid. It was

23

liquid. It was cider, and when I licked it off it tasted good and strong. It was making a pool all around me, up to my ankles. Laura came to the waterfall. She said:

'Lotte's gone. I'll drink it. We need bottles.' She put down a basket of bright bottles, brown glass, green glass, and pink glass.

'I've never seen pink glass bottles before, Laura. Aren't they pretty?'

'From the bottle factory. That's where we'll be if we fail our O levels, Essie.'

'We shan't fail. We can't fail. I don't want to work in the bottle factory. Here, start filling this one.' I handed her the first pink one.

Then we forced the necks down into the pool of cider, which slurped in, glugging and spluttering as the air in the bottles bubbled out. We filled and filled until we had sixteen bottles each, without any stoppers.

Suddenly it changed. The school domestic science room. Laura and me with all the bottles. In walked Ms Richards, with whom I was in love. That was a secret, except to Laura, who used to listen to me going on and on about Ms Richards' views on the Middle East, the Far East, the American elections, the local elections.

'I'm surprised at you, Esther,' said Ms Richards, more sad than angry. I went bright red, and Laura put on her defiant look.

'Why?' asked Laura.

'Cider was not your homework. I asked you to look up the Korean War in Keesing's *Contemporary Archives*.'

'Oh, I will, Ms Richards, I will,' I spluttered, making more froth than all the cider bottles together. 'I was spinning, and it all went wrong. I didn't mean to spin cider. I just sort of, er, it just sort of happened.' Pause. 'I will get my homework in on time, I promise.'

Ms Richards smiled. I wanted to hug her. Laura still looked tough, a big angry. I knew she didn't think as much of Ms Richards as I did, even though she was my best friend. Laura, I mean.

'Politics is the art of the possible,' sang Ms Richards, and I couldn't think just then exactly what she meant or what it had to do with spinning cider or the bottle factory, so I decided to ask Laura later, and not show myself up in front of Ms Richards, because I wanted her to think I was mature, knowing as much as she did about the rest of the world and socialism and communism too, even if I hadn't finished reading all the books she had lent me.

I started to clear away the bottles and she winked at me and took one for later, saying: 'Well at least this is drinkable, you two. Now no more wasting time, or you really will fail those exams. Besides I want that talk prepared for the general studies lesson, and you've only another ten days, so you've got your work cut out. See you in the history class tomorrow.'

'Oh Laura,' I mouthed, as Ms Richards left, 'Isn't she fair. She could have given us a double detention for spinning cider in school.'

'We didn't. You span it and you weren't in school you were by the waterfall,' she laughed.

'But she *is* fair, isn't she, Laura?'

'Mmm. Come on Ess, stop mooning. Give us a hand clearing this lot up.'

Then I woke up, and Densley High and Laura at sixteen seemed so far away, from South East London, now. And so did Ms Richards, bless her bright red boots.

In Densley there were dozens of terraces of brick houses like ours, with outside toilets and walkways called ginnels which separated the blocks, giving access to the backyards. The bedroom that I shared with Lotte was built over the ginnel and was freezing even in summer because the air was sucked fast through the gap under us.

Here and there the back yards had privet hedges smothered from years of soot. Some yards had pigeon sheds and others had blazes of colour from well loved displays of garden flowers. A few were grass patches or were bare with paving slabs or bricks with moss in the cracks.

My favourite was the yard to the corner shop. It was a tumble jumble of paint-box browns and reds, stacked with crates of empty bottles. Green glass, brown and white; flat bottoms, curved bottoms, some with spiders in, some catching the rain and holding it. A forbidden place for us children. More magic because of that.

My den looks down a long garden, ten times the size of my childhood back yard.

The tradition in Grandma Clegg's family was that the miners were the breadwinners, but my Grandma Clegg always worked, knitting garments by hand, pegging rugs, and sewing soft toys.

She told us that at Christmas she felt snowed under with wool, so that I imagined her with just her eyes and nose poking out.

Knitting gave her her own money, no questions asked, and she enjoyed that independence. She could choose a better joint for Sunday lunch and would buy leather shoes when she could for herself and her five children. She was angry if ever anyone called it pin money. She said that her money was a basic part of her housekeeping.

She usually worked on her knitting for over fifty hours a week. Sometimes when money was especially tight, my grandad would work nights down the pit to make more, and Grandma Clegg would work too till maybe three in the morning and manage nightly on four hours' sleep for weeks at a time.

She used her money to buy fruit to make her own puddings which she stored away for Christmas; and a real fruit cake; and a piece of ham for Boxing Day.

When the war came in '39, Grandma Clegg went to work in Densley bottle factory, for the duration of the war. She found the noise incredible and many women lost their hearing. That's why she had not allowed her only daughter Rene to work in a factory before the war. Rene's four brothers all worked down the pit. They were not called up on account of the nation's need for coal.

It was during wartime that my mum, Rene Clegg, suddenly decided to leave Densley. She went to work in the Yorkshire Dales with Aunt Edith, Grandma Clegg's youngest sister, who had been widowed at the beginning of the war and had been left with three tiny children under the age of four.

I've always written like this in my diary, but nobody else in my family liked diary writing, nor, according to Grandma Clegg, ever gave such a thing a thought until Mass Observation asked people to keep everyday civilian records during wartime. But Grandma Clegg said that she didn't go much on diaries because she could never think what to write. Instead she wrote twice a week to her own daughter away in the Dales, and enjoyed getting Rene's letters back. After the war she kept the letters, and from time to time, if she was in the right mood, she might show bits and pieces to myself and Lotte. She said she could write and write because she knew Rene through and through. It was interesting, she said, although it was sad, and she told us that it helped her to get through her fears.

Deanne

Nell and I took the bus to Mereford. An hour's ride from Downingham. We jolted through lanes where the army'd never been during wartime, while we were safe in Mereford. The hills were too steep, too narrow and curving for jeeps.

'Memory Lane,' grinned Nell. I noticed the laughter-line still pulled across her cheek. She was copper-haired as always, taller now and thin. With the same dark brown eyes.

'You're thin as ever aren't you? But the grin's the same.'

'You've changed, Dee. You've got years on you. Years.'

I winced. But I wasn't going to start explaining, until we arrived.

The bus dropped us off. We stepped down with our suitcases, back to ten years ago. As if someone posed us there in an old photo.

'*Déjà vu,*' said Nell.

'French? You've gone up in the world.'

'Leave it off. I got it off of work, didn't I? I'm on the dolls-eye. That's me switchboard. Like that old doll on the farm. All broken. The one we found in that box.'

'Somebody'd put it in a hot bath and melted its joints.'

'Yeah, well we could see its eyes rolling, click, click, yeah?'

'Uckgh!' It used to make me shiver.'

'Well, me switchboard has rows o' them. All clicking round.'

'Bloody hell.'

'It's all right. Got used to it. Well, if the person comes through speaking French, I have to say "Hold the line please" in French, right?'

'What then? You fluent?'

'Neah. I passes 'em through to his Lordship's personal secretary, what's trained . . .' (she held her lips in a pucker, upper-class style) '. . . to speak in French. I listens in, sometimes. Interestin'.'

We were laughing and relaxing, getting used to each other again. We'd shared a secret, passing our letters for so long. I'd often wondered over the years if she might fade out, or get found out. But she needed me too. Her letters used to start with a capital 'D' for Dear Deanne, and finish with a full stop. There was no knowing what might happen in between. But they came, through the years, and we were now here. It was quite something, just knowing that.

We walked down by the river. The pussy willow was trimmed back. A foot or two higher. Otherwise nothing was new.

We spread the blanket Corrine gave me, on the ground. Took off our shoes. Unhooked our stockings. Trailed our feet in the Mere.

It was slow, where we sat, by the curve. A brown gold mirror. There was sunshine on the surface. Everything was very slow. Sun and shadows rippled on the willow twigs.

We were small children again. I imagined us in the mirror. In winceyette nighties. No mothers.

'I'm sad about your mother, Nell.'

'I miss her. I thought about you while she was dying. You was so tough when yours died. I couldn't do nothin' for you, Dee.'

'You did. I told myself I was your sister, looking after you. I told myself that, Nell, and it got me through.'

'I wished you was me real sister. I hated our Joan, hated her. I was glad she was too big to get evacuated. I wanted a bomb to get her.'

'She was a bully.'

'I still got the scar from that piece of wood wiv a nail in, look.' She hitched up her frock. The long scar was still there. It ran down her thigh like a thread of almost transparent cotton. She caught my eye and grinned, pulling the laughter-line across her cheek.

I wanted her to know ALL about me and still love me. I loved her again then, like a real sister.

We started on the fish paste sandwiches. Nell remembered the picnics on the farm. She grinned to herself, then to me.

'Funny what you like to eat as kids eh?'

'Salad cream and dripping sarnies!' I laughed.

'They was me favourite for years and years.' She sighed, half laughing.

'Mercy, Nell, don't. It makes me heave just thinking of them.'

'Tell me about your Dora, then.'

Always the same, was Nell, unexpected and straight to it. I wanted her to know, and didn't at the same time. I said, 'It's a long story.'

'I got time, Dee.'

So I started telling her. I had to fill her in on events from a few years ago, so I could make sense of it all.

'D'you remember me writing years ago, that Dora had her nose in a book whenever she could?' Nell nodded. I felt encouraged by her sitting there very close to me, listening, watching the Mere. Slow.

I took a long breath and carried on: 'I didn't go much on books, Nell. Never was one for all them words. Not really. But I used to draw on a proper sketch pad. Told you that in my letters. People said I had the knack for it.

'Besides, the Bronnester was the perfect place for watching people. Visitors and staff. I used to try and catch the expressions.

'One Christmas, I think we'd been there for maybe four years, Corrine bought me a proper artist set. Tubes. Real hair brushes. Watercolours. In a lovely wooden box. To keep them neat. I was in my element. She bought Dora a book called *How To Study*.

'Dora was restless at the hotel. But I was happy there. I wrote to you I wanted to learn reception work. They said they'd train me. Corrine found Dora a new job. Through some contacts of the Dove. It was in an accountant's office. In Southampton. Making the tea, basic filing. They said they'd teach her on the job about book-keeping.'

'She had you under her wing, then?'

'S'pose so. She was family.'

'Sugar mommy.'

'Sort of. She had Dove as her sugar daddy.'

Nell said, 'Introduce me,' and then rolled her eyes into her eyebrows, like her switchboard. I winced and shuddered inside. Not because of the 'eyes'; because of Dove. I hope she hadn't noticed. I was getting better at covering over.

Then I thought that it was funny sometimes how the thoughts would come at me sideways round the back corners, when I really didn't want them to at all. There were too many. I'd have liked to put them away in a box, like the old doll on the farm.

In all my letters to Nell, I'd always written as though Dora was very close to me. Important. I'd never actually said we were lovers. I somehow felt it was unnecessary; that Nell knew and I didn't have to spell it out. But now it had come to the time to make it all crystal clear. I needed to know exactly how Nell felt; exactly what she did know.

If I was wrong, had misjudged it, then I might find myself unable to talk to Nell about anything at all. My last letter to her had said things were hard for me and Dora at the moment.

I was quiet for a while, wondering how to ask Nell what she knew, how much to confide, and what our friendship was really all about.

Nell was gentle. Giving me plenty of time. She wouldn't want to add

29

to the hurts. I knew that. She would try to lighten me up a bit to help me. She didn't have to be perfect. I didn't want that. I just wanted her to be as she was. There.

So we ate our sandwiches for a while. I was thinking that Corrine was much more to me than a sugar mommy. She was my older sister and mum all in one. I'd often wondered, if we'd been nearer in age, whether we'd have been girlfriends like me and Dora. But she'd been twenty-six and I'd been thirteen, when we first met. Different generations. I wasn't sure how to carry on. Nell asked, 'So you was all set then, set to make yer fortunes?'

'I thought so. I thought we were happy. I mean, I knew she was restless but I thought it was just the studying.

'She's got a good head for numbers. If she'd had the chance, she could have gone to college just like that.' I snapped my fingers. 'That's how it all started.

'Dora began coming back late from work. Said she'd been in the main library in Southampton. She had piles and piles of library books.

'I wanted to believe her. I didn't ask her anything. She was changing. Changing in herself. Changing towards me, too. Ever so moody. Like a cloud that couldn't even find a hill to rain on.'

Nell was listening, concentrating. Suddenly she asked me, 'You did it with Dora, didn't you?'

I nodded, and I could hardly meet her eyes, I was so scared.

She talked softly then, realised she was getting warmer, like in Hunt-the-Thimble. 'I liked your letters, Dee,' she said. 'You was right about me at the farm. I did guess. But I didn't know what I was guessing, if you get me.' I nodded. 'I was too young really to know what it was all about, but I could hear you making happy sounds and I liked that. Being in bed with you both made me safer. You were kind to me when I was a scaredy cat. Both of you. I knew you was both growing up. So I started to train meself not to wet. So as I'd not have to bother you. I worked it out after. When I was old enough to know it.'

She thought for a minute or two. I waited. She said, 'There's a girl like you down my office. We go down the Silver Coach wiv her an' her mates, now and then. There's lots like you in London, Dee. If you know where to look.

'I got nothing against your ways or that girl in my office. But that's not me style. It's just not me style, that's all.

'I got no romantic notions about Fred,' said Nell. 'I told him: "You want it, you got to marry me first." ' She rolled her eyes till I laughed and then she added, 'I'm having that bit o' paper. Or I ain't doing IT and he ain't having IT.'

She raised her coffee drink, and toasted me.

'Here's to both of us, Dee. To us being real good friends, Dee.'

'Cheers, Nell. I'll drink to that.' I did, with the top from my flask.

Then she said that when I became a fully trained receptionist we'd maybe be able to talk to each other on the office telephone. We both laughed at first, thinking of it. But Nell is also very canny. She said, 'Your secret's safe with me, Dee, as if you didn't know. It's more'n my job's worth to go mouthing off to anyone at work, innit? I mean to say, what's the point of letting that lot in? What you do wiv your life's *your* business, innit Dee?'

'You haven't told that girl in your office, have you?'

'Course I haven't – what d'yer take me for? It's none of her business, either, what you do with Dora, is it? Slomner'd get rid of her like a shot, if he knew about her girlfriend, too. *That's* no different in London, Dee. No different at all. Nah. All I said to her was you and me was evacuated together. That's all I'd ever say 'bout me knowing you, Dee. You'd have to tell her yourself, wouldn't you?'

I was relieved. Felt safer when we'd sorted that out. It *would* be lovely to talk to Nell from time to time on a free phone. What a funny twist of fate.

I wanted her to know it all, but I couldn't talk too free. Nell wasn't like Corrine. Or Dora. She wasn't like the girl in her office. She was going to be a married woman playing the role of Fred's wife. Heaven help her, I thought, though I doubted she'd get any help from up there.

So I wasn't going to be able to tell about all of it. But her marriage to Fred made me pause a minute, thinking carefully about marriage and roles.

(I asked Corrine sometimes about her and Maggie. Did they play roles, things like that. She told me they didn't. That they were both everything to each other. That made me feel all right. I'd not ever wanted to be like a man, and Dora didn't either. But we'd catch nasty jokes about women like us, sometimes, in the hotel, overhearing things in the cinemas, too. Sometimes there were bad jokes on the screen, people mouthing off about homos and lessies. I only once, in the very early days, asked Corrine, 'Are you a lesbian?' She said, 'Why?' I said, 'Seems to be something bad, whenever I hear it.' She said, 'I was, Dee, with Maggie and I am now, with Mol.' Then she added, and looked into my face, 'It's not bad. Do you hear me? Anything else is second best.' If Nell had been like us – with women – then I could maybe have talked with her about roles. Me and Dora never did have roles. We'd been everything to each other.)

I looked at Nell then. She asked, 'Has it all gone wrong then, Dee?'

'Yes, it has gone wrong. She doesn't want me ... er, for ... er in bed. Says we should just be friends.'

Nell looked sad and poured us both some coffee. She fished a box out of her bag. She'd treated us to mint chocolate and cream cakes.

I think she was trying to slow us down. So as we could take it all in. Meeting. After so long. Wanting to be close, but living lives that didn't really touch any more.

So we nibbled the mint chocolate and licked the cream in tiny licks off the cakes. To make them last a long time.

We watched the river, not talking. A vole darted out. His nose twitched for the chcolate. Like something from *Wind in the Willows*. We had enjoyed that book in Mereford School.

That made both of us smile. Watching him. Then I thought, I wonder if it's a she?

'Will you ever come back to London, Dee?'

'I couldn't stand the noise. All the hustle and bustle. I'm used to having the country here. Besides, I like walking. I've got myself some real boots now.

'I dream about a place with a garden. Nothing posh, Nell. But I'd love a little garden. My dream place has a huge one. Acres.'

'Now who wants to go up in the world?' She laughed. So did I. It was lovely to have a laugh.

'I did say I was only dreaming, Nell.' I didn't tell her that usually when I had that dream I'd wake to discover that Dora had been in it and I'd lie there facing the day; empty.

'The library was closed by eight. So when Dora came in at midnight, I knew it wasn't just the long journey back that kept her. I guessed she must be seeing someone else.

'Then one night she didn't come back. I was beside myself. I even threw up in the lav. Had to take the next day off.

'She came home at three in the afternoon. She was greybeige. She could hardly stand up. She almost fell in through the door. Into my arms. She'd been in Southampton. She'd had an abortion.'

Nell barely moved a muscle. She watched the river, still she sat, and still listening.

'Corrine came over. She was furious with Dora. Said she'd risked her life, doing it like that. Down by the docks, in a back kitchen.

'Corrine stormed around our two rooms, muttering about how

Dora could've gone to see Mol instead of going behind our backs down to the docks; muttering about rich men and abortions; how they fixed it for "their" women; but not for the Doras.

'Really Nell, to hear Corrine, you'd have thought she never ever did it with Dove, she hated him and his kind so much.

'Then Corrine went out to see Mol and came back with some pills. "For the infection," she said. I stayed home a week, making Dora take them. I thought she might die. I was terrified. She actually came through quite quickly, though. Then I had the time to get angry. I couldn't at first. I was too frightened.

'Then I think it all hit me. Dora had swopped me for a man. We rowed and I raged and raged. She just kept saying she'd needed a fling. To see what they were like.'

Nell looked away from the river. Looked at the sky and the trees. Thinking, maybe about Fred. I don't know. Then she looked full at me. Her copper hair was really red. Funny how you sometimes notice things. Her eyes were brown as voles. Soft, too.

'Go on, Dee.'

She smiled. I hadn't seen that smile before. It was like her talking sad. No words.

'She has had another fling, Nell.'

'I thought you was going to say that. Go on.'

'This man was eight years older than Dora. He said he wanted her to marry him. I never met him. He came to use the reference library in Southampton. Was studying economics. She still lived in the two rooms with me. Said she loved me. Didn't want to make love with me. Then she got pregnant.

'I was going berserk, Nell. Trying to work out what to do. What did my life have in front of me. She was six months on when he left her. He told her he was already a married man with children.'

'That's too far gone. She'd have to have it then.'

I nodded and said, 'The baby was born this January, the week your mum died. I wanted to hate that brat. I tried hating it. I tried for two weeks. But in between that, I used to have to hold it. It's a girl. Dora wanted it called Isobel. Fancy name. Never mind. I had to hold her. Feed her with a bottle because Dora wouldn't touch her. Wouldn't look at her or change her. I couldn't leave a baby without food. That'd be murder. So I had to pick her up. Wash her. Wipe her face.

'Then I kissed her. I don't know why I did. I just one day kissed her. Then it all came pouring out. She was something that needed kissing. I knew what that was like. I was starved for it.

'So I kissed Dora's baby. I kissed Isobel. Then I couldn't hate her properly. Izzie, I mean. That hating didn't work, Nell. I liked her. It was wonderful. Silly that. But it just went right into me.'

Nell was sipping cold coffee. She didn't speak.

'Dora won't touch the baby. Wants to put her in a home. You know how I'd feel about *that*. I'd never ever forgive myself. Dora still won't talk to me, or to Corrine. She sits all day and looks at the walls. Or she cries with no noise. She's been like it the whole time since Isobel was born.'

'Where's the baby, I mean Izzie, now?'

'There's a woman down the road, called Glenis. She has her in the daytime. Corrine's not working this week, and so she has her in the evenings. We daren't leave Dora with her.'

She put her hand over her mouth and her eyes were large. She didn't speak. The tension was tight in me. Like a spring winding. Like one of those damn clocks back in Downingham. It should have been called Clockingham. I could feel the coils about to snap and then they did and the words came through in a rush. And just before they did I felt the same in Nell. Her knuckles went all white like they always did when she was expecting a showdown or a row.

'There's more. The baby, Isobel I mean, she's brown. Her father was from Trinidad.'

'How brown?' It came out like a cuckoo. Straight on cue. Door flies open and out.

'What do you mean?' A lie in a question. I knew. I knew because of how I'd been over it at first. But I thought I'd come a long way in a year and that I was changed, so I was flaming red to the nape of my neck. Sorry at us. And sorry didn't make it right.

But she wasn't letting me away. Not easy. Not so easy.

'I mean how brown. That's what. You shouldn't have kept it. You should send it back. Back where it came from.'

It. How could she say 'it'? It had a sex. It had a name. How dare she call Izzie an it. Because Izzie was brown. She'd not have itt-ed it if Izzie had been white.

'Life's not like that. Izzie is alive and there is nowhere else and I don't want to.' (I was yelling now.) 'I don't want to.'

But she didn't yell. She stayed cold and hard. Where was the sister bit now, uhm?

'Well you should. It's not fair on 'em. You should fetch it down our way. Somebody'd have it.'

'She's not a bloody parcel, Nell. Post early for Christmas. She's a

34

real person. Real. You are talking about a real live person.'

'She won't thank you. You mark my words, Dee. Your place is white as the north pole. You got no right, Dee.'

'You sound like I did. Taking my words. I said all them. I said all them over and over to Dora. Then he left her. And it wasn't about anybody's rights. She was six months on. You just said that to me. Just now. I said terrible things then. I thought I might kill her. Or the baby. Or both. Me. Use your imagination. Gay woman murders lover and child. Headlines. Huh. Then Izzie came. Posh name. I didn't care. She arrived. Of course she is brown. Look. Look.' (I pulled her picture from my pocket.) 'This is Izzie last month.' (I felt myself start to cry.) 'I have nursed this baby through influenza. You know what February was like this year. It's too . . . too late . . . for me to start on about rights . . . She just *is*.'

I was crying. Nell said 'Oh my God. Oh dear God I wouldn't be in your shoes. Or hers. Not where you live. Oh dear God.'

I wept then. The first time since Izzie was born. Enough to flood the Mere. Break its banks.

Nell wasn't a hugging kind of woman. She put her arms around me though, and kept them there till I'd done.

Lotte

Lovely woman, my mum. I can just imagine her on the market, before the war, can't I? Calling out, 'Roll up, roll up! China cheap and cheerful. Tea sets, dinner sets, you name it we sell it. Roll up, roll up! Top quality, bottom prices. Now then love, what can I do for you?'

And Red Heather there next to her, her with her hats, a different one for each day. They must have been a right good team mustn't they?

Mum was only fourteen you know when she was picked to work with Red Heather. Mind you, there wasn't half a family fight over it. Whew, I'd say so. You see my Grandad Clegg didn't want his only daughter going on the market. Oh no. It was quite a come-down for his side of the family. Whereas my Grandma Clegg was more used to the idea, because her mother had been the lavender seller, hadn't she? Well you might think that *she* wouldn't want Rene, that's my mum, her daughter, going backwards, back to the hard life out of doors. But it didn't work like that in Grandma Clegg's mind, because it was the depression and Rene had to have a job, didn't she? Grandma Clegg, you know it's funny but we always called her that. Don't ask me why. I couldn't tell you. My friends said just Gran or just Grandma or more often, Nanan, but somehow we didn't. We actually said Grammaclegg, like that. Not Grand hyphen ma hyphen Clegg, you know. Gramma-clegg. Anyroadup, my Grammaclegg had this bumble bee in her bonnet, that Rene must not go into the bottle factory. It's sad really to think that she went there herself when war came, isn't it? So, she saw Rene's golden opportunity and worked on my Grandad till he gave in as much as he ever gave into anything, poor old soul. Actually he was a stubborn old bugger, but lovable with it, my Grammaclegg said, and he was never ever violent and she said that counted for a lot in them days. Well it did, didn't it? So when Red Heather chose Rene out of forty girls who wanted the job, which wasn't bad going on my mum's part, I'd say, Rene stuck to her guns and Grammaclegg stuck to hers and the master of the house, who wasn't really that at all because my Grammaclegg ruled over us all with an orb and sceptre, well the master had to climb down.

Now one of the reasons he hadn't wanted Rene to work with Red Heather, was that Heather's nickname was no coincidence. Nobody's name in Densely was a thing to be taken lightly. Densley people love names and they can tear you to pieces or boost you up to the sky with their tongues, no kidding, and without swearing once. I mean if a teapot is, well, let's say fat-bellied and a good pourer, then you can say so and sell it for a real good price, and you don't have to say it's a bloody teapot too. My Grammaclegg had such a thing about swearing, only it was a problem for Rene sometimes (and for me because I take after my mum) and sometimes there's nowt like a good swear-off. If Rene was angry, and we all have good hot tempers in my family, well if Rene got the steam up she'd not dare let out swear words in front of her parents. So she'd fly out the house and down the yard to the lav and sit there having a good old go. Or she'd sometimes get sent out by her mum and that was to the coal house. In there she'd swear slam swear slam swear slam with the shovel against the wall 'till it had all worn off and then the family would all be laughing again.

My mum loved working with Red Heather. Oh I lost my thread, didn't I? I was going to say that she was too red for Grandad. They were in the Labour Party and of course Grandad was a strong union man, like all the clan, but Heather was far far left of him; really she should have been in the Communists, but she said there was a lot of work to be done in the Labour Party in the depression.

Rene was secretly interested in the Communists, and she knew her dad suspected that, didn't she, so she kept very quiet about all that while she and Grammaclegg were working on him. Anyway they won.

There were five children and three bedrooms so as Rene was the youngest she had a fold-up bed in the living room. I could never work that out, myself, as they would all be up after she needed to sleep but Grammaclegg said that when Rene was little she'd put Rene to sleep in her own bed (I mean Grammaclegg's bed) and then carry her down when the family trooped upstairs. But of course with them all growing up, it was all so crowded that after two months on the market deciding she liked it, Mum took up Red Heather's offer that she should live in. Later she did all the book-keeping for Red Heather.

She never told us what went wrong, but she took the chance to go to the Yorkshire Dales to help Aunt Edith when the evacuation from the cities started. I'm like Mum. I don't usually go much on writing letters, but I'd have written to my mum three times a week just like she did, and she wrote back to Red Heather too.

I can't imagine wartime. Not really. I don't suppose anybody can from mine and Essie's generation.

I used to give our Esther a hard time. I used to say 'You're a foreigner, our Ess.'

Then she'd get so hoity-toity. Right on her high horse. We was such good friends when we was young. Real close and that's why I could wind her up like that if we was having a row.

My mum went to San Francisco after the war, married to this American GI. That's where Esther was born, wasn't it? Now my Grammaclegg, still slogging away in the bottle factory, was the breadwinner and all the brothers had married and had their own places and some had babies, and Grandad was bedridden with emphysema from all his years in the pit. Well that was hard times for my Grammaclegg, wasn't it? Mind you, she told me later that she never once went a day without meat because all her sons got themselves organised and each one of them brought her meat on different days. I mean you hardly heard of vegetarians and health foods in those days. So meat was a big thing and very expensive and it was on rations still after the war, and they all shared theirs and made sure Grandad had liver. That was supposed to be specially good for him. Build him up and such like.

It fair chokes me up to think of them doing that. You know, all the time we were growing up our Essie said she'd never want her own children and I just couldn't understand that. I loved being in the clan. Well, tribe, call it what you like. There was uncles and aunts and hordes o' cousins. Our Essie didn't bother with all that.

Our Essie was eighteen months old and I was waiting to be born (not that I remember much about it, well would you?) and Mum had this terrible letter from Grammaclegg saying to come quick to Densley if she wanted to see Grandad alive. It was 1948. Rene's husband wouldn't come with her on the trip. That must've hurt. It would've hurt me. To think that someone I was close to didn't understand how important that trip would be. All my mum's brothers had split the fares between them and that's saying something about how much they loved their younger sister, isn't it?

So Mum came, holding Essie by the hand and pregnant with me. She saw Grandad for about four weeks. He'd gone down to six stone and he had to try breathing out into this bag thing to test the volume, you know, and he couldn't do it. Not much would come out and he'd be pink and purple with the effort.

Now our Essie's name was chosen from the Old Testament to please Grammaclegg who was very religious. Methodist. Mum said it was like an umbilical coard across the Atlantic. Actually I could see what she meant, but it made me feel squeamish.

Later when Essie 'got politics' after she went to the Grammar and had this crush on Miss Richards, she was furious about her name and said that the family had no right to steal names from Jewish people like that. There was a row about it.

'You might have suffered in the war but you didn't lose all your family like thousands of them did, did you? You haven't been persecuted down the centuries, have you? You should have thought what you were doing. Miss Richards says it was just plain theft, and what's new about that?'

Well my Grammaclegg went pale and started to cry and my mum went flushed and said our Essie should be ashamed, hurting Grammaclegg like that; after all she'd been through with her own husband killed by his job; and who did Miss Richards think she was trying to teach politics in *our* family. Where was she in the General Strike HUH? Not even a twinkle in her mother's eye.

Then Essie stood up strong and went on and on standing there shouting about oppression and you shouldn't steal even if you were oppressed. I ran out to my Aunty Joyce's and stayed the night.

My name was chosen for Grandad, but he died before I was born. He wanted me named after a famous Yorkshire woman he said, Charlotte Brontë.

Mum and Grammaclegg thought it was a bit posh for the likes of us, but he was adamant and they didn't want to make him wheeze. So they agreed, didn't they, and here I am though they always called me Lotte. I like it. I'll never be a writer, though. Too much like school.

When I was six weeks old, Grammaclegg told my mum it was time she returned to her husband. Mum replied that her life was in Densley now. Grammaclegg was shocked, being a devoted wife herself and such a strong Methodist. But Mum said surely Grammaclegg had noticed that the letters were hardly coming any more, and her husband had not been pleased that I was a girl. In fact he'd been very disappointed, hadn't he? Mum said she thought that was actually a cover up. She just felt in her heart that he had a new woman over there and couldn't see him staying loyal.

It turned out that Mum was right, though she only found out two years later, when one of our cousins married a man from the States, and they knew people in San Francisco and made enquiries for Mum. Then her divorce came and she changed our names back to Clegg.

She never talked about my father. She told me she was very glad to have two girls, especially as we got on so well in the early years.

So that's how we came to live in Grammaclegg's house where the Coal Board let her stay on.

But ill-health caught up with her after all the strain of the factory and nursing Grandad at the same time. When I was six months the doctor said she had to stop the factory work or she'd soon follow Grandad. So she took up her needles again and I hardly remember seeing her with no needle in her hand, do I, needles of all kinds. Our Essie took after her. I didn't have the interest. It was cooking that I liked. She taught me to make jam roly-poly and Yorkshire pudding and potato cakes. She found me a high stool, don't know where from, but it was always called Lotte's stool and that's how I got to hear all the stories while we did the cooking.

I think we did have a happy childhood. We knew we were loved and that is what can never be taken away.

My mum had to be our breadwinner then. She started on the buses and she made lots of friends. But Red Heather wasn't on the market any more. She had a sad end actually. She was collecting pots and things from the warehouse in Sheffield. It was right near the centre where the roundabout is now that Sheffield people call the 'Hole in the Road'. Actually they say, 'Oyel in't royad'. They fished her out the rubble after the bombers had gone. She was completely surrounded by sherds of shattered china. My Grammaclegg told me that. My mum never talked about it.

Mum was thin, active and always laughing. She had the same dark curly hair as me, though I always liked mine shoulder length and she had hers short. We both have brown eyes, but Grammaclegg's are blue and our Essie's are sometimes blue, sometimes green and sometimes grey. My hair's stayed the same colour all my life, but Essie's started off yellow and became bright light brown by the time she took the eleven-plus.

When I was little it was a family tradition that Mum made the best custard, Grammaclegg the best gravy, and I made the best chocolate sponge. Grammaclegg had the most stories to tell us, because she was the oldest, but Mum and Essie had the best dreams.

And I thought mine was the best family in the whole world, didn't I?

Deanne

The visit from Nell was my first holiday, ever. Hers too. I wondered, after the shock of seeing one another, if we'd run out of things to say, but we didn't.

We stayed in pubs and inns. Made thirty hours of each day. We visited the farm. Mrs Gilbert had died. It had changed hands. The new people gave us tea and scones.

We played darts in the evenings if the pubs weren't too busy. Nell played in London. She was good, very good. She enjoyed performing. We usually had a small crowd around while we played.

For each of us the holiday was different. I had to play it straight, as a companion for Nell who was heterosexual. She enjoyed the repartee with the men who were watching us play darts. I didn't buy pints like I usually would, because of the comments I'd have had to put up with. I wished it was The Feathers with me surrounded by the gay women there, but it wasn't. I wanted to be loyal to Nell as my friend but it made me invisible. Sometimes I pretended I was in the Bronnester. I was used to dealing with the men there, and the peculiar thing was that I didn't have to work so hard with the men on holiday because Nell was doing it for me.

We talked about it a couple of times. If we hadn't, I'd have started to resent Nell, and I'd rather have my feelings out in the open with her, so we could get to know each other properly. She said the men didn't mean any harm; but she also said that it unnerved her travelling with another woman, without a man. I said I'd never travelled anywhere with any man. Those were useful talks. Brought us closer together.

In the daytime we walked by the river, and along country lanes. We talked several times more, about Izzie. Nell was frank with me. She told me that I'd given her plenty to think about when she finished this holiday. Said those were the first talks she'd ever had about prejudice. We tried to understand each other. I felt as if she really was my sister.

41

At night we always had twin beds. After the first day neither of us talked again about being little girls, Nell, Dora and me. The three of us, in long soft nighties.

Back in Coombebury, I poured my love into Dora's child. She was my replacement for her mother. Dora withdrew from everyone. She wouldn't wash her clothes. She wouldn't wash herself. She'd hardly even speak.

I began to lose weight. By the time Izzie was thirteen months, I was two stone lighter. Half a stone under weight. I didn't know what else I could do for Dora. I'd tried everything. Patience, anger, talking, silence.

By that time I'd begun to believe Dora's doctor. He'd been telling me that the hospital could help her.

So, in the late spring of 1954, Dora was committed to Fairview Mental Hospital. I hoped they could help her quickly.

I asked myself over and over again if I'd done the right thing in keeping Isobel. Could I have helped Dora more if Izzie had been gone? Might Dora have come back quicker to loving herself, and her baby? I didn't think so. Corrine didn't think so.

Isobel's chances of being adopted in Coombebury were almost nil. Instead of being in a home for a few weeks, she'd have rotted there for years.

The rich white couples would go there to look for a white baby. Passing by the coffee or honey ones like Isobel, even if they were as beautiful as the River Mere, like she was. They'd be there good and smiley, and like her, passed over. That hurt me, knowing that. I didn't want that to hurt Isobel too.

I was absorbing new ways of talking, now, as a receptionist. I now thought of Isobel as my daughter by proxy. She was a joy to me. She helped me to remember how to laugh.

Once a fortnight, on Sundays, I went to visit Dora.

We took to sitting there holding hands. Her smiling all the while at the colours in the flowers I took for her. That would be for the whole two hours. Then I'd go home and put Isobel to bed and be so tired that I'd go direct to bed myself.

There was nothing else. Except watch Dora lose the will to go on. Like a living dead person from an American horror movie. She was gone from me, from herself.

She used to have such a lot of spirit. I thought a lot about that word: spirit. Dora used to laugh with me in the thin room; to get excited by new things, like the accounts work; to read and read, telling me about the books.

42

Once, before she became pregnant, I'd drawn a picture of us. More like a cartoon. I drew her as my reflection, kissing me in a mirror.

But now, in Fairview Hospital, Dora seemed to have an empty body. Empty but not see-through. She was like a mirror that's in a ghost house, covered with a grey cloth cover.

There was no god to pray to. No one to cry to. My aim was survival. It was my link with Nell. We'd both been brought up to survive, whatever way we could. Nell's way was different. So was Corrine's.

My way was with women, or alone. I would never turn to men. After all, I didn't want their money, could get along without, and what else could they possibly offer that I wanted? I'd bring up Dora's daughter. I would not go out with a man to make money to pay for a doctor for Dora. I did not owe her that.

Every day I went to my job as receptionist at the Bronnester. It was my security. I wasn't bored there because of all the different people.

I decided I didn't want to live in the same rooms that I'd gone through hell in with Dora. I needed a change. I also needed a separate bedroom for Izzie. But the problem was that renting anything bigger or permanent was a nightmare in Coombebury, because of the seasonal tourist trade. Many places were not rented on long lets in the summer. I'd known other people put out on the streets in April.

By then I had a few friends through the Bronnester, and the others down The Feathers. Corrine was still my closest. She said, 'Why don't you talk to Stuart about it? He's a builder after all, must come in touch with people with houses to let.'

That was how I realised that I'd been overlooking Stuart and his contacts through the grapevine. He was one of the gay men that I'd met through Corrine. That grapevine is there in every town, but hidden till something makes it obvious.

'Why not buy somewhere?' asked Stuart, and I laughed clean high laughter right in his face.

'Oh come on, Deanne,' he retaliated, though half laughing with me. 'Somewhere half derelict, that needs some work on it. You think about it.'

I didn't want anywhere posh, in the best part of town. Not like Corrine who'd been bought a two-bedroom flat by Dove on the west side.

I didn't have a Dove in my life, perish the thought. I would shudder sometimes at what Corrine did to get that flat and still had to do to keep it.

Besides, I was used to living by the railway on the east side, and that was near to Glenis, who minded Isobel. Glenis was married; a mother with three children all under school age. Glenis needed the money and she wanted to carry on. I needed her, too, if I was going to stay on at the hotel.

It took weeks to find a small house, near Glenis, and one I could get a mortgage for. *That* was another story. The building societies just didn't want to know. Me being single.

I found Twenty-three Station Road. Like Stuart suggested, it was half derelict. He said he would do the work to make it sound, such as damp-proofing and the roof, but the snag was the mortgage. Time ran on and the people selling threatened to pull out.

Then Corrine twisted my arm and fixed up a 'business' lunch between me, Stuart, herself and Dove. (Not at the Bronnester.) I hadn't liked Dove before, and I didn't like him then, either. He had a smile like a walrus. But he said he would put up the money as a private mortgage, with legal papers. Whew.

So I moved in when Izzie was two.

Station Road was posh compared to the flats back in Rotherhithe. I was the bee's knees. Most of the houses came straight in off the pavement. Some like Twenty-three had a path two strides long, and a plot between the pavement and the house.

That became Izzie's plot, later. She liked the blue flowers best. I remember we went to the nurseries, and all the plants had types and names. Like hardy perennials, half-hardy annuals, things like that. I was in my element. We chose all blue ones; Forget-me-nots, Johnson's blue geraniums (fancy geraniums being blue, not red), Lobelia, Aubretia and purple violets.

'They've got faces, Dee,' she said. 'I do like the faces.'

I was choked then. I remembered Mereford Woods and the faces on the violets there, and sitting with Dora, planning to run away, so that we could stay together. Now I was buying plants with her daughter for a plot that Dora couldn't see.

I remade that tiny house. Two up, two down, with a bathroom stuck on the back through the kitchen downstairs. Stuart built that, and then we had an indoor toilet.

It wasn't my dream place with three acres. But it was home for Izzie and me. I learned how to replace windows, build shelves and cupboards, do papering and painting.

There was no 'passage'. We came straight from the front door into the front room. Then, directly opposite, another door led to the kitchen, with a three-foot space between the two rooms for the stairs to

44

go up to a front and back bedroom.

I had the back bedroom. From the window I looked down on to the bathroom roof. Then one day I thought, if that window was replaced with a glass door, I could use that roof.

It was a sunny roof. I put window boxes like a small wall round the edge, and a tub or two with flowers. Then, after Corrine bought Tibs as a kitten when Izzie was four, it became Tibs' favourite spot, there in the sun. Later when Izzie was older, and careful of the edge, she was allowed out there too.

The back yard was ten feet by ten feet. I dug it up. I made it into a blaze of colour. Before that I didn't know that I could get shrubs and climbers that would flower in winter, in England. So, sometimes when the pain of Dora was very strong, I'd go and potter out there, tidying, weeding, taking cuttings, moving things. It helped.

I'd be at home with Tibs on my knee sometimes of an evening, Izzie asleep upstairs. I'd think of all the times chambermaiding when I'd fallen into bed, no time to put my feet up; I'd think of times now when I'd take five minutes after work, sometimes ten. Cats encourage you like that, they say they're good for folks' blood pressure because they slow you down. I'd be there and I'd think that I'd got no landlord putting the rent up, no landlady poking her nose in. I'd got a fair mortgage, all sewn up, no legal hassles with it; and a child and some friends.

Then I'd feel that in spite of all the pain, my fortune was really made.

Dora was fed, washed and left. Fed, washed and left. No one did anything else for her.

It felt to me like a terrible punishment that she inflicted on herself. That made me sad, but it also made me horribly angry because I felt she was punishing me too.

It was much slower than jumping off a cliff.

It was much worse for Dora when she was clear, and for me and Corrine when she was not. So I longed for an end.

Children weren't allowed to visit Fairview. That was a blessing really. It saved me having to make up my mind to take Izzie to see her real mother.

Dora didn't want to see Isobel, but I used to wonder if Izzie had a right to see Dora. Though to see Dora in that state would also have been bad for Izzie.

Izzie started to ask about her real mummy (she called me Dee) when she was about five, because the other children in school had two parents.

I told her that Dora had lost her memory in a car accident and I showed her some old photos. Corrine had a camera, a present from Dove. I said that Dora loved her baby, but couldn't remember anything, so now she was in a hospital for people like her. That she could be looked after, there.

'Tell me about my dad, Dee.'

I told her he came from Trinidad to study. That was true. I told her he was in the car crash with Dora, but he died. That was a lie. I wanted it to be true. I wanted Dora's other lover to be dead. But I regretted that lie, as soon as I let it out.

'Were you and my mum really good friends then, Dee? Were you best friends with my mum?'

'Yes. Your mum and me were best friends, Izzie. For years and years and years.'

'I'm glad. I love you, Dee. Night-night, Dee.'

'I love you too, Izzie. Night-night.'

I still did shift work. Nights too. I paid Glenis to have Izzie some nights, and other times I had no choice but to put Izzie to bed and go out to work. Corrine helped out when she could. If she finished at midnight, then she'd go back to Station Road and sleep in my bed, but she couldn't do that often. One week in four was nights. All the hotels fixed it differently. I used to worry, leaving Izzie, like some working mothers have to if they're on their own.

But the gossip I'd hear at work never made me change my mind about that. Even if there'd been a man in my life, I couldn't have just left Isobel with him. There are lots of the turds who take a shine to little girls. Izzie was safer asleep on her own.

It wasn't just at work I'd hear such things. Cases like that used to get into the dailies now and then. So I counted Izzie's and my blessings and not for the first time. But I was calmer working days.

Twenty-one Station Road was students. Coming and going all the time. I never properly made friends with any of them. Some were pleasant. Then they'd leave. I tried not to let it unsettle me. My neighbour the other side was Mrs Young. She understood about me having to leave Izzie. Mrs Young was in her sixties, but she'd had to do the same thing with her son, after the first world war, because she'd been widowed. She'd been anxious like me, and it was such a blessing that she wasn't judging me. But she did ask me why Izzie called me Dee. I told her Dora, Izzie's mother, was in hospital. She said it wasn't my fault then that Izzie was coloured. That hurt. I snapped her head off. Told her I thought Izzie was beautiful. We didn't talk for a month.

46

Then she needed to borrow some eggs and I offered to feed her cat when she went to her son's for a week. She never mentioned Izzie's colour again.

'Don't worry so much, Dee,' said Corrine. 'Izzie'll be all right. She's growing up just fine. She's tough. She'll come through all right, you mark my words.'

'Let's hope so. At least they're pleased with the start she's made at school. Seems to be picking things up quick enough. I hope to hell it stays this way. That's all I can say.'

I think all mothers must get tense sometimes. It's 'No, you can't have this' and 'No, you can't have that.' The children pout and sulk and you have to be so tough not giving in to them all the time. We weren't perfect, either of us. So of course we had rows. But we also laughed a lot, talked, and hugged each other.

In Coombebury I had some ways of surviving. One of them was The Feathers.

Going down The Feathers wasn't so easy when Isobel was young. It meant Corrine and I couldn't go together if she was babysitting. It meant less time with Izzie. That was already a problem because of my shifts. It meant juggling and jiggling with plans and it meant sometimes buying rounds.

Mol and Pol came round to Station Road sometimes. So did Micky and Pol. Sunday lunch there'd sometimes be a crowd of us, and Izzie, squashed round the table, all laughing and talking at once.

I was never short on company, but sometimes I'd have liked to have got out of the house for a change.

We all lost contact with Charlie. She left Coombebury to go and work in London as a gardener. She didn't phone though she had my work number. I didn't get my own phone till years later.

Corrine and Mol did it, you know, for years on and off. It seemed to suit them both. Mol said she never could bear to be tied to one woman. Liked to spread her talents around, she said. I never asked how she managed to block out the image of Dove's body when she and Corrine were in bed. I didn't ask Corrine either. That was her business. But we did talk about being gays. Corrine was the only one that still had a man. For money. None of the rest of us ever gave straight men the time of day if we could help it.

Micky and Pol set up house together for a short time, living as they put it, man and wife. Now that did intrigue me. I couldn't be doing with that at all. I was all of it and so was Dora. Mol and Corrine were like me and Dora. But it takes all sorts to make a world.

After six months, Micky and Pol made a pact to move back in with Mol, living in the rooms behind the clinic. You never know what's behind those nice net curtains in Coombebury. Myself, I hated nets. They made the rooms dark so I only had them on the front room so the passers-by couldn't look in. The living room-cum-kitchen at the back looked down the path past the bathroom into the backyard. I didn't have nets there at the back. I had my armchair by the back window. I could look at the climbing roses out there and the virginia creeper red in autumn.

I couldn't make the system work for Isobel. She was alone. There was no one her colour in any of the streets around. Coombebury was white, mainly conservative, very traditional.

'Tell me again, Dee. Tell me a story about the people that lived near you when you were six.'

I told her everything I could remember. That they came from all over the world. That they'd been in that part of London as long as my family had, which was about two hundred years.

Sometimes we had knives in our teeth, if she came home from junior school in pieces. Children taunting her, telling her to jump in bleach and such like.

Sticks and stones can break your bones
But words can never hurt you.

That's a lie.

Izzie would keep the hurt and anger inside just long enough to slam the front door and then we'd both get it.

'Why did my mummy make me brown? Why aren't you my mummy, Dee? I hate my mummy. I hate you, Dee. I do! I do!'

Then huge tears would roll down, and she wouldn't let me touch her. It could go on for days.

Do you have to be able to hate, to understand about love? I'd be so angry. I wanted to put the other children in a sack and drop them off the end of the pier. And all their happy families with them.

It would bring it all back. How I wanted to hate Dora; how I did sometimes. Izzie's worst times were mine, too. Times when we hardly knew how to help each other. Too late for me to start wondering if I should be bringing Izzie up in a place like Coombebury, in the fifties, or if I should be bringing her up at all. We were already linked.

The relationship between Izzie and me was not a circle; we were not a straight line. We were more like a zigzag, like the path down the cliffs to the beach. To the wide open sea. Familiar but dangerous. Changing through storms.

When I talked with Nell in Mereford after Izzie was born I thought I was doing well. Thought I'd come a long way from the person I'd been. I thought that the part of me that had loathed Izzie's father was gone. I felt I'd changed and was glad.

I was so naïve. About myself. About Coombebury. About what Izzie would need and how people would react to her.

I was gay. I had wanted to be childless. Now I had a child and although she brought me joy, she made my gayness invisible.

Wherever we went, people assumed that she was my child. They saw me as her mother. They called her coloured and they made their own assumptions about me as a result. That I was not gay. That I had chosen (or perhaps not) to go with her father.

I wanted to blot him out but it was not so easy. People thought I had had a man. Only another gay woman could possibly know what that meant to me. Me, who had only ever slept with a woman. With Dora. These days I slept with no one.

Tourists who knew nothing about either me or Izzie would see us on the beach or shopping in the summer and would stare. Those stares were like eclipses. They completely blotted out my love for Dora; my nights in bed with Dora. My years of knowing I was gay and living it.

All gays were invisible in my town. Except to each other. I suppose many minded that but couldn't tackle it outright. Some used it. They wanted to stay invisible. I did too, at work for instance. But to all the people who were not gay, I looked like someone who had gone through the whole thing of having my own baby. That I had never been and never *might* have been gay. It hurt and hurt and hurt.

Izzie, though, suffered from *never* being invisible. First when we were out and about together they would call her my little girl. Call me her mummy in front of her.

'Dee's not my mummy. Dee looks after me 'cos my mummy's in hospital.'

She would see them look from her to me and back again. There was no peace for her. If they didn't do that then they would ignore her as if she wasn't there; pretending that they didn't notice that she was different. All the time they showed they had questions that they daren't ask. Like their faces were books with words written on. Silent words. Sometimes that was worse for her and worse for me. It is hard to be proud if people are publicly pretending to ignore you. I wanted her to be proud. Being proud is like breathing.

I started to love Izzie without having a clue what I was up to. I thought I knew. That it was enough to have that bond. I couldn't have been more wrong. More naïve. I had no idea what it would be like for her to be on the receiving end of other people's prejudice. Race prejudice. I learned just by being with her, in as much as a white woman can learn. I had a hell of a lot of learning to do. Year in, year out watching how she tried to cope, defend herself, and be proud. As long as I live I will never actually know what it feels like to be her. I sometimes felt I became the woman I am at her expense, on her back. And at the same time she was a child holding my hands, a weight pulling me down under the waves of the sea.

I sometimes thought that it was one of those relationships that is never never free of difficulties and struggling. But women and children learn to keep on loving and starting over again and we did that. We lived with the River Mere in between us. Sometimes the ford was low and we could go across for a while. But actually we lived on different banks and sometimes it flowed too fast. Then we had to call across and get on with it.

If I had left Dora after her first fling, my life would have been very different. But I had not. I used to wonder if my life would actually have been simpler. I don't think so. Izzie's life was complicated from the day she was born. She hadn't chosen to be born. You'd sometimes hear posh people on the wireless talking about babies choosing to be born. To me that was a load of codswallop. I didn't choose to be born into poverty in Rotherhithe any more than Izzie chose to come out of Dora, into Coombebury. I was proud to be from my background. I refused to be ashamed though I was made aware of *those kind* of differences from being young enough to think. So was Nell. I was pig ignorant about race though. While Izzie was little and then as she reached juniors and ready for the eleven-plus, I changed through living with her. It takes years for women like me and Nell. Our race ignorance was like those sand worms on the beach. They show up every low tide. Not just once, or twice. High tide comes and they look as if they have gone. But they haven't. It's just that they were buried so deep.

I wrote in my letters to Nell how I was changing, and all my feelings. We didn't meet often. She had to face up to my new way of life, or not bother any more with me. Sometimes I sent cartoons. She said they made her think. She wanted four children, but didn't seem to fall for them easy.

Funny old life Dee you and Izzie down there and me flat as a bloody pancake and bleeding every month sure as hell fire. I told Fred we must be doing it all wrong but he said dont be daft Nellie and then I told me doctor and he done test after test and cant find nothing wrong youd think all them scientists could fix me up wouldnt you after all they can make atom bombs so why the hell cant they sort me out? I wood settle for just one baby though I wood still like four though what you say makes me wonder how ever my gran brought up six mind you I spose the old uns dragged up the young uns and so on but I wont make mine do that I dont think so any way I got to go now take care Dee and I liked the picture of you and Izzie she is very nice looking and you dont look so tired as you used to praps you are gettin used to it after all none of us are gettin any younger are we and I hope they sort me out fore long I worry I will be in the change before Ive had my first one love Nell.

Izzie won a scholarship to Coombebury Grammar when she was eleven. It was a direct grant school, and most of the girls were fee-paying. Isobel had a free place, or she couldn't have gone.

Her place was dependent on the scholarship, but we didn't have a grant for school uniform or school dinners. All of that had to be paid for. I was happier to pay. I didn't want Izzie to suffer the stigma of a free-dinners girl. Not in a school like that.

She liked some subjects and she was good at them all. So Corrine said she had a natural talent for learning. But I didn't believe in talent, only in privilege. After all, Dora could do numbers, just like that. But she didn't get a chance. But Corrine believed in talent. We even had rows about it.

'You've got a talent for drawing, Dee, why not face it?'

'I like drawing Corrine, always did, but then so do lots and lots of children. Just think, if we'd been so poor that my mum never bought me a crayon, I'd not have started, would I? And lots of women like you can sing, only you couldn't afford a nice singing school to get a qualification. You think on, before you start on about talent.'

I was so furious I could hardly trust myself not to say something that I'd regret later. I did think a lot about Isobel and her doing well at school. I encouraged her as best I could, though she soon passed me in maths and such. I found I'd give her lots of extra encouragement with science and maths. I must have been thinking of Dora, though I didn't always admit it to myself.

Dora said, 'I don't like reading any more, Dee. The lines wobble, Dee.'

While I was there in Fairview on visiting days, her hands would twitch occasionally. Her eyes would wander. She didn't always remember what I'd been saying. So I stopped taking books to her. It had to be the drugs they fed her.

I tried to find out what she was on, but the staff said that the doctors 'weren't available'. The ward nurses said they couldn't talk to me.

I tried then to ask Dora, without upsetting her. She only understood 'that it's the medication, Dee. They say we have to. It's for everyone.'

Sometimes she'd stammer and stutter. More often she didn't talk at all. That was the same as before she was committed. Her hand would be there on the arm of her day chair, and just the odd twitch to tell me she was under the influence.

Mainly, it was her eyes that told me. Her eyes lost a certain lightness that they'd had even after Isobel was born, before Fairview.

Then I tried taking her in a bright painting or two instead. She could tell the colours, and I made sure to take the ones that were bold, no tiny details that would wobble. Those were the few times when she'd smile the smile that I used to know in her.

I tried a good few more times with the people in charge of Fairview. But I was unable to find out anything. I didn't have the means to get Dora out of there and into a private place. Only the Ralph Edmund Doves have money like that. Little did he know he had been paying through the years for Glenis' child-minding wages. Corrine'd always insisted on giving me money for that. But there was no way that we could buy private medical care.

Of course, I knew that sometimes working women like me got windfalls. Winning the pools, or an unexpected insurance handout. But there wasn't any likelihood of anything for Dora. It was Fairview or nothing.

In the autumn of 1966, when Izzie was nearly fourteen, Dora was persuaded to sign, in Fairview, for electric shock treatment. She had by then been one of their experiments for the new drugs for almost seven years. As far as I know, they did not drag out of her the truth about having been gay. It was hidden to Dora herself, and it's my view that the drugs finished off the cover up.

She didn't say much about it, except that it burned her head. I looked in her eyes and there was blankness. Like looking into the Mere and no reflections. No brown gold. No pussy willow. Just gaping, but not really empty.

I only once before saw eyes like that. They were Nell's eyes when she had the terrors about her mum, in Mereford.

The official cause of Dora's death was heart failure. I know she died of terror when men came at her with their cables and electrodes. Did they think they might cure Dora by plugging her into the national grid?

It would have cost them too much money to keep on drugging her. She might have gone on in there for years. It was quicker and cheaper to kill her from terror. That was their punishment. Their final solution.

On the day before Dora's funeral, Isobel asked if she could see her mother's body. She explained to me that she had a desperate need to know how her mother looked. Until then, all she had had to go on were my drawings of Dora and some photos that had been taken long ago by Corrine.

I phoned the private chapel of rest where Dora's body was being looked after. I arranged that we, Isobel and I, could have an appointment for three that afternoon. Isobel was off school anyway and had been for a few days.

I remember every detail of it.

It was a short bus ride, across Coombebury. The funeral directors who owned the chapel of rest were on the north west edge of the town. The street was steep, with glimpses of the sea down behind us, as we walked side by side up to the place.

We were met at the front reception counter by Mr Pascall, one of the two brothers who now ran the business. They were the fourth generation of Coombebury Pascalls, undertakers. This brother was a small man, immaculately pressed and dressed. He had a shock of white hair and gold-rimmed glasses. He always wore a dark navy blue suit with a matching waistcoat. It had a fob watch, the old-fashioned sort.

He was dignified, quiet and polite. He shook Izzie's hand, and smiled at her. He spoke directly to her. He asked her to follow him, and I followed Izzie. At the door of the chapel of rest, he left us. Then we held hands. We went in together, without Mr Pascall.

It was a wood-panelled room, with a sloping roof. The lower part of the ceiling was painted cream, but the upper part had a sloping window of frosted glass so that the effect in the room was of low lighting from concealed lights, and of natural lighting too. It felt peaceful to me.

Izzie was quiet. I wondered if she would start to tremble. But her hand was calm in mine.

We moved across to the oak trestle on which Dora's coffin was placed. Her eyes were closed, her face calm. Her short hair was neatly combed. She was pale, no signs of pain, nothing to shock an observer with what Dora had suffered.

Dora's shoulders and the rest of her body were covered in a white thick linen cover. From her waist the hinged lid of the coffin was folded back so that we could only see the smooth wood surface, with a small bowl of pink flowers on it. Dora had liked pink. I remember that when I took pictures into Fairview for Dora, I'd discovered over the years that she smiled the most when my pictures had bold blocks of pink, red, yellow and white. No doubt some psych would have made something of that if I ever said it, but I didn't care about them. Not about their ideas, their so-called theories, or their treatments. One of the results was in front of me in that chapel of rest.

I made up my mind when I saw those flowers that I'd been right to insist that for tomorrow's funeral there'd be solid blocks of colour too. Wonderful flowers for Dora. The colours she would have smiled the most at.

Izzie and I still held hands. Still. Isobel Beale and Deanne Derby. Looking down at Dora. The coffin was about waist high to both of us. I thought that I should tell Isobel who this woman had been that she was now looking at. No sounds there, except me and Izzie breathing. I was wondering how she was feeling. You can think you know how someone else feels, but you don't actually know. Not unless she tells you; so long as she is not lying. I wanted to stop lying. To Izzie. About Dora. So I wondered how Izzie was feeling.

She had no memories of Dora, alive. She hadn't been able to stop Dora from dying: and through all the years she hadn't been allowed into the hospital to see her.

I thought back to my own mother's death; and my father's too. And to the moment when Dora heard her own news, that she was an orphan now. And as I longed then and there to tell Izzie about the amazing years when Dora and I had been happy, as women, loving one another, I also felt the moments moving past me, without my speaking my thoughts. And then I heard Izzie saying, 'Can I be with her on my own now please? Just for a little while?'

'I'll wait outside for you, then.'

She nodded, taking her hand from mine. We seemed each aware of every tiny movement. P'raps because Dora couldn't move. I don't know. Three females in one room. And only two of us alive.

Izzie stepped aside. My memory as I turned away is of her standing, both hands touching the coffin's edge, resting lightly but just slightly curved over the edge, as she looked down at the face of her mother. I never asked her how she felt in that particular moment, because it was so private and really I shouldn't even have shared it. And, although we were so close, she has never felt the need to tell me what that moment meant to her.

Next morning, Corrine stayed at home in Station Road with Izzie while I went to the station to meet Nell.

Those were no longer the days of steam trains and the place reeked of diesel fumes. Nell had had to take a day's leave without pay. I'd been off a week. My doctor put me down as sick and for once they were sympathetic at the Bronnester, because they had known Dora and they said I must be sick from shock.

'You all right, Dee? You look tired out. How's Izzie coping?'

'Good to see you. I'm all right. Coping. Izzie's doing well. She's very strong. She amazes me.'

'I bet she'll be as tall as me now. Three years is a long time, innit Dee?'

'Mmmm. Strange meeting up like this, for this. Good to see you even if the reason's not. It's weird. Weird time for all of us, Nell. Corrine's been wonderful.'

'You been keepin' busy? They say it helps.'

'Yes. It does. There's been so much to do. Surprised me just how much. I haven't had time to grieve. It'll hit me later, I know it will.'

'Glad you came to meet me. Ten minutes walk's a good thing. That why you takin' me the long way round?'

'Yes. I was glad of the air. I haven't let myself do much thinking, except yesterday. I took Izzie to the chapel of rest.'

'All right was it?'

'Yes. Peaceful. I think it was good for both of us. You said that, didn't you, when you saw your mum?'

'I'll never forget it. They laid her out lovely. It did me good after what I'd seen. Dora's not in any more pain now, Dee. It's a merciful release, Dee. She'd had a long time in there.'

'I know. Well here we are. Come on in, Nell.'

In the chapel of the crematorium we made a small cluster of seven at noon that day. Us and the wonderful flowers. Blocks and blocks of them. Not mixed or scattered. Just bold and strong. Red yellow pink and white. For Dora. The small rooms shone with them. Corrine held Izzie's left hand, and I held her right.

On my right was Nell, but we didn't touch each other. We never had done, and I didn't miss it. But I was glad for the warmth of Izzie's hand, and I felt linked through her to Corrine on the other side. Behind us were Mol, Pol and Micky. They were holding hands.

I noticed that we all had wet cheeks, though none of us were properly crying, and in a way we didn't want to because for Dora this was the end of pain and unhappiness. I promised myself that one day I would tell Izzie the truth, the whole truth, and nothing but the truth. One day.

My anger was my outlet. It kept me sane. I thought briefly of going to seek legal advice from James Slomner, up in London, where Nell worked as a telephonist.

Nell had told me he was a bit of an old rogue, but very sound with the legal advice he gave. He was widely respected and dealt especially with international divorce cases. That was why some of his clients came through speaking in French.

So, if I'd been needing his help for a marriage, or divorce, that would have been the place to go, the person to see.

But Dora was not my husband or my wife. She was my woman-lover. The Southampton branch of the Slomner clan were regulars at my work place. George Slomner, the influential Southampton business man, was the brother of James Slomner senior, Nell's boss in London. Also, it was more than just a coincidence, or just a family link. They were all masons too and had close connections with Ralph Edmund Dove. The Southampton and the Coombebury masons used the Bronnester for the annual Ladies Nights.

When Dora and I had been young waitresses we hadn't known all the guests' names. This was partly because we had been too busy, and partly because the head waiter took over and picked up the tabs. But even in those days, and they seemed a long time ago, we had known that the Slomners were BIG in Southampton and graced the Bronnester with their presence.

Over the years Nell and I had talked and laughed about the links, using the phones for free calls now and then, though I hadn't dared too often. But to go and see Nell's boss, even if he could give me the best legal advice in the City of London, would put my lifestyle on the line and my job at risk. I could lie and say that Dora was my cousin, I intended to lie anyway, but if he took the case, he'd have to dig. Then I'd be exposed and jobless.

There were gays all over the south of England, and probably the rest of the country as well, but we were only safe in our jobs if we stayed there in the closet where they'd put us. We knew the rules, all of us, whoever we were, wherever we were. It made us angry.

Nell put on her thinking cap and sorted through the other respected solicitors in London and came up with Wright and Partners. So that's where I went.

I saw Mr William Wright, who was white-haired and reminded me of Ralph Edmund Dove. I shuddered to think of anyone doing it with him, even for love.

He was charming, though, and his office was lovely. It had wooden walls and a deep pile beige carpet like the best suites at the Bronnester. There were long green curtains, very tasteful, green plants by the windows.

'And are you, Miss Derby, a relative of the deceased?'

'Her first cousin,' I lied smoothly. 'The others were killed in the war.'

'Aah. Well now, Miss Derby, I have examined the possibilities. I have to advise you that the BMA has its own solicitors for matters such as this. In my professional opinion, the chances of your bringing a successful case against the hospital are absolutely nil. Furthermore, Miss Derby, the costs would be, er, phenomenal.'

'You are very sure, Mr Wright?' I almost added 'Sir'.

'I am. Very sure.'

'Thank you for your time.' (For which I had paid . . .)

He leant forward in his chair and for a moment he dropped his mask a little. He even looked quite kind. He looked as if he really did care, and even as if he could see that there'd been suffering.

'I'm sorry, Miss Derby, for what your cousin must have gone through. I wish you well. Thank you for coming to see this firm.'

I stood up, as he did, and we shook hands. All I could think of was that they'd killed Dora and I'd never be able to prove it.

It was Nell's lunch hour by then. We went on our first and only visit to the Catholic Cathedral.

We lit candles for Dora, and I sent a message without words to her. That her spirit might rest quiet from now on.

Esther

Wednesday, 30 March 1983

If Nell wrote her life down, it would read like fire in the sand. 'Who, me?' she hooted, with a laugh like broken glass. 'I ain't arf got a tale to tell, eh, Ess?' I said, 'Why don't you?' She replied, 'I ain't no writer, Ess. You do it fer both of us, you write a book 'bout us being sisters 'n' all.'

That was in the early years, just after we first met, when we were swopping tales about our lives, and we felt like we were family, though she was a Londoner and I'd grown up in Yorkshire; and I'd been to college and she hadn't. She was the older sister I'd always wanted, no question about it. I love her now, like I did then; there's nothing new about anger between women who feel they're sisters. That much I do know because of my relationship with my real sister, Lotte. Nell is family and I do not want to lose her. That's my starting point.

I am so cross with that woman. She knows it. She is furious with me.

I am so dismayed at myself. She does not know that. Maybe she guesses. She is a canny woman after all. But I haven't told her how my feelings about myself threaten to ignite me, however much I try to hide in sand; and she hasn't told me whether she burns with shame at her own actions.

I came to Reeve Juniors when I was thirty, in the autumn of '76 because it was on a working class estate and the teachers were committed to anti-racist, anti-sexist work. The school had a clear policy including those ideas in its aims, and it was well known for the exciting new classroom teaching there. Some of the juniors had been designing anti-racist reading books for the infants, and the library was well stocked and forward looking too.

I was also hoping to meet local women like Nell. Never dreaming I'd find 'family' though. I wasn't in a relationship with anyone and wasn't searching, except for Nell, unconsciously. I'd just moved into this bedsit, in this old house that backs on to Reeve council estate, and I remember it was Sunday afternoon and I was emulsioning. I heard yelling and fighting in the garden.

I hurried out there to see what was happening. I went past the young silver birch tree, and the leaves were sharp gold and shivering because there was just a small breeze. It was a bright autumn day. I saw the leaves and suddenly felt nostalgic. There were two little girls squabbling out there, my side of the fence, and I saw through them back to me and Lotte fighting over the gold chocolate money at Christmas that Grandma Clegg hung in a little net bag on a hook by the kitchen door. It was the gold leaves on the tree that made the link. Funny how small seeds can lie dormant in your mind and come up years later.

At the end of the garden, in the holly bush, was a crumpled teddy bear. There was a furious girl of about nine trying to get it back, and a younger one crying 'Gimme it, Trace, gimme it.'

That's how I met Nell's daughters, Tracey and Sally. That's how I met Nell, whose council house on Reeve Green is ten minutes' walk away, near Reeve Park, Lewisham.

Nell is twelve years older than me, and we've had some very different life experiences. We've spent seven years, almost, talking non-stop before and after work, evenings, weekends, until now.

When I first met her, we grafted together our memories of childhood and adolescence, and our everyday lives as adult women who needed each other for family. (To graft knitting wool, Grandma Clegg would fray the end of the old ounce and then fray the raw start of the new one. Then she'd put them alongside each other and roll them steadily between finger and thumb to make an invisible join. There were no lumpy knots in Grandma Clegg's sweaters. She could fetch a good amount of money for a Methodist Xmas raffle with one of her mohairs as the prize.)

Nell told me she'd only once before felt like a sister to someone. They were children together in London's dockland, evacuated together just after the war started.

Nell's a Londoner through and through. She'd hate to live in the country. She said that in Mereford the stars at night used to stretch for ever, and that terrified her because she didn't see stars in London. At night in Mereford there was such a deep quiet that Nell couldn't sleep. She longed to hear footsteps on the balconies of the flats back near her home, to hear people yelling and talking. She was used to the echoes, because it meant there were people. Night-time in Mereford made her feel as if there'd soon be no one left in the whole world, except the three little girls all on their own.

The morning that Deanne left the note was the end of Nell's childhood. She stuffed the note in her nightie pocket, put her head under the pillow, and shoved her sleeve into her mouth. She lay still as a dead mouse and concentrated hard at not screaming.

Deanne lives in Coombebury now, and they still keep in touch. Nell said it was scary at first, writing letters, posting them secretly. She did it because Deanne was special and it was something naughty that her mum didn't know about. She was nearly found out twice when Deanne's first two letters came. Then she got crafty. She asked Deanne to send them to the post office near her new secondary modern school, and she went there to collect them. She said it made her feel important, and she'd do it again like a shot.

Thursday, 31 March 1983

During the war, all around Rotherhithe, most of the flats and small terraces of back-to-back houses had been reduced to heaps of rat-infested rubble. Nell told me that it was during one such bombing raid that Deanne's mother was killed on the way home from the biscuit factory. No one knew why Nell's block had been spared. Her block was scheduled to be dismantled and re-built as part of the complex of maisonettes and flats. But no one knew when the work would begin. So, when she was returned home after the evacuation, Nell lived in the old block with her mother, Hannah, and her real sister, Joan. Then after a year, Joan married and moved away. Nell heaved a sigh of relief and stayed on, with her mother, just the two of them, sharing the place. A new family had moved into Deanne's old flat. They had a dog that dirtied the communal landing, and yapped at five in the morning.

Now and again, through the late forties, Nell's father returned to the old flats after one or other of his 'wanderings'. She said that once he came in a second-hand Ford car. The three of them piled in and it grumbled its way to the pub nearest Brands Hatch. Nell and Hannah sat outside under an umbrella that shaded a wooden table. For two hours they supped lemonade and beer and ate their sandwiches while Nell's father propped up the bar. At three he lurched towards them and somehow they all climbed in again. The car swayed them home and quite how they arrived, Nell can't remember. They didn't see her father for five months after that.

Nell told me that one of her mother's favourite sayings was, 'You take care of yourself girl, no one else will do it for you.' Hannah Woods told Nell also, just the same as my mum told me, 'I don't want you doing factory work, do you hear me, love?'

While Hannah worked on the biscuit line she wore sticky tape round her fingers because her job was to take the sponge fingers out of their tins, which hadn't fully cooled from the ovens. They came along the belt and she packed from the tins direct into the thin cardboard boxes. Rose, next along the line, folded in the lids.

The women used to work to a fine balance with each other. The boxes and wrappers and labels and halves and fillings and tops and bottoms were at speeds set by the supervisors, and all the women had to fit with that. If any new woman came on the line there was a sweating shift while she adjusted to the speed of the line and to the personalities of the other women.

Hannah Woods resented being controlled by machines. She especially hated the factory owners, who had the power to set the speeds to which she and the other women workers must conform.

'Hannah wot carries the banner.' All through Rotherhithe, Hannah Woods was famous for the union work she'd done before the war. She used to recount tales from union history.

Hannah's favourite story was of the Luddites, who resisted rich people's efforts to bring the weaving looms from the weavers' cottages all under one roof – the factory roof.

I could imagine Hannah, together with my Grandma Clegg, leading an army of Luddite women against the factory owners. Women shouting, waving sticks and banners, striding into the factories, hell bent on sabotage. My Grandma Clegg would have been there, modern Luddite, brandishing her poker from the hearth at home, ready to smash into the control boxes of the electric circuits and short-circuit the systems.

But when Hannah Woods crumpled up in agony during her shift on the biscuit line, it was her body, not my Grandma's poker, that caused the blockage. They had to shut down the whole line because the cakes toppled and jumbled all around her, over on to the floor, and everybody's rhythm was put out. Hooters, bells and buzzers went off right through the factory's control panels. Lights winked all over the show. As Hannah lurched over, the tins burned up her arms, especially her right arm which was the side that the tins came from.

Hannah Woods was sent to the hospital, and then sent home. Nell took time off work, at the risk of losing her job, because she knew Hannah was dying. It was cancer of the colon. I've often thought about that. How they sent Nell's mother home to die, even though she had to be looked after night and day, and Nell had to take unpaid leave. Nell's washing flapped against the balcony walls as Hannah lost control of her bladder as well as her bowels.

But by the year of King George's death when Nell Woods was eighteen, her mother was too ill to carry any banner anywhere. When all the streets were lined with people carrying flags, paying tribute to the dead king, Hannah was unable to lift her hand off the candlewick bedspread.

Nell spent Christmas 1952 alone with Hannah, except for frequent visits from Dr Armitage. She was papering the kitchen on one occasion when he arrived on the outside balcony. He stood there, blowing into his hands, shifting his feet as the cold slapped into his soles.

Nell wiped her hands and went to let him in, leading him along the passage to the bedroom. He'd probably have noticed the beige tweed wallpapers throughout the flat.

He talked gently to Nell's mother who looked so small in the double bed. Then he joined Nell in the kitchen for a cuppa which would insulate him from the weather. He gulped, in shock at the apricot roses which flourished on trellises now all over the walls and ceiling of the six-foot-by-seven-foot kitchen. They gleamed and glowed but he never said a word. Too professional, thought Nell, and she didn't enlighten him.

Hannah had arrived home with it, on one of the rare occasions when she felt strong enough to go out.

'It's for the kitchen, Nell. Bring yer hot June days into the bloody cold winter. Cheerful, innit Nell?'

'Bit on the bright side, Mum?'

'Not a bit. Make a nice change. Seen it this mornin' in Moxon's winder. Nice change. Nice and bright. I thinks to meself, we could do with a bit of a sparkle in here.'

Nell was sure that there wasn't much time left for sparkling. She told me that she thought Hannah knew it too, and was just keeping up a cheerful appearance.

They had seen the New Year in together; the apricot roses still glowed hopefully; but Nell buried Hannah before the end of January. It was the year of the coronation, 1953.

Nell was exceptionally lucky to be taken on again, at Slomner and Sherwood, and she knew it. She decided she would after all marry Fred Winters, and she decided she'd carry apricot roses.

Friday, 1 April 1983

Easter holidays, thank goodness. Time to sit here in my den, writing. Words for me. Words for Nell.

Trying to untangle. Sort the colours, the textures, the sequences and patterns of our lives; to write my way into a clear understanding of my relationship with Nell Winters.

After Nell married she carried on working in the offices of the firm of solicitors up in Moorgate. She had four miscarriages and each time the doctors advised her to wait two or three years before trying again. She was the main breadwinner by now because Fred had progressed from a few flutters on the dogs and horses to being an unreliable compulsive gambler, though he was still a likeable man.

Fred's parents were out to better themselves, and had no idea about Fred's gambling. They had moved out of their Lewisham council flat (in which Fred and Nell now lived) into a semi on a mortgage in Bromley. This was what they dreamed of for their only son as well. They saw Nell as having married above her class by trapping a good lad from the grammar school, and nothing Nell might do or say would change their view of her.

The fourth time that Nell was pregnant the issue blew up again.

'You should give up that job and rest at home,' said Fred's mum.

'I'm all right, Mum. Really I am. The doctor says the company's good for me.'

'When I had our Fred . . .' began Mrs Winters.

'When you had our Fred, I was bringing in good money,' said Mr Winters.

'We're all right for money,' said Nell. 'Everything's fine.'

'Destined for better things was our Fred,' said his mother.

'Nice grammar school boy.'

('Not that again,' groaned Nell silently.)

'Nice boy like our Fred should have married someone from the girls' grammar then he wouldn't still be a milkman, would he?'

(Fred's mother was drinking her tea out of a new cup, one of a set she'd just bought from the catalogue, and she rattled the saucer on purpose.)

'Am I supposed to sit here and take that?' spat Nell.

'Some of us likes to get on in the world.'

'Some of us is snobs what forgets who we still is.'

'And one of us is a low-down loud mouth brassy bit from Rotherhithe.'

Whereupon Nell stood, and slowly put on her coat, which didn't button over her belly. She says she smiled like a she-tiger with toothache and she calmly left the room. She lost that baby too, and returned to work. She never allowed Fred's parents across her threshold after that. 'But I shan't gripe if you go, Fred,' she said, ' 'cos, after all, they are yer mum and dad, aren't they?'

The next baby was kept in place for the pregnancy by two small stitches across the cervix and was born by Caesarean. Tracey's birthday was the summer of sixty-seven, when I was twenty-one.

Tracey weighed five pounds four ounces and she thrived. Four years later, Sally was born. The Winters were rehoused by Lewisham Council on Reeve Estate. After that, the doctors told Nell never to have any more children, yet the sods wouldn't sterilise her because they said she was too young. So Nell went on the pill and stayed on the pill though she told me later she thought that's what gave her the pains in her legs.

My connection with Nell, seven years ago, was immediate and strong, because we both like story-telling and we could feel the class links even though I'd been to college.

But with the other women it was not immediate. I met Mo and Hortense through Nell. Both were single mothers at home all day with toddlers and babies. The distrust around class, because I was a junior-school teacher, was bruising in its violence. I was expecting their suspicion even less, because of Nell's acceptance.

'You gotta see it from their side, Ess,' exploded Nell. 'I got me part-time job, and Fred's money coming in, what he don't splurge on the dogs that is, and you've got nice wages now, and "superann" coming when you're retired, right, nice holidays, and a nice diddy little bedsit all on yer todd. Mo and Hort's got a bathroom full of dirty nappies, and a line full of clean ones, and the ones on the rack is airing, right, Ess? I mean, I know you, and yes, I do see you as family, Ess, and all. But they see all teachers as middle-class, right? I got me scrap of freedom, Ess, 'cos I've got me job. All they got is the social security snooping. They daren't even leave a spare toothbrush in the bathroom, if they could afford a spare one, got it?'

I was shaking so much I couldn't speak. Nell wasn't a hugging sort of person, so I just nodded, rushed down my cup of tea, and went home.

I let myself in the front door and stood in my den. I looked down the garden, past the old lavender bushes to the silver birch and the famous holly bush. Then I sat at my desk by my window in that den, and I wept and wept. I felt polluted by Densley bloody High and the teacher training college. It was Education that I'd longed for, that Mum and Grandma Clegg had wanted for me, but it had already split me from Lotte who told me that the swot-rot set in just as soon as I passed the eleven-plus.

After I'd dried my face and made fresh tea, I found an old exercise book and wrote the word – desolate. I kept that book. Adding to it from time to time. Nothing continuous. Fragments, occasionally.

Later, when Nell asked me to help set up a baby sitting circle, I agreed because I wanted to make friends. I still didn't understand then that England hates mothers and children, nor that mothers' liberation is an obstacle race, like trying to run in the Olympics, with a baby on your back.

Friday, 1 April. Late evening

It's dark out in the garden now. But the street lights from the estate throw long shadows of the trees. The space is safe, still, and calm out there tonight.

I write every day now. Words flow from me like thread through a knitter's hands. Letters wind into word shapes as fast as stitches curl themselves around Mo's and Hortense's knitting needles.

But although my urgent need to write seems like an energy drug and feels like breathing, it's made possible by my having a commodity which for many other women is in short supply. I have the *time*.

This is materially different from the lives of Mo and Hortense – the first a white single parent with two daughters; the second a black single parent with one son.

Through babysitting for both of them I have become no longer a stranger but, instead, someone they have started to trust. They both work as homeworkers for Mrs Tilson's wool shop on Reeve Green. They each earn five pence an ounce. They are under continuous pressure of time, and Hortense also studies on the access course at the tech. Fast, accurate knitting is essential. Even the social security snoopers haven't guessed (everyone expects to see mothers knitting). Their work is invisible.

I sit here, with this serene space outside, protected temporarily by fences and by luck. I was one of the few working-class girls let through the education sieve. My work with knitting yarn is a hobby. So is my writing. To have time for hobbies is a luxury, and so is this place, this space, this peacefulness.

Mo, Hortense and I talk about education, for which they both crave. We talk about women's struggles, about class, race and our daily lives. I told them that Grandma Clegg sewed, crocheted, tatted, and knitted all through my childhood. Even while she was cooking, she'd have the needles under her arm, the ball of wool in her apron pocket.

Deanne

Four years after Dora's death, Isobel applied to UCCA, the university clearing house, to do an engineering degree.

It was November, 1970. She was almost eighteen. I'd seen it coming. Trying to prepare myself for the time for truth. I knew they would ask for her birth certificate. Truth would mean anger. Hers and mine. Open. Cutting through the lies like a seagull's cry cracks open the wind.

Whenever I needed to think, I'd go a little way down the zigzag path, on the cliffs.

I remember that it was a stormy day, in a week of November winds. There were coastguard warnings on the cliffs. I stood on the path, a few feet down the cliff. Wet stones either side, hard rain splatting on the rocks, battering on the leaves and on the shrubs, pelting at my bare face, buffeting at my bare head. Salty. The wind was straight off the sea.

I had tried to kill a memory, a person. Her father. Buried him alive. Wiped out half Isobel's family.

Truth meant anger. Hers and mine. I'd brought up Izzie. Made both of us live through it. Punishment for losing Dora? Or reward? Or both?

Far out to sea the sky met the water. Clouds blurred into knives of rain. Grey lines. Smudging out the horizon. It's hard to paint the sea.

Afterwards, Isobel might cut me out of her life. Afterwards. After the truth that her father was not married to her mother, was not killed in a car accident. I had known as I told Izzie the lie about her father that it would not last for ever. I'd known as the words came out my foolish mouth when she was five.

Dora died without Isobel knowing her.

I'd known her. I'd hated Isobel's father as my competitor, I'd wanted to believe he was dead.

That had been a simple lie. Soon we'd get a simple request: birth

67

certificate. I shook. The wind soaked the grey rain through my clothes. I let it. Wind has a howl of its own on the cliffs. It howled at me. I let it.

Supposing I didn't tell her. Half-lied instead. I was good at that. I half-truthed about me and Dora: 'We were best friends for years and years, Izzie. Goodnight. Sleep tight.'

Supposing I said her father was killed in the car accident, but hadn't *actually* been married to Dora, so that's why Izzie's birth certificate had only one ink signature: Dora Beale, mother. Occupation: book-keeper. Status: spinster.

The white lie nailed my skin to my face with sharp rain.

Shrubs were bending, leaves were smashed against each other.

I looked down to the beach below, at grey-white waves. It was the first time I'd thought of walking into the sea. Oblivion.

I went home, wet from the skin out, cold. Izzie would be home late, gone to visit physics labs in Southampton University. I went and had a deep fast bath. Scrubbing hard, to get the circulation going.

Dressed again, put the casserole in, stoked the fire. Truth hurts. She arrived, soaked, grinned hello, went up to change.

I followed her. We talked a while in her blue room, about the labs.

She'd pulled the curtains, blue of course, against the neighbours opposite, put on the table lamp, and the two-bar electric fire.

I remember noticing how faded the blue carpet was in patches where the morning sun came in. We both liked it – its pattern of small white flowers. She had a blue bedspread.

I remember the huge poster on the wall above the bed. Abstract. Like looking into a hole in the sky, streams of light coming through.

She hugged me again, excited about the future. She'd chosen Birmingham as first option. She caught my tension though.

'What's the matter, Dee? I'm sorry. I've been prattling on all about me. Have you had a bad day, or something?'

I looked at her. It was going to slice through her bones like the cheese wire through cheese in the corner shop. I said I needed to talk. She knew me very well. She sensed trouble. Said she'd need a cigarette. I hadn't realised how much she smoked, until then. I sat on her upright chair, curtains closed behind me, her table lamp on. She was opposite, on the bed, leaning back on a huge cushion. We were both wearing jeans and sloppy sweaters.

'I love you, Izzie. So I don't know where to start. It's about me and Dora, and your father.'

She waited, knocking ash into a blue glass ashtray.

Best to come straight out with it. Get it over.

'They'll be wanting your birth certificate, soon. I lied to you about your father being married to Dora and, worse, about him being killed in a car accident. There wasn't a car accident at all.'

Her eyes scorched holes through my clothes, burning into my skin. 'Tell me.'

'He was over here studying. Your mother fell in love with him. You were a love child, like in the song.* He couldn't have been a bad person. Your mother loved him. But he was lying. I'm sure he loved her too. She was so lovable. But he was married, Izzie. Already. To someone back home. He had daughters there, and one son. That's all I know. That's all he told Dora. He went back when she was six months pregnant.'

Anger was the glue which set her bones together. 'You mean I have black sisters and I didn't know. You didn't tell me that I have sisters. I don't understand. I don't understand why, why if you were Mum's best friend, you didn't tell me.'

'I was not just her best friend.' Just. What a stupid word. 'I wanted to believe your father was dead. I wanted to kill him myself. I was Dora's woman-lover, from when we were thirteen years old. We ran away from Mereford together. Well, you know we did. It was because we were lovers. It was because we were lovers.'

She threw the words back at me like the sea hurls broken rocks.

'You were my mother's lover?'

'I was. I am proud of that.'

She began to shake. Wet poured down her face. All her limbs shook separately. The tears streamed. She looked at me all the time. She didn't move her eyes. They poured brine down, her mouth hung open, trembling. She didn't try to speak. Her hands were shaking.

She'd always known it. She knew all my friends. Knew I never had men in the house, except Stuart, who didn't count in that way.

I had wiped out half her family. The black ones that she needed. I didn't even know what harm I'd really done. I didn't know any other mothers with girls like Izzie to ask what they did, how they felt, what they said.

The sounds when they came were from the bottom of the sea. It seemed like that. They came out of her so deep.

We were there, looking at each other. Dora's lover; Dora's

---

* Love Child: Diana Ross. Released 1968/9 Motown label.

69

daughter. Her father's competitor; her father's love-child. The one he hadn't bothered to name.

My fears were steam behind my eyes. Threatening to burst my eyeballs open, I couldn't cry. My mouth hung open, too. We didn't touch. I could not be the first one to touch her. I didn't have the right to. It's not at all hard to remember it. It's like a film. I know every second of it.

For probably ten full minutes we sat apart like that. She having silent hysterics, with sounds coming up like whales to breathe. I with hot salt water scalding ravines behind my eyes. She reached out her hand. I shifted my chair, till I could catch hold. She held my hand very tight. A couple of seconds. She let go.

A voice so low that didn't belong to me, but was mine, said 'Shall we have some tea?' She nodded. I went down to put the kettle on. We were always like that if we were angry. It boiled out, then we made tea, then we talked. That was her and me, used to living together. I stood waiting for the kettle.

I felt like I'd been burying my head in sand. A fool ostrich. I was trailing years beind Isobel in understanding many things. It was more than a generation gap. I needed to see the world through her eyes, now. At least to try.

Right through the sixties with the rise of the black movement in America she'd become interested in black politics, kept cuttings, watched television. Why can't we see what we need before a crisis?

Why do we put it off so long? The kettle whistled. I took the tea upstairs. We were always like that. We needed a breather. We did it with the tea. We always did.

Her mother was dead, gone mad, my lover. It was enough to cope with. It wasn't all there was though. Her father was alive, somewhere. He was black. She was black. I hadn't told her merely a little white lie. I'd done a complete whitewash job. I could see it now, looking at her as I brought in the tray of tea. This woman – that baby, that I'd wanted to hate – was almost eighteen. Someone I loved.

Her table was covered with her A-level books. Physics, maths and further maths. Her teachers said she was in the running for three A grades. Isobel once said to me: 'I'll show 'em. I'll bloody show 'em, Dee.'

She sat there. Tough, bright, angry. I handed her the tea. Sat again in the chair opposite.

'I learned a lot of lessons since I was four years old, Dee. I ought to hate you, but it's not that easy is it? Why didn't you hate me?'

'I tried. For two weeks. I tried very, very hard to hate you. You didn't help me, damn you. You didn't bloody cry, make a fuss. You didn't wake too often in the night. You were lovely to look at, you made it really hard. Dora was in a bad state, staring at walls.'

'Why didn't you dump me on a doorstep. I'm surprised you didn't just get rid of me.'

'Would you have wanted that?'

'I don't know. I wish you'd been black. At least there'd have been two of us.'

Her mouth was angry, hard. I hardly ever saw it so hard. The anger ran along her mouth, along her jawbone. I'd live with that all my life now, till I was dead, now that I'd seen it.

'It never occurred to me to dump you. In a home, yes. Except that I couldn't. But not on a doorstep. It just never occurred to me. I did think about you being black – they all called it coloured in those days – you were a lovely-looking child. I thought that might be enough. You live and learn.'

'Yes you do, Dee. I learned to fight. You taught me. I learned to love and to hate here in Coombebury. You know that. The day they sat me next to Raymond Phelpps. I was the only black child in that infant school. You know that. He wasn't blond. His hair was white. Not blond, white. They sat me next to him. Of all people they sat me next to him. That's when I knew about hate, and anger. The words came later. Do you remember teaching me how to fight, when they called me names?'

I nodded, choked.

'How to get my sharp nails in their eyes and yank down hard? How to kick sideways into an ankle bone? Get my hands up, defend my face. D'you remember when Mrs Phelpps came to the house?'

Two mothers screaming at each other. Me on the doorstep, her at the gate. Six feet apart with Izzie's flowers like blue clouds on the soil.

'If your son touches my Izzie, so much as touches her again, I'll break every damn bone in his body, myself, personal, get it?'

I didn't want Izzie's anger. She didn't want mine. She began speaking again. Her voice was different. Anger still behind it, but it sounded slower.

'Many girls in Coombebury High really hated their mothers. White girls with rich white mothers. They have a hell of a life at home. No love, no affection, no one to really talk to. It's all "Pass the salt" and "Here's some money, go and buy a dress", meaning bugger off and don't bother me. We're not like that here. It would be really hard to hate you, Dee.' She paused, our eyes telling stories, do-you-remember stories, across the carpet between the bed and the chair. 'I ought to hate you, like I hate white England, white America, too. I ought to. It would be comfortable to be able to hate you. The painful thing is, Dee, I don't want to hate you but I *need* black people. I need other black people round me like air and food. I've known that a long, long time. But you don't have words for all these things when you're little. You just have the feelings and they churn you up.' She looked at me with a softer mouth, as if it ached with anger and hurt, but softer. I needed to see that.

'I think Dora was churned, till she couldn't cope. I don't think it. I *know* it. She just couldn't hold it all together. Hatred ate her up, Izzie. But it won't eat you. I'm not the only one who thinks that. Corrine does, too.'

Izzie shrugged. (Her shrug seemed to say:) Dangerous ground. Red flags. Keep away.

'At the moment we hurt like hell, Dee.' She looked at me. I nodded. 'This is my room, it's been my home, Dee. I still need you. I don't know what I'd have done if I'd been you. I mean, I think I could kill in revenge. I think when I love it will be deep. I haven't let myself love anyone yet. I couldn't in this place. It's all ahead of me. They tease me at school sometimes. I tell them I'm saving myself for Mr Right.' (I flinched.) 'That shuts them up. They try to fix me up from time to time, but I couldn't go with a white man. I do know my choices, Dee. I know all your friends. I know how they live. It's an open question. You haven't shared your bed with anybody for years, Dee. What are you going to do? It's four years since my mother died. I really care 'bout you, Dee. I know I'd feel terrible if there was somebody living in here, in this room.'

'There won't be. It's yours as long as you want it. I'm all right. You look after yourself. I'm all right.'

We were very tired then. Drained. We didn't want the casserole. We were in bed asleep, quite exhausted, by ten.

Isobel gained two As and one B. She was disappointed with the B. She went to Birmingham, returning for parts of vacations. She brought work home. There was nothing else for her in Coombebury. She gained her upper second honours degree in June 1974. She left England for Mozambique, to work there on an irrigation project. Some mornings when I'd open the curtains in her room, I'd watch the sun fall on the faded patches. I'd stand between the chair and the bed, feel the love and anger, strong as waves, and light pour through the poster, a hole in the sky.

Lotte

After she went up to the Grammar, our Esther was always studying. I used to try to jolly her out of it.

'You're meant to have a bit of fun, Ess. You're not meant to be stuck up in our bedroom all the time. You've got to have time to go out and have a laugh, Ess. Like we used to. What's the use of waking up every day if you can't have a laugh by night time?'

Esther said I had it easier being the younger one. Perhaps that was right. For her it was all school and homework. I couldn't be doing with it.

I didn't have a lot of homework. But then I didn't go to school every day, did I? I was a bloody good forger so I wrote myself endless absence notes. I was doing a four-day week long before they brought it into the Densley firms. Not that there were that many firms in Densley. There wasn't that much work for the women.

I didn't go to the Grammar like our Ess. I went to the secondary mod. Four days a week. I had what they called Fridayitis. So I surprised everybody in the place when I passed my thirteen-plus and off I goes to the technical school. That's how I got a chance to do my O-levels. Me and Sara Wilcox, that I'd come up from the secondary mod with. Then they asked me to stay on into the sixth form. I laughed in their faces. When you feel as if you've been doing time for five years like I did – well, you can just imagine me in the dock, can't you? 'I been only five years sewing mail bags, yer honour. I beg yer worship's pardon, but I'd like two years more.'

Not me. No thank you very much. I wanted money and I wanted to see the world. Have a bit of fun. Look on the light side. I loved my mum though and I didn't want to leave her on her own. I suppose, looking back, that's one of the reasons I liked Peter Glade. I could see Mum was happy and he didn't half make a difference to the money coming in. I went to work in Wells the Chemists for nearly a year and I was happy. It was hard work. They had little seats behind the counters and a two-foot-six copy of the Shops Act in the rest rooms, that said you could sit on them, but you wouldn't dare. Somebody would quick as lightning come and ask you to fill shelves or do the price tags. The chemist was right next to the bus stop. I've known people dash in, yell for a packet of Aspros and throw the money at me for me to catch, never even stopping for change. Still, we had a good laugh. I met three of the 'Saturdays' there: the gang met in the bus station at the Thrupenny-Bit Kiosk. (It was always nicknamed that though it had eight sides, not twelve, like a threepenny piece.) We'd hop on the bus out to Chalworth about three miles away and there we'd meet the blokes with their motor bikes. I loved the bikes. We went to the sidecar championships sometimes to watch Beryl Green. She was the sidecar champ, leaning out flat over the edge as they took the corners at dizzy speeds. Mum'd have had apoplexy if she'd known. I became good friends with Beryl Green.

I liked Densley and I liked Densley people, but the shopwork at Wells the Chemists was boring after the novelty wore off.

I didn't seem to be getting very far with seeing the world.

You wouldn't think an ordinary visit to the dentist could be a turning point, would you? But it was, for me.

There I was, leafing through an old copy of *The Lady*. You only ever saw it if you went to the dentist. Piles of them next to *Country Life* and *Homes and Gardens*. Not the breakfast dailies for most Densley people.

Anyway, in *The Lady*, I saw an ad for an agency in Sheffield that wanted *au pairs* and nannies.

I thought: bloody heck, there's money in dirt. Not for them as gets dirty, but for them as gets off on it all. Owners, bosses, friends, and hangers-on what can afford au pairs.

Any road up, when no one was looking, I ripped out the ad from *The Lady* and I stuffed it in me shoulder bag.

I phoned the agency and I went on the bus to Sheffield on me day off to make enquiries and arrangements.

Mum had braced herself for the time when I would leave home. She told me she was glad for me, you know, all little birdies have to fly the nest sometime. I was upset at leaving, but Mum wouldn't be on her own because she had Peter, didn't she? Mind you, when the actual day came we didn't know whether to smile at each other or cry. It seemed such a change, breaking away from Mum. I know she felt it too. She came with me to the bus station, and we both said, you know in unison, you open your mouth and the other person does too, and out comes the same words, 'I remember us seeing our Essie off, do you?' Then neither of us was dry-eyed. Mum had one of Peter's hankies in her pocket. Good job too. We soaked it, didn't we? Then we grinned at each other and hugged, and I said I'd come and see her on me days off, and she said 'Yes, of course you enjoy yourself too our Lotte, and remember the door's always open if it doesn't work out.'

The long and short of it is – I went to work as a nanny living in at the house of one of the lecturers at the university.

They were middle-class people, through and through. You could tell that from their furniture. It was handed down on both sides, but always kept in the family. Know the sort of thing? Bookcases with little lift-up glass windows in front of each shelf. I'd never seen bookcases with windows before. The whole house was decorated with high and low bookcases, all shapes and sizes and they nearly all had windows. They had a daily in to polish them. It was like living in a library.

Meg and Edward liked me and were very good to me. I soon realised I loved children and wanted children of my own. Some au pairs are really just skivvies but I was lucky. Meg and Edward didn't make my hours too bad.

The household was easy-going and very friendly. You see, they didn't have airs and graces or try to put me down. They weren't poor people made good, the sort that go all lah-de-dah and keep trying to prove that they are what they're trying to be.

I especially liked Meg. She was half French and so the children spoke it fluently. Funnily enough, French was the one subject I tried never to miss at school. I liked the way it sounded. Besides, we had this dishy teacher. Good job I never had French on Fridays. Anyway, Meg gave me French books to read and I was soon going at it quite fast. But I told myself I wasn't ever doing no more exams, couldn't be doing with it.

'You want to see the world though, don't you? It's just an idea, Lotte. If you could speak colloquial French, you could do this kind of work in France. We'd miss you, but you'll leave us one day in any case. You could travel more easily with French. Besides, some families would want you to have at least once A-level. I hope you'll rethink it, Lotte.'

It went in, her idea. I thought, well, maybe I'd give it a go. No harm in trying and I could always give up if I was bored. I surprised myself. I found I actually liked A-level French. I wasn't bored at all. Quite the opposite. I enjoyed the literature. We had parts of the set books on tape, and we had earphones in the language laboratories. And I started to tune in to the World Service and the French channels like Meg did. They would broadcast literary programmes and I could follow the texts in Meg and Edward's books from their collection downstairs. I just loved that. And of course I'd always liked cooking, hadn't I? Well Meg lent me her cookery books in French, you know, to encourage me. She was very good to me. I'd not have done it if it hadn't been all around me like that, would I? But I was in the right place at the right time. All a matter of luck really.

I liked being a nanny but I also needed a lot of money if I wanted to travel. I thought I might be able to get some temping work, typing. So I borrowed Meg's old typewriter, bought a typing book, and taught myself to touch-type. Lots of things were going well for me. Meg and Edward were quite Bohemian. They called it 'progressive'. They wanted me to learn about different foods and sometimes they had dinner parties with knives and forks in ranks. Silver soldiers. War on food, though I didn't say so. I was learning fast. Wine and posh meals. Take mushrooms, for instance. I never knew about mushrooms till I met Meg and Edward, did I? At first, I couldn't eat them, soggy things.

'They're an acquired taste, Lotte, like garlic. You'll get used to them,' predicted Meg.

I did, too. Even got to *like* mushrooms. On the night I met James Slomner, Junior, Meg served them in *vol-au-vents*.

By that particular night, I'd come to some conclusions about myself and what I wanted. First, I didn't want to be alone. Second, I wanted children. Third, I didn't want ever to be poor again or get myself trapped bringing up children on my own like my mother had to do, bless her. You see, our Esther underestimated me. She used to tease me about having a bun in the oven but I was too sassy for that. I wanted the life that Meg and Edward were showing me.

Meg and Edward asked me to join them for cocktails and *petit fours* at the end-of-term leaving party for Edward's law students. James Slomner was finishing his law degree and was everything I was looking for. He was good-looking, quite clever (he thought he was the bee's knees); and he had a solid career (with plenty of cash) in front of him.

I decided to marry him because he could take me to posh places, knew about wine and took *vol-au-vents* for granted.

It wasn't hard to catch a man like James. I expected I'd have to try harder than I did. We laughed a lot together. I married him in 1970, when I was twenty-two. That was the year he started at his father's firm, Slomner and Sherwood, in Moorgate. So I left Meg and Edward and their brood, and came south to London. James said he adored the fact that I spoke fluent French. He quite often travelled in Europe for his father's firm and so I went with him on the business trips. There were new people all the time, new ways of eating in quaint restaurants. We danced in night clubs. I was wild. He liked that side of me, the wild side. He said any girl that could overcome her class as I'd done had to be wild. He liked that in a woman.

I didn't like the way he said that, really I didn't. I couldn't get used to some of his ideas at all.

James's hobby was dabbling in oils. He said he didn't have enough money to collect paintings, but he would some day if he worked hard enough. He took me on business trips to Paris, Rome, Venice and Vienna and then we went round the galleries. He said that anyone who worked could have a life like we had. I didn't like him saying that.

'My mum works, James, but she don't live like we do.'

'Doesn't.'

'I mean doesn't. She doesn't live like us.'

'Choices, Lotte. It's about choices. She doesn't choose to spend her money like we do.'

'She don't, doesn't, *have* the money, James.'

'Let's not spoil a beautiful evening by talking about our mothers, hmmm?'

He'd leave it there. Always leaving it. On those nights I doubted everything. I especially doubted him going on about the way I *talked*. I found myself resisting him on that one thing. The rest I gave in to. I wanted what James and his way of life could offer, didn't I?'

James' work frequently took him to Southampton. Sometimes we'd go there together, staying at James' uncle's house and going sailing with his cousins. In the evening we'd have late dinner at home or we'd drive to the Bronnester Hotel in Coombebury.

The Bronnester had deep red carpets and low red lights with satin red lampshades. They looked like miniature crinoline skirts over wire hoops with small silk tassels on. There'd be ten or twelve of us laughing and talking about sailing and travel – I could do that now – and wine and food. The ranks of silver soldiers were no threat to me by then and I'd learned long ago to call egg and bacon pie *quiche lorraine*. I found that keeping my accent was working out all right. Everyone liked me. I was a bit different.

Sometimes James' father and mother would come down from London for a family gathering in Southampton. Of all the Slomner women, I especially liked James' mother. She had a similar background to me, and was always laughing. James' father was so busy with the responsibilities of being the head of a large firm of lawyers that he was rarely at home, but James' mother didn't seem to mind. She made me at home when we visited her house, and when she came with James Senior to Southampton with us (which wasn't often) she was the one who made me feel the most relaxed. She was the one who actually said she liked my speech. She said she'd always liked northern people because we were warm and straight to the point.

There was money everywhere. In our bedroom in the Southampton house, we had tissues to match the bedspread, and you could use them for everything. If you spilled the Martini on the shaggy carpet, you wouldn't dream of going to find a floor cloth. You used as many tissues as you needed and the box would be replaced next day. (My mum wouldn't buy tissues unless she won the pools.)

There were Christy towels with a pile as deep as the carpets, some so big they'd go twice round you when you stepped out of the shower. Beside the bed were piles of glossy magazines. Many's the time I've grinned to myself at the copies of *The Lady* beside *my* side of the bed. Where would I be without them?

Life was fun. The rich life. I missed Mum and Densley but I can't say I missed the scrimping and saving, would you? James and I were living rent free in a flat that belonged to his father in Camden.

One of the pleasures of marriage to James, was having my own kitchen and learning to cater for our dinner parties.

Some of the people he invited were boring as stale bread, but I always enjoyed the cooking and all the preparation. I had my menu cards indexed and colour coded, so that I surprised each set of guests each time; and of course part of the fun was that I had the cheque book. I've even been known to buy my taramosalata from Harrods' food hall. Not that I liked pink fish eggs, but James' guests did. I liked the gateaux and all their fancy names such as Schwarzwälderkirschtorte – that's a Black Forest cherry cake.

It seems a bit extreme to dismiss all James' guests in one sweep of the hand, doesn't it? I mean, people are people, aren't they, and there's good and bad in all types of people. It's just that the men were all go-getters, if you know what I mean, all up-and-coming executives and solicitors, bigger houses and faster cars, into money. Wasn't I into money too? Well, yes in a way, but not in another way. I tried to get to know some of the wives and there were one or two that I would have liked to make friends with but they soon moved away when their husbands got promotions. Other wives were pregnant and some had babies. That upset me, for a start. Others had a habit of saying 'I want' or 'I'm having' and then you'd have to listen to a shopping list. New lace petticoat from Liberty's, gold bracelet from Burlington Arcade. Oh and so much ogling over the ten-bedroomed houses in *Country Life*.

We hadn't many daytime neighbours in Camden. Ours was a flat in an arty street. Women were out at work in town all day. College lecturers, antique dealers; nice enough if you met them in the market on a Saturday, but not to make friends with; not to pop in and have a cuppa with. So my life revolved round James.

I wanted a baby, but James said we should wait. He said he wanted to become established. To move to our own house with a garden. I could see the logic of that. I had a longing for children of my own, and I've found that longings won't fit inside calm talkings, 'discussions', and logic. James could be so logical.

'You're a fly-by-night, Lotte. It's a good thing one of us can take responsibility in this marriage. You're beautiful, darling, and we have such fun, but you're not exactly being rational about this baby thing are you?'

'You said you wanted children as much as I did. You promised we wouldn't be long before we started a family, James. You're breaking your promise, aren't you?'

'Don't twist my meaning, Lotte. How like a woman to misunderstand what a man is saying. I'm just trying to explain why we should wait. Come here and be my rabbit, mmm?'

'Don't rabbit me when we're talking like this. It confuses me. You promised and you're breaking your promise and that's all I know.'

'Don't go over the top, darling. A couple of years from now our mortgage will be secure and we could try then, mmm? You know you don't like the boring money stuff. You hate it when I'm doing our accounts.'

He sounded so calm and I hated him then. I didn't want to but it welled up in me with despair and disgust. I was a nanny when he met me and I had always wanted children the whole time I'd known him.

I challenged him again about it some months later, when the longings were coming through to me very intensely. I couldn't go on ignoring my body. I know not all women want babies but if you're one of them that does, like me, then it's hell every time you bleed because of the waiting. Waiting. Finally in yet another of our rows he said, 'I'm not ready to be a family man. We're too young for thinking about babies. They're just a tube with a yell at one end and no sense of responsibility at the other.'

So then I was sane again. I *knew* that the money had been an excuse. I felt better now that I knew where I was. Because, well, if someone is constantly telling you one thing and you know that they mean something else, then that's crazy-making, isn't it?

That was the beginning of a different phase in my life. It was 1972. We bought a house in Carshalton Beeches with a deposit from James' father. I thought if I made the house ready then he'd agree to having children. I was like a fly on the wall watching myself go through with it all. I was looking forward to the decorating. You see the Slomner women weren't supposed to work outside the home, and well, it sounds silly, doesn't it, but I didn't have the same level of confidence in myself that I'd had before I met James. So I concentrated on nest-building. Then the rows really started. I couldn't understand why he didn't want me to do it. After all, I was at home all day. The women of Densley always did the decorating. Some of the miners' wives made a living by going round doing other peoples' houses. Painting and papering. It was always the women – they were quick and humorous and it suited everyone. I made a really good meal and brought up the topic after an excellent chocolate mousse. He immediately said: 'No wife of mine is going to do that kind of work.'

'Why, James? I would enjoy it and be good at it.'

'This is not Densley, Lotte. This is Carshalton Beeches.'

'I know where we live, James. I live here, remember.'

'Don't resort to sarcasm, darling. Whoever heard of a solicitor's wife decorating?'

'We can be different. It'd be fun. Make a change. An adventure. I'd love it, I would really.'

'The answer's *no*, Lotte. You wouldn't know the difference between a plumb line and a paint brush. Is that coffee ready now?'

He had, from way back, that habit of dismissing me. I should have seen the warning signs when we were engaged, but I was proud of my success in achieving my life plan, so I didn't. I remember on one occasion I challenged back, just after we got engaged, and it went like this:

'If we both want to go to the cinema,' said James, 'to different pictures, then I think the man's decision should settle it.'

'Oh, I don't agree with that, darling. I think we should take it in turns. That'd be more equal.'

'What do you mean, equal?'

'Well, like you said before, we should see ourselves as complementary, shouldn't we? When we're married. I'm the female and you're the male and we need each other, don't we?'

'Yes, of course. Men and women are different. *Vive la différence.* Another lager and lime, rabbit?'

'Yes, thanks.' I waited for him to come back with the drinks, then I added: 'So I should make the decisions as well.'

'Yes, of course, Lotte. We have to share things. But in the end I'm the breadwinner when we have the children.'

'Yes. But you haven't said we'll take turns with the decisions.'

'You've got spunk, Lotte. You stick up for yourself. I like that in a woman. Well, all right then, we'll take turns.'

'Good.'

'Drink up, the show starts soon.'

I felt empty inside but I didn't know why. He'd agreed and that meant he understood, didn't it? But by the time we had the rows over decorating in the new house in Carshalton Beeches, I realised the hadn't listened to a word I said. He had agreed only to shut me up. So then the longing for a baby to fill the commuter-land days returned, and the days seemed longer then – waiting.

Each autumn I went home to Yorkshire to see Mum. I was never there when Essie was. She always went for Christmas. Mum seemed contented and I tried not to show how distressed I was. It was ever so strange to be home again. Every room seemed small. There was no carpet in the bathroom; and I froze upstairs by mid-evening because there was no central heating.

'You've gone soft, my girl. A bit of honest to goodness hard work wouldn't do you no harm.'

'James says the Slomner wives have never worked.'

'Are you happy, Lotte – love?'

'Course I'm happy. I've got a lovely husband and a lovely home.'

'Humph. Still making you wait is he?'

'We can't afford it. We aren't ready.'

'Don't you give me none of your brave faces, our Lotte. When your heart's set on a child, our Lots, nothing else will do. Money doesn't make for happiness.'

She had her new blue crimplene on and it suited her. The convex mirror above the mantelpiece caught both of us. The room was eleven feet wide from the mirror to the opposite wall and was almost square, although it was curved in the mirror as I sat on the settee with Mum. Behind us was the polished sideboard that was Mum's pride and joy. On my left was the window ledge, and the daylight winked and blinked on the rows of glass animals that Essie and I used to buy her each Christmas when we were kids. I had a sudden memory of Essie telling

81

me stories to keep me safe at night. I'd be about nine. That was before Ess went up to the Grammar and the swot-rot set in.

'Are *you* happy, Mum?'

'Every day's enough,' she replied: 'There's only two things I wish for and one's not possible. I wish your Grammaclegg hadn't died just before Ess went to college like that. I'd have liked to have made her old age really comfortable, bless her. Given her a treat. Hired a taxi and taken her to see her sister in Bradford. She wanted to go and see her sister. And as for the other thing,' (I knew what was coming) 'I wish you and Essie would patch it up and start trusting each other.'

'You did all you could for Grammaclegg, Mum. You did all you could.'

'It's not only what you do, our Lotte. It's how you feel while you are doing it. She grieved about her sister. I know it though she didn't say so. There's some things women just know. You don't need words. I used to hear her sitting up in bed praying. Touched me to the quick she did with her praying. Sitting up in bed all on her own there in the dark. Her voice was like a child's voice, trusting. She used to pray for her sister. I grieved for her. And I grieve for you and Ess.'

'No use praying for our Ess. She's a lost cause, Mum, really she is. She's had four boyfriends in four years and she won't settle with any of them. She comes to dinner with me and James and I invite James' friends, the ones that are single, and she hides in the kitchen doing the washing up. Says she's in her element.'

'P'raps she is.'

'Honestly, Mum, it's hopeless with our Essie. It's Marx this and Engels that and by the time she's gone I have to calm James down for two hours. He had one of his medical friends round last time. She asked him how many of his women patients were on tranks. She gets up my nose.'

'All right. All right, I'm sorry I asked. Let's drop it, shall we? No point in spoiling your visit over absent family is it? We've got a couple of hours before Peter comes in. You coming down the market?'

Before I left Mum asked me if I'd thought of doing a secretarial course in the daytime, while James was at work. She said it might help take my mind off things, meaning babies, but not saying so. I said I'd think about it.

The problems between me and Esther were made worse because James and Essie didn't like each other at all.

I'd have loved them both to get along. I'd daydream about our Essie finding somebody I liked. Well, lots of families want that don't they?

I'd dream about her and James making friends, and Essie settling down with somebody, and all of us getting together in a foursome. P'raps a holiday sailing, with James' cousins in Southampton and their wives. But it seemed less and less likely as time went on.

I applied to the nearest private secretarial school, and was accepted first time round. The course would involve four mornings and afternoons a week, from September 1974 and about an hour and a half homework on three nights. It would last two terms, deposit non-returnable. I paid the deposit out of my dress allowance, aware that money came to me because of James, and because I didn't have the babies to spend it on. I remembered Grammaclegg telling me: 'Money doesn't make for happiness, Lotte, but it helps.'

There were twenty women on the course. Some of them were friendly, especially Hazel and Marie. I thought about what Mum once said: 'There are some things women just know.' Then I thought about women friends and for the first time since I got married I began to look, for new friends, for women friends. I never said a word to James about the course or my woman friends there. It was the first time I'd been so secretive with him and I felt funny about it, but stronger.

I didn't tell Mum or Essie about the course because I didn't know if I'd be able to complete it. I didn't want to disappoint Mum, so I decided I'd tell her if it all went on all right. I didn't want Essie to be looking over my shoulder at how I was getting on. I wanted to do it all by myself. I used to feel like that when we'd been at home in Densley together, too. I'd always been following on behind, tagging along, so to speak. This time I was on my own, and I kept it entirely to myself.

It became very awkward with Essie from then on. I wanted to sort out my life, myself. And I wanted my own ideas, separate from hers. She used to ram her ideas down my throat. Used to make me furious, didn't it? But I felt sad about it, because she was lovable, too. And I didn't half miss the times when she'd joked and told whopping good stories. So it bothered me, but you can't have everything. I just thought, well that's how the cookie crumbles, isn't it?

There was heaps more homework than they'd told us there'd be. Well, it didn't worry me too much because James never got in till seven-thirty, sometimes later, so I just practised secretly while he was still out, didn't I? But it was hard for the other two, what with Hazel having three children and Marie four. They were really tired with it. Marie nearly gave it up but we all got through together. I don't think we would have done if we hadn't had each other.

Marie and her husband wanted to move out of the south east, and start up a Bed and Breakfast place in Scotland. That's where they'd both come from originally. They were devoted to one another and to their four children. But B and B's are a dicey business and so Marie decided that if she could type she'd be able to take in work, you know, typing while the children were in school. So that's why she was doing the course.

And Hazel? She was very different from both me and Marie. She read all the time. She was interested in, oh, everything to do with psychology, child development, personal growth and health foods. All things like that. She said she could easily let the housework go hang if she had her nose in a book. But you couldn't make money reading, could you, so she wanted some sort of part-time job, and a friend of hers was thinking of starting up a small secretarial agency. Letter headings, some lay-out work, a bit of graphics, and any kind of typing. So she told Hazel that if she got her finger out, well fingers actually, and learned to type, she could do a few hours a week. So that was a chance too good to miss, and Hazel enrolled the same time as me. Mind you, both of them were hard put to pay the fees, but they were looking to the future, and there we all were.

Hazel often brought in books to lend to Marie and me. You name it, she'd heard of it. She always knew who'd won the Pulitzer or the Booker prize. I said she should've been on television on the book programme.

She brought in Betty Friedan's book, *The Feminine Mystique*, and we all talked about that. Not that any of us were very interested in women's lib, not at all, but whatever Hazel was reading, she'd talk to us about, wouldn't she? It was all for her family, she said. If she was happy then they were all happy, and so on. I was looking forward to the time when I'd have my own children, so it was like being a bit of an apprentice on the sly, really. Of course, I wasn't going to let on about that to them, was I? Also I could see that after the course we'd go our separate ways, but that while we were together we had a lot that we could learn from each other, and I read plenty more books than I'd ever have bothered with if I hadn't met someone like Hazel.

Then Hazel brought in a copy of *The Female Eunuch*. I read it three times before I gave it back. I was pretty shocked by it. It made me think of James' lies about us having children. But I didn't want to be a revolutionary, or a single woman, and I wouldn't want to live on my own, at all.

Anyway, it was the first time I'd thought about leaving James. So of course I was shocked. You bet I didn't tell Essie. She'd have said, 'I told you so,' going on and on about the bourgeoisie and such like.

I didn't want to lose Essie just because I was married to James. I thought I should maybe try to see her in the evenings after my course or at weekends at her place on my own, but that was nigh on impossible. James did his nut if I wasn't there when he was, on account of his long hours.

It was just after I started my course, and before Essie went to teach at Reeve Juniors, that she and I had a row.

She had been to dinner at our house on the Saturday night, and had slept in our spare bedroom. I was driving her home to north London on Sunday afternoon, and we were in the car on Tower Bridge when the argument began.

'I can't come to any more of your dinners where there is a spare man floating around like a piece of driftwood looking for an oil-free beach,' said Essie.

'Don't be crude, Essie. Staying single's not doing you any good – any good at all. Look at you. No make-up, pale as a moon on a bleak night.'

'Look, Lotte, I'm prepared to make an effort with James, even if it is a real struggle, but I can't stand this matching business. I feel like a maiden aunt being looked over. I could come to see you on my own. That'd be much better.'

'James won't have it.'

'Won't have what?'

'He says it looks unnatural you coming here all on your own. He says you are too choosy, Essie, and it makes him uncomfortable.'

'Oh, I see. My purpose in coming to see you was to make your husband feel comfortable. I hadn't realised. I thought you wanted me for me. You know? Me. Essie. Your sister, remember?'

'Look, it's not like that. I want you to come to us. It's just that . . .'

'That James runs that house with a rod of iron or whatever it is he keeps in his trousers. I'll choose my own lovers, thank you very much. Some of us are not for sale.'

'That does it, Ess. You can bloody walk the rest of the way.'

She was crying. I was about to start. I leant across her and opened the passenger door, shaking.

She looked at me, tears rolling down her cheeks. I hoped she wouldn't say sorry. She'd be lying. She was upset, but she did mean what she said.

She got out of the car without hugging me. She didn't say anything. I didn't call her back. I wanted to but I didn't.

She didn't slam the car door. She walked away quickly, in the direction of the tube. She never looked back over her shoulder. If she had, she would have seen me crying.

It takes a long time for a woman like me to look at her life and realise she's made a mistake. Know what I mean? For me it meant facing that my wonderful husband was a liar and a cheat. That made me feel stupid, for not realising from the beginning. Anyway, I did realise and I grew about ten extra skins to save my own life before it was too late.

I heard that James' father's secretary was leaving to have a baby. She was planning on *not* going back to work if everything went all right. I chose a week when James was going to be in Southampton on business and then I rang to make an appointment with Mr James Slomner, Senior. Of course, if I used my own voice I'd be recognised. I knew everyone in the firm including the telephonist, Nell Winters, because when I went shopping in the town I'd call in and meet James for lunch. So anyway I rang and spoke in fluent French to Nell, who said, 'Hold the line please,' in French, and passed me straight through to my father-in-law's secretary. I gave my name as Francoise de la Loire.

I arrived on the arranged day, dressed to impress, wearing a dark wig, dark glasses and speaking excellent French.

The secretary closed the door behind me, and then James Senior offered me a seat. I lit a Gitane in a long cigarette holder and chatted pleasantly about Paris for a few minutes. I could see that he was delighted. He never could resist a Frenchwoman, the old rake.

I slowly took off the glasses and grinned hello.

'Lotte, my dear Lotte, what are you up to?'

'I wanted an entrée, Father. I wanted to entertain you and I've something to ask you.'

I was enjoying the adventure. From his real leather chair he ogled me. I hadn't had so much amusement for years. (All the laughter had gone out of my marriage. I was left with the lies and the posh house and empty heart.)

'I'd like you to employ me as your personal secretary when Valerie leaves. I am out of my mind with boredom at home. I want to use my language skills for your firm. Keep it in the family, you might say. I can type using both a French and an English typewriter and I'm hard-working and efficient.' (I wanted to say that James wouldn't ever have taken my suggestion seriously, and just desired me for a decoration in his home, but my father-in-law was a shrewd old bugger. I let him come to that conclusion himself.) 'We've had some really good talks, you and I, Father, and I want to use my brain, really use it. I'm not afraid of hard work. All my family began as you did, Father, with grinding hard work. James loves the firm, too. He understands exactly how you feel about us waiting before we have a family, but he doesn't understand about *me*. Whereas I think you might.'

Abruptly I came to the end of my performance. I'd been rehearsing it over and over at home, but now my chest was thumping. He might have rejected me, there and then, but he didn't. Then I knew I *had* beguiled him and I could see that the thought of me accompanying him on business trips didn't at all displease him. He liked legs, the old Casanova.

The long, off-white curtains swung slowly. There were green plants by the windows. Green is a colour for hope. God, I thought, Lotte, you're going poetic, concentrate on the job for heaven's sake. Then I watched him consider the possibilities. He leaned back in his chair, laughed long and heartily, and then stood in that erect masonic style (that I thought ridiculous). A proper upright prick of a man. He came towards me and took my hand. I remembered not to flinch.

'My dear, you could charm the back leg off a mule and I am no mule.'

'You'll think about it, then?' (I remembered 'the smile' and I smiled.)

'It is absolutely outrageous and I am an old fool not to have thought about it myself.'

I could imagine his other thoughts quite clearly. Too clearly. I put some of them back in the filing cabinet while I kept out the file labelled: 'One-upmanship: older man scores one over his son'.

'It's yours, Lotte, on one condition.'

'What's that?'

'You take me to dinner on your first salary cheque.'

I was going to have to play this part very carefully. I stepped back theatrically and offered my hand. He, just as dramatically, raised it to his lips. I decided that most of his intentions towards me were in his head only. If I had really called his bluff he'd have run a mile, thank God. But he would enjoy the idea of a chase as did all his kind. He reminded me and not for the first time of Ralph Edmund Dove, his brother's friend in Southampton.

There's a first time for everything isn't there? James Junior knocked me from one side of the bedroom to the other when he found out. I couldn't walk for a week afterwards. And he still wanted sex with me. I wasn't in a fit state to refuse. I lay there, thanking God that I *didn't* have any children.

James showed many emotions, from fury that I'd gone behind his back, to weeping that I didn't love him. But I had my plans now and besides, even my pity was gone after the beating.

It wasn't the last time he hit me, but until I had some earnings of my own behind me, I wasn't ready to leave. Mentally I had left him, however long I might have to stay to see through my leaving plans. So I was especially careful with the pill. I had longed for children until it became an obsession. Now, there was an emptiness where the longings had been. I was dead there however James might want me to perform.

James didn't want children any more than he wanted me as a real woman with needs and vulnerabilities. He wanted a body from the neck down that was silent from the neck up. Unless it was laughing. He wanted me in bits like snapshots in the porn magazines he wanted me to read. Some of them were torsos of living women, with no faces. The world outside my house could call it 'marriage' if they liked. Inside those expensive walls so tastefully decorated (not by me, I wasn't allowed) – inside there, I couldn't feel much difference between me and a model in a porno movie. Except perhaps I got more money.

I started work at Slomner and Sherwood and I concentrated on doing the job efficiently. I was punctual, reliable, and sometimes funny. James couldn't do anything to stop me, could he? After all, he didn't have the power in the firm to do anything that went against his father. Everyone knew that. I began to see that no one much liked James. He wanted to be the cockerel in the farmyard and crow about his feathers. People were much fonder of his father. I think they could all identify with the old rogue. At least rogues are human.

There'd be a twinkle in Nell's eye sometimes as James Senior passed by her switchboard on the way to his office. But she had only a polite smile for my husband.

There was no one I could talk to about my home life, so I kept silent. I planned to save some money to see me through, then leave England for a year and try and get jobs around the world. Eventually I was going to settle in Paris.

I enjoyed working for my father-in-law. I worked through the lunch hour sometimes (he paid me overtime) and quite frequently I worked late in the evenings. I always left the meal at home for James to heat through: he couldn't take that out on me. I didn't refuse him in bed except when I feigned a bad period. I didn't challange his porn magazines either, though I hated them.

I kept in touch with Mum. I wouldn't let James interfere with that. I went to see her as usual for a week in the autmn of '76.

'I'm leaving James one day soon, Mum, when I'm ready,' I announced, and she looked at me with tears right to the corners of her eyes. She gave me a huge hug, like she would when I was little. She didn't offer me any advice, bless her. She just said, 'Are you sure, Lotte?'

'It's just a matter of time, Mum. I'm saving up. I think I'll leave the country for a while, go and find temping work in Paris, maybe. I'm just not quite ready. I need some cash to take with me.'

She knew I wasn't hinting for money. Our family didn't hint. We'd come straight out with it, wouldn't we, where cash was concerned? Besides, it'd be me helping Mum out if I could, not the other way round, but she was too proud to accept it.

Mum asked me if I'd any plans to see Essie. But I hadn't. I was estranged from Essie; it was a habit hard to break.

I'd registered that she'd moved to South London to teach, and I listened to Mum's delight about our Essie's new bedsit, with a garage that she'd made into a den. Mum loved Essie's long letters. She had to make do with phone calls from me. I never was one for letter writing, was I?

Essie's letter, full of nice surprises, came to Mum while I was there.

'Guess what, Mum. I've just met our Lotte's telephonist. Small world, isn't it? She's called Nell Winters, and she's the mother of a nine-year-old in Reeve Juniors. Her other daughter's five, just started in the infants. Nell says she can't wait to see Lotte's face when Lotte gets back to work on Monday.'

I needed that news like a hole in the head. I liked Nell, but hardly knew her. I certainly didn't want our Essie crowding in anywhere near my work at Slomner's; not now I was planning to put the cat among the pigeons by leaving. I could quite cheerfully have clobbered our Essie one for making friends with Nell.

Esther
Saturday, 2 April 1983

For weeks last winter Nell and Tracey's pressure was rising like on a BBC weather map. The hot and cold air currents coming from their front room would make an interesting satellite picture. Storm hour was one wet Saturday at three pm while Nell was ironing.

Tracey emerged from the bathroom with red hair poking up only half an inch over her head. The rest was growing on the wet bathmat like instant mustard and cress on soggy cotton wool.

Nell grabbed the Argos catalogue and slung it at her daughter's face. It caught Tracey's chin. She reeled and slumped on the settee.

Nell's knuckles around the handle of the steam iron were white with hard blue ridges. She whacked into Fred's shirts.

'You hurt me with that thing,' shouted Tracey, volume up.

'I meant to. It might bring you to your senses,' shouted Nell back.

'You could get done, you know. Violence to the younger generation.'

'Don't you bloody "younger generation" me. Look at you!'

'It's *my* hair.'

'Look my girl, I don't care if you're the bloody Queen of England, you can't go out looking like that.'

'I'm going to the disco. You promised, Mum.'

'So did you, Trace. You said last time you weren't ever going to dye it green again and now look at you.'

'It's not green.'

'Don't you give me none of your lip. Why the hell you have to turn yourself into a human hedgehog I'll never know.'

'It's *my* hair. I'll turn it into what I bloody well want to.'

'Why can't you just settle down, Trace. Stop all this punk stuff and find some nice friends.'

'I know what you mean, Mum. I don't want to settle down, as you

90

put it. Do you really want me to look like the other girls on this estate. What 'bout Janie Lendy. You want me like that?'

'I never said that, Trace. I just don't understand you. I just want you to be more, well, settled.'

'Yeah. I bet that's what Janie Lendy's mum wanted. Just settle down, dear. Get yourself a nice boyfriend. She was such a good girl, wasn't she? Did just what her mum said. Seventeen wasn't he? Or was it nineteen, Mum? She *was* all settled. Till he left her. And what's she got now, Mum? She went on the pill for him and now she opens her legs to anyone. 'Cos he left her, didn't he, and now every bloke in the youth club thinks she's game. And she bloody is, Mum. 'Cos she's looking for love, i'nt she? Like you was. With my dad.'

'You leave your dad out of this. He's never laid a finger on you, you young bitch.'

'I might be a bitch, but I'm not a slag too. The only reason my dad doesn't hit me like you is 'cos he's only got two speeds. Dead slow and stop. And you bloody know it.'

'I said none o' your lip. Why can't you find some nice friends? I just don't understand you, Trace.'

'I have got nice friends. Best I could get. And I ain't sticking round here for any more insults, just because I don't want a boyfriend.'

'Well, with hair like that, you're not going to find one, are you?'

Tracey hissed and steamed louder than the iron and pushed past the wash rack to the lobby. Nell heard her hoovering up the hairs and sighed, but instead of starting on her tenth shirt, she came round to me and told me the whole story, desperate to understand it all.

'I just don't know how she is going to end up, Ess. I've enough problems without her thing with these girls. I want my Trace to get some sense in her head.'

'Maybe she has.'

'Go on.'

'The friendships are solid, like ours.'

'Leave it off, Ess. You ain't got your head done up like a porcupine, and you ain't askin' to sleep on my bloody floor.'

'I know, Nell. But times have changed since I was in *my* teens and you're twelve years older than me.' I paused, thinking how to carry on, and Nell waited. 'We all needed a bit of space at Tracey's age, didn't we? You were writing secret letters to Deanne, and I was studying with Laura, driving my mum up the wall, and writing down my thoughts, and my dreams, in a secret diary. It's Tracey's turn, Nell. You love her, and I think she knows that, deep down, even if she's not loving you

91

back in the ways you want. She'll go her own way, anyway, just like you did, and I did. She needs some space, Nell.'

'You're a lot of help you are, Ess. I been givin' her space, as you call it. Till I'm blue in the bloody face. I've had it with her. I tell you Ess, things is building up in our house. There'll be a bloody explosion one day. Space or not. She's winding me up, and she bloody knows it. Whose side're you on, anyway?'

'You're my friend. Family. I need you Nell. But I think you're being too hard on Trace. And time'll tell, for everyone.'

Nell left my place, and I felt wretched. Dishonest. Vulnerable. I didn't stay in the den, but instead I made up the coal fire in my bed-sit and sat for a long time watching it, remembering all the early mornings writing diaries in Densley, when I had tiptoed downstairs into the kitchen, opened up the all-night burner whose coals were still glowing, and stoked it up until it was bright.

Nell and I were like coals blending in a real fire. Fires are never just red. That's only how Reeve School children paint them. Probably some fool adult once said to them: 'Paint me a nice red fire'. But my fires are never so dull. Mine and Nell's friendship burned orange yellow blue and crimson. Splashings of green and slices of cream. Changing all the time, alive and bright. I needed her. I didn't want my friendship to turn to ashes. I could still hear her voice saying: 'You're a lot of help, you are, Ess.' I wanted to be there for her, but would she want to be there for me, if she heard my honest reactions?

I had loved to be alone in the warm Densley kitchen before the others were awake, when the house was mine.

Not like other times of the day:

'You are not the centre of the world, Ess. I want you to be happy and to study, if that will make you happy, but I have my life to lead as well. There's nothing but rows in this house these days.'

'I'm sorry, Mum, but Lotte just won't leave me alone.'

'You used to be such good friends, you and Lotte.'

'I know that, Mum, but she's wild. I never was allowed out late like she is. When she's in, it's make-up and radio till my head's bursting.'

'There's three of us as well as you. We can't live here in a tomb just so you can do your homework in peace, you know.'

'I can't find *any* peace. I have to go next door.'

'If we aren't good enough then go next door and don't come back.'

How had Mum really coped with my rebellions? My differences rom her, and her life? She'd rebelled too, hadn't she, from her parents, by working with Red Heather on the market? I wish I knew more about Red Heather. And about how Grandma Clegg had felt about my mum. I wonder if Ms Richards was close to her mother. And so on, and so on. Mum certainly wouldn't have chosen Laura Randall as a best friend for me. That's for certain.

I met Laura on a Saturday, in September, just after I'd started in the fourth year at Densley High.

Mum was working the afternoon shift; Grandma Clegg was baking; and Lotte was out down the backs somewhere with her crowd. I was lonely, missing my friends who were scattered in the villages and towns around. I was reading upstairs in the bedroom over the ginnel, and it was cold up there as usual. I was thinking about Miss Richards, and trying to concentrate on the book she'd lent me. Not succeeding.

I heard a van trundle along the street and stop outside next door. At the same time, Grandma Clegg, who was quite deaf and wouldn't have heard the van, called up to me to go and get some extra cooking apples from the corner shop, because she'd run out. 'And you can buy yourself a bag of something, here you are, love.'

'Oh, thanks. Lemon sherberts,' I grinned, giving her a quick hug, because the errand money was a secret, and I went out the front door slamming it behind me. Then I saw the new neighbours. And I stopped.

There weren't a lot of black people in Densley in those years, but there were some, and a few black girls at mine and Lotte's schools. But I didn't know any to live near or be friends with. There'd been a lot of talk, on account of Jimmy King beating up two immigrant brothers in the secondary modern school. Everybody called black people 'coloureds' in those days. Except for Jimmy King and his gang of thugs who yelled curses at them and called them blackies or darkies.

I must have been staring. A father, a mother and a girl, who was my height and my age, and very, very beautiful. The parents had gone in and that left her and me, standing there, either side of the small fence that separated her front path from mine.

'Want a photo?'

'Oh. Er, hello. I'm Esther Clegg. Are you moving in? I live here.' I still couldn't take my eyes off her very dark brown wonderful face, and I must've smiled right from my toes, opening my whole face, because her tone changed, and her expression.

'I'm Laura Randall.' She was wary, but I was still smiling, and she must've seen that I wasn't kidding, putting it on, or anything, because she started to smile, and there we stood, eye to eye, only about four feet away from one another.

'I've to fetch an errand, for my Grandma. Will you be here, later?' Then I thought, daft thing, Essie, she's going to live here, and she must've thought something similar, and said:

'I'm going to live here.'

'Oh, yes, daft thing. Me, I mean. Oh, I'll see you later, then.'

I know each detail of that day. I ran all the way to the corner shop, bought the apples and sweets, and ran back without pausing for breath, pounding down the ginnel and in the back door and asked Grandma Clegg if I could take one of her plates of cakes next door.

'They're for your mum's tea, Ess. What's up next door?'

'They've moved in, and she's my age, Grandma Clegg. She's the same height and age and everything.' Which I knew was a lie.

'Who's she? The cat's mother?'

'No. Sorry. She's called Laura Randall and she's amazing to look at. She's beautiful, Grandma Clegg. She's beautiful. Can I make friends, please can I have some of your cakes. Please, just this once.'

'A body'd think I never gave nowt away, to hear you talk, our Ess.' But she gave me the cakes, laughing, and I went out the front, down our path, and up Laura's, and knocked, my heart playing tricks.

The van had gone. They couldn't have had much stuff, I was thinking. Laura answered. I stood there, holding Grandma Clegg's plate of iced fancies, to make friends.

Laura's mother appeared behind her, just a couple of inches taller than Laura, and she invited me in. We went through to the kitchen, where the packing cases were, our footsteps echoing on the floorboards. Her father was in there, fixing the gas cooker. He stood up as I came in. He wasn't very tall, not much taller than Mrs Randall. I was there with my offering and suddenly felt silly, shy, having acted on impulse. I felt my smile fix and I didn't know what to do next.

Then something happened to the four of us, as they took over. Mrs Randall asked if I'd like a cup of tea, and Laura started to fill the kettle. Mr Randall covered a packing case with a blanket and asked me to sit down. Mrs Randall produced the teapot and caddy out of a cardboard box, and Laura opened a bottle of milk.

'Oh, thank you. I didn't mean to be any trouble,' I stammered.

'You're our first guest in Densley,' said Laura's father, 'we never had a welcome like this before, did we?' he asked, turning to Laura. Then he held out his hand to me and shook mine till I thought mine might drop off. At that, I coughed, and he laughed and let go, which made us all laugh. Our laughter broke the tension. I was glad that I'd acted on impulse, and took one of the cakes that Laura's mother offered to me.

'Have you lived here long?' she asked.

'All my life. Well most of it anyway. I was actually born in San Francisco, that's where my father still lives. But we live here with my Grandma Clegg now.'

'We're from Kingston, Jamaica. We've been in Leeds for a year, then we heard through a friend that this house was for rent.'

'Yes. My Grandma Clegg knew the people before. I remember that the man who rents this out lives in Leeds. I can't remember his name though. Ours is from the coal board. Grandad was a miner, you see.'

I wanted to ask lots of things but I knew it wasn't polite, and that I mustn't outstay my welcome as Grandma Clegg would say. So I finished my tea, and said I'd better go home. Laura saw me to the door.

'Thanks for the cakes, Esther. We were renting furnished rooms in Leeds. So we're bare till our furniture comes, but when it does I'll have my own room to study in. Would you like to come and see me again, then?'

'Yes, do you really like studying? I can hardly believe my luck. You're a girl and my age and you like studying. Seems too good to be true.'

She laughed then, we both did. I knew I'd remember that afternoon with us both laughing there in the echoing front room, exactly eye to eye.

'I want to go to Densley High, but I don't know if there's a place. I've got to take tests.'

'That's where I go.'

'I didn't like to ask.'

'I hope you get in. Oh I hope so. I could show you my school books, if it'd help with your tests.'

'Oh, yes, thanks. It might. We kept on moving house, in Leeds. I went to three different schools. It might help a lot. I'd better ask. Will you wait a minute?'

She went back and talked to her parents. I was so excited I could hardly think. When she came back she said I was invited round the next afternoon, if that was all right. I said of course, and I'd see her again then. Then I ran in next door full of it all.

Back in our kitchen I rattled on a mile a minute about them having no furniture till it was delivered; and Mr Randall fixing the cooker and I thought he must be a mechanic, some sort; and him shaking my hand,

and all of us laughing; and about Densley High and the next day's invitation; and then I dropped it in that they were from Jamaica. Ouch.

'Coloured?'

'Mmmm. They're from, Kingston, Jamaica, Grandma Clegg.'

'Sit down, Esther.'

'What? I mean, pardon, Grandma Clegg.'

'Sit down. Now tell me again that I have just given a plate of iced fancies to a coloured family next door.'

'I'm sorry. I didn't think you'd mind,' I lied. 'You don't mind, do you?'

'I mind you not saying first time round, Essie.'

'Why?'

'I just mind, our Essie. You took me by surprise.'

'Well, you won't be surprised now when you meet them, will you?'

I started to cry, and ran out of the kitchen and up to mine and Lotte's bedroom.

Mum came in from work; and Lotte arrived home for tea; and the story was re-told by Grandma Clegg each time. We had a plate of ham with a tomato, followed by bread and butter and Grandma Clegg's cakes. And we talked, or rather they did. I felt like choking over each mouthful.

'Nobody's saying nothing wrong 'bout the Randalls, our Essie, but you shouldn't have kept it secret from your Grandma Clegg, taking her iced fancies like that. Now should you?'

'No, Mum.'

'I've nothing against any of them,' said Grandma Clegg. 'They don't bother me.'

'We're a good union family, our Essie,' said Mum. 'A good solid Labour voting family. You could put up a goat wi' a red rosette on it round here, and people'd vote for it. Not that I'm saying our MP's an old goat, mind you. But the point is Essie, that this family is not stupid. You shouldn't be lumping us in with Jimmy King's family, you know. We are not like them. Even if none of us has had the benefit of your Miss Richards and all her books. Humph. I shall be pleasant to the Randalls, all of them. You can take my word for that. I have always got on with my neighbours, whatever they were like. Isn't that so, Grandma Clegg?' Grandma Clegg nodded, looking granite-faced.

'Can we have the fruitcake now, please?' asked Lotte, which was the first and only time she spoke during the whole meal.

'Yes you can, Lotte, and you too Essie, and let's all get back to normal and enjoy what's left of Saturday evening shall we?' said Mum.

'Now who's for another cuppa?' asked Grandma Clegg, and that was that.

Next day I went through my text books with Laura, sitting on her bed. She was going to have a table and chair to work on, up there, and I could barely conceal my envy. A whole quiet room to do her homework in.

'You're my first friend in England,' she said after we'd worked for two hours.

'But you've been here for a year, Laura.'

'Yes. And you're my first friend, Ess. I've tried now and then to make friends. But always there was a wall.

'What sort of wall?'

'Lots. Different walls. Sometimes white people make an effort, but at the back of their minds they feel superior. They are white. And something happens or some feelings start to show, telling me that they think that really I want to be white too, or paler, something nearer to them. And I don't want to. I do not want to be white, pale skinned, paler than I am. I think that's why I love my mother and father so much. They want me to study, do well, but they don't want to be white themselves, and they don't want me to be, either.'

'Don't you think I'm like the other white girls, then?'

'We'll find out, won't we. But I like you Ess. I'd like to be your friend.'

'I'm glad. I want to be your friend too.'

That night I dreamed that I was walking with Miss Richards in the municipal gardens, on the edge of Densley. She had been playing tennis with Miss Edgely, with whom she shared a house in the nearby village of Chalworth. Miss Richards was wearing her tennis dress, her knee-high red boots, and a brown Densley High School blazer. I tried not to laugh when I saw her. After the tennis, Miss Edgely had popped into town to the market, which left me alone with Miss Richards.

We walked to the ornamental ponds, which were small but very pretty, rather romantic, for someone as much in love with Miss Richards as I was, and the water was falling gently from the higher ponds to the lower levels.

Beyond the ponds should have been the putting green. However, it was a quayside instead, with deep blue ocean water, and a huge liner bearing the name *The Kingston* on it. It had arrived by the afternoon tide, and was moored at the docks by the ladies' cloakrooms.

The ticket lady from the changing rooms was now the customs

official who was busy checking Laura's bags and those of her parents.

'Pass along the bus, please,' she was saying and I laughed because she was confused about her job, and had muddled herself up with my mum's bus. 'Pass along this way please, to the uniform room.'

There, she started to give out three uniforms, one for Laura and one for each of her parents. 'Just a minute,' said Laura, starting to laugh at her, 'we only need one for me. My mum's going to the bottle factory and she wears different clothes there. And my dad has his overalls.'

The Randalls started to laugh, and so did Miss Richards and so did I. We were all laughing and joking so much at the customs lady that I woke myself up, laughing.

Lotte was tossing in the next bed, but my laughter hadn't woken her. She maybe almost surfaced then feel deep asleep again. I was sure my dream meant that Laura would be my friend and go to Densley High. We had some things in common already. She loved her parents, and I loved my family, warts and all, as Lotte would say, and both families liked to laugh a lot. Laura wanted to study. So did I. She wanted a friend. So did I. I lay in the dark for a while, confused from the dreaming, but happy.

When I fell back asleep I dreamed again of the ponds, in the same gardens. Laura was playing tennis with Ms Richards. The boat and quayside had gone, and the putting green was there again. I could see the tennis courts, from where I stood by the ponds. The raquets were huge wooden spoons like Grandma Clegg used to bake with.

I knelt by the pond, running my fingers in, disturbing some fish, who darted out. Deep brown fish. I looked for some more but didn't see any. In the water I saw my own face, my reflection, but it was rippling where I'd disturbed the fish, and my features were moving, changing. Then looking up at me was not my face, but Laura's, her features clear, as beautiful as in real life, exactly her face. She was laughing.

Someone called to me from the tennis courts. I ran towards them. Laura and Ms Richards were still playing tennis and eating iced fancies at the same time. They had a supply in the pockets of their tennis skirts, like people do when they're about to serve, and they have to keep the second tennis ball handy. But the tennis balls which they were actually playing with weren't iced cakes; instead they were large green cooking apples. Or, at least that's how it seemed to me, and Laura said: 'Hi, Essie. They're green apples. Here, it bounced in off the tree of knowledge, quick catch it.'

I reached out to catch the tennis ball, apple of the tree of knowledge, and woke up.

I crept downstairs and with well rehearsed stealth I put coals quickly into the all-night burner, and watched as they caught alight, their sounds huge in the silent kitchen. Then I recorded my dreams in my diary, wondering if I really would read them in later years.

Laura's education in Jamaica had been more thoroughly English than ours (hers and mine) was at Densley High. She knew the kings and queens of England better than I did: the wild flowers that grew along the edges of the wheatfields, before the Wimpey* measles arrived; and the works of Keats, Shelley and Shakespeare.

'It was all "the Mother Country",' she said: 'They advertised for people like my father to come here and help rebuild. I never thought it would be so . . . so hostile, and so wet and cold.'

Evenings came and went with me and her sitting at her table in her room, looking up now and again through the bedroom window, which looked out over the railway line to the farms beyond. Those were the few remaining years before the fields were sold to property developers. The land was gradually built over in a rash of red-roofed bungalows. Then Densley became a far-flung dormitory of Sheffield, without the advantages of the city's museums, libraries, swimming-pools, concert hall and bowling alley.

In the summer, Laura and I would be studying, continually interrupted by Lotte and her friends whooping it up round the backs and down the ginnels.

'Go round the bloody fronts and leave us in peace,' I'd yell out of the window.

'Swot-swots shit a lot,' she'd swear back until Grandma Clegg heard her and made her put a penny in the swear box. No one could hear me; I was upstairs next door. I'd pull my head back in, slam the window, and waste my time and Laura's fuming instead of revising.

Lotte wanted a father. I didn't. I was quite happy with the routine the way it was.

Mum wanted company. Lotte was smug with satisfaction. Peter Glade was Mum's new boyfriend. Not that she had 'old' ones. She didn't bring anyone home until Peter.

He was a widower in his fifties, a bus driver where Mum worked, and his kids were grown up. But I wanted just Mum and Grandma Clegg,

---

* Wimpey's was a construction company building housing estates.

Laura next door, and I'd have liked *not* to have Lotte around.

'What am I supposed to do?' demanded Mum. 'Tell me this, Essie. What am I supposed to do? Sit around and wait for Miss England and Miss Jamaica to swan off to university?'

'You'll be sorry when I'm gone. One more year and I'll have left this godforsaken hole and I shan't bother you any more.'

'Oh and what will you do in vacations? Mmmm? If that's your attitude then don't come here expecting us to keep you, you ungrateful young bitch.'

'Us. Us. I don't want to live here when Peter moves in. I shan't need your money, or his. I'll get jobs.'

'You're too hard on him, Essie. He's a good man, with a good mind, and he likes you. I think you could make an effort.'

'All right Mum. I'm sorry. I'll try.'

In the middle of all the tension, Grandma Clegg fell out of bed and became very cold, chilled through to her bone barrow. She was taken to Densley hospital with pneumonia. She died two weeks later.

Lotte wanted Mum to get married. She thought I was being unduly selfish and she said so in no uncertain terms:

'You're supposed to care about people. You're always going on about workers and prejudice against people like the Randalls. Well, you should care more about Mum. I think you're horrid. You're greedy and selfish and you don't give a damn. All you care about is your special friend and getting me out of the way so you two can be hushed-up, in her room. Well, I think you're like one of your Tory pigs, so there.'

'What the hell do you know about politics? You don't care about anything important yourself. It's all make-up and Saturday jobs and boys. You'll end up with a bun in the oven, like Josie Briggs.'

Mum came in to find us both with our eyes blotchy, and our faces streaming with desperate tears. 'I will *not* have this noise, do you hear? You should be ashamed of yourselves, with your Grandma Clegg not long buried, and you two shrieking, as if the walls aren't thin enough already. I suppose you want the whole of Densley to know our business. Why not put it in the *Densley Evening News*, mmm? Shout a bit louder and you won't need to. Now stop it, both of you, and for heaven's sake let's get some sleep. Some of us are working tomorrow.'

For the first time we could remember she went out without kissing us. She never usually let us sleep on an argument. She had this thing that we should start each day anew. Which we did – usually. But that night, Lotte spat the word 'see' and humped over on the single bed with her back to me.

Peter started to call in to keep Mum company for a couple of hours mid-evening. He didn't stay the night. He liked to do the crosswords in the *Densley Evening News*, and sometimes he brought *The Times*, saying it was fascinating how anyone made up those crosswords in the first place. He played scrabble with Mum, and Lotte joined in sometimes, but I was busy with homework.

One Tuesday, not usually Peter's night, while I was preparing our evening meal, I heard his knock.

'I bought you this, Essie.' He gave me a package, wrapped in tissue paper. 'I called 'specially, hoping you'd be here.'

'Oh heavens. What's in it? Thanks. Come in.'

'Open it and see. Where's Rene?'

'Shopping. Lotte needs some new things. They'll be back by six. Oh. Oh it is just the book I was wanting. Thank you, Peter. How did you know?'

'Rene mentioned it. I admire your guts Essie. My Janet was bright like you. Married now, three kids. I mean to make your mum happy you know. Don't you think she deserves it?'

'Mmm. You shouldn't have to have bought this to make friends, Peter. I needed time, I s'pose. I was used to things just the way they'd been. It's, it's amazing you getting this. I've been longing for my own one. Will you shake on it then?'

So we shook hands, me and Mum's boyfriend. And I read that book over and over. It was Virginia Woolf's *To the Lighthouse*.

Easter Sunday, 1983

I was confident about passing all my A-levels right up to the moment when the question paper for the first one lay open in front of me.

I should have seen it as a gift of a paper. It had every question that I had wanted. But absolutely no words would flow from my brain out on to the blank white paper for about three-quarters of an hour.

I somehow managed to get through the rest of the three hours without breaking down in the exam room, making a fool of myself, and ruining everyone else's chances in there as well as my own. I knew that if I kept calm and did very well on the rest of the papers I might reach good grades for the others and, on balance, get my promised university place. Laura and I had such dreams of sharing lodgings in Bristol. My future with my studies, and with her, depended upon my staying calm, and that became an enormous weight. It made me shake and feel an intensity of fright that I had never experienced before. I could feel that the panic was slowing me up, and the time it took me to overcome it, against the clock, in all my other exams was making me slip grades.

Miss Richards could not understand what had come over me but was kind and tried to steady me. Laura tried to reassure me but I remained convinced that I had done badly. I was miserable the whole nine weeks of waiting for the dreaded results.

They were predictable. I gained three Ds and Laura gained two As and a B.

When misery is at its height our memories cannot always be relied upon. So, there were days at the end of that summer before Laura and I parted that make no meaningful pictures in my mind, however hard I try to re-focus on them.

If I remember that we went for walks, in Summer Hill woods, I cannot recall what we talked about; if I assume that, as usual, we visited the market, I cannot conjure up images of us in our usual coffee bar; if I try to think of us in Laura's room, the walls swirl and blur into fields and woods, which fade and re-form into the market again.

So is it my wishful thinking or do I truly remember her face? That the bright black of her eyes was deeper then than it had been; that the angle of her jaw was harder and softer at the same time; that the lines of her mouth were confused, because her hopes were my disappointments.

I am clear about just one incident.

We were taking comfort in hanging out her mother's washing. We stood in the back yard pulling the ends of the sheets level. It was a scrunching movement in which I'd tug then she'd tug, to and fro, to stretch the sheet until it was sharply right-angled at all four corners, the washer having tangled it. So we tugged; between her future and mine; her needs and mine; our shared past and our separated futures.

We stood sheets apart, silent a few seconds, each aware of the other, aware of the familiarity of that pattern of movement; aware that there would be no more of those kinds of sharings.

The next action, usually, was that we walked towards each other to fold the sheet double. Then one of us took all four corners and the other picked up the peg bag.

As girls we were used to each other and to doing the washing. In our hoped-for flat in Bristol we would have shared that too. She passed her corners to me, quickly, and then I watched as she put one hand to her

102

mouth and the blood drained from her cheeks. There were tears coming and she said:

'Essie. Oh Essie, it will be so lonely for us.'

I was holding the sheet like a child with its comforter. A fool child, wet and cold like the washing. I was crying now.

'I'm sorry, I'm sorry,' I cried out and the words were there which she didn't want and hadn't asked for. No taking back words. I'd let myself down; let her down. It was how I felt; it was how things were. I shoved the sheet in a crumpled heap into the wash basket and ran; out the back gate, down the ginnel; ran and ran in a wet blur to Summer Hill woods where I wept under a tree. Someone had ripped down the No Trespassers sign, and slung it in the bushes. But universities have ways of maintaining their signs and the one that faced me read No Entry.

The question of what next for me did not and could not include staying on in the third-year sixth with the luxury of re-taking the exams in the following November. There was no way I could ask Mum to keep me till then, and if I went into the bottle factory, or into shop work, and studied in the evenings, then the possibility of missing grades again was a real one, because I would be tired out as well as frightened.

One evening, Mum found me sitting in the bedroom, staring at the sheet of results for the ninetieth time. Up till then she had tried to be hopeful and had not been harsh. But that evening she lost her temper.

'Now you listen to me, our Ess. You have been misery in person for three weeks, since that damn list came, and we've all had enough. I know you're upset, Ess, but you can't sit round here mooching about and talking about failing . . .'

'I have failed,' I interrupted her.

'Only in your eyes. It's all relative, Essie. Relative. Most girls in Densley would laugh you to the moon, you calling yourself a failure with three A-levels to your name, so you just pull yourself together. I've had enough, Ess. True as grass is green.

'I don't go much on this grades and failure business, Ess. Otherwise what does that make me and the other women what's on the buses, eh? All you've done is drop some grades. Half the girls round here would sell their own mums for the chances you've still got ahead of you. Now you'd better look sharp and get shot of all this nonsense or I shall be having a few up and downers with you my girl. Life's too damn short for this way of going on, Essie. Too damn short.

'I have never stood in the way of you studying, our Ess. In a way I do understand it.' Her voice lost its anger, and she looked at me more gently. 'I was just like you at eighteen. I like to see myself in you. Bright. Determined. I was doing the accounts for Red Heather at the time. I lived in her little house.' Mum's eyes filled with tears. 'Oh don't think I don't know about dreams. Because I do. I've nothing against dreams, Ess. We can all dream. But I'll not tolerate me own flesh and blood putting me and my kind down. All this "failure" nonsense. I am about up to here with it.' She put her hand to her throat. Like a hatchet. 'About ready to explode, and I shan't be a pretty sight, so there.'

Mum had a way, when she was angry, of still letting you know you were cared about. I still felt a failure. But I kept my big gob shut for once. Funny thing is, I haven't used the word 'gob' for years and years.

'There's a side of you that you've let slide with all this exam work, Essie.'

(I was grateful that she didn't call it exam 'lark'. I couldn't have kept quiet if she'd said that. And I wanted to be silent and small; to be her little child again, and have her make everything all right, put a plaster on, and give me a toffee to stop the hurting.)

'You know, Ess, you are very good with your hands, when you put yourself to it. I know there is a lot of tension here, Ess. And you're not happy right now. You're good with your story-dreams when you're happy and we haven't had as much as a weak laugh from you for goodness knows how long. Have we? I haven't seen you knitting or sewing these past few weeks, and you used to be always at it.

'I worried about you going away to that university. I fretted that they'd not touch anything 'cept your head, Ess. And I doubted they'd let you keep *that* 'n all. Fill you with their arty farty ideas, and set you apart from the likes of your people here, living like we do. But you were so dead sure it was for you. I couldn't reach you, Essie. But now I've some plain talking to do. Like your Grandma Clegg would have. God rest her soul. Now there was a woman for plain talking, if ever there was one. No stuff and nonsense with her.'

Mum paused as if to make certain she knew what to say next and p'raps to make sure she had my full attention. I had started to cry soundlessly. She was taking huge risks with me. It could have been terrible for her if I had resented her trying to talk to me: and it was years later that I was able to look back and explain to Nell that my mum was trying to help me to save my own life; and that although I was not communicating back to her outwardly, she could probably sense that I wanted her to go on talking to me like that.

'I wouldn't go on like this if I didn't care, our Ess. Me and your

Grandma Clegg sat for three nights with all them college prospectuses so as you might have a second string to your fiddle. And you only filled in the forms and signed 'em to please us and get us off your back. Don't think we didn't know it. No don't you go shaking your head Essie. I'm not as daft as I'm cabbage looking. You are very good with your hands as well as your head our Ess, and I want you to give this college a try. It's all there in the booklet only you were so set on Bristol so you never even read it. But I did and so did your Grandma Clegg. She said to me then: "They've got looms and a pottery, Rene, and our Essie'd be in her right element, she would".'

'I haven't ever talked hard like this to you 'fore Ess. I don't believe in it usually. But I know you, and I know there's dreams in you and I'm proud of you. You don't have to get B grades to make me proud, Ess. If your Grandma Clegg lived she'd say the same.'

Mum did not have to talk to me about leaving home. We would have fought if I had stayed and I loved her and I did not want either to stay in Densley, or to war with Mum. I had planned to go and go I must. She was offering me a way of going and keeping the peace and, I thought, some self respect too. I was low on self respect. What she gave me back by saying that she was proud of me, I never forgot even when I felt light years away from her at different times. She wanted me to take up my place at Chaffinch Hill College in north London. I decided that I would. I wonder how many teachers wade thankfully on to the same beach, for the same inadequate reasons, and with the same lack of curiosity. Thank heavens for Miss Richards. For all the Miss Richardses.

I have no more detailed memories of saying goodbye to Laura. We had not enough life experience then to understand the kind of fire that our friendship in our teens had been; nor having kindled it, how we could learn to nourish and tend it, like a beacon in wild hills, or a bonfire on a lonely beach.

So we parted, promising each of us to write; and it was not enough to make us happy but it was at that time all there was to offer.

My mum, Rene Clegg, had always been physically demonstrative to Lotte and me. I had lost all my confidence that anyone might even feel I was worth hugging, and I was going away to some huge and possibly hugless place; so Mum hugged me a great deal just before I left. It helped. I tried not to think ahead too far to Mum's marriage to Peter Glade, or to my college course. I was glad to be hugged and I hugged her back, fiercely.

Mum and Lotte came with me to the coach station to see me off to

Chaffinch Hill. I was amazed at them both. Lotte had spent her Saturday-girl wages on a pair of warm slippers and a dressing-gown for me. Mum had bought me a Timex watch. I was overwhelmed with the gifts. Peter gave me a book token towards my first textbooks. I think that Mum probably asked Peter not to come to the coach station. I don't know. Anyway he didn't, and I was glad. Mum and Lotte stood there waving as the coach swung away and I waved back, and all of us smiled, though I didn't feel at all like smiling.

I was leaving for a course I did not want, in a city I did not know, without Laura, who had gone a week before; and all this for the sake of 'No Other Plan For My Life'.

That summer marked the beginning of a period of detachment and drift.

The detachment was from home and class.

The drift was like that of a bright hydrogen balloon. We used to buy them at Grandma Clegg's Methodist Xmas bazaars, and in the fairground when the annual summer fair came to Densley.

We would pay two pence to have them filled from a hydrogen cylinder. We would buy them and write our name and address hopefully on the label. We would release them, and watch as they sailed high over the pit tip, they would land in France. But I felt as if I'd become separated from my label, and had failed to meet the challenge of the first storm or wind. I had burst and fallen into the sea where I drifted, aimless and bedraggled. I had lost my confidence and lightness; my potential for flying.

So I went to London and started my teacher training. I was lucky. I liked the junior age children that I met on teaching practice and they mostly liked me. They enjoyed my story-telling; and I used to make up dreams to amuse them and to get them writing and painting; and I began to rediscover my self through them, in a small way.

I still felt I'd failed and I didn't cope well with Laura's letters.

1 November 1964, Bristol

Dear Essie,

I waited for a reply to my last later, but decided that it was like waiting for them to get a man on the moon, so p'raps you'll get off your arse and answer this one. Are you all right, Essie? I hadn't heard from my mother that anything untoward had happened to you in Chaffinch Hill, so I can't think that the delay in your writing has been caused by any particular event or incident.

Essie, are you very angry with me, or with yourself? Is that why I'm not hearing from you? I'm missing you, and our day-to-day friendship. No one to talk to here. Like being at university with a load of martians.

Enough about that. The course is quite interesting but they seem to be hellbent on measuring people. I'm biding my time before I launch in with criticisms, because I want to be clear what it is they are really up to, trying to prove, etc etc.

If I don't hear from you I'll see you at Christmas but it would brighten up my weeks to have your letters to read.

1 February 1965, Bristol

Dear Essie,

It's the first of February today, and I had been hoping to hear from you, but still no letter. I have Christmas and New Year to look back on, and of course it was wonderful to catch up a bit on your news but how you seem to have changed. I'm longing for the old Essie, the sparkle and the laughter. Chaffinch Hill has a lot going for it if you can put a lot in, Essie, and at least you're enjoying the crafts. Can't wait to see some of your finished things. How about a finished letter, uh? News from here is that I'm now well and truly visible, since a seminar last week. Whew. Did I tell them what I thought. You'd have thought they'd never heard of the Civil Rights movement, nor anything else happening in the rest of the world. Some of them have travelled too, been to the places that I've only read about. But the status quo suits them, I suppose, since they come from conservative backgrounds and have a whiter than white future ahead of them in the family firms.

Honestly, Essie, I think they must be doing this course for a holiday — them seem to be permanently on vacation as far as I can see.

Come on Ess, 'give us a letter, love,' to quote your mum. I assume you do actually lift up a pen and scribble a few lines to *Her*.

4 May 1965, Bristol

Dear Essie,

Loneliness drove me to the drama club last week. And I met him there. His name is Joseph and he is black like me. That was a bond for a start and when we started talking we found that we had in common a disillusionment with white university studies. He calls it white man's knowledge. I have a friend here now, and it feels better than it's felt since I arrived in this ivory-tower wilderness. Someone to talk to. I told him about you, about how much our friendship has meant to me and still does.

Essie, you were my first friend in this godforsaken country, and if you think I'm letting go of you so easily just because I'm here and you're there, where you didn't choose to be, then you are misunderstanding the depth of my feelings for you. I miss you. So write to me, soon.

3 November 1965, Bristol

Dear Essie,

Over a year since we left Densley for so called Higher Education. Remember how we used to say: we're girls, in the north, and our aim is Education, capital E? Well they can keep it.

Of course I am getting something out of it. I can't knock it all. I do get a buzz from philosophy, and we are reading Marx in the originals, and Lenin. Founding fathers. Huh. Old white men with long white beards. But, snide cynicism aside, Essie, I do love the academic rigour, the logic, the sequencing of all my ideas.

I don't love the students, or the so-called students' union. A lot of booze, a lot of hot air, and most of them have never known anyone who worked in a factory, let alone done so themselves for holiday money.

It was good to hear from you. Your occasional letters mean so much to me. But nothing of politics . . . where is your head these days? Politically you seem passive, and I wonder is that really you? Or is it that in the luxury of an all-white college you blend in, Essie, and are not choosing to challenge the ideas and structures like you used to? Perhaps I'm being too harsh. Perhaps you really are needing these years to drift, and you still have scars that aren't healed, because you still feel you've failed. I had a few glimpses of those when we were together in Densley this summer. My job in Bristol with the young black people was wonderful, and I'm hoping there'll be a chance for some more work like that next summer in the long vac. I admired you sticking out those weeks in the bottle factory. You're amazing Essie. I love you, you know, and you are still my very dear friend. Getting emotional now aren't I. But no one can replace you or what we went through together, and I long to hear regularly from you.

Dear Essie,

Just a quick note as second year exams are galloping towards me, like a chariot out of control. Not quite. I have been revising for weeks, and we've had some good heavy hints about the questions.

I'm writing to let you know that I'm getting engaged after the exams and I'm very, very happy. Joseph is a kind and funny man. He wants a stable family life and children just as I do, and although it may be unusual these days, with all the talk of sexual freedom, I want a long-term one-to-one relationship, and I feel sure that the friendship we have will be a good building foundation for the love that has grown from it. I love this man, Essie, and you're the first person I've told after my parents.

We'll get married next summer after finals, and I shan't work in the social sciences. They aren't moving forward anywhere near quickly enough for me. Joseph has a new job, starting after Easter lecturing in a Further Education college here in the city, and mainly in Geography which is what he wanted.

I'm going to be working with the young black people's drama project again this summer. Terrible pay. But I hope to see you, and talk, really talk, when I'm in Densley at the beginning of July. Will you be home at that time? Are you working during the vacation? Any chance of you coming to see me in Bristol? Or is your money dire, like mine?

10 September 1967, Bristol

Dear Essie,

Well we've done it. Got ourselves Educated. And you're going to Islington to work, and I'm on the project as I hoped. The department's very disappointed that I'm not doing research. I am sure they wanted to be able to say they had a *black* Ph.D research student. Well they won't be able to will they, as yours truly Mrs Joseph Phillips is throwing in her lot with the black youth of the west country . . . etc etc.

Essie, when I saw you at my wedding, my heart went to you, and I can see exactly what you mean about being wrapped around by that damn cloak of indifference that you wove for yourself when you started at Chaffinch Hill. But your Islington school will help you lose that cloak, and I know you want to, lose it I mean, and that that's why you've chosen a working-class school, with black and white children.

Those children Essie were born here, almost all of them. And you will find yourself and your politics again through them, I know it. In some ways we are making similar choices, you and I. Avoiding what your mum would call arty farty people, with arty farty ideas!

There is a welcome in mine and Joseph's home for you, and when the time is right for you I know we'll be seeing you in Bristol. Take care.

Love Laura.

I put all my energies into that job and the children. The nearest anyone at Chaffinch Hill had ever come to the word 'radical' was the word 'progressive'. Islington was entirely different. I had never wanted marriage or children, but teaching gave me a meaning and a pattern that the drift of college had not prepared me for. I joined the union and found my occasional lovers there. Kind men with kind faces and well-meaning ways and good careers in front of them. Those without degrees became my competitors for junior school promotions. Those with degrees hardly lowered themselves to our place in the pecking order.

Meanwhile Lotte married James Slomner, Junior, and moved to London in 1970. I tried to renew our contact. I didn't like her husband. It was mutual. I was too involved in the union for his liking. Lotte and I tried to joke it away. I needed her.

I went often to Bristol to see Laura and Joseph. The difference in their relationship and my sister's marriage was shocking. Laura and Joseph had creativity, laughter and politics. We three did all right together. Laura and I began at last to relax with each other, to really talk, and to re-connect. I felt at last that I was growing up.

Laura said to me: 'I thought I had lost you for good, Ess. It's taken us five years to get through somehow to one another. I was beginning to believe you were like all the other whites I've tried to trust and been let down by, one by one. I've stopped trying. It's not usually worth the time and effort.'

We talked then. Walking the Bristol streets as the early seventies became the mid-seventies. I was finding a new self inside me. I had something to offer to friends again. I was more stable. It was the end of drift.

With Lotte, I could not make the connections. I could not talk deeply with her as I'd have liked to, about how she felt about growing up working-class. Even if I came sideways to the theme, she saw me as ramming my socialist politics down her throat, and said so.

110

Easter Monday morning 1983

Well that was quite a marathon yesterday. I've read and re-read my diary entries. Sitting up in bed, watching the fire, from which the smoke rises like dragon smoke from sleeping dragon logs.

Myself and Laura at sixteen. Tracey now at sixteen. Then and now. The shuttle moves. Threading across time, through herstory.

No words left. Mind empty, body tired. Let it flow. Let it go. More sleep, then some knitting.

Lotte, 1977

My father-in-law was due to retire in December 1977. Uncle George from Southampton rang me and told me they would be arranging a large dinner and retirement evening and inviting his friends and business acquaintances in that part of the country. I agreed to do the liaison in secret with the hotel so we could present James Senior with an organised surprise. I was the perfect choice, he said, for the London liaison, because I knew the Southampton people well.

First I went to see my mother-in-law. I was very fond of her. She had always been kind to me and I thought she had a heart of gold. What she was doing married to a turd like my father-in-law I didn't want to imagine. James was her oldest son. She had three others and she treated me like a daughter.

I called James' mum, Mother, as they all did. I don't think she relied much on James Senior for company. I thought about that a lot while we were planning the 'event' together. She had very many women friends and she saw them every day. There was usually someone having coffee with her whenever I phoned or dropped in. The place was spotless and always tidy. She never had any help in the house though it was huge. There were six bedrooms and the whole place was full of old oak furniture that was burnished till it gleamed. There were lots of little solid silver ornaments that twinkled and glinked like my mum's glass bits and pieces on the window ledges in Densley.

She was grey-haired and rosy-faced and she always hugged me like my mum did. She called James Senior 'Jimmy' and when she was talking to me she usually used his name in every other sentence.

'Jimmy worked so hard for this. Chrysanthemums would be suitable, wouldn't they dear? Jimmy would love those, don't you think?'

'I think so, Mother. I'm glad we can plan this together.'

'It's been such a joy to him, you working in that firm, Lotte. Jimmy has never been as happy as these months since you came there. Well, I should say years really. Nearly two, isn't it?'

'I'm glad you're pleased Mother. I did worry about it, you know, in case you'd mind.'

'Mind? Good gracious no, Lotte. Time's are changing. I'd have liked to work but then I'm too set in my ways to change to that kind of thing now. I've made my own life, Lotte. You have to. I've got some wonderful woman friends, Lotte. Wonderful friends. My friends are *everything* to me, Lotte. Everything.'

She looked at me searchingly, as if for a response. I thought there was something she was trying to tell me, but I didn't know what. I was being too secretive about my own plans to dare to ask her what she meant.

'I miss my women friends from the secretarial course,' I said.

'You've got real initiative, my dear, doing that. I admire you. My son is not an easy man, Lotte. Most mothers wouldn't say that now, would they?'

'No. I didn't expect to hear it from you, Mother.'

'He never was an easy child, and he will never be easy. He's hard. He's a lucky man, marrying you, Lotte. You've made a big difference to him. He's not like the others. I wonder where I went wrong, really I do. Hard. He's hard. You've softened him.'

There were tears in her eyes and I was very moved. I went to her and hugged her tight. Her arms came round me naturally and we stayed there. I wondered if she possibly guessed about the babies. She never ever talked to me about the lack of them and this was the first time she'd opened up to me about James. While we were hugging there, her friend Amelia called in. They beamed at each other and then, catching the hugging mood, they hugged too, and then laughed a very free laughter that I only heard when Amelia came there. Then the three of us sat over coffee; and the two of them took me out to lunch in the wine bar in the high street. I can't remember the conversation, but I went home feeling loved. Funnily, the word cherished came to mind much later. I often thought of that afternoon, looking back with hindsight.

I was owed one day's leave in lieu of a couple of late evenings. I knew that James Junior was overworked with *his* clients in London and that he couldn't take Friday off. He would be in Birmingham on business all weekend. I told him that I needed a rest, so I was going to stay for a long weekend with his aunt in Southampton and that I would make the arrangements for his father's 'do', on the Friday afternoon while I was down there.

Usually we went down to Southampton by train, first class, but I had a fad for this being different. James Junior thought I was off my head, didn't he, when I announced I was going by coach.

I felt safer on the coach. No men in pinstripes and bowlers. I left from Victoria Coach Station, Thursday evening. It was full of middle-aged women who looked like my mum. I wondered if they were all hanging on for the next toilet stop, like me.

It was grey, raining cats and dogs, driven by the wind.

Aunt Clara met me from the coach and fussed over me, delighted to see me. I had a quiet dinner with her and Uncle George.

I slept like a dead dog. Just me in the wide bed.

Aunt Clara herself brought me early morning tea. She'd been up with George, to take him to the station.

'So, my dear, you're off to fix it all up today?'

I smiled, trying not to make my yawn public, and failed. It oohed out and I stretched lazily. We both laughed.

'The bus leaves at ten. I've an appointment at two. Deanne Derby. Do you know her?'

'Only by sight dear. I've heard she's very efficient.'

'The funny thing is, Aunt Clara, that our telephonist, Nell Winters, used to live next door to her in London, before the war. They were evacuated together. Funny isn't it?'

'It's such a small world, isn't it dear? Poor little things. What they must've gone through.'

'Yes. I can't imagine it, really. I thought if I finished early I might just look up an old school-friend on the way home. Sara. I get a card every Christmas. She's in Havenport. That's easy from Coombebury, isn't it?' She nodded. 'She's got four children, three dogs, two tortoises, five rabbits and five goldfish. She said she's always home.'

We both laughed. We could picture Sara in Noah's Ark, surrounded by cricket bats!

'What a menagerie, Lotte. Well dear, I hope it keeps dry for you. The barometer says rain later. I hope it's not like yesterday.'

'Siling down, wasn't it. Ugh.'

'You and your Yorkshire. Still, it's nice you've not lost it all dear.'

'I don't know about that. I say glarse instead of glass these days.' We both laughed. 'What's the time? Help. I'd better leap into the shower. Thanks ever so for the tea. You are good to me, Aunt Clara. I'm proper spoiled when I come down here.'

Not a silly detail of any of that escapes me, because of the rest of that day.

114

I walked along Coombebury beach. The sea was rough though the rain had gone.

Everything was closed up for the winter, but the waves carried on. White horses that I always liked to watch. Mum used to take us to the sea for day trips sometimes. Bridlington and Filey. The sea's rough there, on the rocks. I thought about Mum and her bringing us up as a single parent.

That's something I'd never be. If I got pregnant now by James, it would be a horrid mistake, and I'd get rid of it. Soon, when the time was right, I'd leave him and Slomner and Sherwood, and start my travels.

Mum travelled, half way across the world with my dad, but he wouldn't come back to England with her when she came with Essie, pregnant with me. I don't know why. She'd never, never talk about it. She just said it didn't work out.

I used to wonder if perhaps my father was disappointed with me being another baby girl. Some men only want sons, don't they. I bet, if I ever *had* got pregnant, James would have wanted only sons. He'd even have blamed me if I'd had girls. My desire for babies was gone. I wasn't going to start that now. Dreams change.

So I walked by the edge of the sea. The very edge. Daring the waves to wet me. Sometimes they'd almost catch me out and I'd have to run for it. I was wearing my flat shoes and a smart new belted raincoat in deep blue. But the sea wasn't at all blue. It was greyish green, and wild, with those white horses. Wild. Soon I'd be wild again. Untameable. I was never ever going to let another man near me.

Deanne Derby was lean with a grace and beauty deep in her eyes. I saw her as a woman who must have had a lot of pain in her life, but warm, open and kind. I was completely unprepared for the warmth and charm of that woman. I was twenty-nine and childless. She was forty-five.

'Look, er, shouldn't we start using first names? Seems a bit too formal all this Miss & Mrs, doesn't it? Please call me Lotte,' I said.

'Yes. I'd like to Lotte. I'm Deanne. You could call me Dee, if you like. Most people do.'

'All right, Dee. Oh that sounds better.'

We both laughed.

She went through the details of the menu with me, and we checked all the arrangements painstakingly. We had plenty of laughter.

'Where are you staying while you're down here, Lotte?'

'James' aunt's, in Southampton.'

'Would you like to come for a meal at my house, tonight, Lotte? I'd like to talk some more, would you?'

'Yes. Yes, I would. I would.' I was stammering like a child, and I blushed.

'Seven o'clock then?' She gave me the address. I lied to my aunt on the phone. Said I'd rung Sara and she'd asked me for dinner. I said I'd get a taxi back, and might be late.

The houses down by the railway were done in stone-textured paint, mainly white or cream. A few were pale pink or blue. All were in small terraces, two up, two down. Some still had late roses in the front plots and a few houses came straight in off the pavement.

I walked light and bouncy. I had a new friend. Someone who would get to know me. I knew I wouldn't have to hide. Then I remembered Mum telling me that there are some things a woman just knows. I knew it was a time when I could trust this new woman friend and it was all right.

Deanne's was easy to find. I could imagine that in summer there'd be blue flowers like clouds on the soil, as she put it. I'd not heard anyone speak in pictures like Deanne, since our Essie went peculiar after the grammar school got her. Before that, she told me stories to make me feel safe at night. Funny that Deanne could make me think of Essie doing that.

She opened the door wearing jeans and a soft sky-blue shirt.

'I brought these,' I grinned, offering her the chocolates and a bottle of red wine from the offie on the corner. I stood there like a teenage girl, shy on a date. The Thrupenny-Bit-Kiosk where I used to meet the gang to go to Chalworth, had nothing on this.

'Come in,' she laughed, looking delighted to see me. 'These are my favourites. Come in, Lotte.'

We were four hours talking. She smoked roll-ups but I didn't mind. I didn't mind anything. She could have started picking her nose for all I'd have minded. Every time she spoke she was speaking into my mind, into my thoughts. She might have been living inside my head for years, I felt so excited and secure. All the details of our lives were there and with no need to hurry or skip over anything.

We were making coffee in the kitchen. Tibs was smoothing round my legs, purring.

'Do you speak French, Dee?'

'*Un peu, un petit peu.*' She laughed, gesturing with her arms, moulding her lips for the accent, which was terrible.

'I'd like to go with you to Paris,' I blurted. 'On holiday. I'd like . . .'

116

I was standing next to her while we waited for the kettle to boil. My breasts were growing tight and sparkly, making me want to take everything off and I wanted her to feel the same. If they'd been able to sing, my breasts that is, they'd have been high and sweet and loud. Whew. I wanted to kiss her mouth, too, and touch the skin along her wrists and arms. I wanted to touch her all over. I couldn't concentrate on anything and all the time my breasts sparkling. Then she turned and came into my arms and it seemed the most natural thing we'd been waiting for.

I phoned James' aunt, lying my head off, sounding so happy to be having dinner with Sara and her menagerie in Havenport.

'And she says, why not stay over. We have so much catching up to do, so I won't disturb you both by getting a taxi late. We thought we'd do some shopping in town, tomorrow. Is that OK, Aunt?' I paused. 'Oh good. Bye now.'

I turned from the telephone, still laughing.

'I did it. She's pleased.'

'Do you think she would be if . . .'

'I doubt it.'

'She probably thinks you've met a man and you're having an affair.'

We shrieked with laughter all the way upstairs. We were still laughing when we lit the candles. We kept the candles alight for the two hours after so we could see the wanting in one another's faces.

We were amazing. Beautiful. Kind and calm and wild, all at once. I wanted her, and I wanted every woman in the world to know our feelings.

There I go, waxing poetic again. 'Honest to goodness, Lotte,' I told myself, 'you may not be a poet, but the name for this is joy.'

Deanne, 1977

I don't go much on high romance. I wasn't looking for a 'gay' Mills and Boon. So I woke next morning astonished. I lay awake, in bed next to an almost total stranger who was still officially married to Nell Winters' boss. The Saturday morning light was dawning on me, so to speak.

Lotte was still asleep, dark brown curls tumbled round; she was even snoring slightly. Not as loud as Izzie used to. Lotte's snoring was actually quite smooth. Above the sound of it, I could hear the seabirds. That is one of the best things I know about waking up in a seaside town. I never tire of it, nor of seeing the gulls perching on one leg, on slate roofs.

She was sound, out for the count. I rolled out very gently, found my 'jamas and dressing-gown, picked up my slippers and padded out, down to the bathroom, to the indoor toilet.

I didn't flush the thing, because I wanted time to think, without waking Lotte.

I padded round the kitchen, with the door to upstairs shut. It was warm, real luxury that. Stuart had put the central heating in for me. Never could get over the pampered feeling. I made real coffee, treating myself, and a roll-up, and then sat, smoking, looking down the path, past the bathroom to the back yard. It was red with virginia creeper, and berries on the firethorn. Mine. My safe home where I'd brought up Isobel, fed and talked to Corrine, listened to the radio and telly. A real good fortune place.

There were letters from Nell, Isobel, and Eileen on the rack on my wall. Eileen's had an Aussie stamp. Isobel was still in Mozambique.

I met Eileen in 1975. She came over here to visit Stuart, her cousin. That's how we happened to meet. She was my age, had been a dyke for years. She always called herself that. She laughed a huge, loud laugh that matched her size. She was a big woman, wonderful strong body. She was proud of that. Had made good as a swimming instructor, down under.

She was over here for six months. That gave her the freedom to risk a relationship with me, and me the freedom to risk starting again with a woman after so long.

We had some wonderful laughs together. We loved each other well for that six months. We made love beautifully. After she left I crash-landed. Suddenly bereft. Physically, I was awakened. I wanted a new lover. Something real.

My coffee went cold, and I made more. Another roll-up too. I sat there thinking – what if for Lotte this was just a fling? A night? A long weekend? So the dreams began. The fears came with them.

Perhaps it was just a fling. But I didn't think so. She hated James, and said she'd never ever go to bed willingly with a man again.

Lotte would have to go back to her aunt's, for the Sunday night, to keep up appearances, and then back to James and plan and lie like crazy. The thought of her going back to James made my skin creep as if I'd got woodlice under it. I didn't want him to touch her; she didn't want him to touch her. But he hadn't finished with her. She was on the point of leaving James when she met me. She wouldn't dare leave immediately or he'd connect it direct with a dirty weekend in Coombebury.

Lotte hadn't been away before without James, except to see her mother in Yorkshire. So if she left James now, he'd know it was something to do with Coombebury.

If she left right now, she'd blow the cover sky high. James would burn bright for revenge. He was an arrogant male. He'd assume that Lotte had found another man. Someone who'd give her children.

So I sat and smoked and tried to clear my head for all the links and the problems. I knew I wanted Lotte. I wanted her so bad. So good.

Lotte was much closer in age to Isobel than to me; barely four years older. I needed to think about it. I read parts of Isobel's latest letter.

Isobel had been on the engineering scheme three years by now. She met Marion, born and bred in Leicester, black like herself, but there on part of the irrigation project that was funded by the World Health Organisation. Marion specialised in control of malaria. She was studying the effects of different methods of controlling the larvae in the water.

I've some very fine friends here Dee. Africans from all over the continent.

My passion was and still is, my work. Marion understands that. She understands political passion.

We were acquaintances for months, before we recognised the depth of our friendship. There's so much work to do here. We share the same house now, which is a comfort to us both. Quite honestly, if we didn't live in the same bungalow, we'd hardly see each other, given the distances we have to travel and the long hours.

Marion's as committed to her scientific work as I am, Dee, but she's quite different from me in the fact that she writes. Poetry, I mean. She describes this land and the people superbly. I can hear her anger through the words. I was never involved in literature at school as you know, and I hated history, but this is different. She writes just like a camera, as if she's making pictures of each moment, part of a moving film. I've been using the camera in my work a great deal recently, recording the project as it develops (pun, ugh!! – not intentional!!), and her words seem to catch things like photographs. She reads to me at night. My feelings come into sharp focus, when she reads to me.

'I write with a glass-tipped arrow. My ink contains quinine.' (I'm quoting from her now.)

Dee, do you remember all those times you told me of the River Mere, its reflections? Silly question, not a question at all, of course.

At night we sit together on the veranda. There is no twilight as in England. The sun goes. The whole sky is dark lavender. Colours that you never see in Coombebury, though I used to enjoy the sunsets there. Here the sky deepens to purple in minutes, and the stars come up. There's nothing romantic about the work here, nor the reasons for it, but there are times when my work, and my friends, in this very beautiful country, are more than I could have hoped for.

There were several pages of Isobel's letter. Long descriptions of the day-to-day work on the project, the countryside, the heat, the people. She finished it lightly.

. . . glad to hear the allotment's coming along well. All that work. I used to love my blue plot at the front but I'm not one for gardening really. I still have problems with creepy-crawlies. They're Marion's 'province'. She says I'm a hopeless case. Sigh, give me a slide rule, or a calculator any day. Or even a nice solid clay brick.

Take care, Dee. I think of you so often. Do write soon.

Much love, Isobel.

I went and had a long slow bath, moving the water around lazily with my toe. Corrine gave me blue bath oil. I watched it move. Blue lights on the water.

Dora had once been lively and loving. Until self-hatred ate her up. She was irreplaceable.

Isobel was still irreplaceable. Engineer. Traveller. I had a strong sense that Lotte would be irreplaceable too. No wonder I was frightened.

I let the water out a good while later. Some of my fears went back down the drain, where they belonged.

I opened the door to the stairs. I could hear Lotte still snoring. I was relieved.

I sat there smoking, with new coffee, and tried to look at the situation through James Slomner Junior's eyes. What would he do if Lotte left him?

I was sure she would. I wanted her to live with me. The more I went through the puzzle and maze, the more I wanted that. That was clearing, too.

She fascinated me. Her struggles to get her mind back from the Slomner clan; her struggles to get her body free of James; from men.

If James wanted to know who Lotte spent the night with, he'd come and quiz the receptionist at the Bronnester. It was perfectly logical for him to do that.

What did Lotte's Aunt Clara know? Only that she'd gone to meet me to make arrangements. That was true. That was safe.

But Lotte hadn't gone home. So where had she stayed?

Aunt Clara thought she was with Sara. Sara, of course, was oblivious to that. Lotte didn't know Sara well enough for Sara to be asked to lie.

The lie about Sara and the children, dogs and tortoises, not forgetting the goldfish, was convenient, but it'd never hold up to a closer look by James. If James ever hunted out Sara, Sara would look blank and say she'd not seen Lotte for three years. Because that was the truth.

That was as far as I'd worked it out, when Lotte came downstairs. The tangle of her hair, and her soft, just-woken face, turned me on till my toes curled. I wanted her right then. She came and kissed me, looking concerned.

'Are you all right, Dee? You look thoroughly frazzled.'

'I'm better for kissing you,' I laughed. 'Do you want some coffee?'

'Will you talk to me about it?'

'What, the coffee? It's Sainsbury's.'

'No, daft ha'p'th. Why you're feeling frazzed. You are, aren't you?'

I nodded, grinning and pouring the coffee.

Then we sat and talked it through almost all morning.

We were an unusual combination: we knew what we had was rare. I don't mean two women together. I knew that wasn't rare, even if it was hidden. I mean that we could build on a trust from the start; could ask each other what we wanted, and what was possible. We could see inside each other's pain without making it worse.

I don't believe in love at first sight. I can't say I fell in love with her at first sight. I was fascinated at first sight. With more than a touch of lust. The loving came later, as we started to talk, to get to know each other.

It was a lazy Saturday morning, in spite of the careful talking. We seemed to find it possible to get inside the problems and talk about the details. Just as we had done last night.

By late afternoon the chemistry took over again. Years and years of need in both of us; for affection, laughter, company, sex, gentleness and wildness again.

But what about Nell?

We'd been shocked, both Lotte and myself, recognising last night that my oldest friend knew her sister. I'd heard of Essie from Nell; and I'd seen most of the Slomner wives, presumably including Lotte, from time to time in the hotel. None of it had mattered. It had all been distant, irrelevant. Now it had become interlocked, near, altogether too close for comfort.

Lotte said, 'I don't think even James would try to get at my mum, but he hates Essie already, and she lives on her own. I think he'd call her on the phone, call at her flat, and I wouldn't put it past him, if he gets nowhere with that, to get somebody to put a brick through her window if he thinks she knows something. Honestly, he's evil. I know we had a final row, but she's still my sister. I don't want James bullying her. So what I'm thinking is, if he cottons on to the fact that she really doesn't know anything, he'll eventually lay off. So I have to make sure she doesn't know. God, all these lies. Just because a man's violent. I don't want Ess to know. That means Nell shouldn't know either, doesn't it?'

'It's a huge one, Lotte. I need time to work it out.'

It would take me weeks of thinking, worrying. Obviously Rene would have to have a safe address for Lotte. Obviously Ess would get the address off her. It was awful that we didn't know whether Esther would mind Lotte's giving up men. And so on.

If only Nell and Esther didn't know each other . . . What a bramble bush! I did want Lotte to come and live with me. I wanted the closeness. I was ready for that. I wanted that for Lotte. The trust was there, we both knew it.

I wanted Lotte in my life. It occurred to me, sideways, that if she'd had children, he'd have got at her through them. I didn't know any 'Lottes-with-children'. I thought, bloody hell, if we're going through all this, what must *their* leaving plans be like?

We couldn't plan it all during that weekend. There was too much, so the phone bill over the next two months into the spring was a mile long.

We met twice again within the next month. Once on a Tuesday and once on a Wednesday, both days and nights when James was out of town, on business in Birmingham. We met up, both times, at eleven in the morning, once in a small village near Guildford, the other time near Farnham. We stayed overnight, going straight back to work from there the next day. We pottered around teashops and junk shops, joking and making up crazy dreams about our ships coming home, and all the knick-knacks we'd fill our home with. We stayed in old pubs, treating ourselves to simple, old-fashioned food. We paid for bed and breakfast, and had rooms with twin beds. We daren't ask for a double, though we were damn sure we weren't the first women they'd had there, insisting on sleeping double.

But we didn't want to draw attention to ourselves, and besides, we'd both brought a piece of strong, thin rope to tie the beds together. That's an old, old trick. We knew we hadn't invented *that* either.

Esther

Tuesday, 5 April, morning

Another letter from Mum arrived this morning. Why did they tell me in sociology lectures in college that working-class people don't communicate with letters?

Whatever the tensions and gaps, Mum has kept writing over the years.

Mum must have been strong, to bring up Lotte and me. I've realised that since I've been living alone here, because I've had to toughen up, though I don't always feel strong.

What surprised me was that she – Mum – didn't *show* much grief after Peter died last March. I thought for a while about her coming to live with me in London, but when I broached the subject with her, she was adamant: 'I'm Yorkshire through and through, Ess. Densley's where I was born and bred, and Densley's where I'll end my days. I know the people here, Ess. What would I *do* in London? There's enough going on up here to grace the *News of the World*. Like it says on the front, "all of life is here". It's good on yer luv, but I'll stay where I am.'

Mum had said: 'No fuss, you two. Ethel's staying at the house with me. I'm glad you and Lotte will be at the funeral, but I don't want you to stay. Too much tension with you both in the house. I'd much rather have somebody me own age with me. Now don't get me wrong. I know you mean well, both of you, but this is how I want it.' So I saw Lotte for maybe two hours. Just enough to stir up memories. Not enough to understand each other's lives.

Mum's off on holiday next month, on a package tour to Greece. Mum's first time abroad at sixty-one: 'Well, you see, Ess, I've got a bit put by and there's not much point in taking it with me when I go, is there? So I'm having a little spree, with Ethel. We should get on all right, after all, I've known her since I started classes, when you were nine, haven't I?'

Whenever Mum could fit it in with her shifts on the buses she went to pottery classes at Densley Tech. Grandma Clegg told me, and then regretted it, that the pottery teacher gave Mum the clay free, or Mum couldn't have gone. Then Grandma looked rather red and made me swear never to tell Mum that I knew, and hugged me too hard. That night she made a treacle pie (my favourite) for tea.

Ethel was a cleaner in the school for deaf children. She lived with her mother, then alone after her mother died. I always liked her. Her flat's got to be done up because of subsidence. Mum wrote that the street under Ethel's place is like a honeycomb these days. Densley people are used to it, and the Coal Board spent millions in compensation. The timing has been a shock to Ethel. She'd have expected it in the summer of '76 when the drought caused havoc in the honeycomb, but not all these years later, just after her retirement. Let's hope the holiday away will be good for them both.

Grandma Clegg used to cook for all of us the night Mum 'went to class'. We joked at Mum about Bill and Ben, flowerpot men, and Little Weed. Grandma Clegg scolded us and if that didn't work, she went on strike, saying all workers had the right to down tools and if the miners' wives like her had been in charge of the unions, the General Strike would not have been lost. 'No more puddings till you two behave.'

Then she'd grate nutmeg on top of the puddings and bake them with knobs of marg so there was a soft brown layer that was crisp at the edge where it curled up the side of the Pyrex.

Mum was a very good potter and I wanted her to have her own kiln. I dreamed about saving up my sixpence sweets money that Grandma Clegg slipped me and Lotte on Saturdays. But the bars of chocolate and the forbidden bubblegum, huge in patterned pink and purple and blue wrappers with writing on, always got the better of me. I only once shared the dream with Mum, just after I passed the eleven-plus.

'Don't be daft girl,' she scolded, 'You want a uniform don't you, and a real satchel?'

'I have to Mum, it's on the school list.'

'I know that, our Ess. I can read. Come here luv, and give us a hug. There now. Now, let's be having no more pie in the sky ideas about spending on kilns, all right?'

When she said 'all right' in that tone, it meant 'no more'.

I've never been interested in making pots but I've always used cloth and thread. On Densley market, Laura and I used to buy the remnants from the mills and make our skirts, dresses and blouses. I made all my dresses from the age of fifteen on Grandma Clegg's old Singer sewing machine. It was the only way to keep up with fashion. I couldn't make coats. I'd have needed tailoring lessons for those.

Wednesday, 6 April 1983

I didn't use the word creativity until I went to college. It was a popular word there, in the sixties, when so-called progressive primary teaching was in its heyday.

At college, I took the 'craft' option, to help me later in schools, and weaving was part of it. It had an ancient feel, even then, before I'd come across feminism or women's history. I sat there in the college working the loom shafts with bare feet, slamming the weft to beat it even. They were old Maxwell looms, seasoned from years and years of use. My teacher there said they never failed to run true. Sometimes in new ones there's a twist in the frame, and the uneven tension transfers on to the new warp. 'You can't weave a true rhythm on an uneven warp,' she said, 'but on a true warp, a good yarn will almost weave itself. If the weaver knows what she's doing.'

When I moved to this bedsit, I was lonely. I joined an informal women's history group at a local community centre; and I went to two spinning and weaving workshops run by a feminist weaver.

I started to hunt through books on the history of textiles for references to spinning, weaving and knitting. I found that spinning came first, around 8000 BC. I was astonished. That was seven thousand years before the so-called ancient Greeks and Romans that we did in Densley High.

I pulled out strands of my own hair, wet them, twisted them, and let them dry. They dried still twisted. If I'd been a stone-age woman, I could have used them to sew skins. I watched myself repeating the action. Twisting hair went back to before the ice age. It was ten times older than the ancient Greeks.

I'm aiming to spin new threads with a good strong twist that won't unravel; to reconnect; to find out which strands are at present only frayed and can be mended, and which ones cannot. I want a new warp, strong enough to dance on, with the central threads clear and long, to weave new relationships on.

Deanne, 1977–78

I could see two serious stumbling blocks along my way to living with Lotte. Like the barriers you see in war films. They've plodded on for miles. They're just coming to the last three hundred yards; there, across the road, there's a white pole with red slashes across it, hinged at one side. There's always a man in a look-out box beside the barrier. He can put a finger on the button and up goes the pole and they're across. Or he can put his finger on the trigger and the goodies are splattered. Just bodies all across the road, *this* side of the boundary.

We had the party to get through. Then when Lotte left we'd have, sure as hell fire, a visit to the Bronnester from his lordship, James Slomner Junior.

I must admit the hotel looked wonderful. It was decorated for Christmas. We'd gone to town with soft lighting and red candles. Keeping a good eye out on the fire hazards. Work seemed like forever, without breaks, from the beginning of December onwards. We always had a resident hairdresser for women and a barber for the men in December. The store-rooms and freezers were loaded. Everywhere had a face lift, even my office.

Lotte sent me a wonderful poinsettia. It glowed red on my office desk every day. Every time I looked at it, I knew that Lotte was there. In books – when they're overdoing it on the romance kick – they get way-out expensive presents. Pendants and gold watches, bracelets and earrings. I didn't want her to think she had to buy me things to make me believe she *was* leaving James. I said so. I didn't want 'things' to prove our feelings. They didn't need proving. Besides, I didn't want anything coming second-hand from James Slomner via Lotte, neither did she. She had only the money she earned as a secretary. We needed nearly all her money put by, for emergencies.

So, for my birthday in December, she bought me a plain digital watch, quite small and with a plain leather strap. It was just right for

127

work. That meant I could wear it everyday. It said 'love Lotte' on the back.

I was to be on duty in the Bronnester the night of the Slomner 'event'. Everyone would know that Lotte and I had organised this together. They'd be quite prepared for us to be friendly as business acquaintances. Our problem was that we were so much more. Our question was, how could we hide the magic at the party? We knew that everyone would have a lot to drink. They'd all be high and that would help us. We intended to stay stone-cold sober. That would be our defence. Then we could choose to play merry with the right guests at the right times. We'd be in charge. We had to make it work.

I made sure that the head waiter knew that Mrs Slomner Junior didn't like to drink. That would be seen as unusual by itself in the Bronnester, so I told him she was having tests for a rare blood disorder and had specially asked to have bitter lemon or orange without alcohol. There was to be no hassle for her or heads would roll. He was duly warned. He took the hint, and said he'd attend to her personally. I said it was quite possible that people might offer her other drinks by mistake and she might want to change them. She didn't want to be seen to be doing so.

For myself, it was no problem. I was at work. I had a rule about drinking and working. We all did.

It was hard for me, dressing to go to work that night. I had a new suit, thin wool, warm and cool at the same time. It was a deep mulberry colour. I felt festive but not overdone. It wasn't a night when I could get away with ordinary work clothes. The skirt was just below knee length, comfortable, and I felt confident in it. I wore Lotte's watch, and low-heeled shoes. I never could walk on the Bronnester carpets in very high heels.

I arrived early. I was ready for them all. I wanted them to see me as efficient and rather charming. I felt a bit like the people in *The Sound of Music*, hiding behind stone statues without even daring to sneeze, with the searchlights on them. They had to be blended right into the shadows, while the glare of the light was on them.

The evening was a buffet, all the trimmings, rather than a sit-down meal. James Senior would want to circulate.

From seven they began to arrive. I saw James and Lotte walk up the main steps. They had come the short ride from Uncle George's. James was carrying their overnight case with their ordinary clothes in. Lotte was on his right arm, the friendly wife. It was unnerving to see that. I didn't want him touching her. She didn't want him touching her. She was wearing a full-length dark blue evening dress, with cap sleeves, simple and effective. It had a V-neck and short, stand-up collar. She wore no jewellery at all except her wedding ring. She didn't need to, the dress was expensive and said it all. We were going to give it to the charity shop in Dorchester afterwards. If only James knew. They'd get a good price for it there. Her shoes matched exactly. Completely plain. Not a frill in sight. She'd said on the phone, 'It's a no-frills evening for me, Dee.'

He looked like a typical rugby player: thick-set and jaunty; sure of himself in his posh tuxedo. I went forward to greet them both.

We smiled, she and I, like distant people who'd chanced to meet through work. My heart was doing 'dum-dum-dumdum-dumdum'. I held out my hand, to him first, and his grip was metal.

'You've done us proud, Deanne. You and my wife. On behalf of my father, I am grateful to you.'

'Thank you, Mr Slomner.' I almost said 'sir'. 'It's been a pleasure.'

'Do call me James.'

'Thank you.'

Then it was her turn. She just held out her hand as if we'd talked only on the phone since her first and only visit, and said quietly, 'Hello Deanne. Is everything all right here?'

'Hello Lotte. Yes, thank you. We're all ready. Did you have a good journey?'

'Yes thank you. The drive is quiet at night.'

Those words meant that she was calm and ready, too.

I took their coats and handed them to the cloakroom attendant. We had a second to meet each other's eyes. Hers were clear. We will do this, and do it well, they said. I love you, they said.

I was needed by the next guests and so I left Lotte then. The head waiter was already dancing attendance.

I was glad I was working. I had a well-defined set of jobs for the whole evening and I put my mind to them.

She was there in the distance circulating. I could see she was succeeding. Other guests were being put at ease by Slomner's charming wife. Minds would be thinking how suitable she would be as the foil for James when, after this night, he took over as head of the clan in London. For father and son, it had a special meaning: like a coronation or a passing on of titles.

One of my more pleasant tasks was giving all the women fresh flowers to wear, and buttonholes to the men. I met Aunt Clara and then the wife of James Senior. I didn't know her name. I'd forgotten to ask. I kept my breathing slow and steady.

I made sure not to hurry round. I had given Lotte those tips too. Things Corrine taught me in the early days when I was waitressing. How to appear fresh and not agitated whatever's going on at the tables.

Corrine used to say it was a bit like singing – most of it's down to good breathing, and how you use your chest and shoulders.

It would be a six-hour marathon. For Lotte and me.

They began with cocktails and chitchat. I could hear men's loud voices everywhere, quieter, higher women's voices. Dove arrived with his wife, Elizabeth. She wore a lace two-piece, with a long skirt. I used always to think how she wore her humiliation with dignity in public. I was glad Corrine was not there. I felt sad that the women were set against each other, Corrine and Elizabeth, for a low-down prize like Dove. He was a skunk. Not even a bad smell to warn everyone.

There were business colleagues from Southampton. I thought sourly that half the masons from that city were there. I wondered if they all really did wear suspenders.

Meantime I kept smiling and talking, nothing talk, to all the guests, as if I was really part of the wallpaper. A piece of the pattern that came off and walked round chatting for a while.

By eight they were all there, even those whose journeys had hiccoughs, with traffic jams the wrong side of Southampton, near the new road works.

The room began to fill with smoke and talk and occasional belly laughter; and tittering. Long before the food was served at eight-thirty, there were the different smells of cigars and pipes and French cigarettes and English ones; of gin and orange, and sherry and the rum-based cocktails; of maraschino cherries and slices of lemon; of olives and nuts. Slowly, Lotte's perfume and that of the other women mingled, until it came to smell like any other posh party.

But she was there, working too. Recording in her head the bits and pieces of family news, business news, and what-the-firm-will-be-like-in-the-future news. There were the male jokes to put up with, and the hints about James and his future. I could see her working. Bringing out the right answer, the repartee, the laugh in the best place.

We were a double act and we knew it. It kept us going, though we dared not meet, exchange winks or a grin, show any eye contact, touch hands or brush fingers in passing. We daren't risk going to the powder room at the same time, being near the buffet tables together, near the waiters or waitresses at the same moment.

130

We had six hours on schedule. Not a minute to take a holiday. If we did, we might end up in the same part of the room, and our need for a smile would come pouring out like the weight of pressing water behind a patched-up wall holding back a reservoir.

I checked with Sam that Lotte's drinks were all right. He nodded and said she'd thanked him, and was 'well pleased'.

I listened to the sounds of people eating; china chinking and the noise of knives and forks; tables and tumblers; the sound of crockery on the wooden table mats; chair legs scraping; the sound of liquid being poured out of bottles, and of the neck of the bottles clinking slightly on the tops of glasses; and of glass against glass as people met and made their own informal toasts to each other.

She was there, passing *vol-au-vents*, as if she'd had them all her life. Mushroom *vol-au-vents*. There were dips and spreads; chicken drumsticks done this way and that; shellfish and patés; jellied salads, American style; and a whole carvery with four waiters carving. There was salmon and caviare. Every kind of salad, all with greenery out of season. You wouldn't have thought it was December. It all looked wonderful, even when it was being attacked by the party, and it cost a bomb.

I could imagine drawing a cartoon of these people – a plague of locusts devouring a field. Isobel wrote that Marian's work was with pest control. Mmm, I thought, looking at the Slomner clan. Wouldn't I just love to spray this lot.

Lotte was there, eating and drinking carefully. Careful what she ate with what, mindful not to overeat from nerves, meticulous to make it easy for everyone else. Making sure everyone noticed her being a relaxed calm junior hostess.

I watched her with the women, especially her mother-in-law. They obviously were fond of each other. I almost envied her then, having a family.

I saw how Elizabeth Dove was drinking, steadily. Double gin before the buffet, and very much red wine during it. I pitied her, for not daring to go against her Catholic priest and divorce Dove. She was such a wonderful looking woman, too. Grey-white waving hair, cut so that it fitted the shape of her face exactly. Her face was heart-shaped. She had dark green eyes. What a waste when she could have been a dyke, I thought. She believed fervently in God and His Almighty Son. She had coverted to Catholicism not long after marrying Dove. Dove had it good. I resented him, when I caught his loud laughter there, above the other sounds, from time to time. He never lacked for clean shirts or clean sheets, nor bodies to iron them, nor bodies to bed him.

They were all there in their tuxedos. Every button sewed on by some poor blighters who got a pittance. I could see all of them, the tuxedo bullies, taking an evening off from running the country. I'd have loved to have cartooned them, but of course it wasn't possible and it would be a waste of paper.

The women I minded, caught up in it all, bullied, some of them. Others, like Lotte's mother-in-law, finding their own ways of getting through. They'd be Tory voters down to the last pencil tick. Not Lotte. She'd kept her Labour allegiance, although she hadn't told James. That would have definitely meant a beating.

It wasn't my place to be there for the speeches and in a way I was glad. I didn't want to listen to James smarming, or Dove being jocular. Or George Slomner boasting, or the cousins coming along like an outing from the sailing club.

My work in the party room was over by about ten. After that I was down the corridor twenty-five feet away, with two and a half hours relief duty on the main desk. It was part of my evening rota. We were busy in the main part of the hotel because it was close to Christmas. The hotel was easily large enough to absorb a private party as well as the usual dining rooms and weekend bookings.

At twelve-thirty, I would reappear to make sure all the guests who were leaving had their taxis or cars, their coats, and lost belongings, and that the others had keys to their rooms, if by chance they'd arrived too late to go to their rooms before the gathering or, like Lotte and James, hadn't chosen to.

The time on the desk was worse than the rest of the evening. I couldn't see if Lotte was all right, or what was going on in the party. I could hear the dance music, of course, but I could only imagine her with James' sweaty arms around her and his whisky breath down her ear.

I wanted Lotte to fly right out of there, like Cinderella on the stroke of midnight. I didn't care for James-bloody-charming. I cared for Lotte. If I could, I'd have waved a wand and castrated James on the spot.

Midnight came: no coach, white mice, pumpkin. I thought to myself that real Cinderellas don't come through so easily.

They started to leave, so I flipped into my role 'off the wallpaper' again. All smiles and cheerfulness.

The Doves were among the first to leave. She was blotto, trying to disguise it. He was about full, too. His words were slurred. They weren't staying over, so I called their cab round. They were followed by the cousins, all three of them, with their wives, all three sheets to the wind and laughing fit to sink a schooner.

Then came the various businessmen from Coombebury and Southampton and Havenport, wives and girlfriends in tow. Slightly toppled. I felt like a packer in a supermarket, wrapping them all up and boxing them into taxis, four at a time.

Some came out in dribs and drabs, others in small groups. Some were so far gone they couldn't see through a ladder. Cork high and bottle deep the lot of them.

They were raucous and whimsical and genteelly disorderly. We wanted them out, of course, without a hassle. The manager came through and began to beam and wish them Merry Christmas, happy holidays, and so forth.

Aunt Clara and Uncle George were staying at the hotel, so were James' parents and James and Lotte. I was sleeping there too.

Lotte looked calm, and clear. She was letting herself giggle, to fit in with the others. I knew she was doing that on purpose. James was pickled as a gherkin, gone somewhat green around the ears. Unfortunately, he wasn't on his last legs. I wanted to rush at him with the visitors' book, cracking him a nice one over his right eye. But I just stood aside waiting while the party-goers unjumbled themselves, all calling goodnight, and more Merry Christmasses.

I wanted to catch Lotte's eye and I could feel her need of mine, but we daren't and we knew it. We could have shown it, or blown it, caught off guard because we were tired and we'd done nearly a full shift.

There were enough alcohol fumes to go up like nitroglycerine in that entrance hall. I wondered that any of them dare light up. There were several puffing away as if their lives depended on it. I was dying for a roll-up myself, but I knew how the manager regarded that.

It was almost one am. Somehow the ones who were staying were easied towards the lift, by the manager, and the last I saw of Lotte was her turning to say 'Goodnight Deanne.' She was the last to enter the lift. At that moment we realised the others were too busy with each other to notice us. James was helping his mother. Lotte was, just for a couple of seconds, free. So we met each other's eyes then. We were still wary, couldn't be too careful, but the look said, from both of us, I love you, well done.

If it had all been finished, then I could maybe have slept better. I rapidly checked the desk, put the emergency phone through to the manager, and the desk phone through to my room, and went upstairs.

My room was at the back of the building, overlooking the delivery yards and the ventilator shafts that whirred all night. I shared the room with Moe Harding who worked opposite shifts to me. We shared a kettle. There was always tea or coffee in there. We had to bring it ourselves. The Bronnester didn't provide it.

I put in my ear plugs as usual when I slept in there, and took two Mogadons. I knew I'd need them to knock me out, stop me thinking. I had my light out by one-o-five.

I never had sleeping pills usually, so I'd been sure they'd have a strong effect. Nil. Absolutely nothing at all. I hadn't a book with me, or anything to doodle with. Anyway, I never felt less like doodling. I put the light on. Got up. Put on a dressing-gown.

I made tea, with the bedside light on. Made a roll-up. Then I turned off the light and opened the curtains. They were dark blue, plain. The room was still warm. The heating had only been off since one am. I sat on the only chair, an old, small but quite comfortable armless chair. Funny how the details were clear. Important too. The chair was an old Parker Knoll. I heard a church clock somewhere in Coombe-bury (not the parish church, because its bell had broken), chime one-thirty.

I went out to the toilet down the corridor a couple of times when the tea ran through. Came back. Made more tea and another roll-up. Then I turned off the light, again. I was awake. Aware.

I knew when Lotte was trying to persuade him he was tired; knew he was telling her that tonight he intended to continue the family line; knew her disgusted replies that anyway she was on the pill; knew that he said she shouldn't mind then, should she? Knew she was trying to persuade him to sleep; knew when he was trying to accuse her of having another man; almost heard her evading his questions.

The tower, I still couldn't make out which one, chimed two. There was something different. New signals. I couldn't work them out. I was very, very troubled. I couldn't see what else we could have done, except go through with the wretched party as we had, but now I felt we should have planned it differently. The price was too high.

I was getting distress signals coming through like waves on Coombebury beach in a thunderstorm. I was going to have to intervene, regardless of the consequences. I couldn't go through the night risking Lotte. I didn't know what James was actually doing. I was four floors away from their room. I was sure he thought she'd found another man. That's why she wouldn't let him shoot his load into her. I could feel their row. I knew he was shouting: 'If I can't have you, no other man is going to. I'm going to make damn sure no other man'll want you!'

I flew for my clothes, scrambling. My watch said two twenty-two. Love, Lotte.

I ran out, locking the small door behind me. To get to Lotte I would have to go past the main desk. I didn't know how I'd explain it. I didn't care. I was sure he was beating her up. I had to stop him before he maimed or killed her.

I arrived in the foyer. Aunt Clara was there, and James' mother, crying. An ambulance was coming, the siren wailing, up the drive. The manager was on the phone, the one that went through to my room. Someone, Lotte, was on a chair under a hotel blanket. I wobbled, wanting to be sick.

'Deanne, we've just been ringing for you,' said the manager.

'I couldn't sleep,' I said. 'I didn't hear the bell, must have left my room just before you rang for me. I just couldn't sleep. Funny that. What happened to Mrs Slomner?' I rushed my words out.

'She got out, to her aunt's room. The men have gone in to him. They called me on the direct line.'

The ambulancemen came in, started to see to Lotte. I wanted to hold her.

'She'll be all right, Miss,' said one of the ambulancemen. 'You work here?'

'Receptionist.'

'She can't talk, Miss. But she'll be all right. We're just taking her to St Mathilda's.'

'Can I go with her?' I asked.

James' mother hadn't stopped crying, but Aunt Clara was calming down.

'I was just going to get dressed, dear,' she said.

'I don't mind, really. I'd be pleased to do it. I'm dressed already and I'm off duty at six anyway.' I looked at the manager. 'It seems more sensible,' I added, 'doesn't it?'

He thought, then nodded. He turned to Aunt Clara. 'Perhaps Mrs Slomner Senior might be glad of your company . . .'

Aunt Clara's face was wet. I guessed it was salty. She looked at me and nodded. 'Thank you, Deanne. We're obliged.'

So that's how I got to go with Lotte to St Mathilda's on the last night that she ever spent with James.

Lotte could not see me for three days because her eyes were so swollen.

She could hear me, though. I stayed with her on Sunday for most of the day, just talking to her quietly, asking her to squeeze my hand when she wanted me to leave. Talking was possible for only a minute or two at a time because her mouth and jaw were very bruised. She was almost unrecognisable.

When she did speak, it was to the doctor. She just said, 'Don't let my husband near.'

Aunt Clara came, and so did Lotte's mother-in-law.

They both stood, silent, tears pouring down their cheeks. 'Can she hear me?' asked Sandra Slomner. It was the first time I'd learned her name. I'd never bothered to ask before.

I just nodded. She leaned over to Lotte and took her hand.

'I'm sorry, Lotte. That my son could have done this.'

Lotte just turned her head away. Sandra Slomner might be sorry but she would never let this spoil James Junior's chances in the firm.

They left not long after.

I worked days, Monday and Tuesday. Visiting in the evenings. They knew me for 'a friend' now. There were no questions. I'd come with her from the hotel 'officially' in the first place so I suppose that helped. I had not done anything about Lotte's mother, though I thought Rene ought to know. I felt that I should wait till Lotte could talk.

She was healing quickly. By day three she could just see. The colour was purple-cum-red, with darker patches round her eyes. She could talk by then.

'Good job I've got some savings, eh, Dee?'

I just nodded, wondering what the hell we could do now.

'I need somewhere for a couple of weeks till this lot's cleared,' she said. 'Then I'll go home to Mum for a while. I phoned her last night, Dee. They brought me that trolley phone.'

'How long will you stay?'

'Long enough to sort out an injunction. It can be done. The doctors here will give me the papers I need. He's got to be stopped from ever coming near me again, Dee. I'll start divorce proceedings straight away. The lot. I'm going to throw the book at him. It will take about four months.'

'You're brave. I love you. What about costs?'

'I'll win. I can't lose. Not with *this* face. Not this time. This time he's really gone and done it. So costs will be down to him. It won't be a very long process because I shan't make any claim on his bloody money or the house or anything. I don't want his money, even if I did earn it. If I went for any of his property then it'd take for ever. Slomner's can't

136

bear it if some upstart wants their money. Not even my mother-in-law would support me in that, you know. She's sorted out her life. I don't blame her for that, but Slomners close ranks when there's trouble. "The family" comes first and I'm on the outside now.'

'It makes me boil up, Lotte. He did that to you and you come out without a penny?'

'Unless you want it dragging on for two years, Dee.'

Of course I didn't. I wanted her well and strong again. Free of that sod, and living with me. The point then was, where?

I'd thought about Lotte and myself having to do a dramatic exit. Me leaving the hotel, us both finding new jobs, setting up home together some new place. But she talked me through that. She said they wouldn't be looking for a woman, only a man. James was obsessed with that idea, hence the row. None of the Slomners clan bothered with Coombebury by day. We'd be as safe there as most places, because it was not at all what anyone would expect. Whereas, if I suddenly left my job, it would look peculiar, given the timing.

I knew of a good bed and breakfast in Lyme Regis. I rang, explaining that my friend had been in a car accident and needed a rest, and booked her in.

We were too far gone on feelings almost to miss each other. That might sound funny, but I find I'm like that sometimes. I just need to go it alone, get myself back together, and before too long I'm fine again. I learned that while Dora was in Fairview.

I thought we were damn lucky that Lotte had savings, and no children. When she came home, eventually, we'd have to start all over again, just her wages and mine. While she was in St Mathilda's, one of the nurses told me about women's aid refuges. I hadn't known about them. I thought it was wonderful, what women could do from nothing. Against all odds. We'd been lucky in comparison with many. Lotte could afford Lyme Regis, and then the train to her mother. That was sheer good fortune. I thought about Corrine and Maggie, and how me and Dora had started.

It went round and round and back again. I had already made my decision not to contact Esther, behind Lotte's back. We'd never have got over that. Lotte's anger, if I'd done that, would have finished us. Though when she was in St Mathilda's, couldn't move, couldn't talk, couldn't see, I was tempted. I'd not ever had 'family' after the war. It seemed dreadful to have them and not to let them know.

I knew it would be safe to tell Corrine – essential too. She'd not give me away. The Slomners would never tell anyone – and that included

Lotte's mum. I knew they'd keep their rotten secret, like maggots hiding in bad apples.

Lotte said she'd write to her mum from Lyme Regis, and she did.

I saw her off from Southampton station. We were too exhausted with it all even to hug too closely. We knew who we could be for each other. Who we would be. But not for a while, till we'd flung off the fury, and the grief, and till she had her decree absolute.

We both knew too much about pure rage. If I'd seen James, I'd have killed him. So would she. I was bloody glad she hadn't. God help us, we didn't have to face that kind of mess.

It was a while before I cried. Maybe two months. Then one night, it came when I woke from a dream, reliving the party night in the hotel.

It was all there in my dream. Every detail. It came like the crack finally gave, in the dam. It flooded. I got a dry towel from the airing cupboard and let it flow. My nose bled too. It poured. All over the pillow, bringing back chambermaid memories of the Bronnester. I was sobbing, gobbing, sobbing, some more. I felt that somewhere there were other Lottes going through what Lotte Clegg had gone through. Rich men, poor men, beggarmen, thieves. Venting their spleen on women, and then their sperm. Different reasons, different ways of doing it. I didn't care about the details.

When the crying was done, in maybe an hour, a bit less perhaps, my nose felt like the national blood bank. It was huge, still bleeding. I had to throw away the towel, get another. Put a bag of frozen peas on my nose (I didn't have any ice), and lie back looking into the sky through the open curtains, like I'd done that hotel night.

It stopped less than twenty minutes later. Then I slept.

When I woke, it was eleven. I'd missed my shift. I had to ring in to say I was ill. Had had a fantastic nosebleed. They were okay. I never usually was ill. Never had taken time off for myself, if I could possibly help it. Not even as a mother, with Izzie. Especially not then or they'd keep too close an eye and I might have risked losing the job. (I had had to save time off for when Izzie was ill.)

Late afternoon, I went down on the beach. Walking, like Lotte said, along the edge of the waves.

Esther

Thursday, 7 April 1983

It's Nell who has brought Tracey up. Nell who wanted to let go and dare not. Nell who loved her enough to check where she was and who she was with, and that's what Tracey resented most.

Nell told me that during term time when the girls were at school all day, the pressure was off a bit.

Nell still catches the forty-seven bus at half past two, up to Slomner and Sherwood in Moorgate, works four hours and arrives home at seven-thirty.

She said it was a straitjacket of clockwatching, making a face as she told me and rolling her eyes in that way that always makes everyone laugh. She'd have been a star on stage.

The living room is the same size as Mum's one back in Densley. Two paces from one side to the other and you land in the settee. Three paces from the window to the door to the lobby and kitchen. It takes so much effort, unconsciously all the time, to be in that room with all those people, and stay private, happy, relaxed, calm and whole. There's no physical space around to protect you from the others.

I know because it was the same for us at home in Densley. I used to envy Laura her own room. I colonised it, and made it mine, too. I don't like that recognition.

Nell hasn't tried for a full-time job. She knows that if Fred could, he'd rely on her money and spend all his. In Nell's case, part-time is her survival method. She makes sure the rent is paid, so in effect she's the one keeping a roof over all their heads. His Lordship pays the bills, including the gas bill, for the fire, and gives over some of his money for the food. Nell clothes the three women. His Lordship buys his own.

She makes him tidy up, now. 'Used to be that he'd leave his pants and socks just where he took them off. But *I* put them *all* in a sack for the dustman, so he had to kit himself out from the skin up.'

Another time he kept leaving his greasy plate by his chair. So she

139

served his egg and chips on paper plates and kept re-using them with-out washing them up. He threw up in the toilet, and now he takes his dirties back to the draining board. He doesn't wash up, though. After all, he says, he's got daughters and why have a dog and bark for it?

Nell is canny. Fred is quite clear about one thing – one finger on Nell or the young ones and she'd leave, taking them, with or without anywhere to go. Neither of them have ever said it. They don't have to.

Friday, 8 April 1983

By the year 1976, when I first met Nell, I had left far behind the period of being passive. I was growing fast, always restless and now always curious. Laura was part of that curiosity. She had believed in my potential to explore, to dare to ask myself questions that had dangerous answers, or no answers, and to feed off self-change. Sometimes it takes another woman friend to keep up the challenge. She had been that woman for me. It was a joyful recognition.

Laura and I began to see each other several times during each year. We talked on the phone when we could. After her children, Melody and Sophie, were born in 1974 and 1975, it was easier if I travelled there rather than have her and Joseph trail to London with all the paraphernalia of cots and potties and half of Mothercare (to use her phrase for it). I watched Melody and Sophie growing and changing and I wanted to be able to learn as fast, to take the level of risk that babies and toddlers take, every day. I was used to school-age children. Watching much younger children was new, and interesting.

Laura still worked. It was her life-force, she said. Melody and Sophie must fit in around her work – she would not be able to breathe without it.

She made me recognise her, so, when I became interested in women's history I couldn't help but wonder at Laura's. I was shocked at my ignorance about her heritage; at the ways I'd colluded in blanking out her past just by not questioning mine. The fact that men have buried both, was no excuse for me burying Laura's.

When I started reading, about spinning and weaving, I began discovering goddess names in some continents. Ukemochi from Japan, the source of all agriculture and silk works; Uttu from Sumer (long before Arachne who spun thread in ancient Greece), and Tlazolteotl, the Mexican goddess of domestic arts.

I was so excited, bouncing up and down, naively wanting to rush into school and start Navajo projects with the children, telling the stories of Spider Grandmother.

But all of it left out Laura from the history of the world. I was recognising that her friendship was a profound source of love through my teenage years, as important to my wholeness now, and my creativity now, as Mum's work on the buses had been, and my Grandma Clegg's huggings. (My relationship with Lotte was a whole other story, from the time that the eleven-plus 'got' me.)

All I'd ever been told of Laura's ancestors, other than through her own personal history because of our friendship, was of a dark Africa opened up up Europeans.

Nothing of the African women who ran the markets, planned the festivals, and organised the ancient towns of Zimbabwe. Nothing of the black women warriors, explorers along the inland waterways. Nothing of the queens, religious leaders, women workers in the fields. Women's history didn't begin with men in charge, and white women were not the focus of the matriarchal times. The strength and experiences of the yellow women, the brown women, the red women and the black women were woven into a tapestry that was exuberant, lavish, celebratory. It was musical and agricultural; it was muscular and it was refined; it was textile-based and pottery-making; it was based on movement, music and healing; it was astrological and astronomical; it was economical; it was fruitful, yet derived from struggle; it was fat and it was lean; it was tall and short. It was.

Yet through the excitement there ran a disappointment that became anger. In all the books I came across on goddesses, the white explorers, travellers, anthropologists and historians, hadn't recorded the vast numbers of African ones. Africa is huge compared to Europe, absolutely vast. But the lists of goddesses were tiny and I knew that was a lie. The same books had the minutest of details for piddling little European ones. Where were the weaving goddesses of Africa?

In my women's history group, in 1977, I asked this question. They weren't enthusiastic about ancient history anyway, and when I tried to describe my anger they seemed to think I was off my head. Then came the response. How dare I make claims about women's heritage without evidence? Didn't I realise that kind of talk would discredit women's history in the eyes of men? Didn't I have any standards of research? Didn't I realise I should be much more careful?

I'd been so celebratory. So jolly and bubbly. Quite like my old self before Densley High. I'd been excited and happy, searching and reading. Slap.

I'd dabbled in fire. I hurt the ends of my fingers and the pain went up to my heart. So history was still white, still European, still only going back to the eighteen hundreds. I left the group. I never went back. I felt more lonely than before I'd joined. Another reaching out, another failure. How naive could I get? Did Laura see me as a narrow-minded Englishwoman, too?

I realised then that it was no use trying to talk to some white Englishwomen about world history. Most of us didn't really care. How was I going to find my questions or my answers by searching through books by white women and men? How could I completely re-teach myself? By readings from the Caribbean, from Africa, from Asia and South America? I'd have to read poetry and fiction, myth and legend. I was on a long journey but I had a few signposts. One day, was I going to find someone to share the journey with?

If I couldn't find out through history, could I search through the poets? Poetry was not something for working-class girls in Densley High. It was for poets. They were all men. Shelley, Byron, Keats, Shakespeare. All white. But I taught the seven-year-olds in Reeve Juniors to write poems, didn't I? Had I really kept that outside me? Doing that without knowing what I was up to?

Working-class children, black and white, on a working-class estate, wrote about their lives. I, Esther, came from generations of storytellers. It was history by word of mouth. It was poetry. I'd lived it without knowing it. I'd known it through class.

In the spring of 1978, I sat here in my den, and wrote to Laura. It was the longest letter I'd composed to her for years. I ended with the words:

I don't want you to pat me on the back, but I'd like you to know what I'm up to. I know it's not your job to teach me, but if you could point me in the right direction, with a few books, it would speed me up.

She did. She wrote:

Don't get muddled up by guilt, Essie. Just get on with the work, okay? Some of the ones on the list are probably out of print, but there are loads of new novels and poetry books coming out because of the new publishing houses. Joseph's sending you the reading list from one of his courses – it's mixed, black and white, so it's okay for me to send it. And you know, Ess, I'm glad you're doing all this, okay, but just for the record, I don't want our friendship to be all about this. It's a good thing you remembered to ask about Melody's foot. She's driving us all crazy fetching and carrying for her. I don't know how much compensation she'll get from the insurance, but it can't ever make up for the months of her life that she's had to spend sitting down. If I ever meet the driver face-to-face, I'll kill her, then she'll never be able to hurt another child. But the hospital says it's healing well and although she'll limp for a while, there won't be permanent damage. We're all thankful for that. I used to think the problems would ease up as Melody and Sophie grew older, but they don't, they just change. We are hoping that Melody will be walking quite normally by the time she starts school this September. She asks after you. So, I was hoping you'd be able to come down and see us when the weather warms up. Why not write with some possible dates. Think about it. Hoping to see you soon. Love, Laura.

PS. Don't be discouraged, Ess. It makes me very angry whenever I hear the so-called academic women pulling rank over everyone else's studies. It's not just holding up the system that we are struggling to challenge, Ess, it is also inherently racist. The system is white. It is very very painful to me to hear of white women talking about standards. Whose standards? You and I will have a long session together about all this. I want to talk to you about evidence, research, and all the ways in which we make out rational arguments for our ideas. Our growing commitment to feminism, Ess, yours and mine, will take us late into the night on your visits, wont it? Do come and see us soon. This is much more than a PS, but *time* is so incredibly short at the moment, because of Melody's accident. L.

Her comment about feminism gave me plenty to think about, during that spring. I was nervous of groups, but wanting still to reach out. I continued to read as widely as I could, and to meet more often with Mo and Hortense, talking all the time, about class, race, children, and studying.

Mo and Hortense also shared ideas with me about knitting. Different stitches, very complicated to learn, sometimes.

I hoped that in the long run the same would hold true for my emerging feminism. That I wouldn't have to follow other women's patterns without questioning them or wanting to change them. I'd be able to experiment, stitch by stitch, like Mo and Hortense. Take some more risks, learn to redesign, so that my feminism would be a good fit, and a suitable shape for me, Essie Clegg. Me.

Deanne, 1978

Lotte stayed in Densley from January until March, and then she went to rent a room from Rose, a friend of Corrine, near Downingham.

Rose lived with her sister. They ran a wool shop with a sub-post office. They had a huge Alsation dog, who was a comfort to Lotte after he had accepted her. She found a job, temping for a local agency; and we waited for her decree absolute to come through.

I still half expected James to turn up at the Bronnester, but he didn't. I eyed more than one client there, wondering if he was a private detective, but I wasn't asked any questions.

Whenever Lotte and I wanted to sleep together, we went to a B and B. We decided we'd rather have the occasional weekends, more often, than keep our holiday money and have a fortnight somewhere.

At the time, it was a strain. Looking back, we found we'd been glad of the times apart, so that we could be sure about the step we were taking, deciding to live together. She planned to do temping in Coombebury, and I would stay at the hotel. I didn't have age on my side for job-hunting.

James had already found a new rabbit to bully. He intended to marry as soon as the divorce came through. Nell gossiped to me on the phone.

The new fiancée was twenty-one years old. Her engagement ring was a huge diamond solitaire.

Lotte and I went on a two-day trip to Lulworth. It was May. Just before the bank holiday, before the tourists. A bright sunshine, but windy. Waves were coming up the steep beach. Falling back again. They had to drop three feet. The froth looked like old lace petticoats. Shingle sucked and pulled. A couple of families were picnicking like us, but a distance away. We were going to walk up and over the cliffs to Durdle Door.

She had walking boots on, like mine, and a yellow anorak. She looked like sunshine on legs. Nobody took any notice of us. The fact that we were two women, scheming to live together, wasn't a world-shattering event in Lulworth Cove.

We sat on Lulworth beach, throwing stones into the sea, laughing and joking. We'd made love all night. We were fascinated with each other. It seemed like nine years since we'd met, or nine minutes, but not nine months.

The petticoats frothed and slid away. Returning. I told Lotte. She wanted me to draw them for her. I didn't know if I could because it's hard to draw the sea. She laughed and said 'try'. I had my sketch pad and coloured pencils in my anorak. But I wanted to talk, and said I'd try and draw it later, back in the B and B.

We packed up the remains of lunch, and crunched back to the lane, up through Lulworth Village, to the walk over the cliffs.

On the walk I talked about my friendship with Nell. I told Lotte I couldn't sacrifice Nell. I had no family as such, except Isobel, Nell and Corrine. If I trusted Corrine not to tell Dove, then I ought to trust Nell with our relationship. She was putting Esther in no danger now, whether Ess knew or not.

Lotte insisted Ess must not know. 'I want to make my own decisions without my older sister in on the act. I feel crowded by our Essie. Ever since our Essie went to the Grammar and I didn't, I've struggled to run my own life. I must do it my way.'

'All right. But Nell is my friend. I love you Lotte, I want you in my life. But I must tell Nell, or it'll go sour between you and me. I've been months thinking about it, Lotte.'

'Maybe you're right then, Dee. We'll have to try it and see, won't we? Just think, Dee, we'll be living together by October.'

We walked on. Over the stiles and up the final hill to the top of Durdle Door. We were content. Our minds were made up. I would tell Nell. But Esther would not know. I felt sad for Lotte and Ess.

We sat through early evening watching the waves around the 'door'. Wearing away at the rocks. I thought that the rocks must be weary with it.

The sunset was red orange and pink. Velvet ribbons and satin too. Strung out from the sun, like spokes from the hub of a wheel. The setting sun was a red disc.

There'd been an old cartwheel sloped against the farmhouse wall in Mereford on the south side of the house. The wheel's rim stood in the narrow bed of flowers that ran all around the farmhouse.

The hub and the spokes had been painted scarlet once, but parts had

145

dulled, a deep red, where the hot sun on the south wall had flaked off the paint. The flowers that grew up through the spokes were snapdragons. Each year they glowed, red orange yellow and pink, hiding a few of the spokes completely. I'd been in love with Dora then.

Now, above me, the sun's disc was the centre of a different wheel. A sun wheel. My wheel of fortune, turned full circle for me, in love with Lotte.

I reached for her hand, and we watched without talking, as our eyes saw the sun slip slowly into the ocean as easily as a bright new penny into a slot machine. It was so ordinary that it amused me. There must have been a hole in the horizon, waiting. So spectacular that it took me by surprise.

As it touched the water it dissolved. It cast its velvet towards us, turning the surface into a scarlet mirror. Half the hub of the wheel still in the sky, half in the sea. Ribbons rippling, the colours fused, blended. Past and future held there for us. Held in one moment for the present, now, a perfect moment, shared with Lotte.

Esther

Friday, 8 April 1983

Writing all through the night.

In the summer of '78, I saw the ad I'd been waiting for. (It hadn't occurred to *me* to advertise.) A new women's group was being formed in my area, and it gave a phone number. Most of the women, said the ad, were working-class.

Would they accept me as working-class though I had been to college? They did. Two others had also been through further or higher education. The group lasted five months and was very important to me. We met every Sunday evening in somebody's house or flat. There were nine of us, ages from twenty-three to thirty-five and we were all white.

In the working-class women's group we talked about family love and family strife; and about the struggle to remake broken family ties; and I became close to two women, Mary and Janet, because of that.

I'd sometimes talked with Laura about how Densley High encouraged the girls to leave their families, feeding an urgent desire to flee from Densley. Not that I regretted leaving. But I understood better now, how the process had worked, and where it was based on class and race. Over the years Mum and I had talked for hours too.

In Chaffinch Hill College, there had been no radical thinking – no criticism of schools as part of the state; of the ways in which schools controlled the creativity of working-class children; nor how they defused children's anger about class conditions and did nothing to undermine the racist assumptions of both children and adults.

Sometimes, faced with the size of the issues, I felt about as useful as a donkey peeing into the sea. It seemed hopelessly futile and romantic sometimes, imagining that I, as a junior school teacher, could make any difference.

Locally, I talked on and off to Nell about the series of cuts and setbacks which the schools were starting to face. In both Islington and

Reeve there were other teachers who wanted changes, but the heyday of spending was now over.

At Reeve Juniors the PTA hoped to start an after-school activities club for children whose mums or dads did not come home from work till six pm or six-thirty. Plans had been on the school staff-meeting agenda since before I arrived at Reeve, and were backed by the unions. The money for staffing and equipment was not forthcoming. I saw it as political work. I wanted it to happen. Many children went home to wait for adults to arrive, and we were always worried about bullying from older brothers and sisters; about accidents; and about sexual violence from adults who knew that young girls and boys were in on their own, or were (in the winter) walking home alone in the dark. I had read reports. I knew that 'adult' means 'adult male'. That sexual abuse of girls was by men, not women, in ninety-nine per cent of cases. We had been involved with cases in school. It was impossible for me not to make connections with my emerging feminism. I wanted an after-school club for the protection of the girls more than the boys in Reeve. I talked about it to Nell, though in general – without names or examples. Even the social service departments were muttering about child abuse. It was the huge and growing problem of the social workers' case loads, and it went across all classes; though middle-class people have ways of keeping their violence hidden and social workers have more ways of interfering in working-class lives.

By '79, though, I was a new and excited feminist. I talked to Nell about 'changes and possibilities'. She said, 'I ain't no college girl like you Ess, but I do like to get things done. I'm good at that, and I ain't afraid of nobody. I think we should get on with this club thing. Start it now. Or my girls'll be on pensions while that lot's still making agendas. Agendas. My arse. Forget about havin' it in the school, Ess, and go for the community centre.'

I laughed and laughed. It was obvious, though I hadn't seen it.

It was so exciting, so much caring, commitment and energy. And for me it was an expression of active grass roots feminism. I felt I could put my body and soul into that work in that group, face the setbacks, struggle with the other women to divert resources to working class mothers and to their little girls whose safety I cared about more than the little boys. I didn't say those things in the group, nor in the school staff room. In Reeve Juniors I was the most visible feminist, always bringing up girls' needs.

My feminism was a cliff edge sometimes. One slip and I'd fall off, labelled as 'extremist' with none of my words and ideas taken seriously.

We used to take turns to meet in the mothers' front rooms. Seven of us, all local women, and coffee mugs and grant application forms, in triplicate, all of us bundled together on the settee and the floor, trying to avoid getting too near the wonky gas fire.

They were modern fires with a wood surround, nothing old or objectionable about them. But the brackets didn't hinge safely to the walls and the ignitions sometimes failed to strike.

Nell and the others had badgered the Council and the Gas Board to fix the fires and to attend to the others like them on Reeve Green, where everyone was complaining about the fires and worrying about the children and the cats, who calmly stalked through the living rooms trying to find a warm clear safe piece of floor to lie on not too near and not too far from the warmth.

But the Council blamed the Gas Board and the Gas Board declared it was the responsibility of the Council and no progress was being made.

Nell was sure there'd be an explosion and an injury before they'd get it sorted out.

So there we used to sit, listening to the gas filaments clinking and clanking, as if trying to get a word in edgeways. But with seven women and five sides of forms and questions, sub-sections and parts of sub-sections to deal with, the gas fire was relegated to fourth division after the children and the cats.

We were all nervous of the forms, and even more of standing in front of the Joint Working Party of the Council to make our case.

Hortense came up with the idea of taking the photos from the open day we had had for the club.

'They keep saying they want to do something for black people in this area. Well, we'll show them these and they'll see that me and Beth and half the kids is black, won't they? Shame the buggers into it, that's what I say.'

'Yeah, let them put their money where their mouth is,' added Beth.

'Had the woman from the social round today. Nosey bitch. Smiling all the time. I tell you, I'd smile on her wages,' said Sharon.

'Salary,' grinned Hortense.

'Beggin' her pardon, there's a pig in my garden.'

'Here pass this coffee to Nell. Blue one's for Beth. How many sugars, Ess?'

'None. Sweet enough.'

'Says you. Here you are, superman's for Sharon.'

'I should be so lucky,' laughed Sharon. 'You tell that to my Tony.'

The forms had to be done in triplicate and we'd never done them before. We planned to pass on what we learned to the next group but it was harder for us being the first ones. I slipped as much as I could through the school copier, which was part of my job in the group.

'The blokes was on Reeve Green again today, with them theodolites, so I gets me shoes on, and off I goes out to talk to 'em. I says: "What's this then?" He says, "More trees".' Mo paused for effect.

We were all thinking about the passages between the houses where the uneven concrete had hollows that filled with water; the wallpapers that wouldn't stick to damp walls; the windows that didn't shut; and of course the gas fires. Mo went on.

'So I says to 'im, "What about me gas fire then?" "Oh," he says, "different department. We're doing trees." I says, "What d'yer think we are, a load o' bloody monkeys?" '

Amidst the laughter, Sally put her head round and asked for a bath. She tried to move across us to the bathroom that was downstairs, next to the kitchen. She was only a foot from the lobby door when the mug went over, sending coffee across one of the finished pages.

'Oh Gawd. Get a cloth. Clean it up.'

Sally rushed out for the cloth, trying to be sorry and invisible all at the same time. Nell rolled her eyes to the roof and I know she was thinking, 'If we can do all this like this when most of us have nothing, what couldn't we do with half a chance?'

We voted Hortense and Nell in as the spokeswomen. They laughed, saying no one was going to scare them off when it came to the money.

'But the bloody thing starts at seven. How are we all going to get there by then? I don't get home till seven,' said Sharon.

'Who'd bleedin' put on a meetin' at seven 'cept a load of men in suits?' frothed Mo.

Sharon worked shifts on the checkout in the supermarket (cash in hand, no questions asked. She hadn't told the social that); Beth and Linda were child-minders; Nell worked up in town in the job they all envied, because it was paid quite well for part-time; Hortense was doing an access course, because Mark was now at school.

I was the only non-mother there. Most of the group couldn't get sitters, so had to have neighbours to listen out for the pre-school children that were already asleep. They'd pop in every hour or so, to check things were okay, till the mothers came home. It was a nervy business and the mothers hated it, but there wasn't a chance to meet any other time because most were child-minding or on shifts in the day time. Jobs like Nell's were rare.

'Jammy cow. Wouldn't you just know Nell'd land a job like that?'

'Give my right arm for one like that, I would.'

'Who'd have the baby?'

'Me mum'd do it, she says. I need the money. There's no jobs though.'

'What's this clause three?'

'We don't do three, we go straight to five because two was "Yes".'

'Oh, I see. No, I don't. Come again. Bleedin' forms.'

'All this slog for a poxy . . .'

'We should get the Queen Mother to sell one of her rings. That'd pay for it.'

We tried our patience for another half hour with the lists of questions, until Hortense suddenly said: 'Shit, I've had enough of this for tonight. Besides, I'm still thinking about them royals. All them jewels. Money and class, money and class, like a bloody merry-go-round.'

Beth replied: 'We're doing all right Horts, though. We're just tired, that's all. We'll come through okay, I just know it. 'Cos we're bloody determined.'

Horts said: 'Maybe, maybe not. I need a sleep, I know that.' (We all nodded and laughed as she rolled her eyes like Nell sometimes did, and let out a giant yawn.) 'But we can be as determined as we like, we're maybe up against too much. That's what's going round. I get so tired in these meetings I can't see beyond the bloody lists.'

'We've got them photos as well as forms and questions. You've got to keep on looking on the bright side Horts. We can't give up now,' said Beth again, leaning over to grab Hortense's arm, and looking really anxiously at her.

'Look, I need a sleep, all right? Who said anything about bloody giving up. And take your hand off me arm. I don't need no 'ffection, I just need a morning without me kid waking me at the crack o' dawn.' She stood up and started for the door. But before she got there Mo interrupted her:

'Hang on a minute Horts. You started all this. Money and class, money and class, remember? I don't want you to just go this minute. If you'll hang on five minutes while we just finish off we can go together like we always do.' She waited while Hortense sat on the arm of the settee by the door, everyone's eyes moving and changing, none of us happy, all of us exhausted. I thought Horts had really talked for us all.

151

I felt stuck through like a horse on a pole on a carousel; only instead of fairground music, we had papers and coffee cups rustling and clinking. Jangling our heads up all the same. Round and round.

'Just hang on. Just finish off. It's always just just just,' snapped Hortense, squatting on the arm of the settee, higher than most of us. 'I'm not just anything. I'm tired and cross. Cross with the bloody Council. Bloody forms. Royals with nannies galore. When do they ever have a so-called' (she pursed her lips and imitated royal speech) 'child-care problem?'

'I know that,' snapped Beth back. 'Mo knows that. We all fucking know that. I just wanna get on with it. See it through. Get the fucking money like the rest of you.'

'Just wanna get on with it,' repeated Hortense. 'I don't want no more justs. I want Justice. I want Thatcher to struggle like me on an access course. I want the DHSS to lose her bloody file. I want her woken every bloody night for months on end.'

'We've a right to that money,' began Nell, who'd been quiet which was unusual for her. She looked drained and drawn, with shadows too, under her eyes: 'Know what I'd like? I'd like to storm into that council hall. . .'

'Chamber,' said Linda, reading from one of the instruction lists in her hands.

Nell smirked: 'Chamber. Storm in there and shout "Look you lot, there in yer stuffy suits, this is a big thing for us, a giant . . ." (she rolled her eyes and we all roared with laughter in spite of ourselves) "a giant step for womankind". (Nell rolled her tongue around 'womankind' and we began to relax and roared again. Even Horts was caught up in it, as if she was relieved that Nell had started clowning for us. I loved Nell deeper in that moment than I had for quite a while.) "Don't you sit there pon-tif-ic-atin' on our app-lic-ayy-shun. We are not just a bunch of women you know. We are not just any thing. So there. We are gettin' our nerve up. So just you all" (she rolled again and talked with her hands now too) "watch OUT. We want Justice. We mean to 'ave Justice. And we do NOT intend to leave this chamber" (she winked at Linda) "until we 'ave Justice." ' Nell paused, for effect. I saw Horts and Beth grin at each other, and Horts' shoulders were a fraction looser.

I wanted to clap and I bet some of the others might have too, but maybe it'd be a bit over the top so I didn't. Neither did they. But we all started shuffling up and collecting bags and coats and I felt easier about it all than I'd done all evening. Like Horts had said, maybe,

maybe not, but we went home with a bit more hope after Nell's performance. Besides, when we turned up for the next meeting, Horts had recovered and said that being so angry was going to help her. She said she was going to give those Council men hell about what women needed in the borough. She said: 'They might win, sod 'em. But we're going to have a damn good go at 'em, and see if they just' (we all laughed) 'just dare ignore us.'

Usually Tracey's friends, Jane and Anita and Bev, were upstairs in Tracey's room when the meetings were at Nell's house, downstairs. They didn't make that much fuss, really, and we didn't often have to shout for their disco tapes to be turned down. But sometimes when they put their heads round to call goodnight, Nell would unconsciously let slip her dislike of them. It troubled me, but I wasn't honest enough to confront Nell with the fact that she wasn't making much effort with Tracey's friends. Sometimes Tracey would meet me at the front door, just before a meeting.

'Can I come and see yer, Ess?'

'Are you all right, Trace?'

'Sure I am. It's her in there that's not all right.'

'Give us a break, Trace. Nell's my friend.'

'Well, she don't understand. I wanna come and see yer, Ess. Can I?'

'Yes. Tomorrow, after school?'

'Thanks. Will you talk to my mum?'

'I'll try, Tracey. Take it easy, will you?'

'I am. It's just we had another row.'

'Not another, Tracey?'

'She won't leave orf. Going on and on . . .'

'Okay. We'll talk tomorrow, just you and me, all right?'

'Yeah. Thanks Ess.'

So it went on. Me, the wise older friend. Joke.

Saturday, 9 April 1983

Slept in late this morning, after writing till almost five am As soon as I woke, I was in the kitchen, making tea and toast, then into the bath, thinking about what I'd been writing, and about what is happening to me. I have thread fever. Making the weft and warp and weaving the words as if I have waited for this flow to be released. Little did I know this would happen, when I began the diary back in February. At the moment I can't stop it. I feel as if there is a tape recorder in my head. I can hear the voices of the women in the after-school club, I can listen in on recordings of me and Mum, and myself and Laura. If I could communicate the excitement of this to the children in Reeve school in such a way as to release their words from them, about their lives, it would be so powerful. To move like this between woven cloth and finished words on paper, I never thought would happen to me.

If I could communicate like this with Lotte, would we have a chance to re-create our friendship? Was this how I was as a child? This passionate excitement, this sense of making something?

Saturday afternoon

So after a quick late breakfast here I am, not knowing where the exploration will take me, but certain I have to go with it.

It was Sunday morning, February 20th, this year.

Tracey came to my den, wandering round the walls, peering again at photos, staring again at my books. I tried to potter, making tea, not hurrying. Eventually she settled in my rocking chair, tipping and rising in an agitated rhythm. She had heard the Reeve school gossip earlier that week. I'd confiscated shoes from two boys found fighting behind the lavs in the playground. They spent the day sullen and busy, doing jobs for me in my classroom. So, searching for neutral territory, Tracey started with that.

'I heard about Neil and Gary's shoes. D'you remember when I was ten and Phil Smith hit me?'

'I remember that you won. I should think he still has the scars, doesn't he?' My laugh was false. High. Tinny.

'He never hurt me again.' She paused. 'Me and Bev and Jane's started self-defence now.'

'Who teaches that?' I showed patronising interest and was ashamed.

'Miss Lawson. The one that's a bit of a feminist like you. She does Women's History too, on Thursdays, only we're fifths so we can't go. I'm leaving anyway, after my CSEs.'

'Why Trace?' As if I didn't know.

'I wanna leave home, Ess. Bev's sister's in a co-op. She can get me, Anita and Bev a room.'

'Oh. One or two sugars?' I kept my face bland.

'Two. Thanks. Mum don't know about me leavin'. She's on and on about me going down the youth club, find a boyfriend. Well, I ain't settlin' down wiv a boyfriend. I ain't getting married, ever. That's for sure.'

'Do you know why?' Write your answers clearly on this exam paper, state your reasons, and draw a map.

'Yeah, I know why. Besides you haven't. Why don't you get married, Ess?' Sweet sixteen. A bar of candy. Seaside rock. The word in sharp pink letters. Right through. It read CHALLENGE.

I pretended to drink my tea.

The rhythm of her rocking chair seemed to echo a spinning woman's foot on the treadle of a spinning wheel. To and fro. To and fro. Like spider woman, Tracey sat there, spinning her questions at me like truths from the centre of herself. I yearned then, at thirty-seven, to spin like that: my own strong threads. To spin words into phrases, to unravel, to untangle, making miles of truth. I longed to stop hiding from myself, and to share my spun words, with Tracey and with Nell.

She, Tracey, shocked me with her level of self-awareness, especially when I looked back at myself at sixteen. Was she typical of other sixteen-year-olds in the eighties? I didn't know. She had been born the year I had left Chaffinch Hill College. So her birth had coincided with the birth of this cycle of the women's liberation wheel which had been spinning round unevenly for centuries. Evolving. Revolving. Evolution and revolution. The concepts spun around me until I felt like a fly caught in Tracey's spider-web.

I was changing, but I wasn't ready to tell anyone. I wanted more time. Time to feel sure of myself; time to decide who to talk to about myself.

I thought: I'm still spinning unevenly, and the fibres come from my mouth like dental floss, rasping along the edges of my teeth, like string made bloody with insecurities, grating my gums red raw.

I'm not one of the three Norns, sitting on a rock near a waterfall, spinning threads of wisdom and life. I'm not the ancient legendary basket-maker, throwing a strand of fibre to heaven for people to walk on. I'm not the rainbow serpent, arching my body over the earth, flowing with water threads of colour.

If I were those beings, would I know myself, my centre, the movements of the past, the moments of the present, the possibilities for the future? Would I be able to weave trust and knowledge, with Tracey?

Her rocking chair rhythm while she waited for me was not smooth, but she had a calm glow around her which made her very attractive suddenly to me. I felt sick then, as if the rocking was a boat at sea; and was appalled because she was my friend's daughter and had come to

155

my flat asking for help. But I was still drawn towards her, allured. It was intense. Shocking.

She seemed suddenly to be the older one of us two. Older and infinitely more honest, vulnerable like me, but braver.

'I'm a loner,' I said, 'I'm just not the marrying kind.'

There was still plenty of time left, wasn't there?

She left home four days later.

Deanne, 1979

After Lotte moved in, novelty swept us along for almost a year. I thought of it sometimes as the two of us playing house. There was joking and laughing. It was amazing.

Take, for instance, a Saturday when I wasn't working a shift. I'd be making a banana cake, for Corrine, for tea. Lotte'd be at the sink, washing up, humming out of tune. I never heard her hum in tune once, but I was used to her. Wouldn't have had her stop. She'd dry her hands, still humming. Then she'd sneak past me and steal a fingerful of the cake mixture before I could stop her.

But instead of licking it herself, she'd surprise me, offering it to me, putting her arm around my shoulder and kissing the side of my neck.

I'd take my time licking that mixture off that finger.

There were moments like that when we weren't working, moments that I'd remember. Like birthday gift-boxes. Just traces of scent. So faint you'd only just be able to tell. And the gift not even started.

In the first year that Lotte and I lived together, Ralph Edmund Dove died. He left Corrine nothing except the flat he'd bought her. Didn't surprise me. So much for the headlines in the papers that try to make out that women like Corrine live off rich men. He left a sound business, which was okay for me. My mortgage papers were all legal and not based on him being in charge.

Corrine was happier after Dove died. Taking a new lease of life, she said. 'I shan't give you all a chance to have a retirement party for *me*. I shall burn bright like a candle, and fade just as quick. I shall sing till I'm ninety.'

We did have a sixtieth birthday party for her. There were a dozen of us at my house. Stuart came, and Ian. Lotte, of course; Mol, Pol and Micky; Agatha, Mo and Freda from Salisbury; and Rose and Amy and Vivienne from the singing group that Corrine started in Dorchester. It was midweek so as not to clash with the 'do' for her at the Bronnester. Ours was more informal and, I thought, more fun.

Corrine had a zest for life. She looked changes full in the eye. She wasn't afraid of being afraid. She said, 'It's part of life to be frightened. It's what you do with it that matters.' She refused to turn her fears inside like Dora did. That was the difference between her and Dora.

Corrine gave me the strength to go on year by year when Dora was in Fairview; and to go on after Dora died in there.

I have lots of drawings and cartoons of Corrine. She's like a high-spirited mare, flying at the five-bar fences; she topples some bars and knocks her feet on others; then she waits a moment, steadies herself and carries on.

She said sixty was young, a chance to find out more about herself. She looked beautiful, and there were laughter lines around her mouth.

I had tapes, as well as drawings. The singing group in Dorchester recorded themselves. The voices made me see ripples on the River Mere when a kingfisher darted in.

Two of the singing group lived in an amazing old house in one of the villages, about four miles out of Dorchester. Lotte called it 'The Froggery', on account of the stream in the garden. The house was all nooks and crannies, full of antiques, like a Victorian museum. The two women had lived together for years. The villagers called them companions. We called them 'the V&A'. You'd think one of them would have changed her name from Viv or Amy, but they didn't. Neither of them needed to work. How the other half lives!

At Corrine's party, something became public. Very public. Viv wanted Corrine. That's the night they started. Then they lived as a threesome, and Corrine was there most of the week. She still went to see Mol from time to time. I don't know whether they really found it so simple, but they seemed to get along fine. It was beyond me to see how they worked it all out, but they did.

Finding a job for Lotte wasn't difficult because there were still jobs around then. She started temping, through an agency. There was a post in one of the international language schools in Coombebury. They were so pleased with her they asked her to stay on.

Rates were hefty in seaside towns. My rates were as high as Lotte's mum's rent and rates put together. It made a difference having a second wage coming on.

There were times when I felt really crowded though. So used to living alone. I think it made me cranky and cantankerous. Small things would irritate me.

Like she tore the orange juice carton tops instead of cutting them, then they didn't pour and she cursed all over the kitchen mopping up the drips. The thing that really got me was her turning down the corners of the *Radio Times*. It fidgeted me till I could near explode with it.

She did that *once* with one of my gardening books. Now, I love my plot out the back, and my allotment. It means a lot to me. I don't go much on books, but I paid good money for those. One day I found one of the corners turned down, at section D. D for Daphne. Pretty stuff. Pink in early spring when you're least expecting anything in flower. I did my nut over that page. I had steam coming out of my ears. My book. She turned down a page in *my* book.

Petty revenge. I was so mad. Spoilt brat. Too much money for too long.

I was tempted to put her best handwash lambswool sweater in the washer. Then I thought that was going a bit over the top, so I took it out again without switching on. Instead, I took the laces off her posh new trainers and used them to tie up my honeysuckle.

She came home that night with a root of Daphne. We laugh now when it flowers in the spring.

The first of our rows, a real humdinger, came in April 1980, uninvited.

Lotte suddenly mentioned to me about taking a three-week holiday in France. She wanted to show me Paris. I didn't catch on at first to what she was saying.

'You can't take three weeks off, can you, from the language centre,' I said.

'Well, it's just that I'd like longer than two.'

'I don't think I could manage longer than two, Lotte.'

'I thought they let you have three together, now that you've been there this long?'

'It'd be a bit awkward. But *you* can't anyway.'

'Oh, I thought I'd hand in me notice,' she said, offhand.

'You what?'

'And go temping again when I got back.'

'What? Give up your job for a holiday? You must be off your head.'

Worse was to come. She wanted us to go in September.

'How am I going to request three weeks off work in September?'

'But I thought the high season'd be over then.'

'Not in Coombebury. You know that.'

'No I don't.'

'Well, you bloody should.'

'Why?'

'Because we live together and I work in a busy hotel, here in this town.'

'I thought you'd be pleased.'

'Well I'm not. I can't see where your head is.'

'On my effing shoulders, where it's always been.'

'Well you wouldn't think so, from what it's mouthing.'

'Thanks a billion. You've been looking tired, that's all.'

'Looking my age more like.'

'That's not what I said.'

'Isn't it?'

'No, it bloody is *not*. It's not me that frets about the age gap.'

'You agree there's a gap then?'

'Don't be daft.'

'Senile too now?'

'Oh for crying out loud. I suggest a holiday and all I get is a heap of shit.'

'You didn't just suggest a holiday, sweetheart. You wanted me to leave a busy hotel for three weeks in the tourist season.'

'So I'm sorry. I didn't mean to upset you.'

'Well you bloody have. I don't want you to soft soap me about being tired. I want a bit more honesty than that.'

'I'm not lying. You've been working all the hours there are, that's all.'

'No that's not all. You knew what you were taking on when you came to live here. Hours and hours talking it out, remember?'

'Of course.'

'Well then?'

'Well what?'

'Well you knew what my hours were like. I'm a shift worker. You knew that.'

'Have I ever complained?'

'You'd better not damn well try.'

'Oh? Rules now, is it?'

'Well you're quite used to having your own way, Lotte.'

'Jesus Christ, Dee. What *is* this?'

'I just don't see how you can think, even think, of walking out of a good job, when there's no jobs left in Coombebury.'

'There are still jobs left. Besides, I've got more experience now.'

'Aren't you the lucky one? One year here, another there? Get bored quickly, do you?'

'I work bloody hard and you know it. How dare you hint, even hint at me about not sticking at work. After the struggle I had to get trained, change my whole life, live here.'

'Bored with this too?'

'No, I haven't got time. I'm too busy arguing. You're twisting everything. I wanted a holiday. With you. A *real* holiday. The first we've had. You know? *Together.* Or are you fed up with me? Are you? See me as a spoilt pet? Something like that? Do you? I'm sorry about September. I made a bad mistake. Judgement of error.'

'You mean error of judgement, dear.'

'I know what I mean. Don't you bloody patronise me. I don't need your patronage. I'm not a rabbit any more, you know. My name's Clegg now, not effing Slomner.'

She stormed out and spent the night God knows where.

I shook. True I was tired. I looked like I needed three months, not three weeks. I stood at the mirror. The resentment poured out of my face. I thought I'd be eaten alive with it. Like that woman who survived an air crash. In Brazil. She struggled through the jungle with maggots in her skin. But my jealousy came from *not* having travelled to faraway places, nor had adventures, nor exotic meals.

Next night, when I arrived home, there was a note: 'Down on the beach. I love you. Lotte.'

What did I expect? Her to come home first and make a meal? Candle-lit dinner for two? Red napkins in the glasses and a menu? It's as well I didn't. That would be how she'd had to deal with James. Cordon bleu dinner, chocolate mousse. Then, please? I wasn't James. I wasn't a bloke. She wasn't married to *me*.

I changed out of my work clothes into jeans and trainers. I didn't hurry. She wouldn't want me to. So I fed Tibs (the third) and had a quick cuppa, and then set off.

It was light outside, late April. I knew where she'd be. Our favourite spot. Ten minutes along from the pier.

I was at the cliffs sooner than I'd expected. I must have been walking quite fast, in spite of myself. I reached the zigzag path down. I could just make her out, down there, walking with her shoes off, along the edge of the waves. She loved to do that. My heart was going dumdum dumdum, dumdum. The wind was blowing my hair. That made me a bit on the wild side too, like Lotte.

I walked down the zigzag path to the beach. Then a sharp memory came up, like a stone on the cliff, jagged and rough. Dora down there, walking on the beach, pregnant with Izzie.

I zigzagged on down. Lichens grew on some stones. Even new shrubs had taken root. I was too shaken to be that hopeful. I reached the last steps down to the sand, afraid of memories, of losing a woman-lover again.

She heard me. Turned. Waited. Held out her arms. I went to her. We held close. Didn't kiss, too raw, too afraid.

'Shall we walk?' she asked. I nodded. We linked arms like any tourists, walking, listening to the waves and the sound of our trainers on the sand. We were walking maybe four minutes, it seemed fourteen.

'So now we know how to hurt each other, don't we?' I nodded. 'I didn't mean to hurt you, Dee,' she said sadly. 'I'm so sorry, Dee.'

I was silent, waiting.

'Funny, isn't it? I'd never have dared spend money like that when I was with James. But last night, I knew I had to be on my own and it was my own money. And nobody could tell me not to. I couldn't get over that. I was awake almost all night, thinking. I'm stupid sometimes, Dee. I hated James and what he stood for, didn't I, but I wanted it all too. Holidays. Money. Things. I thought I'd left all that behind. Last night I found out that I hadn't.'

I looked at her direct. I was almost struck silent. My voice went down into my knees. But I'd come this far. I wasn't going to give in now. If she wanted it all back, it was best to *know*. Now. While I still had that wonderful year to look back on. Before the bitterness came, and more lies, from both of us. I watched the sea, and we walked on slowly.

'Do you want it back, Lotte?'

'Sometimes. Yes, if I'm honest I do. Look at me, Dee, please. But it's only some of the *things*, that I sometimes hanker for. Not the people or the houses or way of life. I got too used to the things. Like the chance of a long holiday with you. With you. I want you.'

I was swallowing hard. There were tears down my face. I realized I must be crying. I think the last time I cried like that was when Izzie's letter, the good one, came. The one about her and Marion.

'I want you too,' I said.

She licked the salt off my face, murmuring. 'I want this,' she said. 'I want to go on with you. To make a life together.'

'That's a lot to offer. We said we wouldn't make plans. In case we let each other down.'

'I know,' she said, 'but it's how I feel. Anyway, I need to tell you, because that's not *all* of it. I need to say that *first*.'

I thought, Oh my dear life, she wants to take up with someone else as well. Like Corrine with the V and A.

'You've come over all funny, Dee. What's the matter?'

'Does it show?'

'Summat does. What's up?' She often went back to a strong accent when she was anxious.

'I was thinking about V and A,' I said.

She went white. 'Bloody hell. Is that what you want? I don't understand. I thought you wanted just us?'

'I *do*. I'm not sure you do.'

'Oh bloody heck. This is a can of worms. A threesome's fine for *Corrine*.' I nodded. I was nodding faster than a silly dog on a rear window shelf.

'Corrine can do whatever she bloody pleases,' added Lotte, 'but I just want you. Just us. You've not exactly ... Well, I mean, you've got no reason to see me different from that, have you?'

'No.'

'Well then, you are going to have to bloody believe more in me and more in yourself, aren't you? I know why you get scared, Dee. But I'm not Corrine, and I'm *not Dora*. I'm not jumping through hoops to prove it. I jumped through hoops for James and I'm not jumping for anyone ever again. If you don't believe in you, and in me, and in us, then I can't make you. Nobody can do that for you, Dee, except you. Deanne Derby.'

'Well, you said there was something else you wanted to tell me.'

'Well, if you'll let me spit it out, instead of jumping to conclusions.'

'Go on then. Let's be having it, as you say.'

'Well, you used to live alone all those years, and I'm a bit surprised that you don't feel I'm in the way sometimes. I get frightened that you'll feel overcrowded. Like I arrived in a whirlwind, and then suddenly there's two of us living together, when you were used to being on your own for years. And your house isn't very big and, well, don't get me wrong about this will you?'

'I'm trying not to,' I said, my teeth sharp.

'I love the house, Dee, and I love you. Sometimes, though, I think you must feel crowded with me, and sometimes I wonder if we will always be here, in Coombebury together. Usually I go from day to day, happy and glad, but this row, and the night on my own, brought up all these things to think about.'

163

'I think about moving, too.'

'Do you, Dee. Do you really?'

'Yes . . . Sometimes I feel ready for a new place, a new start. No hurry. But they were muttering about starting a Bronnester in Brighton. It was a five-year plan, a string of sister-hotels, and it set me thinking. If we hadn't had the row I was going to mention it that night. They could be wanting some of the experienced staff to move. There would be plenty of work for you there, we could think about a slightly bigger place, one that was ours, a shared mortgage. We could have a spare room for friends to come and stay, and Izzie if she came on leave. Then you'd not feel it was so much *my* house, would you?'

'Brighton? Do you really mean that? What about Corrine?'

'It's not that far away. There'd be weekend trips for us. I think I'd like that, would you?'

'Yes. Like you said, I could find work there. And there is a lesbian night life there, isn't there? And it would be possible to go up to London from there. Easier than from here.'

There was no hurry, but we decided we'd think about it. I would make some enquiries at work. We'd look carefully at all the pros and cons. The wind came up, sharp off the sea. We made our way home then, starving hungry. In Hollywood movies they fall in bed, to make it up. But we weren't the 'have-a-good-row-and-make-for-the-bedroom' sort. We didn't make love in fact until two nights later. Then it happened out of the blue, and it was passion.

Lotte, 1979

Dee was a good lover, gentle and funny. Kind and wild. I'm not saying it was easy, a bed of roses. Besides, even roses have thorns.

It's hard to talk about our sex life because we don't have enough words, do we? Besides, the words we *do* have have been mucked around by men.

There we are in bed and I'm wanting to say you've got a beautiful . . . But I feel silly saying 'vagina' (and she hates that anyway), and I can't say 'cunt' because of James. And I can't say 'fanny' because of all the lads in the Thrupenny-Bit-Kiosk gang, who said it every other word. One of them used it instead of commas. He did really. He said it at least as often as he said 'fuck'. And he said that all the time.

I'm a bit too far gone, feeling all passionate; so's she, and there we are, no words. 'You've got a beautiful blah de blah de blah,' I said. Then we both started laughing, though really it was no laughing matter, was it, and do you know, we couldn't do it that night. I started laughing and she started laughing, and you know how your hands go all weak if you laugh too much? Well, mine did and they were all floppy, my fingers, I mean. And that was that. Well, that time anyway.

It's not that I spent all my time in bed with Dee, well, I would have if I could, but we couldn't because of work and such, no, I mean, it's not that we spent all our time in bed, talking. It's just that there were times when I really did want to say something lovely, and being as I'm no poet that wasn't simple.

I mean, I have never laughed so much in my life in bed as I have laughed with Dee. I never dreamt it could be so much fun.

First of all I'd had all those years wanting babies and having to do it for His fun and no babies.

Then I had months, no, it must have been years actually, if I added it up, yes, years, when I had to do it and I was afraid all the time of having babies.

Years of eating chemicals for His sake, then chemicals for my sake. Almost two years. What sort of a choice is it anyway: pregnancy or cancer?

No wonder that some women who know they don't want children turn lesbian. It's obvious, isn't it? I mean, what *is* the point otherwise with men, unless you have to? I'm not stupid, and I can't see it myself.

The thing that gets me is that no one ever says that being a lesbian is the best form of contraception. I have ploughed through all the agony pages of women's magazines for years and I have never seen it written.

Dear Desperate of Densley,
Has it ever occurred to you that the answer to all your birth control problems might lie in a woman's arms?
Think on. Yours, Aunt Agnes.

Things would be a bit different.

So when I met Mol and I heard that she did it once, just once to get Pol, and I see how happy they all are living there, the three of them, give or take the odd visit from Corrine, you know what I mean, well, when I heard that my mouth fell right open and stuck. 'Shut your mouth, a bus is coming,' said Pol. So I did. But I was thinking that I could have done what Mol did to get a baby, and I'd never have needed James at all. If only the school nurse had said!

Just because we're not up in London on demos and meetings and such, doesn't mean we don't talk about it.

I like most sorts of it with Dee. I never knew there were so many kinds of it. And I was no novice. I mean He had made me try everything hadn't he? As *He* saw it. He had books of pictures. He used to try them out on me. I won't bore you with the details. I need to talk about *those* like I need a hole in the head.

But I was new to women. So I was new to me.

I didn't even know that I've got a super sex spot behind my right shoulder blade. In fact, I've got dozens of super sex spots when I'm in bed with Dee. I couldn't begin to count. I don't need to. I do draw the line at some things, and so does she. It's not 'orgasm at any price' you know, in our bed. I should say not. That's how men see it.

James was a turd. It did take me a long time to realise that, being as how well I was trained not to see it, you know. But better late than never. But once I saw him for what he was, I was on the way out, so to speak. I mean, if he'd been a bit softer, not hard as nails as his mother once said (mind you, that surprised me because mothers don't

166

normally say that about their sons) any road, if James had been one of those gentle ones, like you see on BBC2 plays full of nice middle-class people (I do watch them sometimes, if I want a bit of moving wallpaper); well, then, if he'd been nice and gentle, I don't know how much longer I'd have been poisoning my body to satisfy his needs.

So, in a way, coming through with no babies was the making of me really. Dreams change.

James made me read umpteen magazines. Porn. Only over the years they changed. Much harder. I don't mean he bought different ones. I mean the usual ones went very nasty. They had women and girls writing in them. About how they liked the rough stuff. I thought it was horrible. It seemed like degradation to me. Getting into pain. Painful positions, painful clothes. Men using weapons on women.

Oh, James loved reading about all that stuff. He really got off on it. My bet is that those BBC2 TV types do as well. Trendies. They'll get into anything just for the kicks. Whose kicks? I couldn't see any of that as liberating and I still don't.

Dee was never into any of that. Neither am I.

James liked power. No doubt about that. So it stands to reason he got into all that. That's all I'm saying.

I can't imagine behaving in any ways in bed with Dee that might get her or me into pain. I'd go without sex or affection for the rest of my life rather than go back to men or get into pain, know what I mean?

But there are times when I've got the hots for her, or she's got the hots for me, and gentleness is just not enough. Times when the mood changes and I want her fingers or tongue, or both (I'm greedy, I admit it), harder on me or in me for a while. Same with her. Whew. That takes some saying, doesn't it? You bet somebody who hears that'll get me all wrong and that's their problem. I know what I mean and I don't mean pain, okay?

I heard this Bible-basher in Southampton once. He said gay people were an anathema to him. I went home and looked that up. It means hatred. He was giving out these tracts down by the market. I spat on his foot as I went past. Then, a bit further on, I found one of them blown away in the gutter. 'That's where it belongs,' I thought, but I was curious so I picked it up. Made my blood run hot. How they hate us.

It did me good, though. Made me realise that I'm not even going to try to make out a case for us.

What I'm saying is that the problem is that lot and their super-hatred, not us lot and our lives. It's been very hard to keep the hatred outside me. It creeps in sideways, like round the corners, you know.

Like when I'm in bed with Dee, and I'm rising high, just about to come, and porn comes up in my head and I could scream. I'm so angry. I know where the damn stuff comes from. I know how hard it is to get rid of it, don't I? I've had a lot of rubbish to get out of my head, and not only porn.

I don't want my sex life now to be like sex with James in any way do I? That means everything. Time, caring, loving, keeping promises, feeling safe, feeling free, laughing, oh, everything.

There is absolutely no comparison, for me.

We are superordinarysurvivors, aren't we?

The number of times I've been to bed with Dee, and fallen asleep supertired. Just a peck on the ear and then land of nod. No hassle.

We can't plan it. Any sort of it. It doesn't work like that for us. Planning's a sure dead cert for superfail. All worked up. Great Expectations. If Dickens only knew, he'd never have called it that. But I don't expect Dickens was an expert on lesbian love. I bet Mrs Dickens was. I bet she did it with the woman next door while he was up in the attic writing his *Great Expectations*. Well, the thing is, she'd have known that Great Expectations is sure cert failure. With him or without him.

Well, at first Dee and me were so passionate that I didn't worry too much. My life with James was shoved to the back of my head. I was into Dee in a big way. Nothing in my head in bed except her body. Dee's body is quite enough to fill my head to overflow. *Huh. Whoo.* The first year I just didn't care. I was everything unafraid.

Like I'd come from work and she'd have been on earlies and be out up the allotment. So I'd be sitting rocking, cuppa and Tibs, feet up and she'd come in. Come and bend over me and kiss me. Now when Dee does that in shorts, it puts her blahdeblah on the level with my eyes and nose. And me eyes are fixed there, like they can't move. My heart's going, and Joanna, you know down there, well she wakes up and she's up and going hello? hello? Is that Dee there? And all I can think of is lying on the floor right there and then and waiting for it. I mean waiting. It was worth waiting for.

Next time, out of the skies, or rather out of Dee's face would come this smile that would make my finger-ends itch. I could hardly wait to get my hands on her. I didn't care. I knew what I wanted and it was her. Blahdeblah and all. And she was not at all complaining, was she? I knew all the times when she made small noises in her throat and they meant go inside, and all the times when it meant go slower, go softer, oh all that, know what I mean?

I knew when she was going to be like waves on a beach, one after the other and the times when she was going to superslide. You know, right off the top of the mountains and down to the sea, no stopping. And hit the ocean and vumph, float, till she was asleep.

It was our second year together, after the hell row about the holiday, that my head began to let trickles through. I started having the Big Doubts.

Oh, don't get me wrong. I never thought of going back. I'm not stupid. I just mean I was confused, wasn't I?

And it was my second year with Dee, that James and porn came through. Well, one night we were in bed. She was kissing me all over. Nothing. I couldn't hide or pretend. She knew me much too well. How could I share a bed with her for over a year and suddenly start faking. I couldn't with a woman, not with a woman like Dee.

So I was lying there, all cold inside and frightened. All the fears all there at once. And confusions. Oh, heaps and heaps of the damn things. Heaps and heaps. Did this mean I didn't love her? Didn't she really want me? If she did want me, wouldn't I just know. Shouldn't that be enough to make it all work? Didn't I want her? If I did, wouldn't I just know? Shouldn't that be enough to solve it?

What I'd have *liked* would have been to leap out of bed, laugh a bit, hahaha hey: 'Guess what, I've, er, got this er . . . sexual identity problem.'

Only I couldn't, so I just lay there.

She suddenly got off the bed and put on her dressing gown.

'What are you doing, Dee?'

'Will you get up, Lotte, sweetheart?'

She threw me my dressing-gown.

'What d'you mean, get up?'

'I mean get up, sweetheart, please. I'm no astronaut, Lotte, but I know when there's no lift-off and it's not the first time. Get up, please.'

'All right. All right. I heard you,' I grumbled, feeling superguilty and superfrustrated.

'Tea or coffee?' She was half way down the stairs.

'Double whisky more like,' I muttered.

'Not bloody likely. We need to be sober. Tea or coffee?'

'Tea.' I made a point of not saying 'please'.

Sounds a bit odd, looking back, and even at that time it *was* funny. It was half past one in the morning and she'd been caressing my body for ages. She'd been, as they say, raring to go, when we'd gone to bed. Now, I had a pout long as the pier and she looked . . . determined.

There we were, huddled by the remains of the back-room fire, having our first serious sex-talk. Reminded me of the time when me and Beryl Green, the teenage motor-cycle champ, got it together to go out into the country to look at each other's blahdeblahs. As it happened, we didn't. We just kept our clothes on and practised kissing in the warm grass, so as we'd know what to do when we got boyfriends.

'I get confused, Dee. Confused for wanting it. I get worried, you know, I'm femme or summat.'

'What about when I just lie there panting for you?'

'I get confused then, too. Like I'm butch or summat.'

'What about when we both want it all?'

'Oh, that's okay. I get too far gone to worry.' I had to laugh. 'Then I panic after,' I added, shy as a first date. 'But I get frightened, Dee. It comes over me, how much I want you and you want me, and I get frightened. Really frightened.'

'So do I. So does Corrine with Mol.'

'I didn't know. I thought it was well, maybe, us new ones that were unsure.'

'I'm not that tough, Lotte. Not inside. None of us are. Not if we think about it. It's just we don't all say so.'

'About sex?'

'Yeah. Sometimes about sex. There's nothing out there to help us. Men hate us, if they know; other women are terrified, if they know. Most people in Coombebury don't know why you and I live here, or even that we do live here. Being brave *all* the time. I have to give up on it sometimes. A holiday. From being brave.'

'You get scared, too, about sex? You really mean that?'

'Yeah.'

'How?'

'I can't explain it all that well. I've been wanting to say but I didn't know how. I think a lot, draw a lot, but I don't find words that easy. You know, when you take me up, you know, tops of the mountains, my paintings, the ones with all the colours?'

'Yes. They were lovely. I never had anybody in my whole life make me anything like that . . .'

'It was easier for me in paintings. It always was. Words are harder, much harder. But I think if we're moving along, together, we've got to look at these fears. And you were just lying there, and I knew it wasn't good. I have times when I'm scared, and I think it's better in the open.'

'Dee, I love you. I think it's better out in the open, too. What you afraid of, Dee?'

170

'Lies. It goes way back. The biggest lie I told myself was that I was all right celibate.'

'You mean you weren't all right?'

'I coped. I don't want to again. So I'm afraid of liking sex too much, wanting it too much. I don't want you jumping through hoops as you put it, sweetheart, but you can't have just the fearless bits in me. Otherwise I'm pretending, aren't I?'

'You're not afraid of the roles thing, like me, are you?'

'No. Never have been. I like being all of it too much.'

'So do I, Dee. I feel much better already, Dee. I don't want you to have to pretend. We were down on the beach, right? and I said about hoops, and all.' She nodded. 'Well, what I meant was that I can't *prove* that I'm staying around. I am, staying, I mean, but you'll only know that when I've stayed, won't you? I do know you're scared. You're bound to be. Like you said, nobody's that tough. If you was that tough, Dee, you'd never have let yourself in for this relationship.'

'Do you want some more tea, sweetheart?'

'No. Think I'd like cocoa. Shall we go back to bed to sleep now?'

So we did.

There were plenty more talks after that. It really opened up. If she couldn't talk, she painted it. I loved her doing that. Wouldn't you? If a woman like Dee painted these amazing colours and said she found the colours inside all the loving.

After that first time, then, the next time she was in a state, I dared to say, 'Dee, here's your dressing-gown, will you get up now?' I felt the bee's knees. I knew I could do something for her, help her talk it out.

It especially helped me when Dee said that we all get scared, even the tough ones do. I need someone that won't make me feel silly and won't get more afraid, just because I'm having a downer, don't I? Besides, when you've been there in the pits, really terrified that you are wrong inside, bad or mad, and you get through again, that makes you stronger. Well, I think so anyway. Cups of tea at one in the morning, and all.

I became angry, sometimes very angry. We had to find it all from inside us, all the beauty, the sexual loving. To keep it alive and wonderful, to overcome our fears, to make something new against all the odds. And we did.

There was laughter, too. Like the time I said: 'Besides, you didn't go without sex for ever, did you, Dee? Eventually you started to masturbate again, didn't you?'

'I know that on my good days. On the bad ones I forget.'

'What, how to masturbate?'

We started to laugh. As if any woman could forget how to masturbate. Masturbation's like learning to ride a bike. Even if you haven't been on a bike for ages, you soon remember when you get going.

My body was changing. Opening out. I found passion in me I never knew I had. Energy. My hips widened, my breasts grew larger.

Pictures from James' books came at me sideways. I learned to talk them out of me. It would take a long time. We had time.

The months became years. Passing fast or slow. Like Dee said, seeds on a dandelion clock.

Esther, April 1983

Sunday, 10 April: early morning

I had a dream last night about a valley. At first in the dream, the clouds were hanging low over some huge entrance stones. Then the midnight sky cleared from the earth, right out into deep space. I could see the moon, and called the place, Moon Valley.

There were women talking in ones and twos, and none seemed afraid of being out at night. I didn't see any men in the valley, in my dream.

My mum was there, running a pottery. It was in an eight-sided building with a part that jutted out long and quite narrow like a pan handle. I could hear plenty of laughter around where Mum was working.

Then it was dawn, very deep red across wide sand dunes, which seemed to be to the east side of the valley. There were dogs barking and cats stalking, and I could hear someone putting out milk bottles.

Then it changed, like dreams do, suddenly. In another part of the valley there was a group, black women and white women, sitting around, singing by a tree – a strange tree with evergreen leaves, but paler than any evergreen I've seen. Something like apple green mixed to pale silver green. The leaves were being collected in a net spread on the ground underneath. That surprised me, since the tree was definitely evergreen.

Mum came along then with one of her pots. Instantly we flipped back into the kitchen in Densley, and she was mashing tea, in an old fat-bellied teapot.

'I got these off the Hope Tree. You know it's like magic mushrooms, Essie.'

I can remember being in two layers then. I was listening to Mum, and I was thinking alongside that, separately. I've found I do that in dreams sometimes. I was thinking: I didn't know Mum ever had magic mushrooms.

It switched again. Back to the valley. Women were sitting by a bonfire beyond the dunes on the east shore, just after the spring festivities, waiting for the singing to begin. They were sipping Hope tea, made from the evergreen leaves, and it was being served out of the big brown teapot, by my mum.

'Hope tea is near to ecstasy,' whispered a woman in my right ear, 'better even than going into warm grass with a woman-lover.'

Then I woke up.

Sunday, 10 April. Afternoon

Have spent all morning thinking, and writing. Did some knitting too, drank endless swigs of coffee, hot and strong, wishing it was Hope tea. Disturbed by that dream, because of its layers and layers of meanings, possible meanings anyway. It won't fade. The place, the tree, and the hope and the women.

I wonder how Christine Shipley is this morning. No, I'm not going to try to contact her. We both still hurt too much. Remembered conversations rush through folds in my brain, today.

I met her a while after we had started the group for the after-school activities club. Chris was in the last few months of her clinical training. I broke my leg, and she set it in plaster for me. She was hoping, after she'd finished her training, to specialise in psychiatry, which she went on to do.

She invited me to her place for dinner.

Her flat was the exact opposite to mine. It was high up, looking out over roof tops, near the radio mast at Crystal Palace. She shared it with two other women.

They were out the night I went to dinner, and stayed.

Oh I remember how we talked, she and I. She'd come from the slums of Liverpool, and had run away to London when she was eighteen. She'd done so many jobs I could hardly keep count. She sent money home so that her younger sister Jenny wouldn't have to leave school at sixteen, as she had done, even though she had eight O-levels. Her father was in poor health and the family all depended on her mother's wages.

Then her mother's health had broken down too and when Chris was twenty-two she went back there to look after the two youngest children with Jenny, who had just finished A-levels. Chris loved Jenny dearly, and was grieved to the core when she decided to marry instead of going to Liverpool University. A year later Chris's mother died. The strange thing was that Jenny then turned round and said she and her husband would take their dad off Chris's hands, if Chris would stay and see the two younger ones to the end of school.

'Funny the way life sends you the unexpected, Ess. It ended up with me and the youngest two all doing our A-levels together. And we all passed. All three of us. I did physics, chemistry and biology. I knew how much work there was ahead of me. But I was older and I'd become clear, by then. I'd seen so much suffering. Not just physical Ess. Mental. My dad was in bits after my mum died. He was sort of senile in middle age. Though his body was aged, because his health had been so bad.

'So I came to London, to the best medical school I could find. I didn't want children. I'd done my bit in that direction. I didn't want men. I wanted my own career.'

'Your Brilliant Career. It's like the book, Chris. It's a wonderful story. It really really is.'

I was in love with her from that evening, and it seems that from the start it was mutual and it was doomed. The power and the waste of that thunder and lightning: beautiful energy, and all you get is dead trees.

Could the Hope tree possibly be me, or was I the lightning, or the thunder? Didn't Chris always say I tried too hard to analyse things? There was a beautiful tree where we used to picnic out in Essex.

Its dead trunk was bleached white by the sun and wind, and its insides were still charred from the strike of fire in the storm that sliced it in two. Its roots were huge, still firmly in the soil, and we would lean up against it, feeling its warmth on our backs. There we would eat and talk, and I'd learn the new language which she spoke so often and so fluently.

'Can you relate to my wanting to be rich, Ess?'

We were eating melon slices at the time, and all my erotic senses were on sparkle-alert. Five stars. I wanted her to smile. I loved her smile. She'd sparkle too with it, dazzling my mind, and my thoughts would chase each other quickly, subscriber trunk dialled, straight-through connections. My palms would itch there in public for the feel of her breasts. Relate was a new word and I didn't quite understand it, but if I used it, it would make her smile.

'I can relate to your struggle for education,' I said, 'and to your need to be secure around money.'

'That's significant then,' she replied. Significant was a word I came to use. Came to use was a new phrase too. Privately I called it psycho-speak because I knew it came from the psychiatrists she mixed with. I never told her that. I tried to speak it fast like her.

'I love falling in love with you Ess. I never loved falling so much for any woman until now.'

'Falling usually means pieces,' I laughed. It came out like a slice of high-speed dazzle and we laughed and laughed because we didn't believe we'd end up, either of us, like we did, in pieces.

In London we used to dine out with Veronica, a lesbian friend of Chris, who was from a wealthy medical family; and who regularly lent us her cottage in Essex. In London also I began to meet other friends of Chris.

I'd already made friends with Mary and Janet who I'd originally met in the working-class women's group, and who were now, both of them, out as lesbian-feminists in the women's movement, and now in a relationship with each other.

However, I had an amber light in my head. It cautioned me that I was not yet ready to be 'out' with Mary and Janet, though I was longing to be. But it was such a huge leap for me, that I wanted to be more sure of myself and I evaded any possible questions from them.

Chris neither wanted to go to lesbian clubs on the non-political scene; nor to be part of lesbian-feminist groups or collectives. So we never went to women-only events together, and I missed her whenever I went with Mary and Janet.

As far as work was concerned I kept quiet about my newly discovered sexuality. I thought I knew what kind of reception I'd get if I announced my sexuality in Reeve Juniors; and I decided it would be just as hostile in the after-school activities club planning group. There were sometimes anti-lesbian jokes in that group and I didn't know how to start confronting all that.

It was easy to lie to Nell about my weekends away from my flat, because I was heavily involved in union activities and I would say, if I was asked, that I was at weekend meetings, socials, or conferences. It all seemed plausible. I almost had myself convinced that it was for real. So, I didn't trust myself to share my new lifestyle with either Nell or Laura, and apart from seeing Laura three or four times a year in the same way as before, and Nell almost daily which was normal, I let myself become isolated. I lived for Chris and through Chris and sometimes I had glimpses of resentment. I pushed them away, telling myself how lucky I was to be in that relationship.

'I love my work you know, Ess. I know it makes me seem hard sometimes. I do try to face that. I don't want to trample all over you as you say. Really I don't. I want you to understand things from my point of view. I need you to. I need that from you like I need good food, nutrition. Basic. For my mental well-being. I need a lover who will try to put herself in my shoes when I'm interacting all day in a world of men. Can you begin to imagine how I'd stand, in male psychiatry, if they knew I was a lesbian? I'd get no family work; I'd get no children's work; and they'd not let me near a man in case I magicked his balls off or something.'

We both began to laugh then, scalpel-edged laughter, imagining how easy it would be for women if all we had to do was a little magic and make a world devoid of rapists. How I loved her then for trying to tussle with it all. It seemed so much harder for her than for me. To get to the top and stay there. However brilliant and beautiful she was, she was a female trying to aim for the top in the study of mental health. I wanted her to succeed because I wanted women to be pioneers. But she didn't see herself as a pioneer.

'There you are again Ess, on a crusade. I'm not political like you. I care about people, all people. I want people to be healthy in their minds as well as in their bodies. But I'm not doing this for men-people or women-people. I don't really divide human beings up like that. That's what you have to realise about me Ess. I love women, of course I do. I love you, as a woman, dearly . . .'

'Good. I'm glad . . .'

'You don't doubt that, surely?'

'No-oh. No, of course not Chris. How could I after last night, all the nights?'

'Don't forget the mornings. I often think mornings are the best times, especially when it's sunny outside and it filters through the curtains.'

'Yes. I never made love before in a room with light-coloured curtains. Even with the linings the sun streams in. It's wonderful. So are you. I am trying to understand. The gaps seem so wide sometimes, that's all.'

'Well, of course they do, darling. We're very very different individuals. We'd be bored out of our brains if we were alike in everything surely? I think that's what intrigued me so when I first met you. I'm damn glad I hadn't started my houseman place in the mental hospital before you broke your leg.'

'I'm glad I broke my leg.'

We both laughed again. She teased that it was probably an early warning sign. Serious mental disorder. I tried to laugh. Succeeded. But the joke must have frightened me deep down (or high up somewhere in the parts of my brain where I kept my secret fears or something), because it filtered through in dreams. About that time I read Marge Piercy's *Woman On The Edge of Time*. My dreams became a jumble of hopes and fears about women, mental hospitals and sexuality. Always, running through them, was an unease between myself and Chris. At weekends, in Essex, sometimes, I would watch myself start a conversation about all of this.

'Don't you think, Chris, that if Freud had stuck to his original hunches, things would have been better?'

'How come?'

'Because he started off believing the girls when they told him about their experiences with their fathers. Incest.'

'But his job was to look at the unconscious.'

'Yes. And they were telling him their conscious experiences, and he decided it must be fantasy, because it was so awful.'

'Look, Essie, we're on holiday. It's a lovely day. Why don't we leave Reeve Juniors and my hospital behind. We're both tired, and I need to take a break from Freud.'

'It's a pity we haven't got time to talk it all through, Chris, because Freud meant a lot to me at college, all his dream theory and so forth. I don't want to throw it all out. All right, all right, I heard you. Holiday from thinking, okay? You're right, it is a lovely day. Come on.'

Sometimes we resolved the differences in our attitudes by going to bed and making love. Then, sex would be especially good and happy for both of us, and we'd both feel in harmony with each other again. We'd forget that we'd ever disagreed, or that either of us had felt let down or unfulfilled. I'd mislead myself into believing that we did agree, deep down, really, where it mattered, because sex was whole.

London was work, busy-ness, hustle and bustle, timetables and schedules for both Chris and myself. The cottage was playtime. We played house, and played 'relationships'. It gave us time, and a safe place, a snug romantic nest. We needed that, having searched a long time to find each other, without necessarily knowing that we were searching.

The car journeys back to London became tense transitions back to the world of work where we were both surrounded by heterosexuals and all their assumptions about us as single women living alone, who must surely be looking for men.

I had gone to Reeve Juniors in the first place because the staff had written policies on anti-racist, anti-sexist teaching.

All of us worked our butts off to write, re-write, design and re-design the books, work cards, library resources, and all our visual aids such as pictures, slides and charts. We did this at weekends and in our so called holidays. We loved it. It was a challenge to reflect the lives of all the children in Reeve school, not just the white ones, and to get far far away from the old style teaching where Jane is in the kitchen with mummy and Peter is in the garage with daddy.

Our books had single parents, black and white children, boys and girls doing the housework and using and mending machines. Our girls were active lively and strong.

But. There was always the but. I dare not challenge the fact that everyone in the world of Reeve school's teaching was heterosexual. I was seen as an outspoken active feminist. I lived alone. I went to women's meetings. The whole atmosphere in Reeve Juniors seemed anti-lesbian, anti-gay.

In the cottage and on the long walks by estuaries, in marshlands and along sea walls, I avoided those topics that brought out the tension in Chris and the dis-agreements in our outlooks, including the fact that I wanted my lesbianism to be open within the women's liberation movement. I'd come to an understanding of, recognition of, my sexuality after I'd become a feminist, but Chris hadn't, and did not want my politics near her mind, or her body, or her soul.

For me it was all linked, and so it crept in beside me in bed. I'd be in the middle of making love to Chris, or be rising fine with her tongue between my thighs, and suddenly I'd think of some feminist book I'd like her to read so that we could talk about it; or some lesbian group I'd heard of with a great new campaign, and I'd stop rising, as if a weaving goddess somewhere had dropped a stitch or something. Oops.

I've always laughed a lot in bed, and with Chris it was easy to have fun. So we did have lots of laughter. How many times have I heard Grandma Clegg utter a silent curse (when she thought us children weren't listening) because she was trying to pick up a stitch in a complicated Aran jumper? In the cottage some stitches remained unpicked, unravelling slowly downwards. And we both knew it, though we tried to pretend we didn't, because we loved each other, and desired and needed each other.

Sunday morning in Veronica's cottage in Essex. We were reading the Sunday papers and eating croissants, an occasional treat. Chris brought in a huge pot of real coffee just as I finished a review of a new book that some man had just written about psychoanalysis and sexuality.

'Have you seen this?' I asked.

'Mmm. Thought I'd get it when I'm off on Tuesday.'

'Oh.'

'What's the matter, Ess?'

'It doesn't mention gays or lesbians, not in this review anyway. You'd think they'd move on, wouldn't you. We could do with some positive work, really. By women, for women.'

'What's wrong with a man writing?'

I saw the warning signs. Decided this was *it*, we had to have it all in the open.

'Well I don't see how any man is going to have a cat's chance in hell trying to understand about female sexuality. They've got too much to lose Chris. It's like, well, expecting one of the bosses to write a workers' tract, or something.'

'I know some excellent men in this work, Esther.' (My heavens, this is it, I thought, she's used my full name, that means let battle commence.) 'I am bone tired of your assumptions that male psychiatrists are out to get us.'

'They are certainly out to keep us heterosexual. It amazes me that you can't see that.'

'You're simply wrong, and you don't know this field, not as I do. You are overlooking my years and years of work.'

'No I'm not. I cannot see why you won't challenge the fact that well, Freud, for example, a fairly famous example, didn't believe that men could actually abuse their power. So he made their actions into women's fantasies. You can't get more male than that. It's a typical male ploy. I'm not saying that he's to blame for the whole works but there are women who've had some dreadful things done to them. Lesbians they try to straighten out, things like that. Somebody should take responsibility for criticising that. Whereas this review I've just read does no such thing. There's no sense that there might, just might be a problem. You know what's been done in Freud's name, to lesbians and all the others. He had a hell of a lot of power, Christine.'

I was shaking from the unexpected length of my outburst and the fact that I'd deliberately initiated this confrontation.

She had a body change. From having come in all soft and open after our love-making, and doing her warm friendly actions with the coffee, as if I were truly a delight to wait upon, she was now granite-faced, and her shoulders would have held up the entire BMA buildings like one of those female statues you sometimes see around London.

'My God, Esther, you're arrogant sometimes. You've been a lesbian for all of two minutes' (I gasped, as if she was a surgeon and I was a patient and I'd had no anaesthetic), 'and you start analysing me out of existence. How dare you?'

'Because I love your existence. If you didn't exist I'd not be in this relationship.'

'I'm tired of the constant challenges Esther.'

'But you said yourself there should be challenge.'

'Not all the time for heaven's sake. I get it all the time in my work.'

'So do I, come to that. From the children and from the staff room. I sometimes wonder how all of us at Reeve Juniors cope with all the challenges there.'

'That's as maybe, Esther. I'm not a teacher. I'm not assuming to comment on your staff room. That's why I get so angry when you assume you can comment on my work.'

We both paused for breath. I didn't know how to go on, which way to take it next.

She said: 'I need a bit of peace and quiet sometimes. Work wipes me out. You know that. And I love you. I just cannot take much more pressure from inside' (she waved her hand in a circle from me to her and back again) 'from inside this, us. All this pressure is driving me to the edge.' She stopped abruptly realising that my thoughts were momentarily outside the cottage, outside her words. I was thinking of the bird sanctuaries near the marshlands. She waited, as I realised we were in for a long session and that although I had started it, I was unsure of direction, but I needed to tell her that image.

'With you I have learned the names and songs and cries of the birds of these marshes. Bird sanctuaries. Birds I never recognised before, only heard, without understanding, or naming. And sometimes I feel so full of delight and joy with you' (she started to cry silently) 'learning about myself naming, moving forward. Recognising just like we did together in the bird sanctuary. I love analysis of friendship, of relationships but when I try to link work, yours and mine, with my new name, lesbian, it hurts you. And when I don't, it hurts me.'

She nodded, wiping her eyes with her sleeve, a gesture very loveable and intimate, which I couldn't imagine her ever doing at work.

'When I leave work, Essie' (I noticed the name change) 'I need to really leave. Walk away and forget until I'm next on rota. If I had the hours away from my work that you have free from yours, then maybe I could cope better with the heart-searching. About your work and mine. But I can't . . . I'm exhausted.'

181

'Then why on earth did you choose a complex difficult woman like me?'

'Desire. I fell in love with you, Essie. I wanted you. I still do. You know that, even if we do both drop stitches as you call it. But I don't desire all this analytical stuff. Not in my private life. I still love you just as much. And I've no doubt that you love me.'

'Of course I do. There is no doubt about that. But I also love the whole idea and excitement of women's liberation, the movement, the campaigns, the debates. Especially now that I call myself a lesbian. To myself. To you and your friends. You have loved women for a long long time. I love you for that, Chris.' (She noticed the name change. We reached to one another and touched hands. But we were well beyond falling into bed to solve this one. We both were acutely aware of that.) 'I know you think I'm too quick to judge, a bit over enthusiastic on the feminism. It's part of my urgency because of the route I took to becoming a lesbian. But I love you and your lesbian friends, Chris. Really I do.' (I was now the one to cry softly, as I was speaking.) 'Who am I to harangue you about definitions, boundaries, or naming. You've been calling yourself a lesbian for years.'

'I love you for all your enthusiasms, Ess. And I do respect you for the politics in your friendship with Laura, and with Nell, and the women on Reeve Green. But for me personally I have to maintain a gap between work time and time off. You know what my hours are like. Houseman placements are always like this. I treat people all day whose lives are all over the place. Individuals in fragments, their minds unfocused, their hearts broken, and *all* their boundaries blurred. I have to keep my realities steady in the middle of all that. Or it will be me in pieces, no use to any one. You had a choice too, Essie. You knew what work I was about to embark on when we first met.'

'I fell in love too. And now it doesn't feel like a choice. I'm in a quandry. Your needs or mine.'

'I'm not trying to put it like that.'

'That's how it feels though, whatever you are trying to do.'

'I'm trying to love my work and love you Essie, everyday.'

'I'm not peace and quiet enough for you, Chris.'

'I'm not political enough for you Essie.'

'I'm angry about class and poverty and the social reasons why you have patients in that hospital in the first place. That anger needs expression.'

'Of course it does. I'm not denying that. My job is to care about and treat the individuals who need me there in that hospital. I cannot and will not take on the world. You might do that. But that is not what I want. And the pressure of what you want makes it harder for me, harder everyday.'

'And I cannot bear it that you see the world only in terms of you as an individual and other people only as individuals. I know I'm an individual but I'm part of groups too, and I know which groups are on my side and which groups are not, most definitely not. No, I'll change that. I mean I'm learning about such things, and I want to be talking with other lesbians who are learning those things too. Not stuck out in the wilds of nowhere listening to bloody birdsong and not even having as much voice as me feathered bloody friends. It's getting to me. I know there's another world out there for lesbians and I want to be part of it.'

We were both shaking and crying by then. Even our crying mirrored our differences. Mine was boo-hooing and full of desperately noisy snuffles, and hers was silent, with quiet tears, as if she wanted peace even while she was grieving.

Never in any of my previous crying had my skin hurt as if I were a pin-cushion stuck full of sharp steel ends. It did then, in the cottage. The crying lasted, for both of us, almost all day. We kept looking at each other, as we passed, on the way to the kitchen for more coffee, or to the toilet to let it run through, and the tears ran the questions down our faces, over our chins and sogged into our clothes. If she'd touched me she'd have pushed the pins further in, and the physical pain was already acute. So she didn't touch me and we couldn't ask or answer each other any more. Yet we couldn't leave either. The cottage would have to hold us both until we'd cried it out and I think both of us knew that.

Then by some evil sympathy the rain outside started, pouring streams down the cottage windows, while inside, our tears enclosed us in a globule of salt-soaked time.

I had a foolish image of us then, that I can still remember. It was of a little glass dome, no more than three inches high, with a plastic base, that Lotte was given one Christmas. It had some people and a cottage and was full of liquid. It made a snowstorm when you shook it and then the snow settled again.

Outside our cottage the rain fell, sheets of it slanting until the bushes dripped as if shaken in that toy of Lotte's. I was trapped in the cottage with my lover, and we were splitting down the middle though the rainstorm outside had no thunder or lightning. It didn't need to. We provided our own.

That was two summers ago. Since then, I've been on my own. There have been many different layers of thinking since then. I became furious with her, going over and over the argument in my mind, taping and re-playing the tape.

I blamed her and I called that betrayal. I couldn't bring myself to talk to anyone about it.

But, after a few months when the immediate loss was receding, and I was used to being without sex, and even without hugs, I found that other emotions were coming through.

I started to examine closely that word I'd used too easily – the word 'betrayal'.

I had to ask myself a few hard questions about what I'd been up to, about relationships between women, sexual and non-sexual, and even more about the ways in which we give ourselves away, and let one another down.

It was difficult for me to sort some of it out. I decided to go and talk to another lesbian who was also a therapist. A Christine that was not like Christine. Not at all into male psychiatry. Instead, she provided me with a chance to learn for myself about *my* questions, *my* definitions, *my* anger, *my* labels, and whether I wanted them or needed them. I had five sessions with her, to help me through the crisis.

This time, this April, I want to go through this on my own. I've never used my diary quite like this before, but it *is* helping me. Finally, I've stopped giving Chris even more power by blaming her. Instead, I feel as if her survival methods are merely very different from my own. I still think she's completely up the creek about Freud and male psychiatry. But I don't think she could have had power over me, if I hadn't stood by and given it away. Our betrayals were mutual and complicated.

Just because she's a survivor in a man's world, doesn't make her bad. But it does mean, if her methods and mine aren't compatible, that the warp thread *is* broken, can't be mended, and we can't be lovers or even friends again. And, it's probably just as bad for her to be near me. In other words, I'm bad for her too. Wow. That one hurts. I like to think I'm good for everyone, usually. But I'm not. I'm a human jumble, like lots of us. If I'm nearer to understanding *that*, then I must be nearer to finding out who I am and what I want. That's a start. That's hope, and growth.

I used to think of Chris Shipley as a central person. When I first thought about Chris and weaving, I saw her as a central thread. Now I don't. She was important once. She's important now because I think

I've learned so much about myself through all this. Perhaps any lesbian's first relationship, if it's a deep one, is like this. Probably different for each woman.

I still haven't told Nell that I'm a lesbian. I'm not ready. It has to be *my* timing. I have to cope with the consequences. I haven't told Mum yet, either, or Laura, and of course, I haven't written to Lotte. So I *am* hiding, lying, and yet, through the unravelling, I know that these four women – Mum, Lotte, Laura and Nell – are my central threads.

Lotte, 1979

When I was married to James I couldn't stand those romantic novels where the story ends with them getting together. I didn't know how the hell they managed when they had rows; what kinds of things niggled them; even how they managed through illness and money.

I decided to live with Dee because she fascinated me. I thought there was enough going for both of us to make it possible to set up home together, and I knew she was never ever going to sleep with a man.

It was all very well saying *that*, but the real part of loving – beyond just being in love and wanting to leap into bed, which we did, usually when we least expected it – no, I mean, the real part of loving was working it all out together every day.

We were not just good friends. I fancied her like crazy and she fancied me. Sexual love was part of our lives. But it was not all there was. She said, 'It's just a part, Lotte, not the be-all and end-all.'

I wasn't about to get on a soapbox like our Ess would. I'm not the type at all. But I'd changed over the years and I began to feel that living in Coombebury was not giving me enough chances to meet and talk to other lesbians. It'd been such a change from being het, and I couldn't find anywhere to ask *my* questions. Know what I mean? Like well there was the V and A and Corrine but they were in another world, so were Mol, Pol and Micky, in a different way. I mean, you couldn't get much more different than those two households, could you, money and class-wise, but I could no more talk to Micky about her being married to Pol, I mean married, than I could to the V and A about money. So I was between the devil and the deep blue sea, so to speak.

So after the novelty wore off with Dee and we started to look at the relationship, and how we might want to change it, I thought back to all the changes in my life. Then I wasn't content to keep quiet and get on with things the way Dee and Dora had had to. I knew I didn't *have* to. There were other lesbians like me around if I could find them.

Well, I knew of a couple of clubs up in London where lesbians went, and I knew of one or two women's bookshops, didn't I? So I asked Dee if she'd come with me. For a weekend on the razzle, so to speak. Night on the town, go to a good show, on to a lesbian club.

'You sure you want this, Lotte? I thought you couldn't be doing with all the politics and such like?'

'I can't. I'm not about to get me green wellies and stripey jumper and go on demos, but I'd like to have a good bop and a good *read*, Dee. And I'd like to go to a real lesbian club. Just now and again. Feel part of it, you know?'

So off we went to London for the Big Weekend.

Well, it would have been better if we hadn't both come on, on the Thursday before, but at least that got rid of the premenstrual heebee jeebies. I mean, two of you with the PMT's no joke. One is quite enough but we always come on together. Dee says it's a common thing for women-lovers. I can't get over that. I never ever heard of that while I was married. I like it, except for the PMTs.

I was on the phone to Dee once and I felt myself start and I said to her, 'Hey, Dee, I've started. Have you?'

'I can't tell right now, I'm on the desk.'

'Well, you go and check. I bet you have.'

She had. That was two minutes apart. The closest we'd ever been. That was only three months after we began sharing the house together.

These days we can measure how we're getting along by how many hours and days we're apart. You can bet that if we've had a humdinger of a row, one of us comes on late.

We thoroughly enjoyed that weekend. Our hotel room had a double bed, and they didn't bat an eyelid about us sharing.

I enjoyed all the music in the club, and so many different ages of lesbians there. Sixteen to sixty. I couldn't get over it. Dee picked out the older ones, whispering to me about The Feathers and bar-dykes. But it was the young ones that got to me, wasn't it. Fancy having all those years ahead of you, as a lesbian. No time wasted with men or marriage. Ooh, I was over the moon about that.

I was so excited, more than I'd been when Grammaclegg took me and Essie to see the lights. 'Blackpool illuminations had nothing on this' I whispered to Dee, and she laughed. We hugged tight, there on the dance floor. It was wonderful. Her body, the music, and both of us holding, laughing. I'll never, never forget it.

There aren't that many books by lesbians for lesbians, but the women's bookshop had enough to keep me going. Mainly American stuff. Not very much from this country. But I spent a fortune and I was in there two hours, just browsing, delighted.

Yes, I am angry. Very angry. Like I need a bookshop in Coombebury that sells books for lesbians like me. Written by lesbians like me. That's what I need. That's when Dee named me soapbox Charlotte and we laughed a lot about that.

Back home in Coombebury we loved and laughed and loved and laughed. There were times when I thought I'd burst with it all, because of the years wasted, the changes in my life.

So then I'd go down to the beach and walk right along the edges of the waves, almost letting them catch me. I'd be there for ages all on my own, thinking about what I'd been reading. By then I'd been struggling through some pretty huge tomes. I didn't find it easy. But then, who said it was all going to be easy? Sometimes the loving was easy. Sometimes not.

Esther
Monday, 11 April 1983

After Chris, I became totally self-sufficient as an asexual woman. I didn't let anyone close, not even Nell who was supposed to be my good friend. I went out many times with Mary and Janet. I told them I'd had a relationship with a woman, and that it had ended.

We three decided to join the groups working on violence against women, and I joined the collective of a group of women teachers who wanted to challenge anti-lesbianism in girls' education. I felt wonderful coming out as a lesbian in those groups. Many's the night, with them, that I danced my feet off. But I must have been giving off the danger-don't-come-near-me vibes because no one ever made an invitation to me, and if anyone had she'd have met with zero. I was protected against other women so that I wouldn't let myself fall in love again.

Last spring and summer after Peter died I went to see Mum several times and wrote long letters about work, Nell, Laura and friends in general in between. I never once let Mum into the despair or the joy I'd had over Chris.

My need for Mum and hers for me were equal. We were really glad of each other. If she guessed that I was trying to heal from a relationship she never said so. We had a holiday together too, hiring a car and touring up in the Dales. I was glad I'd learned to drive all those years ago. She took me to the farm where she had looked after Aunt Edith's children during the war.

I remember the small museum in the Dales.

In there, there was a shaft of sunlight coming through the window on to the teeth of a man-trap. Sharp silver. But the teeth were closed, and could not harm anyone anymore. And although the sunshine brought in on to the trap the memories of past hurts, the teeth of the memories were closed and were no longer dangerous.

Wednesday, 13 April 1983

Woke this morning after another dream about Moon Valley. I enjoy falling asleep just because my dreams may take me there again. I remember that when I was a child I would look forward to dreaming, with the same expectation that I feel now.

In last night's dream I was a traveller, rucksack on my back, going along the silk route to China opening up the pathways through the mountains. Dawn over the summits turned the snowcaps pink and rose, and I stopped every so often to write down my explorations so that later, when the silk route was established, young girls would know of my journeys.

I met messengers who gave me news from other continents, and though I knew I was dreaming, the messages were real, and I had to hurry on to Moon Valley to take them to the women there.

So much news. So many messages. From the women travellers of Africa, who explored the ivory routes; women traders of the Sahara; news of the raging rivers of Nigeria, and the sweeping waters of Chad.

Yet I was on the silk route to China, protected by women and we were all so strong that no man dared to offend us.

I saw looms pegged over holes in the ground, and the women were tightening the warp threads. Then the breeze came up, catching in the threads turning them into singing harp strings. The women said: 'This is how we make our musical instruments, Essie.'

Usually there are sounds in my dreams, but this is the first time I've been conscious of music and instruments.

When I reached the valley I was tired. I called through the entrance stones. There was quite a wait there, then Mary and Janet came and helped me over the stones and we walked down the valley together beside the river.

We talked then as I started passing on the news. It was night. The talk flowed like thread without knots, breaks or thin parts. We reached out with words. Our bodies were easy, joyful, though we three were all tired. They told me there'd been some terrible arguments, and the women were trying to sort it all out. It had started because someone gave birth to a boy. And another woman told her that she would have to leave because boy children were not allowed in Moon Valley. Many mothers had been crying.

Some women had gone to pray to the mother of earth and sky, the one who sent rain and harvest, who used the moon as her mirror, who sent the sun each morning.

In the valley the next morning women were subdued. The mothers were to meet and decisions would be made. Mary and Janet and I walked together, by the river, in the morning sunshine, trying to sort out our real feelings, but there were no answers, only more questions.

Suddenly somewhere outside the valley a horn sounded, like one of those car alarms going off; that surprised me because I hadn't seen any cars in Moon Valley.

I woke up and heard a car alarm outside in the road somewhere. I went to my table in my den to write down my dreams, then I wrote these words: we make our myths to help us understand our heritage.

Thursday, 14 April 1983

In the history of the words associated with making cloth, a staple was a piece of wool too short to be spun by itself. But if it could be twisted tightly enough with other pieces, they could be spun together without breaking apart.

Words are my staples. I struggle to connect them. My staple diet, perhaps. Without them I cannot feed from knowledge of my heritage as a working-class lesbian.

I need to be whole, not limited for growth; strong, not afraid of being vulnerable; self-aware not selfish; self-defended, not closed; sexual and woman-loving without competing for control.

Words have become my strands of the thread of life. Strung across the gaps and silences, like silver beads on spider threads reflecting in the moonlight.

Women's words have to be collected here and there like staples of sheep's wool impaled on men's barbed wire fences. Scattered and blown apart. But gathered by us women, and spun together.

Threads from girls, the maidens: curiosity and creativity. Threads from the mothers: power of life, communication, negotiation. Threads from the hags, the crones: sensual eroticism and vision.

I shall become a spinner of words. Independent woman, without a man. Spinster, proud to be, cherishing the gathered staples, spinning them so carefully, not wasting them. Spinning yarn as did my foremothers, and theirs before them, miles and miles of yarn reaching back into the past. Life lines. Ready to be woven into the future.

Friday, 15 April 1983

After telling Mary and Janet, the next stage of my coming out had to be to Laura. I was gaining confidence in myself as a lesbian on the London 'scene' though I avoided making 'invitations' to anyone and still didn't put myself in a position where I might receive any. The shock of the split with Chris still made me recoil from being intimate again, but the identification with Chris and her wonderful body had been real. No amount of hurt could take that away, and indeed it was the intensity of the feelings that caused the hurt in the first place.

I remembered back to the distress and almost physical kinds of pain that Laura and I had had during our separation when I'd missed my grades for university. We'd re-connected since then, and if we could survive that split and come through whole and stronger in our understanding of each other, then couldn't we deal now with my coming-out process?

However I was nervous. I dare not even think of coming out to Mo and Hortense and the others. It was by then the late autumn of 1981. Tracey and her friends were under suspicion from Nell because they stayed together and showed no interest at all in boys. That made them very different from other girls of the same age, and Tracey was making no secret of the fact that she preferred girls' company to boys'. Nell and I hadn't talked at all about what was happening to Tracey. But most of the signs were there eighteen months ago and Nell's attitudes made me terrified of her.

I remember several discussions with Mo and Hortense at the time, especially about how education separates women from each other. I talked to them both about Laura, about my not getting to university, and about my jealousy and resentment that she was a university graduate and I was not.

'Wonder how you'll be then when I get me degree,' said Horts.

'Hey, come on. I've grown up a bit since then, Horts. Give me the benefit of the doubt will you?'

'Oh just testing,' said Horts lightly, but we three knew it wouldn't be that simple when Horts did finish her studies.

'Life's not that simple,' said Mo, speaking straight into our three minds. 'Sometimes the anger churns round and round. I mean I don't know how *I'll* feel when Horts gets hers, and I'm still slogging away through the OU, do I? I know we've lived next door to each other now for years, but there's mud at the bottom of every pond you know. And education stirs it all up, doesn't it?'

'Not half enough stirring yet, though. They don't use a long enough stick. You ask any black person on my course.' Horts paused and looked me direct in the eye. 'Maybe we'll get through it Ess, and maybe we won't – you, me and Mo. Don't you make no rash statements to me about your feelings towards me. 'Cos my bitterness about this country hasn't even scratched your surface, yet.'

192

She started in on a pile of washing up. I was silent. So was Mo. We both saw Hortense often; Mo every day, and I saw her several times a week. We knew that her turning away and starting in on something practical was not a way of saying: now leave my kitchen. It was, though, her way of challenging us that called for some ordinary actions from us, and *no* speech.

I picked up the tea towel and started wiping. Mo packed the pots away in Horts' cupboard, and put the kettle on. We drank the steaming strong brew while we cleared up the surfaces and wiped them down. By the time we'd done, the place was sparkling and the three of us then said our cheerios and Mo and I left. We were used to each other. I couldn't let go of that by coming out. The risk was too great for me, especially as I didn't have a lover then to curl around at night, a sheet anchor in the coming-out storms. That winter there were plenty of similar gale warnings.

However, Bristol and Laura were not Reeve Green.

I hesitated and fretted about how to write. When finally I did at the end of November, telling Laura that I'd been through so many anxieties and delays, and now felt I must share the news with her about my lesbianism and my relationship with Chris, she replied:

'Oh Essie, I despair of you sometimes. After all we've been through, for half our lifetimes together, did you really think I'd abandon you now? For heavens sake get yourself down here next weekend so that we can talk. Love you dearly. Laura.'

I read those words over to myself a hundred times. The last line I read a thousand. Memories jerked like a silent movie in my mind. Images of the old old drift and detachment and that amazing woman reaching out so many times across my fears.

She and Joseph had a car by then, so Laura met me at the station and the girls were waiting too, in the back seat. There were hugs and shrieks from them. I'd bought each of them a box of coloured pencils, or rather a tin. They sniffed the new wood like I used to. There is always something magic about a pencil that no one else has used.

My nervousness had begun to recede.

It came back with a rush on Saturday afternoon. Joseph, who had also greeted me warmly, took Melody and Sophie out to see one of his friends, which gave Laura and me a chance to go shopping in town and to talk.

At three we sat in our usual chairs by our usual window in our favourite coffee shop in town, on the first floor of the largest department store overlooking the comings and goings of the locals and the visitors. Bristol on a Saturday not long before Christmas was teeming full of consumers.

'Tell me about all this, then,' she began, as we were cutting through the largest cream cakes we could find.

She already knew how I'd met Chris and many of the things we'd gone through; that we'd had to part; and that I now called myself a lesbian, but was not at all public about it.

'It seems so logical Laura. After all, I've never found a man I'd like to settle with, most of them were hopeless at any kind of communication, and my feminism's been growing steadily for years. So meeting Chris and moving on to a future based on women seems the logical next step for me.'

'Mmmm.'

'What's Mmmm mean?'

'It means, go on.'

'Well that's it really.'

'Mmmm.'

'Mmmm again? This conversation's going a bit prehistoric.'

'Mmmm.' We both laughed then, uneasily. 'I didn't mean about the logical bit. I meant about Chris, really. Er. How did she know to invite you out?'

'Oh. Well we'd been talking about feminism and we'd been laughing a lot. It takes ages to set a leg you know, and for much of that time we'd been on our own because they were so short-staffed. Cuts and all that. Funny to think we had Thatcher to thank for us getting together. Don't expect it was what Maggie might have had in mind at all.'

'No.' She laughed. A short uncomfortable laugh. My nervousness was coming up alongside my coming-out.

'So she said she'd like to hear some more. Wanted to do some reading, I think she said. Honestly I forget now. Why?'

Laura shrugged. 'Just wondered. Intrigued me.' These did not sound to me like the words of an amazing woman delighted I was now a lesbian. It was the tone that gave her away.

'You're not pleased about all this are you?' I asked.

'Surprised.'

'Why? I said it was logical.'

'Logical's a bit heavy Essie. If it's logical for one . . . and all that.'

'Your letter wasn't like this. Your letter seemed well, er, positive.'

'Did it? Well you're you Essie and you won't change will you? You're still you whatever your, er, preference is, aren't you?'

'Am I?'

'Mmmm.'

We ate in silence. It was in fact the last cream cake I was to eat. Whenever I fancied a cake after that, the memory of the afternoon would come up and I thought I'd choke if I tasted the cream.

'I'm not the same. Not at all. I've become very different. I dress differently – as you can tell. I feel different. I react differently to people and places.'

'Men?'

'Yes.'

'How?'

'I don't want to talk about them. Like now. I don't want them to take up spaces in my head, my speech, my conversations with women friends.'

'Joseph?'

'Yes I know. He's been a good friend, but . . .'

'But he's your enemy?'

'Oh, Laura. Please, I don't want it to be like this.'

'We have to have this conversation Essie. Grunts and all. I said I'd not abandon you. And I won't. But you might as well have gone to the moon Ess. It's further than crossing the Severn Bridge Essie.'

I was determined not to cry in public. I'd done it again. I'd wanted Laura to be something, and I'd wanted Chris to be something . . . and in each case they were themselves. Women who did love me. I was sure of that. It had a little bit of comfort in it. And it was barely enough. But it was all there was, so it would have to do.

I played with the cream cake and finally pushed it sideways. I asked as lightly as I could manage: 'Would you like to finish this? I think I'd like some fresh fruit now.'

She nodded and tried to grin at me.

'Love these,' she said, then, 'Love you too Essie. I do, you know. You don't half ask a lot of me Essie.'

'Do I?'

'Yes.' Not 'Mmmm' this time. But instead something more like the old Laura. Someone I loved, and had loved for years and years.

'I love you too, you know. I regret you find this a lot for me to ask.'

'Do you, Ess?'

'Yes. Because this is who I am, now. I wanted it to feel like coming home. And it bloody doesn't. Because you're part of home.'

'I know. It's true. I am.'

'It *is* true. And if you can't go home, where can you go?'

'Home's never perfect, Essie. Even if it is where the heart is.'

'That's what I'm learning, Laura. Will you tell Joseph?'

'I already have. But not Melody or Sophie.' (I winced, possibly visibly when she uttered this.) 'It's not a possibility in their lives.'

'You wouldn't say that if you were living in London.'

'But I'm not. Nor shall I be. I don't want them to be.'

'Oh Laura. There was such a lot of joy in me when I received your reply to my coming-out letter. But there isn't any now. Not any.'

'I have thought about it you know, Essie. It's not simply my gut reaction. It's how Joseph and I both feel, and it's about what we want for Melody and Sophie and their futures.'

'No dirty white liberal crap, huh?'

'Don't get bitter, Essie. It doesn't suit you.'

'They're your children, but they might not want what you want.'

'I know that. They choose their own friends already. No doubt they'll find out for themselves what they want and don't want. It is just that you're speaking from the moon. And I don't want them learning moon talk.'

'But, Laura, they'll read later on. Black women writers, Laura, lesbians.'

'I'll deal with that. Not you. It is not your place.'

'I'm not saying it *is* my place. Not at all. I'm saying that you are hurting me terribly. Like a conversation I once had with Chris, about boundaries. Boundaries hurt.'

'Yes. I know all about boundaries. They hurt. They always do.'

What had I expected? That she would be arms open, welcoming my choices, my lesbianism? Had that been an expectation, or had it been a deeply embedded hope? From my heart or womb, or both, where I kept my woman-loving?

I couldn't possibly tell what the future held for either Melody or Sophie, nor what they'd choose, nor how, eventually, they would react to me. But I needed and wanted Laura, who did represent part of home. She and I both knew that, and the talk had confirmed that; though I didn't feel as if I lived, or wanted to live, on the moon. But at the same time, I was distressed that if I had dared to share it with her, Laura would have ridiculed my Moon Valley dream.

Saturday, 16 April 1983

In the year that followed, Laura and I wrote more often. Our letters were anguished sometimes with the intensity of the feelings and debates about sexuality and its interpretation in my life and in hers.

196

Months passed. Looking back, I imagine us with a bag of scraps of wool trying to thread them together; or of scraps of cloth, the left-overs from our attempts to make do with the yardage we each had.

At the time I could not conjure up those images. I didn't have dreams about them to help me much, either. But now I view the scraps as uneven in size, texture and thickness, and I marvel that we managed to use them like we did. We didn't make quilts large enough to keep us warm. The winter was harsh.

The women on Reeve Green heard that we had the money for the club, and we had a celebration party. Then we continued to meet to create a management group; to work out job descriptions; and to interview and appoint the new workers. Hortense said it was all a reward for Effort, with a large E. We all laughed and patted one another on the back.

I didn't come out to the group; and I didn't confide in Nell. Perhaps I was quite simply a coward; perhaps I daren't take the risk that I'd taken with Laura because I'd known Laura for longer and she didn't live round the corner; perhaps I was quietly frantic that Nell might prevent me seeing and talking with Tracey and Sally; and perhaps it was a combination of all those.

Anyway, I didn't tell Nell, and as I still couldn't write it to Lotte and was still closed against potential new lovers, I was lonely and unhappy for months on end.

However this spring I had a letter from Laura, saying that Melody had come home from school asking: 'What's a lessie, Mum?'

'It's a word for women who are holding hands, like you in the playground. Just ignore it: or tell the boys to go jump in the river. I'll tell you more about lesbians when you are older, but you're not old enough right now, okay?'

But although I fobbed her off with the 'when you're older' bit, my stomach churned over Essie. You and your Moon talk were in my way. And you are not the only woman talking Moon talk right now in the women's movement are you?

I thought about you so much between Melody's question and sitting down to write to you; about the letters that have flown to and fro, to and fro, since your visit here and that afternoon having coffee and cakes; and about the right you have to be who you want to be Essie.

And so, one day, but I'm not sure when the right time will be, there *will* come a time for you and my daughters to communicate directly about this.

I have never dealt with this in any of the youth groups I've worked with. It hasn't come up, in the ways I work nor in the kinds of groups. It hadn't come into my life, until this week, except through you.

Yet now my own daughter is bringing this to me. I feel that this is a great change around.'

With typical timing, the timing of real life, that letter arrived after Tracey had fled from Reeve Green. I cannot possibly know what effect such a move from Laura might have had on me and on my strength in helping Tracey, had it come before the crisis.

When I was small I read in a fairy tale that a young girl from a very poor family was given an endless ounce of knitting wool. However much she knitted, it wouldn't wind down, nor run out.

I have shared an ounce like that with Laura, since I shared that tale with her, when she moved in next door.

The thread which we began with is still there. The past cannot be changed, nor the ways in which we have hurt one another, but the yarn continues.

Lotte, 1982

They say it comes in threes. First Essie broke her leg and I heard about that from Mum. Then Peter died, and I met Essie briefly at the funeral. Later, I thought it was wonderful of her to offer to bring Mum to live in London. That made me feel very warm to our Essie. I can't explain that. You'd have thought I might have been jealous, but I wasn't. Life's funny that way, sometimes, isn't it. You never quite know what's going to turn up next.

No, I didn't expect it. And when it happened I had a short sharp shock like the Tories want for lads and girls on remand.

I'd been safe. In a cocoon. Just me and Dee, and the local friends, oh and trips up to London, now and then. I wasn't prepared for despair; never gave a thought to losing Dee.

She was walking home from work and he didn't stop; on the panda crossing. It was on the green man and he just drove through it. She had a light blue mac on. You know, wear something light at night. But he didn't see her; or if he did, he didn't care. And it was only just dark, being June. They found her address in her purse. Phoned home. I was in. Wondering why she was late. I used to worry, specially after the pubs came out. She didn't always sleep over, at the Bronnester. So, I used to worry. If she was late.

They said that she was in a coma. Intensive care, they said.

It took me almost twenty-four hours to get a message through to Isobel. She was back in England twenty-four hours later. That made two days altogether, and we didn't know, didn't know if Dee would make it.

I'd been in a cocoon. Just me and Dee. Safe. But now nothing was safe. Dee was unconscious; and Dee's daughter was home. In my home. In her home.

Oh I never was the literary one of the family and I never could bear English lessons at school. But one title stuck in my mind. *The Rivals*. I'd been made to farce around with it in the third year. Couldn't even remember the bloody plot, or if there'd been a plot, but I remembered that silly title, now that Dee's daughter was home. Rivals. In the same kitchen that we'd both shared with Dee. Only this was real, not some silly school play, and it was not funny, not at all.

It was one thing for me to see Isobel's photograph in the front bedroom, and another to have that photo walking around my kitchen. My kitchen. I was used to another body in that place. Dee's body. But there was Izzie instead; Izzie who couldn't find things because she'd been away since 1974 and this was 1981 and we had moved things round.

No good beating about the bush. I had to realise that I'd never bothered to find out much about Isobel. As far as I'd been concerned, she was busy working halfway across the world, and her life didn't affect mine much. Dee sometimes tried to talk about Izzie, but I hadn't been at all curious. But there's nowt like a crisis to make you ask the questions you should have asked all along. For the first time I wondered how many women lived in ignorance like I'd been doing. I had started off wanting to travel all over the world, and now I knew nothing about the country or the people where Isobel lived and worked. Nothing.

And the worst thing to handle was my being so jealous.

Daytimes, I was at work. They don't give compassionate leave for sickness of husbands or parents, let alone lesbian lovers. So each day Isobel went to the hospital to sit beside Dee, and in the evenings I went.

Trouble. Capital T, I'd say. We all needed mothers, but I could hardly run away from Dee back to mine, could I? Isobel was facing the possible death of her second mother, and she needed loving and caring. I was facing the death of my lover, and I needed warmth, hugs and care. And what about Dee? She needed both of us to love and care enough to bring her out of the coma, to make her fit and alive again. It seemed as if none of us had ever needed mothers so badly. Each night when I came home from the bedside I wanted to crawl into a nest and cry until my head stopped spinning, cry until I could get all the despair out of me.

For the first ten days Isobel and I stalked around one another like Tibs used to stalk if another cat dared venture into the back yard. We had our backs up, so to speak, wary and suspicious. I didn't know what she was thinking of me. I didn't ask. She seemed locked tight. I was shut and the door was bolted. No good knocking on me. I was made of wood. Coping.

I didn't know if there was a future. Coombebury – on my own. I'd not faced that, till then. But Dee was much older than me. Even if she lived through this (did I have hope left, after all?), I might have to face Coombebury on my own, mightn't I?

Corrine, Mol, Micky and Pol were not allowed to visit intensive care, so they came to the house to see us. Sometimes they were there when I arrived back from the hospital at nine at night. It increased my stress. I wanted no one. Just a quiet cave to crawl into. I wanted Tibs, and a hot-water bottle and a sleep. I couldn't sleep though. Night after night I lay awake willing Dee better.

I wanted time to think, but there wasn't time. At work I was a moron, clock-watching myself through the hours, till I could leave. They didn't know I was grieving for my lover. So how could they sympathise? To them, I was just a lodger whose landlady had had an accident. It was gossip for a week. Then it was only a nuisance.

I'd have liked it all to turn out like a fairy tale. Izzie riding up on a charger, cutting all the thorns down, rescuing Dee, her surrogate mother. But my life was not a fairy tale or a bed-time story either, come to that.

No one to turn to, except Dee's daughter, who wasn't a daughter anyway. She was somebody I didn't know and I didn't know how to talk to. She was a private person. I didn't know who her boyfriends were back in Mozambique, and she never talked about them, and I hadn't even asked Dee. All I could remember was that Dee said that Isobel was dedicated to her work.

Izzie and I spun down into the pits, in a polite slow spin. If she asked me about Dee, I felt she was intruding. If she didn't, I minded and felt she didn't care. I was shrunk as an old cast-off blanket, matted and tight, hard and itchy.

It was the eleventh day of Dee's coma, that I snapped.

I arrived home, wanting peace and quiet and there were Corrine, Mol, Pol, Micky and Izzie. They were all eating and had saved a place for me. I took one look at all those people crowding out my house and I broke. Small pieces everywhere. I ran upstairs to the back room that I shared with Dee, threw off my clothes, crammed on my pyjamas, shut off the light and slid into the cold bed. I cried there until I almost burst with crying.

I was worn out with wanting to be Dee's mother, looking after Dee, and needing someone to mother me at the same time. I'd had no children of my own; had not even known Dee when *she* was somebody's mother so I hadn't even shared that with her. I was almost the same age as Izzie and yet we were strangers. And now Dee might die, and I was helpless. Helpless to help her, just as she'd been helpless to help Dora. To the outside world, no one would know, would they; and no one would care.

That night it was Isobel who brought me cocoa and a hot-water bottle after all the others had left. She sat on the edge of the double bed, asking me softly if I wanted the bedside light on. I nodded. It made a dull orange glow. Isobel had on winceyette pyjamas and one of Corrine's winter dressing-gowns. It was June but Izzie was cold all the time.

Somebody was mothering me. She talked at me not to me. I could hear her anger under her words, though her words were not loud. They were soft-angry. Have you ever been talked at by somebody you've treated badly and listened to them shake a space in your head? Have you ever started off furious and found yourself glad they were talking and wanted them to go on and on?

'Deanne is not going to die, Lotte. She is not going to die, because you and I are not going to let her. People have been in comas before and have pulled through. She'll pull through. I was powerless to stop my own mother dying; I was only fourteen. But we are not that young. We have the power to stop this woman dying. Don't ask me how I know it. I know it. If I have to spoonfeed her myself, I shall not let her die. You have to use your power too. If you panic you cannot help me. The only way you can help her is to accept that you have the power. You have to help me.'

'Other people die. You've seen many people die. I don't understand.'

'Deanne is not going to die. You should get some sleep now. Goodnight, Lotte.'

She left the room as quietly as she had entered. I don't know why she said what she said. I'll never know. I believed her. That's the truth. I simply believed her.

How did she know what I needed? How could a few short and quietly angry words from a woman who had come from thousands of miles away, be a turning point for me, Lotte Clegg? Why should she be so kind to me when I'd done nothing for her?

I couldn't answer the questions. But she was there, with me, to save Dee's life. It chokes me now to think of it.

The cocoa and the hot-water bottle warmed me; and the talk shook me till all the parts of me fell apart like a jigsaw, and I had to put them together, one by one, if I was going to make Dee stay alive. The only other black person I'd known was Laura. I'd been jealous of her too, and had never faced that before. Now through Isobel I faced it, at the same time as I changed in my whole narrow-minded way of seeing.

I took a week's annual leave. People at work thought I'd gone crazy. I didn't care. Izzie and I held Dee's hands and talked to her. We told her stories over and over again. We played her favourite music. We put headphones on her with the sound of seagulls. Music like the sea. Tapes of Corrine singing. Everything we could think of. Stroking her face, her hands. Whispering in her ears. Kissing her eyes, her mouth. I remember that it was Saturday at 3.35 pm when she came round. She smiled at both of us. I was so overwhelmed I nearly forgot to smile back.

The day we were told that Dee was to be allowed home was a Tuesday. It was yet another turning point in my feelings for Izzie. We talked for a couple of hours that evening about what Dee would want, and what we both wanted.

There wasn't an ambulance for Dee, was there, on account of the cuts. So Izzie offered to go on the bus to the hospital, then order a taxi to bring Dee home; and that made me happy, because I could have the place ready, all spick and span and welcoming, and the kettle on, and a new fruit cake, Dee's favourite, hot out of the oven.

I'll never forget the moments waiting for that taxi – I had the front door ajar, listening. Then suddenly there it was, drawing up outside our gate; and I was rushing down the short path as Izzie was opening the taxi door, and there was Dee, all smiles, fit to bust with it all. Then the taxi left us.

Dee could just about walk, but ever so slow with a zimmer frame thing. We were all laughing and we said to her to go first. So I followed snail pace with Izzie and it seemed a long long time since I'd phoned Mozambique to ask her to come to Coombebury.

Imagine Dee's face when she went in. The front room had a huge pot plant with beautiful, mottled leaves all colours. It had a string on it and a message: Welcome home Dee. Love from Izzie and Lotte. And a book token so she could choose some books; and a new red track suit, easy on her hips.

We sat her in the best armchair and I mashed the tea. It was one of those times, like I had when I was a little girl in Densley. I'd have got my friends with me, and the sky would be all blue and a few fluffy white clouds and I'd *know* I was happy. There was this mountaineering programme once on tele. Sometimes people high up on a mountain get a rainbow in a ring right round them; only it's turned inside out, starting with violet instead of red. They call it 'Sudden Glory', only I'd never heard of it before had I, but when Izzie fetched Dee home, I was on top of that mountain, and then I knew exactly what Sudden Glory was all about.

Isobel stayed five weeks with us then went to London for three weeks, staying with some medical friends. She rang Dee every night from London, and came for a final four days before she went back to Mozambique.

If she had been going to live there for ever, I still might have put her back in my 'out' tray, so to speak, filed and sorted and posted off. I might have forgotten that she and I mothered Dee together in the hospital, talked to her softly for hours, brought her out of her coma. Isobel said it was Dee's turn to be mothered. I might have let all that go by, but I couldn't. Why? Because she said she had already been trying to make up her mind not to renew her contract in Mozambique; to move away from Marion; and had even thought of a total change and a period of living in London.

Dee's coma wasn't the cause of Isobel's decisions. She said that the timing coincided with some rethinking of her plans. That she had never lived in London. It would be a new city for her; and one where black feminist politics was extremely active; where there were many like her, with her ideas; in short, there was work to be done.

So as Izzie left Dee and myself in the early autumn of '81 she said she thought she'd return to England before long.

Dee was steadily getting stronger. Her convalescence would take between six months and a year.

Me? I had had an almighty kick up the backside, and it was long overdue. Isobel Beale had been there with me to breathe life back into the woman I loved best in the world. There was enough tension in me, sorting that out, to break all the fine bone china and cut glass in V and A's dining room at The Froggery.

I didn't enjoy finding that the jealous side of me was so ugly; the side that had resented Laura; the side that had stifled my welcome for Isobel. I didn't like finding out that I was short-sighted and ignorant; and I didn't enjoy taking out my feelings and looking at them in the light of day.

I had one hell of a way to go, now that I knew Isobel would be soon living in England. I'd assumed she'd had boyfriends and I didn't like Dee laughing me to scorn when I was reminded she'd shared the house with Marion. Me of all people assuming that?

Dee said, 'Did you imagine all lesbians were white, then Lotte?'

'I didn't think about it at all.'

'But I told you Isobel lived with Marion – I thought you'd understood, Lotte.'

I went for a walk then, the usual walk, along the sands, trying to piece together all Dee had said, all I'd not bothered to hear.

I was full of questions and full of wants. Full of sorries, and sadness and guilt. Full of awe and wonder and wanting to do something, to start somewhere. I remembered reading a book called *The Women's Room* and had a pang for Myra walking at the end on a far off lonely beach.

It had said on the cover that this book changed lives. Well it had not changed mine. I had. And now a meeting with the surrogate daughter of my lover had changed me again. I was full of questions, full of wants. I had been in a cocoon and was making my way out.

You can't learn those lessons from books. There aren't enough pages in books for all the sorries. I knew, because I'd met Isobel, that wherever there are women, there are women-lovers too. I had phoned Isobel for Dee's sake, but not for Isobel herself. I had used the fact that we lived miles apart as my excuse.

I did not feel strong then, walking by the sea, even though Dee and Isobel were making me realise that women like us were everywhere. Lesbians, I mean. I felt weak and narrow-minded for not knowing. I wanted happy endings for us all. I wanted Isobel to meet someone new in London and I wondered then how difficult it had been for them both in an isolated house in wide-open country. I wondered why it hadn't worked out for them together. I felt sloppy, romantic and couply. And could see how angry Izzie would be at my curiosity when I hadn't been bothered before. I'd be damn furious if some one started prying into my life. I had a lot of sorting out to do.

But because Izzie and I had those weeks to link us, we were linked now, no matter how tense and angry she might feel to me. And I was left wondering who would mother her when she was alone and did not want to be; and was she the sort of woman who might want her own children later on, and would there be support for her? And when would I be able to read her articles about her work and life; and when would Marion's poetry be published?

The sea did me no good that day on the beach. It kept coming back at me, waves and waves of questions about myself and Izzie, and the questions did not flow away like if I'd been walking by a river, carrying my fears and sorries to the sea. Instead, the sea came back and back, waves and waves, again.

Esther

Sunday, 24 April 1983

Back at work one week. Every night I have had another dream about Moon Valley, and I have been very troubled during the daytime, because the women in the dreams have stayed with me.

Friday night I wanted a dreamless sleep. So I took half a bottle of whisky to bed, with me. Grandma Clegg's cure for a cold, which in fact she never tried on Lotte and me, was to put her hat on one bed post, and drink spirits till she could see it on the other one. Then she said she'd wake up feeling fine.

Not me! Not only did it take ages to knock me out, but I woke in a terrible sweat after yet another of my vivid dreams.

I dreamt that Nell arrived at the ox-stones at the main entrance to the valley. Part of the area was well wooded and the river ran downhill, into the valley, swirling into a whirlpool after about three hundred yards.

Nell was clambering through the ox-stones with a rucksack on her back, carrying a Sainsbury's carrier-bag full of shopping. She cursed loudly because the damn handles always started to go on these things just when she was at the end of her tether.

She called to me:

'I came on the forty-seven.' Then the whole of our conversation changed and she was phoning me from work like she usually does in the holidays. In real life, it isn't my holidays any longer, but in the dream it seemed to be.

She stood, then, grinning, talking like a telephonist.

'Hello Ess. It's me, Nell. Hang on Ess.' (I wait.) 'That's it. Now where was I? Oh, hang on again.' (I wait.) 'You still there, Ess?' 'Yes I'm here.' 'Oh good. Can you make the meeting, Ess? Oh. Hang on a minute.' (I wait.) 'You can? Oh good. See you then Ess. I gotta go. It's going to rain.' (Pause.) She looked at the sky as if we were at the bus stop not by the thinking pool. 'It's going to pour. Cats and dogs. Hang on.' (I wait.) 'That's better. Well see you then Ess. Bye for now.'

I woke up.

Questions about Nell (and Tracey who hadn't even been in the dream), were tumbling behind my eyes. Very physical sensations, as if I were a tumble-dryer with my eyelids for the door. Things kept clinking against me, like when the press-studs haven't been done up in the launderette and they clank and twang to and fro.

Nell and Tracey. Linked names. I had the grandmother of all headaches. Nell and Tracey. Tracey and Nell.

Then I remembered another sequence from the dream.

Some women were making fires in the sand dunes. There were blankets near several of the fires so it seemed that some women were going to sleep out, under the stars all night. Nell wasn't there. She'd not wanted to go right into the valley, so she'd gone back over the ox-stones. No, I mean through them, because they were too high to clamber over. She'd gone home on the bus. But Tracey was by one of the fires and she didn't recognise me. I didn't tell her who I was.

Then the sequence blurred. Then someone was stoking one of the fires with lumps of some kind of rock. I decided that the women were fusing silica and sand to make glass. It was very hot near the fire.

It blurred again. Suddenly I was in my classroom in Reeve Juniors, doing a project on how glass is made. Measuring windows, and looking in telescopes and mirrors. Then it jumped. I was sitting by the whirlpool. Its surface was crystal clear, reflecting back my mind. A thinking pool. It was glass. A mirror.

An ordinary mirror. Tracey had another mirror where she sat near the fire, brushing her spiky hair. It was bright red. Nell was nowhere to be seen. I felt sick, in the dream, and ran and ran over the sand dunes until no one else was in sight. I was alone. And it was very very hot.

After writing about that part of the dream I made some coffee. I was thinking about glass being an ordinary everyday thing. Fused from the hottest part of the fire like my friendship with Nell. I was not a dream specialist, but I realised that there'd been other fire images to do with Nell and myself in the past, both in my dreams and in my writing. I didn't understand what all the images meant, but they affected me deeply.

At ten-thirty on Saturday morning, I rang Nell. I told her I had had a dream and I asked her if we could meet. She said she'd like to come round, and that there'd be more chance to talk in my place. She hadn't been sleeping well. Not since Tracey walked out.

I met her at the door. We never hugged because it wasn't her thing. I said: 'Let's go in the den, shall we?' When she nodded we went in there and I switched on the kettle which I had already filled up. I said: 'Tea or coffee?' She chose coffee, though she usually had tea.

'Tell me about your dream then,' she said. So I did, just as I had written it in the diary. By then the kettle was ready so I made the coffee and as soon as I had sat down again, she said: 'I been wanting to see you so bad, Ess. I been missin' yer. I'm glad you phoned me. I been on the point of comin' round so often. Only we was both so angry, wasn't we?'

'Yes. Me too. I've wanted to phone you so many times. But I was angry too. And I was afraid, nervous. I need you to know some stuff about me. It's a long story.'

'I got time, Ess. I got all today and all tomorrer, bein' as it's Saturday.'

'Oh it won't take *that* long.' I managed a laugh. I was thinking that I could really say it in three words. I'm a lesbian. But actually that should be four.

While I'd been waiting for Nell to come round, I'd realised my three choices.

So now she had arrived, and there I was, faced with them.

I could forget all the lesbian nonsense in my life and Tracey's, run away and jump off Tower Bridge: fast death.

I could hide for years and years into the future, from anything further to do with lesbians and lesbianism, comfort Nell whose daughter was strong and clear about sexuality, stay in the closet and go mad: slow death.

I could face all the contradictions and the hatred that had been and always would be heaped upon lesbians in heterosexual society, tell Nell exactly what I thought of my and her behaviour towards Tracey: cope and survive.

I began: 'Do you remember the time I broke my leg, just after we started the after-school club planning group?' She nodded. 'Well I was invited to dinner with the doctor who set it in plaster, and that was a woman, and I fell in love with her . . .

'We were together a year and a half. And it didn't work out. I suppose you could say we agreed to part, on both sides, but it hurt.

'I'm not with anyone now, Nell, and I don't think I shall be for a while longer. I've needed time on my own.

208

'But when I do love again it will be a woman. I couldn't go back to men now. I've changed so much.

'And I told Mary and Janet from that working-class feminist group I once joined. They're both lesbians too, now.

'And Laura. She knows. But nobody else. Then in the middle of me working this all out, Tracey came to me, back in the spring, and I knew what she wanted to tell me, and maybe she knew that I wanted to tell her too. Hell knows she gave me the opening. But I didn't take it.

'I thought there was time. And there wasn't. That was four days before she left.'

I was shaking, though I hadn't wanted to be. I couldn't control it and that maddened me, but maybe better out than in. I'd have laughed at the thought, if I could.

Nell's face had moved from surprise to disbelief and back again. From caring and sympathy to shock and challenge. I don't recall ever having seen so many expressions pass over her face in a short few minutes.

But her emotion was anger, it seemed, as she blurted: 'You could've helped her, you mean. Helped her and me? We was a triangle – you, me and Trace. If you'd told her, she might not've left. You could have maybe stopped her, but you didn't. Is that what you're telling me? You could have talked to Trace and you didn't?'

'And what would you have done then? Mmm? If she'd wanted to come here to live, and wanted to do it here with Bev or Anita, or both? Mmm? Or stayed at home, glorying that I was a lesbian too? You welcoming her and me with open arms. Don't make me laugh.'

'I might have.'

'Come off it. I don't fuckin' believe that.' (I started to get louder and louder.) 'I don't believe that for one fuckin' minute.'

'Don't you swear at me Ess. I didn't come here to have you swear at me.'

'So what did you come here for? Peace and quiet? I'm not the peaceful sort anymore. I don't want reconciliation at that price. The price is too high. I paid in hurt and loneliness for a good while now, deciding when and how to let you into my life.'

'All right Ess. I heard yer. I heard yer. I don't want no peace and quiet 'cause I ain't used to it. Get it. I want my Trace, and I want you. So we got some hard times ahead, you and me. So what's new uhh?'

'I wanted to tell you. I was on the point of it more than once. I wanted to. A lot. But I saw you closing Tracey off. Though you and me *both* knew what was going on. We both knew years ago, not months

209

and we did fuck all to stop her leaving. Either of us. Fuck all. I watched you closing her off; and I knew you'd close me off too.'

'You can't know that. You can't know anything about me. Not if you don't let on to me. You were only thinking. Not knowing.'

'All right. Thinking. That was enough. I was sure you'd close me off. I didn't want to lose you. I still don't. I didn't want lies. Not between you and me. Not after all the hours and hours of telling the truth even when it hurt. I didn't want lies, no more than Tracey did. I know I failed her. I've been trying to live with it. I failed her. I failed you too. And you failed too. Failed. Failed. Failed.'

Then Nell cracked. I saw Nell cry for the first time ever.

'Our Trace is not comin' home Ess. She phones me up. Says: "I'm missin' you Mum. I want you to be happy for me with Bev and Anita. Please Mum. I still want you to be a mum to me. I want you to be pleased. Please Mum. I want you to say you're pleased." So I says: "Give me your phone number Trace so as I can phone you." She says she can't, she's in a short-life house. No phone. So I asks for her address and she says she don't want me coming there making rows. She only wants me to have her address when I say I'm pleased. So, there I am Ess. I'm just sorting out all that. Trying to understand her 'n you drop this one. Only you haven't had much comfort 'ave you Ess? From this Chris woman by the sounds of it. I do want my Trace to be happy. I do still want to be her mum. I didn't bring her up from a premature squalling brat that wouldn't let me sleep nights, all that, just to lose my Trace now, did I?' (Nell was crying noisily by now.) 'It's a big thing this, Ess. Tracey left home 'cause I forced her out. I forced her out 'cause she wants girlfriends. I don't know how to live wiv meself.'

I passed the box of tissues to Nell, noticing that they said Man-Size on the side, and I filled the kettle from a plastic container that I keep in my den. And saw Nell break like an egg, shell in splinters, contents running out. Humpty Winters there, fallen off the wall. But all the king's horses and all the king's men wouldn't have cared less about my friend in bits.

The kettle whistled. I took refuge in the tasks, carefully twisting on the coffee jar lid, slowly filling the mugs. Then I set her mugful on a small wooden stool beside her rocking chair.

She was rocking to and fro, as her daughter had done, in that fateful visit to my den in February. As she rocked, Nell appeared to me to be birthing something, and I wanted it to be a new phase of a creative friendship between her and me. Yet the birthing was destined, it seemed, to have a long labour. She was still crying.

210

I was quiet, drinking my boiling hot coffee slowly, sip by sip. Nell was calming a little. For a short time our communication reverted back to the wordless variety that we'd become used to over the years. So many times we'd spoken directly into one another's thoughts, and we'd often laughed about that.

This time, though, it was also new. So we were on more than one level, at the same time. It was new because it was like a first meeting, and in a way, I thought, that was exactly what it was. My first contact with Nell as an out-lesbian; the first time I'd confronted her with that; and the first time I'd been so clear to myself that this knowledge demanded to be shared between us. Lesbian: take it or leave it.

Suddenly she said 'We used to be like sisters, you and me, Ess. I've been missing you Ess. There's nothing like a sister, is there? Have you told your Lotte all this?'

'I am thinking of writing to Lotte, but I don't know when. She never answers my letters, not since James beat her up at the Bronnester. Well, except when I took Mum to the Dales. She wrote me a nice letter, then.'

'I think you should write to her soon.' The sad face again. Eyes deep brown. Pain-soft eyes. Sharp smooth eyes. Nell's eyes.

'I wish you was really me sister, Ess. I been missing you Ess.' Her crying was continuous but quieter. The edges of the rocking chair were just catching on the edge of Grandma Clegg's proggy rug. The creak on the floor squeaked in contrast to the soft muffles as the rockers tipped forward on the rag pieces of the rug. Squeak–soft. Sharp–smooth. Like a pendulum swinging slowly from distress to comfort. Rhythms relentless like the rhythm of birth. I said slowly, 'I want you to recognise me as a lesbian. But I do feel funny saying it. Like a little girl again almost – as if we're in the playground, Nell, you and me. I used to play "dare dare devil dare", with Lotte. Did you play that?' She gulped. Blew her nose again, her eyes still brimming.

'I used to play with Dee. "Dare dare devil dare" with Dee when we was evacuated to Mereford.' She paused. Something made me wait. Nell seemed to want to go on, but she was holding back, or was being held back. I drank my coffee, hiding in the mug while she collected herself.

'You know Ess, you *was* kind to my Trace. She respected you Ess. She might've gorn off the rails altogether if she hadn't had you to visit. You see, Ess, I panicked when she started all this wiv Anita and Bev, 'cause she was only thirteen. Well that's how it all started in Mereford too. Dee and Dora cuddlin' behind the hay barn while I collected eggs.

They thought they had me fooled. But they didn't. Dee's been a lesbian since then.' (I gasped, choking into the coffee.)

'I couldn't tell yer, Ess. I couldn't. She made me promise not to tell. A promise is a promise, innit, Ess?' (I nodded, feeling as if a metal band was tightening inside my chest and another around my windpipe.)

'There's more Ess. Lots more I'd like to tell. It's been getting to me, not tellin'. You see, Ess, Dee had ever such a hard sad time. She's all right now. I'm glad. It's about time she had a bit o' happiness. But wiv what she went through, I never wanted it for our Trace. I didn't. Even if Dee *is* all right now.

'I don't like lies, Ess. I'm not sorry I've told yer. I'd like to tell you *all* of it, Ess, only I can't . . .'

'I'm not asking.'

'No. But like I said, I don't like lies Ess. Not wiv you. 'Cause we was like sisters. Only you been lyin' to me, and I been lyin' to you, and where's it got us, eh?'

Had I really thought this would be a garden of roses? We had never promised each other a rose garden. I was so upset at Nell having known another lesbian, as a friend, all those years, I could hardly free myself from the metal band. Yet strangely enough I didn't feel at all like crying.

'I've always wanted to meet Dee. How much does she know about Tracey?'

'I told Dee that Tracey respected you, could talk to you. And I said I was sure she was doin' it with Bev and wiv Anita – and wanted to be a lessie.' (I flinched because of the fact she said lessie, not lesbian, and because of the way she said it.)

'I phoned her up, 'n told her. She said Tracey was doin' the right thing. Mind you, I was upset with Dee for saying that, 'n I told her so. But Dee said Tracey must follow her instincts, somethin' like that. 'N she said I hadn't to fret. Tracey would be all right, just like she's – I mean – she's all right now.'

'It hurts, Nell. To think I could've known Dee, maybe met her, talked to her. I needed people to talk to, just like Tracey did. I mean, women. Women – lesbians – who'd understand. But you just never let me near to Dee. If you'd told me about Dee I'd have been able to trust you. Then I might've helped you and Tracey.'

'Well we didn't. Trust each other. 'N now we've failed 'aven't we?'

I was thinking then that if Dee had known her own lesbianism at thirteen, and Tracey had at about the same age, then I could have done too. And later I could have been out in the women's movement instead of waiting for all the other lesbians to make a liberation movement for me to come out into. I hadn't supported Tracey when she needed me. I'd colluded with Nell, and Nell with me, in a whole series of lesbian-hating doubts. In my case I'd kept these doubts closed inside me for years, without confronting them.

Sitting there with Nell that morning I was anguished; but underneath the distress there burned an anger at all forms of lesbian-hating, including my own. And I realised then that my anger would boil to the surface over and over again. Lava. From the fire inside. And I did not intend to waste it in undirected explosions; nor to let myself burn out.

We talked and talked, sorting out what to say to Tracey; when and if each of us, separately, would have the chance to meet her; and how to re-build our relationships with her.

I made lunch for Nell and myself and we decided to go up to town shopping, because Nell didn't want to go home and I wanted to have more time with her. We were done with sitting talking, and the walls of the den were crowding in on us after the intensity of the morning. Shopping seemed a safe thing to do. And it turned out well for us. I bought some new wool and a fairisle pattern; she bought some wallpaper for the front room. Typical for both of us.

As we left one another, early evening, she said:

'Bye then Ess. I'sll think of you when I'm putting up this lot. I been missing yer Ess.'

'I'm glad you came to my place this morning Nell. I've been missing you too. I'll see you soon, then.'

'Yeah. Bye for now, Ess. See yer later.'

Then we parted, and after I'd arrived back at my flat, I cleaned the whole place, floors, windows and everything. I cooked a jacket potato and heaps of vegetables with it. Then I went to bed, shoved a huge pillow behind me, and started my new knitting.

Lotte

April 1983

It was the end of April and I was the first to get in from work. Dee was on lates. There was this letter waiting for me on the mat redirected from Rose's place. It looked a real marathon and I thought: 'What problems might our Essie be coming up with *this* time? She gets up my nose.' So I put on the kettle and change out of me work things into me trousers and trainers and I sat down to cope. Coffee one side and me Benson and Hedges on the other. Well I know I shouldn't have but I did now and then. When me and Dee had a humdinger or suchlike. I was no smoker really. I reckoned I averaged one a week. Not exactly hooked as it were.

So I opened the envelope and was staggered. My sister was coming out to me as a lesbian. Well it was not exactly what I was expecting but then our Essie was never exactly predictable either. So there I was getting through five Bensons straight off, and it was *me* she was telling.

I stubbed out me sixth, walked to the cooker and tried to concentrate on the dinner. I put on the potatoes and I started on the washing up from last night's supper and from that morning's breakfast. Go to work on an egg.

A mug slipped and bounced on the sink. I bent to catch it. I was muttering to meself. The same words over and over. My rubber gloves were all slippery with bubbles. I missed the damn mug, didn't I. It smashed on to the tiled floor in a little pool of washing-up water. I had just dropped seventy pence worth of pottery mug. Six years ago I wouldn't even have noticed the cost.

I left the pieces where they were and the puddle around them. 'My Essie's a dyke. My sister Esther Clegg is a lesbian. Oh heavens. What a thing to tell Dee when she gets in.' Suddenly I was in the air jumping on to the china pieces in the puddle. Deliberately. No warning. Crunch. Suds and china chips flew across the floor. I was letting out this howl of unexploded all pent up . . . joy.

214

I made some more coffee and I sat drinking it trying to calm down. Tibs came and leapt on me. She was going like an engine. 'Our Essie's a dyke. Our Essie's a dyke. Our Essie's a dyke.'

I could see lots of problems. Now that was typical of our Ess. I thought, 'What about Nell? And has Ess told Mum?' and so on. I thought about Tracey running away to live in a co-op, in the East End. Problems galore. But the engine was still going: 'Going to Densley. Going to Densley. Going to Densley.' I couldn't calm down.

Then I smelled the potato water boiling dry so I had to come back to Station Road, didn't I?

I put Tibs off my lap. She complained. I swilled down the rest of the coffee, still with the ridiculous pink rubber gloves on, and began to face the boiled dry (almost) saucepan, the broken bits of pottery mug, and a floor splattered with bubbles.

And it was all down to Essie's letter wasn't it!!?

In between cooking for me and Dee, I re-read Essie's letter.

Dee came in at eight. She found me just dishing up. We went through it all together. She just kept looking at me astonished.

We were both thinking: 'What can be better news from Essie? Or more unexpected? Better than winning the pools – almost.'

At the same time we were churned up. I was churned up because I wished it had been me to break open the lies. It hadn't been. I was going to have to live with that. Wouldn't be simple. Dee was churned up not knowing if Nell had told about us though there was nothing at all in Essie's letter to indicate that. Only that Essie'd told Nell she's a lesbian and she felt much better now it was in the open.

'I've been waiting and waiting for something,' said Dee. 'I've had a sixth sense that I should be phoning Nell and hearing from her. I've gone over it many times. Round and round. I was half decided I'd phone Nell this weekend. I just had this funny feeling that something huge had happened.

'You never said.'

'No I know. It was more an uneasy feeling than anything definite. But I never in a blue moon dreamed it'd be Esther to make the links. Funny how we can be half-there sometimes, isn't it?'

'Mmmm. You were the one on at me to meet Esther way back at the beginning after James got his new wife and you said (d'you remember?) that Essie would be safe from questions now, and you begged me to settle it all and I wouldn't. Then our Essie wrote that letter, well several, but I mean the one to come and visit her and I wrote back and said I didn't think we could accomplish much by visiting.

Well just think on, Dee, she must've already been through it with this Christine woman by then.'

We bitched about Christine for a while. Well we always did love a good bitching session, and I'd done enough about our Essie. 'Bout time I gave the poor love a rest. So I had a go at Christine instead. Oh, I know it's not very noble but then my sister was my sister, wasn't she, and if anybody was going to shit on my sister, it was going to be me.

Lotte

June 1983

It was cold upstairs in Mum's house. I had to dig out the 'lectric single bar from the back of the wardrobe and plug it in. Ess came up with the tea. I was shivering although it was June. She put the tea down.

'You all right?' she asked, red-eyed.

'No. Are you?'

'No. Want a hug.'

'Come here then.'

We stood there hugging for all we were worth. 'Seems like years since your letter, Ess. Not like eight weeks.' That set both of us off again like taps. No washers. Crying on each other's shoulders.

At night we slept together. Mum had put a double bed in the back bedroom when I got married. I s'pose she had hoped James and me would come to see her. He never did. I had always slept in that double on my own when I had gone to see Mum. In June it was a comfort to me and Ess. After all, I was used to curling up round Dee every night, and Ess needed a body to hug.

The walls of the houses in Densley were thin. No privacy from your neighbours day or night. When one turned they all turned.

So when Rene Clegg, my mum, had left home to stay at Red Heather's it had been a relief to Gramma Clegg and it had helped with the overcrowding. The three youngest brothers had slept in a bed like me and Essie, hadn't they, and the oldest brother had slept in the box room. Me and Essie used to fight sometimes in bed when we very small. That's why my mum got us singles.

You remember all these things, things like that, when there's a death. Especially if it's your mum who is dead and you didn't expect it.

Essie was more prepared for it than me. One of Mum's letters to Essie, the one saying she was going away with Ethel to Greece, well, that letter had said 'I can't take it (my savings) with me when I go.'

Well, that set Essie off thinking about Mum 'going'. Looking how our Essie'd taken it mind you, I didn't think being prepared had made that much difference, really. How could any daughter be prepared for her mother's death?

Myself, I wasn't at all prepared for it. I'd always taken Mum's life for granted. Well, no, I don't mean that, I mean her being alive I took for granted, you know.

Ess said that time would help the grief to fade like the summer flowers on Mum's grave. She said we had love underneath the layers of grief. She talked like a poet. I liked it. Took me back years to the good old days before the swot-rot set in.

Deanne sent me two drawings.

There was this one of spiders in the lake. She said it was on telly. How they spin webs in the rushes, under the water. Then they bring down air bubbles and fix them in the web, and hey presto an underwater house, air-conditioned. The air bubbles don't last long. When they're gone the spiders make new ones. They go on doing that, spinning webs and homes in spite of everything.

Ess said Mum's death brought up the hidden meanings. She looked at Dee's drawings and then at me and said p'raps one day she'd find someone to love that was like Dee. Like the spiders. Making somewhere safe to live where you'd least expect it. Mind you, even though I was so sad and upset I couldn't resist a grin as Ess and I fell asleep, arms around one another. Easier than spiders, I thought, where would you put all them legs?

We had to get a move on sorting out the house because the Coal Board had been round. Vultures. They wanted the house back. The Randalls had come to tea after the funeral. Ethel had been there and lots of Mum's friends off the buses. She had so many women friends.

You wouldn't expect Mum to make a will. She wouldn't give it a thought. So me and Ess told all her friends to choose something of hers they'd like. I rang up Women's Aid for the rest. They could use the beds and cooker and such.

While we were in Densley our Essie had more dreams about a place called Moon Valley. She told me in the mornings, before one of us got up to go and make the tea.

She said she dreamt that Mum was there. There was a brick building with eight sides and a long narrow corridor leading in. Sounded a bit like the Thrupenny-bit kiosk, if you see what I mean. In there, Mum made pots and she had her own kiln. Oh, and there were long, long

218

windows so it was very light, sunny, and Mum could see across the dunes to the beach. I liked that bit.

'Well, I'm right glad you haven't got Mum stuck in some awful dull place with the angelic host above,' I said. Ess thought I was joking but actually I wasn't. I was right serious about it. 'I can't see Mum being happy stuck on some cloud in a white frock with a harp. She never was one for harping.'

Ess laughed, the sort of tinny laugh you get when you tie cans on the back of a wedding car. Looking back I could hear them when me and James got married. If I closed me eyes the sound came right there, it did really. Thank heaven it wasn't a custom at funerals.

Before Mum died, me and Essie had begun to get to know each other. She came to see me and Dee. She was full of history. She was wonderful. She always was clever our Ess. Somehow I didn't mind it anymore. After all, I'd been doing a lot of reading. I could keep me end up quite well.

Deanne

Red Heather's letters to Rene Clegg were neatly tied with a brown velvet ribbon. The bundle was in an old large envelope with an exercise book. Rene had roughed out all her replies, some in pencil some in fountain pen. Parts were rubbed out, written over. Others had crossings out, and blotches as if Rene had cried on to them.

May 1940

Rene sweetheart

Why? I won't believe it. Can't believe it. Four years with you, gone. And the last two, in this house, together. Such heaven. Why? I pray and pray you'll change your mind. My love won't lie down and die. Funny sort of war widow, I'd make. Yours truly a cup of tea with salt in.

Tried telling meself you only went to help Aunt Edith. She needs it. But at night the bed's empty. Love cut up in pieces, people dying all over Europe, bombs on cities here in England. I can't sleep, get up and pace the house. See the boxes packed for market, huh, nothing fancy now, but people still need plates and cups. You and me packed up in boxes. You there. Me here. Ready for what? Love put away like cracked pots not wanted.

I'm breathing. That's what matters now. Thousands aren't. What matters is going on, staying alive. But I don't *feel* alive, only breathing.

Come back sweetheart. I love you. I want you to come home.

Your own Heather.

June 1940

Dear Red,

Who is this Heather? I always called you Red. With your fabulous hair and your bright hats.

When we first met, four years ago, and started to fall in love, I said

220

it couldn't be forever. You haven't forgotten the talks we had have you? I don't think so, Red. I promised I would live with you as long as I could. But I always said I wanted to marry. I always wanted babies of my own. Always. You knew that, and I never lied to you.

When the war started everything speeded up. I knew our time would soon be up. I can't marry you and have babies. I only wish we could. But we can't.

I don't regret one minute of being with you. Not one. The love, the laughing, even the times we had rows. You were my Red Heather. I was your girl. I loved you like you loved me, that was true. I miss you and your loving arms now. It hurts badly. I miss you very very badly.

I shall not come back. If I did I should have to start pretending, then we'd start to hate. It's terrible this way but it would be much worse if I'd stayed. Or if I ran back now.

I had to leave you before my lies started. I don't know when I'll find happiness. There's not a lot around, but everyone is in a hurry to find fun, even to find love, before tomorrow. Death and loss in every family. People round here go dancing at the Army bases to try to forget.

I still love you and I'm haunted by ghosts. From the market, the house, and our bed. And from the future. The pull of babies and family life is like a haunting. It comes at night.

Daytime the children fill my time, showing me I was right to take this job with Aunt Edith. She is a kind woman, quite huggy. Very lonely. She misses my uncle badly.

I said before I left I wanted you to look for someone else. I wanted you to be happy with the right girl. Though God knows how does anyone find happiness on this earth now?

If my letter makes it harder, shall I not write any more? Tell me if you want me to stop. God knows I'm in a torment some days, but I mustn't come back.

People find a way through times like this, don't they?

Love Rene.

July 1940

Rene sweetheart,

Don't stop writing. I'm not stopping. So you want me to go and find a girl to take your place? So soon? Oh yes, you said it before you left but I didn't believe you. I didn't think you meant it. What sort of love did we have then? Set of cups and saucers, break one oops find another, any one'll match?

221

Don't talk daft girl. You were my girl. I wanted you. I don't change girls like I change hats. Get a new one, nice and bright. Felt and feathers, fur and frills?

I wanted you. I can't replace you just like that. I'm 'bout as happy as a teapot with a missing lid.

And the tea's gone cold.

Your loving Red.

August 1940

Dear Red,

I haven't written in this long while because I didn't know how to. This is my fifth try.

Your last letter was so angry. But what did I expect? I don't know. You've every right to be angry. I don't s'pose it helps if I tell you I'm suffering too. You could just say: serves Rene right, or summat. P'raps it does. Sad. Everything is sad, except the children. I was right to come here to get to know children. I measure them up against the kitchen wall. The little lines get higher every fortnight. You don't want to read this I know, but being with the children shows me that that side of me is true. I feel cut in half down the middle. Them one side. You and me the other.

I hate this war, but I went dancing to try to forget it. I've known plenty of bad times in my family, small wars at home, but you'd think after one world war this century people would have learned.

What else is there to say? I said it all before. I think a lot about love, and us, and everything. Us being enemies if I'd run back. You and me in our very own war. Is that what you want?

I want you to be loved. I hate all that stuff about cracked china and missing lids. Makes me want to cry. I can't and won't change my mind. However angry you are. I know I left for the right reasons. I left. And it is very hard to live with meself.

Love Rene.

September 1940

Rene sweetheart,

What do you want? Sympathy and tea on a tray? I've done enough moping and crying to fill Densley reservoir times over. Did me good. The bed's still empty and that's the hardest part. Sometimes I wake in the middle of the night and roll over to put my arm around you, but you're gone, and you're not coming back are you?

Your very own Red.

222

Dear Red,

No. One day I hope you'll respect me. Some people live their whole life as one huge lie. They lie to themselves and then to the people around them. But we didn't. Our love was true, and good. No one can take it away. But if I'd stayed and my family had ever realised what was going on between us, our own roof would have come crashing down on us both. Like a bomb in peacetime.

It took courage to walk away from you. It takes courage, more than I think I've got some days, to start again. You are a wonderful good woman Heather Myers, my Red Heather of Densley. Good and brave and true. And yes I want you to find someone worthy of you. You couldn't do that if I'd stayed.

Love Rene.

November 1940

Rene sweetheart,

If you didn't hurt too I'd think you were a real bitch. But you're not are you and I suppose your bed's cold like mine. But you get hugs from the children and Aunt Edith.

I know you are not coming back.

Made myself a vow yesterday. I'm going to find myself some fun soon. Look for a girl. She won't replace you. Nobody could. But nights are cold, nights are long. Never thought I'd be writing this. Thought I'd be on me tod, me on my own for years. I hate being alone at night, in bed.

Don't take a chance and call in to see me, though. I still hanker for you girl, that's why. But yours truly Red Heather is on the mend. Never had to look for long, so maybe me luck'll be in again now. I want to be warm at night.

Grab some happiness if you can. This war takes everyone from everyone. What's the point in hate? I loved you girl, don't you forget it or deny it. I try hard to see into your head. Why bring children into a world like this anyway? When this war's over will we make a good place for the next generation? I didn't get my name just for me hair you know. I got it because I vote for the working class. Is that why you want babies? Is it?

Your Red friend Heather.

Dear Red,

I cried. I have read your letter seventy thousand times. I have cried each time. Thankyou my old love, my sweetheart. There were so many ways I loved you, so many reasons why I did. And I knew it was not only for your hair. How many times have we talked all night?

I hope to God she loves you good. Heaven help if I don't find a man to love me. I'm afraid the war will last forever and I'll turn to stone.

I have learned about love and caring, and shouting and voting from you, Mum and Dad, and now from Aunt Edith and these children. I think Aunt Edith *knows* about us, because sometimes when I read your letters over and over I can't hide how shakey I feel. She never says much, but she is kind and she hugs me.

I'm in a hurry to find somebody, like the other girls round here. Sort of war fever. We've got real food here, not like the towns, and everyone is trying to make fun, so sometimes we succeed. Yesterday tomorrow today. All a blur now, death all around. I feel I want to live everything right now, just in case. Nobody knows, everybody plans, you work to play and play to live.

Love Rene.

Rene sweetheart,

New Year, new girl. Her name's Gladys and she works in the bottle factory. She kept coming to buy small things off the stall. She came so many times I finally noticed her. I mean *noticed*.

She's twenty and she's been around a bit. I quizzed her hard, and she does not want family life. She lost her old love, like me. We talked about that. She never liked men. Her old sweetheart has gone to London. She was older than me, fancy that.

The bed's warm at last. I am sleeping all right now.

She says she had her eye on me in the spring but she's not silly and she knew I'd take a while to turn around after you went.

Gladys is not you. She's got a different place in me heart. I try to keep your place stocked full up with good memories. I am not so angry, not so much with you. Sometimes I'm angry with the world. I'm always angry with the Nazis. I go to plenty of meetings for the Labour Party so we shall be ready when the war is over. Will it ever be?

I never wanted children. I don't know how it feels. You are so different from me. I try to understand. I did try to forget you but Gladys says we don't forget, only glue our bits back, and keep on going. PS I got a new hat. Blue velour, very posh.

Your friend, Red Heather.

June 1943

Dear Rene,

I knew you would be shocked but you'd want to read this for yourself.

They found her under the rubble, when the air raid was over. Like it says in the cutting, she was covered in sherds of shattered china and all of Densley will miss her, won't they?

I know she looked after you like a real mum would, didn't she, and I am very upset. We all are. Where will we be without her on the market, eh?

Her new lodger was a young woman called Gladys. I don't know if you knew about her. She has gone to London to join the army. She didn't want to stay on in the house on her own. I can't say I blame her. I will write more on Sunday but I am in a hurry to catch the post. I hope you are all right. Sheffield is very badly bombed, and the warehouse was right in the middle of it all. I'm very, very sorry love. You've lost an old friend.

Love Mum.

In my back room in Coombebury we three tried to understand. I cradled Tibs in my lap as we talked. We all had cans of beer, the hearthrug was littered with my ashtray, rings from the beer cans, and the pages of the letters. We passed them to and fro reading, re-reading.

'What I'm trying understand,' said Essie, 'is why she kept them. She must've known we'd find them, read them. And what about when she came home with me, pregnant with you, Lotte, they were what she brought with her, otherwise they'd have been left in San Francisco. They must've meant so much.'

Lotte was agitated. She shifted around in her chair, fidgeted with the zip on her tracksuit top, with the laces on her trainers, with the ring from her beer can. She said 'Makes me think she knew she'd not be going home. Things must've been bad with Dad even then.'

'Not a chance of talking to Red Heather, either, Lotte. Perhaps she brought those letters as a way of facing Densley again, keeping up the conversation even though Red Heather was dead. People do do things like that. I can almost understand that. But why keep them afterwards if she knew we'd find them?'

'It's a message,' I said quietly. I was thinking of Dora and Corinne in the New Forest, and Maggie who used to like to touch the stones. Secrets, and secret places.

'Message or not, Dee, I'm so angry with Mum,' said Lotte. 'I never was so angry in all my life with her.' (She turned to Essie.) 'It was always you that was the angry one when we were little, wasn't it Ess?'

'Yes it was. Funny thing. I don't feel angry now. Maybe it'll hit me later.'

'Mum just took her chance and went, Ess. Wanting babies, wanting us. I can't believe it how angry I feel. I know what Dee went through when Dora left her for a man. I hate being one of the babies that she, Mum I mean, left Red Heather for. I hate it.' Lotte started to cry, and I let her. I didn't move to hug her, or she'd have stopped and it was better to let it out.

Essie said: 'Let it out, Lotte. It's better, isn't it Dee.' (I nodded.) 'Then when it's out you can get on with your life. Mum wanted that. If she left those letters for us to find, and I'm becoming more and more certain that's what she did, then p'raps it *was* her way of telling us she knew. About us both. She wasn't anyone's fool.'

'You know, we should go out today,' I said, thinking aloud. 'To the New Forest. Walk and listen. It's always a good place in the early autumn. What d'you think?'

It was beautiful. Under our feet the ground was warm and soft to walk on. Deer sprang away in the distance. Near us the waist-high ferns were dappled beige and cinnamon colours, like the deer.

It was the trees that soothed me. Light bright browns and deep gold browns. I knew then that those colours, like the River Mere, would always give me pictures of Isobel.

Lotte's feelings about her mum had taken me back to all the times that Izzie had been angry with Dora, and with me. Lotte's words had sliced into my scars. Talking with a cooking knife in her teeth. Like Izzie could sometimes: 'Why did my mummy go in hospital? Why did my mummy make me brown? Why aren't you brown like me? Why aren't you my mummy, Dee? Why didn't you die instead of my daddy? I hate you Dee.'

We walked, listening to the birds. Esther could name some of them. She'd learnt through meeting Christine, loving Christine. We heard twigs snap under our feet; and autumn leaves rustle as we swished in

226

them. Through the branches and leaves we could look up to the sky. Blue, the colour of Robin's eggs. An overhead tapestry of blue and brown.

Lotte said: 'I'm glad we came here. Everything is settling down, isn't it, now that autumn's here, and I know it's corny to say so, but it will grow new leaves next year. Even if it is a hard winter. Red Heather grew through the hard times too, didn't she?'

'She was angry with Rene,' I said. 'No use pretending about that. If you hide from your own anger, it gnaws at your inside. It gnawed Dora to death slowly. I want our anger. I think it's good for all of us to be angry.' (Essie nodded, Lotte was walking slowly, looking thoughtful.) 'Tears, laughter, grief, all of it. It's . . . it's part of surviving for women.'

'That's p'raps why we're not supposed to get angry at all,' said Essie and I wondered if she was thinking of Nell and Tracey,' because we're not meant to survive if we're lesbians.'

'So it must hurt you, Essie, to find out that Red Heather died. I can't leave that alone. I keep on gnawing at it. It hurts and hurts,' said Lotte.

'I know, Lotte, but she *was* surviving before men's bombs killed her. She went on alone after Mum left. That's something to hold on to. Some lesbians don't survive, but some do. And those of us that do have to hold on and on. Wouldn't you say so Dee?'

'Then there'll be more of us,' I answered. 'I learned that down The Feathers.'

Lotte spoke more steadily: 'Isobel meant that about you Dee, that night when she came into my room, when I thought you might be dying. She said we had the power to stop you. I believed her. It made me strong again. But afterwards I knew it couldn't have worked unless you had the will to live, had survival inside you. I'm sure of it.'

'We have everything to live for,' I said, 'all three of us. So did Red Heather. The letters show that Rene didn't stop loving Red Heather even though it changed.'

'I didn't stop loving Christine. And I know she still loved me.'

'And Rene loved both of you wonderfully. We've got to live in the present, now, or we'll all go gaga. Rene's life was not a waste. Look at all her women friends, her letters to Ess through the ups and downs. Look at all that.'

Back home after Esther had returned to London, Lotte and I held one another close. We were thinking into one another's minds like we did

227

so often. (Like I'd be in and she'd be at work, and I'd think of her having something to tell me and the phone would ring. It'd be Lotte, telling me.)

'I'm not to blame for my mum's decisions about her and Red Heather.'

'No you're not.'

'Just as Isobel was not to blame for what Dora did.'

'She was not. I don't want to make it all sound simple, Lotte, easy. Men might have simple emotions, I don't know. I don't care. But I do know about women. And women's feelings are complex. It's not either/or. Izzie and me have shared a lot of hurt, and a lot of love too. She is black and she's angry about many things. I'm white. I'm angry about many things. But we love each other. We're part of each other's lives, she and I.'

'Like Mum and me. I'm glad she was my mum.'

'So am I. I love you Lotte. I would survive without you, if I had to, but I don't have to and I'm glad.'

'I'm glad too, Dee. I wake up thinking that, everyday.'

The autumn moved on, and so did the feelings. Changing like the New Forest. September to October.

Isobel wrote: 'This October is an end and a beginning. I feel acutely alone, even when I'm with people I love. It's preparation for the long winter back in London. And it feels positive.

Marion is still very loving, and says that I am the inspiration for the collection of poems that will be published next summer. I told her that I may make Muse my middle name.

It has been hard getting used to her new lover, Zella. Remember the black nurse I wrote you about? She was involved in the liberation struggles here, and now works with the medical progammes for the youngest children. It's been a big adjustment for Marion and for me. Non-monogamy is never easy. And I'm leaving in three weeks anyway.

The flat-share seems to be sorting out very well, through the African friends I stayed with when I was in London after your accident. I needed to be sharing with other black women in London, so I feel that I've been very lucky with the timing of it all.

But, to complete a circle, I have been thinking carefully about when and where to see you. Would you meet me from the plane, Dee? Is it possible, and does that meet your wishes too? I shall be arriving late afternoon/early evening on 25th. It's about ten hours from Maputo, changing Harare. I'll be on BA 052 Harare arriving Heathrow 18.40 hours, and I would love to see you. Much love Isobel.'

Overhead in the arrival lounge the monitor screens flickered: BA 052 Harare Expected 18.40.

Around me a hundred or so people, all waiting on the thick pile carpet; walking with muffled footsteps; talking with a babble of voices.

Light years ago Nell's switchboard, dolls-eye, had clicked and flicked. But now everywhere was high tech.

BA 052 Harare Delayed 18.55.

At the edge of the carpet the shiny airport floors began. For passengers only. They would emerge from open doors in the long blank wall opposite, and walk with luggage and trolleys past the carpets and the crowd, to the open area of the lounge maybe thirty yards away from that door. At the edge of the carpet, a waist-high silver barrier of tubular railings. Some sort of high-tech metal. I didn't know what.

I stood my side of the barrier. My eyes would zig from the screens to the waiting people; zag back to the door in the wall. Customs officials could be seen the other side of it.

I had gone alone to meet her. She had called it full circle.

The silver barrier was cool and smooth to my touch. The screen flicked.

BA 052 Harare Expected 18.55.

I went for coffee, and the toilet. All mod cons, silver and steel.

I came back. My watch said 18.45. Love Lotte. The doors slid open. Families emerged from an earlier flight. Their glances travelled past me, as they looked for familiar faces.

Back in Coombebury my lover, Lotte. My friend, Corinne.

My mind zigzagged from memories of the past to possibilities for the future. More families and couples with children; babies and toddlers were carried. Older children walked alongside the trolleys and some held on to the straps from the luggage.

Around me strangers waved to strangers. People's stories made me curious. Airports capture moments of meetings, glimpses of lives. People arrive and click away like the lines on the display screens. A moment. Then gone.

BA 052 Harare Landed.

I cried, I couldn't help it. I felt silly, very young, very old.

I had my red scarf ready to wave.

It takes time to get through the baggage collection hall, then customs.

I waited. Minutes. Minutes.

BA 052 Harare Baggage in hall.

Time 19.30.

No one emerged.

Time 19.35.

The trickle began. People were dishevelled, travel weary. Families again. Looking into the waving throng of us. On our carpet we represented almost every continent, or so it seemed.

Isobel.

Dressed in blue cords with a heavy padded jacket, bright blue. She had grey and blue trainers. I waved my scarf wildly, but was one of the crowd, and for a moment she stood still, searching. She carried a heavy holdall in each hand, and had a very large travel bag slung from her shoulder. Her eyes moved. She saw me. Her face opened up. She began to walk not along the walk way but across it straight towards me.

She dumped the holdalls, her side. Shrugged off the heavy travel bag. She was laughing. 'Dee, I'm here. I'm here.'

Then, laughing, arms wide, we both reached across the silver metal barrier to each other.

Afterwords: Lotte   Spring 1984

Three Ply Yarn is the name we've chosen together for our book. Essie has edited her own diaries. She did the first edit of the tapes that Dee and I made, and then we all worked together, hours and hours in Twenty-three Station Road. Essie says that we're following the centuries-old working-class tradition of oral history. I put it different. I say, and so does Dee, that there's nothing like listening to someone telling you the story of her life. There's nothing quite like being asked to tell it either, is there?

Afterwords: Deanne

The first time I heard my voice on tape I nearly died of embarrassment. But I soon got used to it. What I enjoyed most was how my voice changed when I was telling my childhood, and I seemed to go back now and then into the old ways of talking. Zigzagging to and fro from me then to me now. A word or phrase slotted in from me, now, into me, then. I've enjoyed doing this book. I'm hoping other working-class lesbians will do the same. The more the better I think. Now these two are on at me to publish my drawings, but as Lotte and I *are* moving to Brighton soon, I shall be too busy for a while in my first garden.

Afterwords: Esther

I don't regret any of the loneliness. Looking back, it's something rich to have gone through. Love to Chris Shipley wherever she is now. We have changed her name and our friends' names and some of the places to protect the women we love. I shouldn't think coming out as a lesbian can ever be easy in a world that wants us to hide. Now that I've made a new start with Lotte and Dee, I shan't stop. Uncovering the herstory that has been deliberately, carefully and brutally hidden. There are too many of us. They can't lose, abuse, use and silence us all.